GOD'S
GIVEN GIFT

RODOLFO WALSS

Copyright © 2019, 2023 Rodolfo Walss.

All rights reserved. No part of this book may be reproduced, stored, or transmitted by any means—whether auditory, graphic, mechanical, or electronic—without written permission of both publisher and author, except in the case of brief excerpts used in critical articles and reviews. Unauthorized reproduction of any part of this work is illegal and is punishable by law.

ISBN: 979-8-89031-773-5 (sc)
ISBN: 979-8-89031-774-2 (hc)
ISBN: 979-8-89031-775-9 (e)

Because of the dynamic nature of the Internet, any web addresses or links contained in this book may have changed since publication and may no longer be valid. The views expressed in this work are solely those of the author and do not necessarily reflect the views of the publisher, and the publisher hereby disclaims any responsibility for them.

One Galleria Blvd., Suite 1900, Metairie, LA 70001
(504) 702-6708

CHAPTER I

The rain drops sparkled as they bounced on the cobblestone that covered the streets, shining in the darkness of the night as they lifted the silver dust that had fallen from the wagons carrying the mineral through centuries of mining.

The trembling light of a kerosene miner's lamp cut through the dark, it moved nervously, creating shadows that danced capriciously as it searched the walls of the narrow streets of Guanajuato. It stopped when it hit a plaque with a name written on it: Dr. Fulgencio Campos. Women and children.

The sound of the rain drops, the whistling of the wind, the murmur of the water running down the streets, the rumble of the thunderstorm, along with the hard knocks on the heavy doors, created a symphony that would have been pleasant to whoever listened to it. But the two men knocking on the doors, their straw hats dripping, their white pants and shirts soaked, their huaraches full of silver mud, didn't care and they pounded the door harder and harder. The rhythm of the poundings were anxious, almost desperate.

"I'm coming, I'm coming," a woman from the inside, yelled. "You don't have to knock that hard, I already heard you."

The heavy door opened with a shrinking noise.

"Well, what is it? What do you want in this hell's night?" She asked as soon as she had opened the door.

"The doctor. We need to talk to the doctor. Please! It's an emergency," one of the men answered, taking off his hat and humbly holding it in front of his chest.

The woman, in her mid-forties, obese and short, her dark hair braided with red and green ribbons, cleansed her hands in her apron, looking at them from the head down. She frowned, as she was holding the door and appeared ready to close it. Socorro Serna, the one who had talked, realized that she had noticed that they were just poor peasants that had recently come to work in the mines, so he pulled two silver coins from the inside of his hat and showed them to her.

The woman looked at the silver, took a deep breath, looked at them again, still doubtful. "I'll call him; wait here," she said after another moment of hesitation.

"Well, what is it? What is so urgent that brings you here in the middle of this horrible storm?" Dr. Campos, a short, chubby, and almost bald man in his fifties, asked.

"Doctor, it's my wife," Socorro said. "She is pregnant, the pains started the day before yesterday and her water broke more than twelve hours ago, but the baby doesn't want to come." His soft, humble voice was sad.

"The women and the midwife that we called to help her have already given up. The midwife says that she is certain the baby has died and that we need a doctor to pull the baby out, otherwise, Maria Teresa, my wife, will also die." He kept his hat in front of his chest as he talked.

"We come to ask for your help, please come with us," his voice now trembled, "although poor, we'll pay for your services." He added as he wiped the rain and tears running down his face.

The Doctor looked at them hesitantly. "It's a hellish night," he said as he paused, to rub his chin. He seemed to be struggling with himself. He looked at them again, searching their faces. He, then, took a deep breath. "Wait here, I'll go, get my umbrella and my tools and we'll be on our way in a moment," he finally said, pretended to smile, turned and walked into the house.

Socorro and his brother, Candelario, guided the doctor through the labyrinth of Guanajuato's narrow streets. As they fought the windy storm, the mud and the darkness, the doctor kept a frown on his face and his jaws were tight. As soon as they arrived, Socorro noticed how Dr. Campos face brightened, the frown on his forehead disappeared, he became alert, paying attention to the details of the house that was clean, built in stone, like most of the houses in that mining town. Socorro and his brother walked him through the first large room that was a combination of kitchen, dining and living room. The room was gloomy, barely illuminated by two oil lamps and a torch. Around a table, women prayed the rosary in a monotonous, rhythmic voice. Children were sleeping in a corner and in another corner men smoked and drank coffee with tequila, mumbling something amongst them. In the dimness, the entire group and their shadows looked phantasmagoric.

Socorro pulled a curtain to enter the adjacent room where Maria Teresa was laboring. She was soaked in sweat, obviously tired. Her face, although pale, showed calmness and determination. She grimaced, "another pain is coming," she said as she lifted herself, grabbed her legs and pushed hard. Her body was covered by plain cotton sheets that were stained by sweat, blood, urine and feces. A woman wiped her forehead, while another mumbled some words of encouragement. "The doctor is here," a third woman said, with a touch of relief in her voice.

The doctor placed his umbrella and his bag of tools in a corner, took off his jacket, rolled up his sleeves, walked to the side of the bed and lifted the sheets, just enough to allow his left arm through. "You'll feel some pressure and discomfort," he said. His voice was calm and gentle. While he examined her, he kept mumbling something to himself. Afterwards he got up, took a towel from his bag and cleansed his arm; his face was now alert, in deep concentration. He searched in his bag and pulled out something that, to Socorro, looked like a small trumpet. He walked again to Maria's bedside, palpated gently her belly. Then, he placed the trumpet like instrument on her abdomen, bent and listened. He smiled, pulled the watch from his vest and looked at it as he continued listening for almost one minute. "This baby's heart is strong," he announced smiling at Socorro. The women sighed in relief, one of them clapped and smiled.

"Go and get plenty of clean water and soap, also clean rags, please," he said to Socorro and his brother.

Then he turned and talked to the women who were standing at the side of the bed. "You two will help me. First help her to slide to the edge of the bed. Each one of you will hold one leg. Spread them apart, so I can maneuver to get this baby's face down. If I am successful, the baby will come out." He turned to another woman, "also we'll need more light, please hold the lamp close, so I can see."

He washed his hands in a basin of clean water that had been brought in by Candelario. Meanwhile, the midwife and the women helped Maria to slide to the edge of the bed, spreading her legs as they had been instructed. He then washed her buttocks thoroughly as he talked to her in a gentle, soothing voice. "Relax and allow yourself to feel some discomfort," he said. "When you feel pressure, push hard; as hard as you have been doing it until now. I'll help by guiding the baby."

One of the women asked Socorro and his brother to wait in the other room. "Doctor, if you don't mind, I would like to stay," Socorro said. The doctor nodded affirmatively. Candelario left and Socorro walked to a corner.

From the corner, Socorro watched how the doctor placed his hands in the basin with water and soap, then, without drying them, slid his soft, chubby, left hand into Maria's private parts, he then twisted his body until his back was towards her. At the same time, he had twisted his left arm, while keeping the hand inside of her. Maria grimaced. "I'm feeling pain," she said. "Push now," the doctor said firmly. She did as she was told and while she was pushing the doctor twisted his body to face her, untwisting with the movement his arm. He kept the hand inside of her feeling carefully. He looked confident. "I think the baby has now turned," he said to her. "Push again, hard, as you have been doing and hopefully this baby will come out." Once again, she obeyed and Socorro could see that something that looked like black hair showed up in her private parts. He started to sweat, his heart pounded in his chest. "It's coming, it's coming," the midwife yelled, clapping at the same time, she then said in a loud and firm voice. "Keep pushing Maria, push hard, the baby is coming." Maria pushed and the baby's head started to come out.

Socorro had his eyes fixed on the doctor's hands, he was impressed seeing the baby's body coming through, as the doctor slowly and gently guided the delivery, holding the baby as it came out. "It's a boy!" The Doctor announced as soon as the full body of the baby was out. He held the baby with the head hanging down and slapped the baby's buttock gently, but the baby didn't respond, his body looked flaccid, with his arms hanging down, motionless. The doctor slapped him again and again, still there was no response. The doctor slapped the baby again and this time there was a gentle movement and a soft, cough-like sound. The doctor slapped again and this time the baby reacted by moving his entire body and with a loud, vigorous cry. The cry reverberated in the stone walls of the room. Socorro felt that his legs couldn't hold him anymore, so he leaned on the wall and overwhelmed by the emotion, he wept.

The women in the room laughed and clapped nervously and Maria Teresa also laughed with tears running down her cheeks. In the other room, having heard the baby cry, the women started singing a religious anthem.

Outside, nature's symphony reached a climax. The skies brightened with the rumbling of the thunder, the clouds poured water, emptying themselves. The heavy rain sang hymns of praise and the rumble of the creeks of silvery water that poured down from the mountains into the streets of the town joined the chorale.

"Doctor, I don't know how to pay you," Socorro said to Doctor Campos when he was getting ready to leave. "But, please take these two silver coins, I wish I had a better way to show my appreciation, but as you can see, we are poor."

The doctor took the coins, put one in the pocket of his vest and gave the other one back to Socorro. "One silver coin is enough. I'm aware of the kind of hard work you must have gone through to be able to save them." He smiled. "Besides, being able to help is always a good payment. Use the other coin for the needs of your family. By the way, how are you going to name this child?"

"Maria Teresa had already decided that if it was a boy, his name would be Fidelio." Socorro replied.

"That's the name of a saint who was wise and lived to the service of others. There must be a good reason why the lord chose to preserve your child's life," the doctor said as he lifted his bag of tools and his umbrella.

"Teach him to grow to be a good Catholic and to help those in need," he added, before opening the umbrella and stepping into the storm.

CHAPTER II

Eight years later, Socorro and his wife were in the kitchen getting ready for dinner. He had just returned home after having worked more than fifteen hours at the mine. The children had eaten their dinner of beans and tortillas, prayed the rosary with their mother and were sleeping peacefully over the wool blankets extended on the cold stone floor.

"Socorro, I'd like to talk to you about something that has been worrying me for some time now." Maria Teresa said as she added a piece of wood to the stove where his dinner of beans and pork with hot sauce, corn tortillas and a pot of fresh coffee were heating.

"What is it?" he asked as he washed his hands and face in a basin. He felt tired, but happy to be home; even if it was late and just for a few hours.

"Well, maybe it's just my imagination," she said as she served the hot stew into a clay bowl.

"You are making me nervous," Socorro said as he dried his face and hands with a piece of cotton cloth. "What is it?"

"It's Fidelio, I know as well as you do, that he is a loving, obedient, child. In short, he is what anyone would call a good boy, and I'm proud of him." She shrugged her shoulders and frowned, as if she was trying to put order in her thought. "It's something else that has me worried." She hesitated for a moment, took a deep breath, before continuing.

"Well, to put it in a few words, he is different from the other children." She finally said.

"What do you mean?" Socorro asked as he sat at the table.

Maria thought for a moment. "Well, for instance, he is always playing alone, but he talks as if some other children were also playing with him, and…" She stopped, looked at Socorro, a concerned look on her face, "he always seems to know when I'm going to ask him to do something. He does it before I even say a word. I know it is a silly idea, but it is almost as if he could read my mind."

"Ha, ha, ha," Socorro laughed. "Come on now, woman. I agree with you, that's a silly idea. Many children like to play by themselves. You know that they have a great imagination and Fidelio is not the exception, so he is just using it." He said, shrugging his shoulders as he talked. "Besides, Fidelio is always around you, we all know how much he loves you and he is always trying to please you. That's why you think that he can read your mind." He paused for a moment, took a tortilla, cut a piece and used it as a spoon to get some of the pork with beans, then he put everything in his mouth. He chewed his food slowly, while thinking. "He is still a young child, he learns quickly and always praises the Lord," he said after he had swallowed.

Maria got a piece of cloth and lifted the hot pot of coffee. "Funny you mention that, because as you know, I've been teaching the children the catechism and although Fidelio is the youngest he learned it quickly and now, he is the one who is teaching and explaining the meaning of the lessons to his older brothers and sisters." She filled Socorro's clay cup with fresh coffee and sat in a chair besides him. "And there is something else," she continued, "he spends a lot of time observing the frogs, birds, squirrels and every animal that passes by. He gets upset when the other children throw stones at them and when a frog or a bird gets hit, he tries to heal them. He also gives them names and the strange thing is that they seem to understand him."

Socorro felt concerned, took another bite, chewed slowly and frowned. The hot pepper in his food made him sweat. He wiped it from his forehead with the back of his hand. "Does he harm the animals in any way?" he asked, after he had swallowed.

"No, but he spends a lot of time watching them, and another strange thing. When he finds any dead animal, he carefully cuts them open with a piece of glass. He does it methodically, examining their internal organs. It's like he knows what to look for. It has me really worried. He is just a little child, but he doesn't act like one." She started to cry in silence.

"Calm, calm, now woman," Socorro said trying to look calm himself. "He is just a curious boy. There is no reason to be worried," he extended his arm to hold her hand. "Soon he'll start going to school and he'll be just fine, learning and playing with the other children. He'll grow up to become something more than a miner or another peasant as we are."

"I hope so," Maria Teresa replied, holding his hand too.

"Fidelio, are you paying attention?" Sister Maria Magdalena, the teacher at the little school in the church of Saint Francis, asked.

"He is always looking at the frogs," one of the older children said, in a sarcastic tone. "He does that so much that he is already looking like one of them." The children laughed.

"Yes, Sister. You were talking about how God created Eve from a rib that he had taken from Adam." Fidelio answered without paying attention to the elder child.

"Well, that's good, Fidelio. You are a good boy and you take the word of God seriously," Sister Maria Magdalena said. "And I wish that all of you would pay as much attention to it as Fidelio does," she added, talking to the class.

"Fidelio is a freak," another of the elder children said. "He never wants to play with us and as Dionaciano said, he is always watching the frogs, the birds and any animal that passes by. He prefers to be with animals rather than with children. We don't like him."

"Yes, that's true", another child intervened. "He gets upset when we use the frogs and birds as targets for our slings and if we hit one of them he cries and tries to heal them. He is indeed a freak. One of these days we are going to throw the stones at him. That way he'll understand."

"Fidelio is a good boy. He loves and praises God's creation," said Enrique Sanchez de la Fuente, the eldest in the class. "If anyone of you ever harms him, you'll have to deal with me." He stood up and looked at all his classmates. "Is that clear?" he asked, with a defiant look.

Fidelio turned and looked at him, feeling thankful.

"Well, enough of that children. Nobody is going to hurt anyone." Sister Maria Magdalena said. "Tomorrow we'll continue with the story of Adam and Eve. Now go home, do your homework and be good boys. God bless you all."

"Thank you for helping me in class," Fidelio told Enrique as they walked home after school. "But there is no need for that. I can take care of myself."

"I know that you can take care of yourself, I've noticed that you are as strong as anyone of us, so there is no need to thank me. But, I like that you love the Lord as much as I do," Enrique answered, smiling to him and padding him on the back. "But, I'm also curious, why do you care so much about the animals?"

Fidelio flushed a bit, shrugged his shoulders. "I like them and also learn from them, that's all." He resisted the temptation to add that he didn't know why he was doing it, but at the same time he enjoyed it.

"It really doesn't matter to me. It's just that you act different from all of us. You don't like to play the balero or the trompo with us. You don't even have a sling like most of us. You are a bit strange. I'm sorry to say that."

Fidelio smiled. "I know that," he said, "but, I really admire how you guys made the trompo dance and I enjoy watching the boys play the balero. I just enjoy learning from the animals, that's all." His voice trembled a bit. He was feeling a bit upset of having to explain something that he considered natural.

"I told you. It doesn't matter," said Enrique, laughing, slapping Fidelio's back again.

"It matters to me," Fidelio replied, smiling. "And yes, I would like to be an altar boy to Father Segura."

Enrique stopped and looked at Fidelio. "I was about to ask you exactly that, but I didn't say anything. How did you know?"

"You didn't? I thought that you had asked." Fidelio was feeling more and more anxious. It had been some time since he had noticed that he had this ability of hearing people's thoughts and it scared him, and since he really appreciated Enrique's friendship, this time it also bothered him.

"Well, you know that Father Segura is my uncle. And since I told you how I appreciate your love for our Lord, you knew that I was going to ask you to join us as an altar boy." Enrique said, pensively.

"Yes, that's it." Said Fidelio, feeling relieved.

"This Saturday, we are going to start the lessons for the new altar boys. Be there at nine. My uncle doesn't like children who are late or lazy," said Enrique, smiling again. "These are the stairs to your home," he added pointing to a narrow, long and steep stone staircase. "Rest and prepare the lesson for tomorrow. I'm sure Madre Maria Magdalena is going to ask you for it. I'll see you there." He waved as he walked down the street.

Fidelio started going up the stairway. After a few steps up, he stopped. Upstairs, the birds were flying in circles and making a lot of noise, there were more frogs than usual; they were noisy, like trying to warn him about something. Looking around he saw that behind one of the corners, flanking the narrow stair, several of his classmates waited for him. He was about to turn around when suddenly, he felt a terrible pain in his forehead and everything became blurred. As he fell down he saw that Dionaciano and the other children were coming at him and there was nothing he could do to escape or fight back.

Like in a fog, Fidelio saw how, suddenly, Enrique appeared and he started fighting with the children. Since Enrique was older and stronger than all of them, the children ran away. Having scared the children, Enrique came and helped him to sit up. Fidelio felt a severe headache. When he touched his forehead, he could feel a large lump with a cut bleeding. Enrique took his handkerchief and used it as a bandage around Fidelio's head.

"It's fortunate that I came back," Enrique said to Fidelio who was still feeling a bit dizzy. "The noise of the birds flying in circles and so many frogs looking in this direction caught my attention. So, I decided to come back and see for myself." He pointed to Fidelio's head. "You are lucky that the stone only scratched your head, had it hit you straight on, it could have killed you."

"Yes, I'm lucky and I thank you," said Fidelio, making an effort to think and speak. "This is not the first time that they have come after me." He touched his forehead and smiled. "My mother is going to be upset when she sees me. She is going to think that I was in a fight again."

"And she is going to be right about that," Enrique said, smiling. "Be careful. I'll see you tomorrow and don't forget about Saturday," he said, waving his hand, before he turned and started walking down the street.

Several months later, Fidelio, who had learned quickly the duties of an altar boy, was helping Father Segura to get ready for the evening mass.

"Fidelio, I'm very happy with you. You have learned much quicker than the other boys the duties of an altar boy, and since you came, the number of people assisting to the church has increased and so has the collection, especially when you are the one passing the collection basket," said Father Segura, as Fidelio handed him the mass garments. "There is something special about you that I hope you'll never loose. You care about people and although still a young child, you try to apply Jesus teachings to your life."

"Thank you, Father," Fidelio answered. "You and Enrique have taught me well and I'm thankful for that."

"You are humble, another of your qualities," Father Segura smiled, as he turned around. "You have been given the gift of a unique talent. Someday, all that is inside you will come together. I just hope that when it happens you will be ready, because it will be a wonder for you, and everyone else," he sighed. "Well, enough conversation. People are waiting for the start of the mass, let's go and do our job."

Shortly after the mass, while Fidelio was getting ready to go back home, Antonia, one of his older sisters, came running, with tears rolling down her face. Fidelio was worried as he knew that she was strong and something serious must have happened.

"Fidelio, Is Father Segura around?" asked Antonia, as soon as she arrived.

"He is outside, talking to some people," Fidelio answered. "But, what's wrong? Why are you crying?" concerned, he asked.

"Mama! She fell and seems to have broken an arm," she answered. "Dr. Campos is not in town and Dr. Urbina has refused to help us when our papa told him that we don't have the money to pay him at this moment, but that we would pay him later. The doctor wants the money before he does anything. I came running to ask father Segura if he could help us with some money so we could pay the doctor to help mama."

"I know that he would help if he could," said Fidelio. "But, the bishop has already sent for the collection money of the week and Father Segura has just given away the little that was left to the poor."

"Oh, God, what are we going to do now?" Antonia asked and started sobbing.

"I don't know, but I'll talk to Father Segura. I'm sure that he would give us good advice. Go home and do your best to keep mama comfortable."

Shortly afterwards Fidelio talked to Father Segura.

"At the moment there is not much I can do to help, Fidelio," Father Segura said. "The only thing I can offer now is a prayer. I know it's not much, but that's all I can do."

"That's a lot." Fidelio replied. "Please do so, God will listen to you. Now, if you don't need me anymore, I'd like to go home."

"Yes, my son, you are right, God will listen. Go home that He will be with you."

Fidelio walked up the hill to his home. He was feeling sad and wondering what he could do to help his mother. When he approached the stairs, he noticed that a man was sitting on the first step. It was an old man, tall, strong, dark complexion with white hair and a beard. He was dressed as a common peasant, white cotton pants and shirt and huaraches. He seemed to be playing with the butterflies flying around him.

"Fidelio," the old man said as Fidelio got close. Fidelio felt as if the man was an old, trusted friend. "Why are you sad? What is bothering you?"

"My mother broke an arm and because we are poor, the doctor refuses to come and help her and I don't know what to do," Fidelio replied, tears rolling down his cheek.

The old man smiled, Fidelio was impressed about how white and clean were the teeth of the old man. "You can help her. I'll tell you what to do."

When Fidelio got home, everyone looked sad and down. Fidelio was feeling full of energy and confidence, as he went straight to his mother. Her left forearm was swollen and bent because of the broken bone. Fidelio took the arm, caressed it carefully, looked at his mother and talked to her in a soothing and gentle tone of voice, while he caressed her broken arm. "Rest now mama," he said. "Rest calm, and relax, your arm is going to be healed, close your eyes and rest." She did as she was asked. "You are going to feel a gentle pull in your arm, just like when you are washing dirty clothes in the cold water and the cold makes your whole arm numb, and then you have to carry a heavy bucket of water." With a swift move, he pulled her arm reducing the bent. Then he asked his father for a piece of wood and used it as a splint wrapping a piece of cloth around the arm to hold it. He then put a large handkerchief around her neck and put the splinted arm to rest on it. "Now mama let your arm rest in there. It will heal, you'll see."

His father, elder brothers and sisters, just looked at him with wide open eyes, but no one questioned or doubted him.

Three weeks later, Maria Teresa was moving her arm like it had never been broken.

CHAPTER III

"This has been a particularly busy lent season," Father Segura said to Fidelio as he pulled out the mass garments. He turned and smiled. "Enrique and you have taken most of the burden by helping me these days. In two days, the procession for the Holy Friday will happen. The organizers assure me that this year will be special. Have you ever seen one before?"

"No Father," Fidelio replied. "But I hope I'll have a chance this year."

"That's something you shouldn't miss, you are already nine-years-old and I'm sure you'll understand it. Since you and Enrique have worked hard all these busy days, I'll let both of you free on Holy Friday."

"Thank you, Father," said Fidelio, cheerfully.

Two days later, Fidelio and Enrique were among the crowd watching the procession in remembrance of the Passion of Jesus. Fidelio felt a sensation of pressure in his chest when he saw Jesus coming up the street with difficulty, bent by the weight of the heavy cross made of raw wood. As the procession approached, Fidelio's heartache worsened when he noticed that on Jesus' forehead there was blood because of the crown of thorns that he was forced to wear.

Fidelio's body got tense with a feeling of rage starting to build up. "Why are they doing this to him?" he asked himself in silence. With a combination of pity, rage and impotence, he saw how Jesus stumbled, the heavy cross falling on him. Although, the spring morning was cold, Fidelio could see that Jesus was sweating, having difficulty pushing the cross away from him and getting up. A couple of tears rolled down Fidelio's cheeks. He felt so much rage that he started biting his lips.

"Get up. Carry your cross and keep going!" The Roman soldier yelled and whipped Jesus a couple of times. Fidelio felt the pain caused by the whipping on his own back, he could hear his own heart, his head was heavy, sweat running down his forehead blurred his vision, his fists tightened; he was trembling, rage continued building up.

With difficulty, Jesus got up, put the cross on his back and continued his painful, sorrowful, walk. When the Roman soldier whipped Jesus again, Fidelio couldn't hold himself any longer. With a quick movement, he pulled the sling out of Enrique's pocket, picked a stone, swung the sling, aimed, and let the stone go. It flew and hit the soldier in the middle of the chest, who grunted and stumbled, falling on his buttocks. The expression of his face was a combination of pain, surprise, perplexity and anger.

Upset, the men who were around Fidelio snatched the sling away from him. One of them held him tight. "Why have you done that!?" Their hands were up, ready to slap him.

"Because he is whipping him for no reason!" Fidelio replied in a firm voice. Defiant, he was ready to fight, if necessary. "He has done nothing to him!" he added.

The men looked at each other, confused. Father Segura arrived at that moment. "Don't worry, I'll take care of it from here. Thank you," he said to the men, taking Fidelio by the arm, guiding him and Enrique towards the church.

"Fidelio: It was only a representation to remind us of Jesus' suffering," Father Segura said after they had walked a few steps away from the men.

"It looked real to me!" Fidelio replied, still angry.

Father Segura looked at him, took a deep breath, sighed and then smiled. "God has made you special," he said as he embraced Fidelio and Enrique. "Let's go home and have a cup of hot chocolate with sweet bread. It will make us feel better."

A few days later, as he arrived at the school, Fidelio was approached by Dionaciano and some of his classmates. The same gang that had attacked him in the recent past.

"Fidelio, let's talk," said Dionaciano, with a firm tone of voice. Judging by the expression in Dionaciano's face, Fidelio felt that the matter could be serious.

"Sure, let's talk," Fidelio replied, feeling cautious.

"We have been talking about what you did during the procession," Dionaciano continued, some of the boys nodded agreeably. "And we want to tell you that we wish we had had the balls to do what you did." He paused, looked down, moving nervously. "Well, in short what I'm trying to say is that we want to be your friends from now on," he finally said smiling and extending his hand to Fidelio.

"Of course!" Fidelio replied, smiling, feeling happy and relieved. He extended his arm to shake hands with Dionaciano. "I'm happy to be your friend," he added looking to the other boys.

"Which one of you is Fidelio?" A short, bulky, muscular man asked.

"Why are you asking?" Enrique, who had been watching, asked the man.

"It's personal. It's something I'll tell only to him." The man answered.

"I'm Fidelio," said Fidelio, before Enrique or any of the other boys could say anything.

The man looked at him, a frown in his face. "So, you are the boy who hit me during the procession," he said.

Enrique, Dionaciano and the other boys moved in front of Fidelio.

"Yes, I'm the one," Fidelio said, taking a couple of steps, not letting the boys stand between him and the man. "I apologize if I caused you any harm."

The man looked at him and smiled. "Not at all," he said. "On the contrary, I'm here to thank you."

The boys looked at each other, surprised. "How is that?" Dionaciano asked.

"I've been a miner since I was your age," the man answered. "I've spent most of my life inside the tunnels. Some time back, I started noticing some difficulty in breathing. Slowly it became more and more difficult for me to breathe, to the point that I couldn't work anymore." He looked at them. "Being in the procession was hard for me. I was having trouble catching my breath and I was afraid that I couldn't finish it." He paused, looked down, as if he was ashamed of himself. "Without noticing, I was channeling my anguish and frustration on the poor man carrying the cross." He paused, looked at the boys, smiled, took a deep breath with fruition. "It was then that the stone hit me," he continued. "Of course, I felt pain at the beginning. But to my surprise, after that, I am no longer short of breath. The difficulty in breathing is gone. I owe it to you and that's why I'm here to thank you."

"Thank God, not me," said Fidelio. "If anything, He has used me as his instrument. But, I really meant to harm you." He added in an apologetic tone of voice.

The man extended his arms, a broad smile on his face. "Well, child, let me tell you. You also succeeded in that, it was painful and I still have a large, tender, bruise. Of course, I'll thank God. But I'll thank him for the gift that he has obviously given to you and for making me the recipient of such blessing."

Fidelio didn't know what to say, he only felt as if someone had put a heavy weight on his shoulders. He didn't enjoy such praise. What he really wanted was to be just like the rest of the children.

Several months later, Fidelio was just outside his parents' home, busy observing the frogs and birds, as he used to do every time he had a chance. It was early in the afternoon, the sun was bright, the sky clear, the birds chirped happily. Everything seemed to be pleasant and peaceful, when suddenly an explosion was heard, followed by a rumble. Scared, the birds flew away and the frogs went under the stones.

"An explosion in the mines! There has been an explosion in one of the mines!" Someone yelled.

Fidelio stood up and as he looked around, he saw a frantic scene. Everyone was leaving their homes and running towards the place of the explosion. His mother, Maria Teresa was among them. She left home, eyes wide open, anguish reflected in her face. She ran towards the steep stairs outside of their home and when she took the first step, she stumbled, and rolled down, leaving a trace of blood. Scared, Fidelio ran after his mother. When he finally got to the bottom she was motionless, her face and head bruised and swollen, her dress stained by blood and dust. Fidelio knelt, lifted her head, caressing her face. As his tears fell on her face, he took the handkerchief—the one that Maria Teresa always put in the pocket of his shirt, and used his tears to wipe her face, gently.

Respectfully, several men approached, one of them tenderly touched Fidelio's shoulder. "Fidelio, we'll have to carry her body home, so the women can clean it." Fidelio heard his voice like a distant murmur. He moved, allowing the men to carry Maria Teresa's body to the home; once in there, the women cleansed her body and changed her clothes. As they worked, they prayed the rosary in a monotonous, murmur like, tone of voice. Like in a foggy dream, Fidelio saw Antonia cleaning the house and started preparing coffee to serve to those coming for the funeral.

Later, Buenaventura, Joaquin and Socorro, Fidelio's older brothers, who were also working at the mines, arrived. Their faces didn't show emotion, but Fidelio, who knew them well, noticed the wetness in their eyes. "We still don't know anything about father," Buenaventura told Fidelio. "He is one of the miners in the tunnel, where the explosion happened," he added. "Let us trust in God and hope for the best," Joaquin said. Socorro nodded. "Hail Mary, full of grace, the Lord is with you..." a woman started praying the rosary, the rest followed. The body of Maria Teresa, cleansed, fully dressed in her best Sunday clothes, was already lying in the center of the main room of the house, somebody had placed four candles around it. The night was falling. Antonia, helped by neighbors, kept busy offering coffee with tequila to those present. The monotonous and rhythmic murmur of the women praying the rosary; the soft, but high pitched sound of the clay coffee cups, the whisper of the voices, the shadows created by the flames of the candles, made Fidelio feel as if he was in an underground tunnel, his mother's spirit flowing towards heaven. For some reason, he now felt peaceful.

It was almost midnight when Father Segura and a group of men walked into the house. Their clothes dirty, soaked with mud, their dark faces covered by a mask of dust that made them look pale. Their callous hands after hours of pulling rocks still showed silvery powder mixed with blood. They all looked serious, sad, concerned with their shoulders sloughed. The praying stopped and all turned and looked at them. Fidelio also turned and felt a knot in his belly. Although he was just a child, he understood the meaning of their attitude.

"Everyone, please listen," Father Segura said, as he rubbed his forehead, looking to the floor, as though he was searching for words. "Well," he finally said, "there is no easy way to say it. So, I will just say it like it is. There are no survivors. These men," he pointed to the miners with him, "have worked hard trying to rescue them, but all of those working in that tunnel are gone. I'm sorry." He sobbed and wiped his nose.

The women screamed, raising her arms in sorrow. Everyone started crying; the men tried, unsuccessfully, to hold their tears from flushing down. Fidelio cried loudly and ran towards Antonia and hugged her. Their brothers joined them. All joined in a collective weeping.

The sound of boots entering the room called everyone's attention. A foreman of the mines, a blond and robust man, walked in. He was escorted by a captain and several armed soldiers. He walked straight to the center of the room, looked at Maria Teresa's body, then turned and looked everyone straight in the eyes. He was slightly crossed eye, and under the flickering light of the candles, his green eyes looked sinister. Fidelio felt a chill down his spine.

"I'm sorry for your loss, it's a tragedy. I understand that. But it's not a reason to stop working. The mines will be open tomorrow as usual and everyone is expected to be there, otherwise you may say good bye to your job. I hope I have made myself clear!" he said and walked out followed by the soldiers.

CHAPTER IV

"Fidelio, it has been five years since you have been working for my uncle at the church," Enrique said. "He is pleased with you. You not only help in the services, clean the church, but also have learned to cook, and have continued school." He smiled for a while and then frowned. "Meanwhile, the mining business has slowed and for the last eighteen months, thanks to the revolution, and the change of government brought by it, the mining business has gone down and, as a consequence of it, I am without a job and probably will have to leave Guanajuato."

Fidelio looked at him. "I'm sorry to hear that. Is there something I could do to help?"

"No, don't worry, I didn't tell you that meaning that I was in need of help. As you are well aware, my parent's still support me." His face turned serious. "Well, as a matter of fact, I already have been offered a job as a book keeper."

"That is good, I'm happy for you, but at the same time sad. Since the loss of my parents, Antonia got married and left town and my brothers have gone to the mines in Pachuca and Real de Catorce. You are more than a friend to me, you have been almost like a father."

"Don't exaggerate, we are friends. The fact that I'm several years older than you doesn't mean much between us. But, precisely I want to talk to you about going with me. I have talked to my uncle and he says that is up to you; but he also said that it would be good for you to travel a little and meet new people."

Fidelio hesitated for a moment. "I'm happy here. Your uncle has also been good to me," he paused, "Where are you going?" He finally asked.

"Not too far. To Morelia. I have relatives there and I am sure I could convince them to hire you to help in the kitchen. Besides, in Morelia, you could continue going to school," Enrique looked at Fidelio, smiling. "So, what do you say?"

Fidelio felt uncertain. He was happy working for Father Segura, but at the same time, the attraction of knowing new places, learning more, and above all, following his friend were important.

"You say that I could work with your family and still continue school?" he asked.

"That's something I can assure you," Enrique answered.

"And you have talked to your uncle and he agrees to it," Fidelio said, still hesitant.

"Yes, and as a matter of fact, remember that he said that it will be good for you; but, the final decision is entirely up to you."

Fidelio sighed, looked to the ceiling, frowning. He felt hesitant, afraid of the change, but at the same time the idea of knowing new places, different people, was tempting. "I'm not sure." He finally said, "could I think about it for a few days?"

"Sure, I'll be leaving in two weeks. We'll talk again in one week. Is that enough time?" Enrique replied.

"More than enough. I promise I'll have an answer by then."

Later, that night, after assisting Father Segura during the evening mass, Fidelio was cleaning behind the altar when he heard loud voices coming from Father Segura's office. The door was open and he could see the Bishop, dressed in his purple robe talking to Father Segura whose face looked pale.

"For the last time, I'm telling you that the entire collection must be sent immediately to my office. I'm tired of hearing that you are using part of it to help those that you think are in need," Fidelio heard the Bishop talking, his voice was not only loud, but he sounded upset. "Besides, who could need more than our Saint Mother the Church? So, once again, the entire collection must be sent immediately to me. I'll decide how is best to use it. Do I make myself clear?"

"Yes, your eminence," Father Segura replied in a soft voice.

"I expect you to obey. You have done a good job in this parish; and I would hate to have to transfer you."

"It will be done as your eminence wishes," Father Segura replied, looking to the floor, although the tone of his voice was sad; from his position, Fidelio clearly saw the muscles of his jaws tightening.

Fidelio felt Father Segura's pain, embarrassment, the desire, without hope, to rebel against an unjust order. He felt upset. Several times he had taken the collection to the episcopal palace. He knew how richly decorated it was, full of expensive furniture and art everywhere. Once, he had been at the private chamber of the bishop and he had felt surprised seen how luxurious it was. Several times, when the bishop had invited someone special for lunch, or dinner, Fidelio had been asked to help in the kitchen; and he had helped to prepare succulent and expensive dishes that quite often were not even tasted, and were later thrown to the dogs. He compared all that waste with the simple and humble way of living of Father Segura. He had to make an effort to control himself and not get in and kick the bishop out.

"Good. You are a good priest and I know you'll do as I ask you to do. Remember that we also must send part of it to Rome." The Bishop said in a softer and calmer voice.

"I understand, your eminence," Father Segura replied.

"Well, I must leave now, receive my blessing my son," the Bishop said extending his right hand so Father Segura could kiss the episcopal ring.

"Father, I apologize but I heard all that conversation. I don't know how you were able to control yourself," Fidelio said after the Bishop had left. "It isn't fair. You use a little of the collection to help the poor and those in need; but, I know that you send the collection without keeping anything for yourself."

"Thank you Fidelio, you have grown to be an intelligent boy. So, I hope you understand that we must obey the bishop, remember that he also has someone above him," Father Segura said, smiling. "But let's forget about that. Has Enrique talked to you about moving to Morelia?"

"Yes, but I'm still undecided. I like it here, working for you. But, I also admit that I like the idea of meeting other people, seeing new places; besides as you know, Enrique is my best friend."

"I appreciate your help, and also enjoy talking to you. Although merely out of childhood, you are already a wise man; I don't know anybody who could explain the word of the Lord as well as you do." He paused, "you are so smart, that you know that pretending not to be would be to your advantage," he smiled, "I know that I'll miss you." Father Segura finally said, his voice trembled a little.

"Father, I haven't decided to go, as a matter of fact, I'll stay here, with you." Fidelio said in a firm voice.

"No Fidelio, you must continue with your life. The change will be good for you. Besides, I already know that what you heard today is only the beginning; the bishop has already decided. I'll be transferred, he is just waiting for an excuse. Go and God bless you."

Fidelio found Morelia different from Guanajuato and he enjoyed that. Although the public buildings were not as impressive as those in Guanajuato, he found Morelia's cathedral and its surrounding plazas beautiful. He also felt free walking the wide and almost straight streets of Morelia, and he thought that the plazas and gardens were better groomed. In the fall and spring, he enjoyed the huge amount of different species of birds and butterflies coming to the town; he spent many hours looking at them. From them he learned to distinguish the subtle changes in nature that presage the coming of a storm, or a change in the weather, also about plants with curative or poisonous properties. To his surprise, he also noticed that the animal behavior frequently is violent and brutal.

The new environment also made him conscious about the strong, acute, almost painful, differences between the few wealthy families and the rest of the population. In Guanajuato, he had already noticed that alongside a few beautiful mansions, with well-kept gardens, and abundance of everything, there were many miserable shacks with scarcity of even the basic. Probably because of the wider streets and the plain terrain, the contrast became obvious in Morelia. It was there that he started paying attention to the social and political changes that were happening in Mexico. General Diaz, who had been the President for decades, had been forced, by a rebellion in the northern state of Chihuahua, to leave the country. Although the new President, a wealthy man from up-north, had brought hope for change, Fidelio noticed that there were people to whom such change was unpleasant and undesirable. But what was a surprise to him was to notice that not only those who had benefited from the previous regime, but also for many who had been oppressed by it were among those who were unhappy.

Thanks to a letter of introduction from Father Segura to some priests in Morelia's cathedral, Fidelio had made friends there. During the weekends, he volunteered teaching catechism to the children and cooking for the poor; thanks to his knowledge about the healing effects of different herbs, and what he had learned observing nature, he also helped in giving advice to those who couldn't afford to see a physician. The rector of the church, who had been a classmate to Father Segura at the seminary, was impressed by Fidelio and sometimes in the evenings, would invite him to join him and the other priests for a conversation while enjoying a cup of hot cocoa. They mainly talked about the social events that were occurring in the country.

"I believe that the circumstances are now favorable to bring back what Vasco de Quiroga accomplished a couple of centuries ago. The time is ripe to put again in practice the teachings written at *The Utopia* by Saint Thomas Moore," Father Casimiro, one of the young priests, enthusiastically, said at one of those reunions.

"What are those teachings? And who were Saint Thomas Moore and Vasco de Quiroga, and what is it that the latter did?" Fidelio asked.

"Saint Thomas Moore was an English philosopher who was executed because he followed his conscience. He wrote *The Utopia*, where he describes how, if a community works in harmony, everyone would benefit from it. Fray Vasco de Quiroga put it in practice in Janitzio and Patzcuaro, in this state, and it was a success, even to this day. The liberal laws that favor individuals, instead of communities, have jeopardized it. Now, it seems that the time to put it again in practice has come."

"Bah, the circumstances are now different and Vasco de Quiroga was a dreamer. Besides what he did would work only in a small community of uncivilized Indians, as are those places where he put it in practice. What is really necessary for the church is to recover the influence over the government, influence that was almost lost with the defeat of the Conservative Party, but that was recovered under President Diaz, with a lot of effort on the part of hierarchy. With this new President, whom I hear is a spiritist, it has been lost again," Father Toribio, a fat priest, said.

Fidelio mostly listened. He agreed with the idea of helping people to come together and help each other out of poverty and servitude; at the same time, he wondered about how could common people benefit from the influence of the church's hierarchy over the government.

One evening at the house of Enrique's relatives - where Fidelio was hired to work as a kitchen aide, Fidelio helped to serve dinner. "I have news from the capital. Madero is dead and General Huerta is now the new President." Fidelio heard Don Tomas de la Fuente, Enrique's uncle, saying at the dinner table, his voice was somber.

"I'm glad," Dona Marina, his wife, said. "Now there will be order again. That Madero was a fool, a dreamer. What we need in this country is a firm hand to control all those filthy peasants, low class people, who are asking for land and equality. How could they be equal to us? They are lazy, and as soon as they have a few cents, they spend it in pulque; their children are full of lice and their women, well, I don't even want to talk about them."

"Yes, Madero was a dreamer," said Enrique in a firm tone of voice. Fidelio could sense he was upset. "But what a wonderful dream. To give everyone the opportunity to improve and move in the social ladder, including those that you aunt, seem to despise.. Open more schools, giving the opportunity for all to receive education and the most important part of his dream, that those who work the land should share its benefits. I believe that all of us should do our part to make it a reality, that's the only hope we have for real progress."

"There are rumors that Madero and Pino-Suarez were cowardly assassinated," Don Tomas said. "That's bad enough. Although Madero was having some difficulties, he had many supporters. I'm afraid that a very difficult time is coming. A social storm could be brewing."

"You are right. I heard that the governors of the states of Coahuila, Chihuahua and Sonora have already declared that they won't recognize Huerta as the President," Enrique said, also serious. "I believe that a civil war is about to start. The hope that the revolution against Diaz brought, must not be lost."

"Enrique, I'm surprised to hear you talking that way. I didn't expect you to be against your own class," Dona Marina said.

"My own class? What are you talking about?" Enrique replied. "The fact that we were lucky to be born in a family wealthy enough to support itself, that we were able to receive an education, doesn't make us better or superior to the peasants, laborers and farmers. As a matter of fact, we need them more than they need us. It's their work that provides most of what we enjoy. If they had the opportunity, many of them would rise to be governors, generals, leaders, and I believe that they would be much more honest than the corrupt leaders we have had."

"Marina, my dear, you know that I supported Madero; and that I was against Diaz' reelection," Don Tomas said in a firm tone of voice. "Huerta has a reputation of heavy drinking and abuse of marihuana. I believe that under him, we are in a dangerous situation. Diaz at least worried about Mexico's progress; but this man cares only about himself and, at the most, will continue protecting those who are already extremely wealthy. The wealth of this country will continue going only to few pockets. With Madero, we had hope of a smooth change, but now, I'm afraid that the already existing social tension will explode."

"Tomas, you scare me."

"My dear, we all should be scared."

Most of this was news to Fidelio. The man who had brought hope for change had been killed, and his assassin was now the new President? Although he knew little about politics and about Madero, he could sense that this man had brought with him hope. During the last few months he had become acutely aware of the unequal social reality of the country, but it was also obvious that there were many who wished to keep things the way they were, and now it seemed that they had the upper hand.

The following days, in the streets, everyone was talking about the recent events. Most of the wealthy supported General Huerta. Fidelio already was aware of that, but he was happily surprised when during the Sunday mass in the cathedral, the Bishop denounced the death of President Madero and Vice President Pino Suarez as a crime. Although the bishop was aware that when General Huerta declared himself in charge of the new government, the bells in Mexico city's cathedral had tolled as a signal of approval, the church could not and did not condone what was obviously a crime. Many of those present stood up and walked out of the church, obviously upset by the Bishops' words. The Bishop finished asking all to stay calm and pray for peace.

Two days later, Enrique and Fidelio were in the kitchen. Fidelio had prepared hot chocolate accompanied with sweet bread. It was October and it was already cold and windy outside; a storm seemed to be brewing. Enrique, who usually enjoyed chocolate, barely looked at it. He was tense, his dark eyes shined, it seemed that he had been crying. Fidelio sensed that an inner storm was brewing in his friend's mind; so, he just sat quietly, sipped his chocolate, and waited.

"Yesterday something happened that has made me reach a decision." Enrique finally said. His face was tense, his voice metallic.

"What is it?" Fidelio asked, feeling a bit worried; he already knew that his friend was reproaching himself about something.

Enrique put his elbows on the table, his fingers rubbed his forehead, jaws tight. "It was ugly," he said looking at Fidelio, "and I couldn't do anything to stop it or prevent it." Fidelio put down his cup of chocolate and listened.

"The foreman of the ranch brought two peons, two Indian peons to the patron, 'el amo', as the foreman calls him," Enrique continued. "Then the patron, after listening to the foreman, ordered the two men to be whipped. It was ugly, ugly, and I just stood there!" He looked at Fidelio, who noticed the fire in the eyes of his friend. "They used lashes with steel balls at the end. At every lash, their skin was deeply cut and blood gushed from their backs. The pain made them scream, a wild, horrendous scream; but it only seemed to excite the beast who was lashing them, he whipped them until he was exhausted. The men, their backs bleeding, were left there, surrounded by flies attracted by the blood." Enrique started crying, his tears flowed down his cheeks. "And I just stood there, didn't say a single word."

"But, tell me, why did the patron do that?" Fidelio asked. He gave Enrique a handkerchief to wipe the tears. Fidelio was perplexed; it was difficult for him to understand how someone could be cruel towards anything, much less another human being.

"The poor men dared, dared. He repeated in a sarcastic tone, to ask for permission to keep part of their crop. The product of their own, hard work!" Enrique yelled, slapping the table, the dishes jumped, spilling the chocolate that Fidelio was drinking. "Harvested in land that used to be communal land, land that used to be theirs; land that has been taken away from them; and, now they are forced to continue working it, but to benefit the new landlord; they no longer receive a fair share for their work. They have become slaves in their own land."

"I don't understand. You are saying that they are working land that should be theirs. How is that?" Fidelio asked

"It's a long and complex story Fidelio," Enrique answered, a sad grin on his face. "I'll try to summarize. Traditionally the towns, along with private property, had a land that was communal, land that everyone in the community would work and share the benefits of the crops. At the same time, there were the haciendas. They used to respect each other. But, in an effort to make the haciendas more productive, laws were created that allowed the big haciendas to take possession of this communal land. It was all legal, even if the community didn't approve of it. This has forced the people from the small farms and towns to work for the big ranchers. That and the fact that they are not really paid for their work, but barely receive what is necessary to merely survive from the hacienda's store, has made them less than serfs. These people are practically owned by the rancher; that's why they call him 'el amo'."

"I understand now why you are upset about it. But, you said that you have made a decision. What is it?"

"Fidelio, we are living in a time of change, we can accept that there is injustice in our world, and pretend that it isn't our concern and look the other way, or we can rebel against it. As a matter of fact, there are men who are already fighting." Enrique took a deep breath, looked at Fidelio straight in the eyes. "I don't want to be just a passive observer while others are fighting for something that is just. I want to be part of it. I'll join them."

"But, do you know who are you going to join?"

"There are several choices, I could go south and join Zapata, or up-north and join the forces of Francisco Villa, or to Sinaloa and join Rafael Buelna." He looked to Fidelio, paused for a moment, "I made up my mind, and I'll go north and join Villa."

Fidelio noticed how Enrique was now boiling with enthusiasm and he felt the same rush inside him, he also wanted to be part of it. But, at the same time, he was conscious that it meant that he would have to take part in war, perhaps even kill someone. He realized that Enrique was right, if change for everyone was to come, it was necessary to fight for it, or become just an observer. Holding Enrique's gaze, he thought for a moment, "I'll go with you," he finally said.

Enrique smiled. "Although barely out of childhood and a bit naive, you are able to understand better than most people. Sure, you are tall and strong, as a matter of fact, you look older. But you despise violence, you are unable to harm even an insect, you are always trying to heal, you don't know how to use a gun. No Fidelio, I appreciate that you want to go with me, but I'm afraid you couldn't help; I am sorry to say it, but you could even become a burden."

"Yes, it's true that I despise violence, but I have already learned that it is part of life. It's also true that I don't know how to use a gun, and I recognize that I don't even care to learn." Fidelio smiled back to Enrique, "but you forget that I know how to take care of wounds, and I know about the use of medicinal herbs. I can assure you that even if I don't use a gun, I won't be a burden, I am sure that these skills will be useful."

"I wouldn't be so sure, but if you are certain, I'm glad to have you on my side." Enrique said, smiling. He took a bite of the sweet bread and sipped the cocoa.

CHAPTER V

It was late in the fall when Fidelio and Enrique arrived at Torreon. A city in the middle of northern Mexico, barely twenty-years-old, but thanks to the cotton, Torreon had become the most important agricultural emporium in Mexico. And if we add that is located at the center of the northern part of the country, with excellent railroad communication, it had become an important strategic position for both, the rebels and the government. When Fidelio and Enrique arrived, the city was under the control of the rebels. There, they hoped to join the forces of what was being called "the northern division," under the command of General Francisco Villa.

"I don't know about you, but I'm hungry, let's find a place to eat," Enrique said as soon as they had left the railroad station.

Fidelio looked around. "Look, there is an open market over there, a few blocks from here, I'm sure we'll find a nice and clean place to eat," he pointed to his left. Indeed, several blocks in the direction Fidelio pointed they could see the open market, it looked busy, lots of people, several eateries could be seen from where they were.

"You are right and it looks like the right place to eat, let's go there," Enrique said. They started walking towards the market. They traveled light, each of them carried only a small bag with few changes of clothes.

"This is truly a modern city, look how wide and straight the streets are, as much as sixteen horses could fit in it, and the sidewalk is also spacious, we can walk side by side and still there is plenty of space for other people and, there is even room for those palm trees, planted in the middle," Enrique said.

"Yes, and also these trees in the sidewalk not only look pretty, but also provide a pleasant shadow," Fidelio replied. When they reached the corner of the street, he stopped to read the plate with the name of the street. "That's strange, look at the name of this street," he pointed to the plate, it read: "Avenida General Porfirio Diaz."

Enrique read it and smiled "The name of the man against whom the revolution started. Probably they haven't had time to change it, or maybe they don't care."

"That might be so," Fidelio replied. When they approached the market place, he pointed to a woman standing behind a large table, where several people sat in front of a plate of a hot red soup. "That pozole smells delicious."

"It might be that I'm hungry," Enrique said, "but to me, it smells like heaven." His belly grunted.

"Two plates of pozole, with plenty of radish and lettuce," Enrique said, as they sat at the table.

"Large or small?" asked the young woman in charge. Her voice was pleasant, musical.

"Large," said Fidelio smiling, feeling happy. The woman turned, looked at him and smiled at him. When Fidelio saw her face, he felt a current running through his entire body. It was a strange, different, never-before felt, sensation. Suddenly, he felt shaky, his hands sweated, his mouth salivated. She was a teenager, with long black hair, braided with green ribbons. Her eyes were large, black, shining, her skin smooth, her cheeks had a natural pink color and her teeth were well aligned and white. Fidelio thought that she was an angelical being, to his eyes all of her glowed.

After a while, she turned, prepared the two plates and put them in front of the two boys. "I put a little more meat in yours," she said, smiling again, to Fidelio. "Where are you from? What's your name?" she asked. Her large eyes sparkled, friendly.

"Fidelio, and this is my friend Enrique. We come from Morelia," he answered, making an effort to overcome the strange sensation.

Looking at her eyes, Fidelio felt like he was looking at the stars in a clear night; but at the same time, he was surprised to find in them a promise, a promise of something new, different. He didn't know what it was, but he felt that it would be exciting and pleasant. He noticed that a part of his body was getting tense and was embarrassed noticing a bulk growing in between his legs.

"Morelia, it sounds like a far-away place," she said, still smiling, keeping her eyes fixed on Fidelio. "You are young, tall, and strong. Did you come looking for work? It would be difficult to find one these days." She saw that there were new customers calling. "I'll be back, we'll continue taking, if you don't have a place where to stay, I know one, clean and cheap."

Enrique pressed Fidelio's arm and made a gesture signaling a man with a military insignia among the other customers.

The man turned, looked at them. "Hey, you two," he yelled, pointing at them. "You are strong, the revolution needs you. Don't even try to move from where you are, because today you are going to join the Northern Division."

Although that was the reason they had come, Fidelio felt surprised, upset. He didn't like to be imposed upon.

"Well, Captain, that is precisely the reason we have traveled here. We want to volunteer," Enrique said, with a friendly smile.

"Ah, that's better. Welcome! For a moment, I thought you were pelones trying to pass as civilians. Finish your meal in peace. Afterwards, I'll take you to meet General Contreras who will assign you," said the man with a friendly smile.

On hearing all of this the young woman turned, looked at Fidelio. Her expression was sad, concerned. She hurried up with what she was doing, and went back to Fidelio.

"It seems that you'll be leaving," she said to him. "I don't even know you, but I already like you. There is something about you, that makes me feel something strange, different, that I had never felt before," she flushed, looked down, embarrassed. "I want to get to know you better, come back whenever you have a chance." She fixed her large, black eyes on Fidelio, who, once again, felt like a current running through his entire body, but happy to know that she was also feeling something for him.

"You said you know a place where we could stay," Fidelio said, making an effort to hide that he was almost shaking. "We might still need it, I'll return later, after we enlist."

She smiled. "I'll be waiting."

"I still don't know your name."

"Candelaria," she said, smiled, and turned to answer the call of another customer.

"Well little boys, let's go." The man said, walking towards them. He was short, chubby, bow legged with a scar on his right cheek. "You are going to meet my General Contreras, who is the one in charge here. He'll assign you where you can be most useful to the cause." He stopped and looked at them. "You two are very young, let me warn you. Sometimes, with novices like you, he likes to scare them and threatens to shoot them or to send them to the firing squad. But, he does that just to see if they have balls." Then he laughed softly, as if he was telling a joke. "Sometimes, however, the firing squad has shot before he orders them to stop. Anyhow, if the boys act sissy, he will let it be." He stopped, laughing and hitting his right thigh with the palm of his hand, it was obvious that he enjoyed talking about it. "By the way, my name is Toribio Renteria, captain in the newly created artillery. Perhaps, you would like to join it."

"My name is Enrique Sanchez de la Fuente," replied Enrique, "and my friend here is Fidelio Serna. I'm much better on the horse and with the rifle and he knows how to take care of the wounded."

"I'm sure General Contreras will find a place for both of you."

After they had walked through several streets, Fidelio who was still feeling like walking on the clouds, under the magic spell of the young woman, was conscious enough to notice how straight the streets were and how well designed the city was, each square measured exactly one hundred meters per side. They finally reached a plaza, clean with a lot of trees on it; a beautiful fountain in each corner, and a kiosk in the middle of it. Around the plaza there were several beautiful buildings, built with pink stones.

"The headquarters are in that building," said the captain pointing to the most beautiful of the buildings, in the middle of the street. Large cooper letters on top of the entrance read: "Casino de La Laguna."

They went up a few marble stairs, crossed the heavy crystal door that had cotton plants chiseled on it. At the end of a corridor a General, along with some other officials, were looking at a military map. A man with the insignia of a Captain on his hat stopped them as soon as they had entered.

"What is your business Captain Renteria? And who are these boys?" He asked.

"These are volunteers that want to join the cause, Captain Michelena," Captain Renteria replied.

"Wait here, I'll let General Contreras know."

The captain went to the table, talked to the men, who looked in the direction where they were waiting. Captain Michelena made a signal to them to approach.

General Contreras came forward to meet them. He was of medium height, slender, still young, around thirty-five-years old, light brown hair cut short, and a thin moustache. Dressed in khaki pants and shirt, a gun hanging on his right thigh, long, leather, military boots.

"Good morning Captain Renteria, it's always nice to greet a good soldier." He then turned and looked at the two young men, his eyes of an olive-green color sparkled. Fidelio sensed that although he seemed to be in a playful mood, he could be harsh, even cruel, but at the same time he could be compassionate. "I see you brought two new recruits," the General said, walking around them, slapping each one on the shoulders. "They seem to be strong. But, how will they behave in combat? Will they be brave, or will they be a sissy?" He paused, stood in front of them, frowning. "Where are you from? Do you come by your own will? Why do you want to join?"

"We are from Guanajuato, but come from Morelia. It was there that we decided to join the revolution because we didn't like what happened to President Madero and because we want a change, justice for all, not only for the rich." Enrique replied

"It's a long way from Morelia to Torreon," Contreras said. "Why didn't you join Zapata, in the south?"

"Because to do so we would have had to travel through the territory controlled by Huerta. It was easier and faster to travel here," Enrique replied.

"That makes sense. Can you ride a horse, shoot a gun and a rifle? Have you ever killed a man? Do you understand that you will have to kill and that you might be killed? Are you willing to sacrifice your life for this cause?"

"I know how to ride a horse, and how to shoot. Yes, we understand that we might be killed and yes, we are willing to sacrifice our lives, if that becomes necessary," Enrique said, and Fidelio nodded approvingly.

Contreras turned to Fidelio, got closer and faced him. "You are tall and strong, but, have a childish face. How old are you? Can you ride a horse, shoot a man and are you willing to sacrifice your youth, your life, for the cause?" he asked, poking on Fidelio's chest.

Fidelio remained calm, looked down, straight into Contreras' eyes. "I'm seventeen, and no, I don't know how to ride a horse, shoot a gun and I will kill a man only if that is absolutely necessary. But, I am willing to sacrifice my life for this cause."

Upset, Contreras looked up, straight into Fidelio's eyes. "Do you take me for a fool? How can you come here and tell me that you want to join the revolution when you don't know how to shoot a gun!" he yelled. "I believe that you are a sissy and I'm going to kill you right here," he pulled his gun and pressed it under Fidelio's jaw.

Fidelio didn't move. Being much taller than the General, he calmly looked down, straight into Contreras' eyes. "I can't shoot a gun, but I can take care of the wounded. I know the use of healing herbs, not only by killing can someone be useful to the cause," he said. Although his voice was high pitched, it was firm, tranquil and poised. Fidelio, however, felt surprised about feeling so tranquil, it was a strange sensation. He was scared, but at the same time something made him feel serene. It felt as if someone else had taken over his body and was putting words in his mouth.

"General Villa has ordered Doctor Villarreal to create a sanitary brigade, probably this boy could be useful there," one of the officers said.

Contreras kept the gun under Fidelio's jaw, they looked straight into each other eyes. "If you really believe that I'm, as you say, a sissy, go ahead and pull the trigger. I'm only afraid of God," Fidelio said, with a voice that was firm, slow, and calm. 'Who is this that is talking for me?' he thought.

The General started breathing heavily, with sweat drops on his forehead, after a short while, he was no longer able to hold Fidelio's gaze. He lowered his head and his hand, put the gun back in the holster, smiled nervously, looked around, before looking back at Fidelio. He now seemed relaxed, and his eyes were friendly. "Indeed, you are brave, and you are also right, a revolution is to create something new, and bring justice for all. Yes, we can make use of men like you. Captain Renteria," he said turning to face the Captain, "enlist them." Then, he pointed to Fidelio, "take the boy to Dr. Villarreal, I'm sure that he will be useful to him." He then pointed to Enrique, "give him a horse, a rifle and enough ammunition. In two days, we are going to join Villa in Chihuahua, for the time being we'll have to leave Torreon to the Federales."

"I'm proud of you," said Enrique slapping Fidelio on the back after they had left. "You were not only brave, but above all, you showed control and remained calm; anyone else, including me, would have been scared."

"Yes, indeed," said Captain Renteria. "All of us were impressed. I'm sure Major Villarreal will be glad to have you in his group; and since General Villa has ordered a train wagon to be prepared for the medical brigade, there is no need for you to ride a horse." He then looked at Enrique. "You will join the cavalry, under Maclovio Herrera, a brave and honest revolutionary. After you get your horse and ammunition, both of you can do whatever you want. But remember in two days we are leaving to join Villa in Chihuahua."

Fidelio said nothing, himself surprised by his attitude. How was it that he remained calm in the face of real danger? The words that he said, who had talked? He knew well that General Contreras had thought that he was a sissy and was about to pull the trigger before he had spoken. Something strange, that he didn't understand, had saved him.

"Well Fidelio, I overheard that you promised to go back to that pretty girl in the pozole stand," Enrique said after they had been enlisted and Captain Renteria had left them. "I'll leave you now. In this matter, it is better if you are alone with the girl, don't worry about me. Captain Renteria, who also heard, has already told me about a place to stay. Maybe we'll meet again in two days, before we leave for Chihuahua." They hugged. "Be careful, you have no experience with women," Enrique said smiling, slapped Fidelio's shoulder in a friendly way and walked across the street.

As Fidelio walked back to the market where they had eaten, the memory of Candelaria caused the same sweet emotion that he had felt when he saw her that morning. In his mind he saw her smile, her lips, her cheeks, her figure, but above all, her large black - with shades of deep blue, eyes. Fidelio saw those eyes everywhere he looked and that sensation made him feel excited and happy; so, happy that he almost danced as he walked. Those who passed by his side seemed to notice his happiness and smiled at him.

As he was approaching the market, Candelaria, who apparently had been looking for him, left the booth to meet him. She almost ran. She looked happy to see him, her face was radiant. Looking at her, Fidelio was impressed. It was as if an angel, like those he had seen in the paintings in the cathedrals of Guanajuato and Morelia, came to greet him.

"I'm so happy you came back. I was afraid you had already forgotten me," she said, as soon as they got close to each other. She took his hands and looked straight into Fidelio's eyes. Her eyes, her touch, caused him to feel again a current flowing through his entire body. The touch of her hands, her bright smile and above all, the radiance of her eyes, caused him to have again these, until now unknown, sensations. The rest of the market stands, the people around them, all disappeared, and he felt and saw only her. He was in a cloud, speechless.

"Say something," said she. "Are you upset that I ran to meet you? Maybe you came for some other reason and I am embarrassing you, if that is so, I am sorry. It's just that I felt so happy when I saw you coming back that I couldn't hold myself and ran to meet you. I'm sorry." She let his hands go and looked down, an expression of sadness in her face, as if she was ready to cry.

"No, no, please don't be sorry. You are the only reason I came back. And, of course, I am glad you came to greet me," said Fidelio, touching her gently on her shoulder and then lifting her chin. "Please smile again, it makes me so happy to see you smile."

She smiled, extended her arm and caressed Fidelio's cheek. "You are so tall, but still beardless," she said. Putting her arm down, she frowned, looked at Fidelio, before asking: "Did you join the revolution? I don't know why I'm afraid, I just met you, but I already care about you. I heard that the federales are coming and you will have to go."

"Yes, I already joined and it's true, we are leaving in two days. I'm glad that you care about me, because I care about you," Fidelio said, smiling. "You said something about a place where I could stay. I'm tired and I would like to rest a little."

"It's just a couple of blocks from here," said Candelaria, pointing in direction of the train station. "General Diaz number twenty-three. You can't miss it, it says clearly 'guest house.' Just tell the hostess that I sent you. But, could I see you later? When we close the stand, I'd like to take a bath and go and see you. But that's only if you want it." Her large black eyes pierced Fidelio, who, once again, felt a current running down his spine.

"Of course, you are the reason I came back. But if you want, just tell me where to go and I'll meet you there." said Fidelio, flushing.

"It will be much easier for both of us if I go and find you at your room tonight," she said, smiling. A woman at the stand yelled, calling her. "I have to go, but wait for me I'll see you tonight at your room," she said tiptoeing and kissing him in the check before leaving. "Wait for me," she said, before running to the stand.

He stood there watching her. He gently caressed the cheek that she had kissed. After he saw her getting into the stand, he turned and walked to the guest house. He felt like floating, walking on a cloud.

He had no difficulty finding the guest house. A short, chubby blond woman was in charge; when Fidelio told her that Candelaria had sent him, the woman smiled at him in a friendly manner.

"Anyone who is a friend of Candelaria is welcome here," said she. "Where are you coming from?"

Fidelio smiled back. "From Morelia, it has been a long trip," he scratched his head. "Is there any way I could have a bath?"

"I'll warm some water and prepare it for you. It will cost you thirty cents," she said, extending her hand.

After the bath, Fidelio felt refreshed, and at the same time, relaxed. He was tired after the long trip and the heavy emotions of the day, so he went into his room and, leaving the kerosene lamp on, slept. A couple of hours later, he was awakened by soft knocks at the door.

"Wait for a minute, I have to get dressed," Fidelio yelled. He jumped out of the bed, looked for his clothes and dressed as fast as he could, rushed to the door, opened it and stopped. He thought an angel was at the door.

Candelaria laughed softly, "What is it?" she said. "Were you expecting someone else? You seem surprised." Her skin was radiant, her black hair sparkling; her large, black eyes shined. Because she had a white dress with embroidered red flowers, her brunette complexion was enhanced. "Please say something, may I come in? It's getting cold."

"Yes, yes, please come in," Fidelio said, moving aside and letting Candelaria walk into the room. Besides the bed, the room had a small table and two chairs. Candelaria walked straight to the table, opened the basket she was carrying, extended a white table cloth, embroidered with flowers and butterflies, placed a dinner pail in the center of the table, two plates, forks, knifes and glasses, opened the dinner pail, served chicken soup and poured Moscato wine in the glasses.

Fidelio who hadn't noticed the basket when she came in, looked at her and everything with wide open eyes. He had to make an effort to prevent his jaw from dropping. Now, he was convinced that she was a celestial being.

"I hope you are hungry," she said, showing him her well aligned white teeth.

Fidelio's bowels rumbled. "Yes, I'm very hungry," he said, laughing. Candelaria also laughed.

They sat at the table. Since he had not eaten or drank since early that morning, he really was thirsty and hungry. He took the glass of Moscato and gulped it to the bottom. Candelaria smiled and filled his glass again. Both were happy, so they ate, drank and talked cheerfully.

Fidelio was amazed about how easy it was to have a conversation with her. They told each other the story of their lives. He admired her when he learned that she had also lost her parents and how she had learned to take care of herself. He loved listening to her and she seemed so happy to have someone who would listen to her and talked almost incessantly.

"Oh! Fidelio it's so easy to talk to you. I don't know what it is about you, but since the moment I saw you, I knew that you are the one I was looking for; and, what is truly amazing is that I didn't know that I was looking for someone until that very moment." She laughed, and that laugh sounded to Fidelio's ears like music.

After the fourth glass of wine, he found her more and more attractive. But now it was not as a celestial being, but as a woman. Her radiant skin, her smile, her lips, had now an attraction that to him was new, different, but that made him feel energized. Fidelio now noticed her breasts moving provocatively under her white blouse every time she breathed, laughed, or moved. He felt a strong desire to touch her, to caress her, to fuse with her, to become one with her. "Let me take those dirty dishes away," she said standing up and getting closer to Fidelio, who feeling her so close, without even thinking about it, extended his arm and passed it around her waist. He noticed how firm she was, like a warm rock.

At his touch, she turned facing him and smiled. Fidelio, with the arm around her waist, gently pulled her towards him. She let it be and let herself sit on his knees. Feeling the weight of her body, he moved his hand up, caressing her back, her neck until, taking the back of her head, gently, pushed her towards his face. She let him do it and once she was close enough, kissed his lips. It was Fidelio's first kiss. A sweet, hot, humid kiss. Candelaria put her hand on his cheek, and continued kissing him. Fidelio felt that his blood was now steaming and started rubbing her entire body; he pulled her skirt up and caressed her firm thighs, her rounded butt. He stood up, lifting her along with him and put her on the bed. He got on top of her; his movements were rough, clumsy.

"Ssshh, relax, calm, go slowly, I'm not going anywhere," she said, holding his hands and smiling to him. "Be gentle, let us relish these moments. I want this to be something special for both of us. I want it to be the most important moment in my life. I want to keep the flavor of your lips in mine forever, to keep the memory of your body in me; but I also want you to keep me in your memory forever." Smiling, Fidelio realized that she was right. He nodded and slowly, gently, started to undress her; she did the same for him. They shared caresses and explored each other's bodies until exhausted, slept; just to restart as soon as they awoke. They had hunger and thirst just for each other's body and continued the whole night, the following day and night, breaking the embrace only when they were forced by nature's call.

"I'm afraid that it's time for me to leave," Fidelio said, at 4 a.m. in the morning of the second dawn they were together.

"I know," Candelaria replied. "Remember the time we have spent together. I will feel you in me forever, and if you are ever back, I'll be here waiting for you. You are the first and the last man in my life, no one will ever touch me. I'm yours forever and, for that same reason I'm letting you go free."

"What are you talking about? I don't want to go, I don't want to leave you, I'll stay at your side forever," he said, putting his body close to hers and embracing her.

"I will not let you become a deserter. Besides, there is something special about you. Maybe you don't know it yet, but I can feel it, there is something in you and that makes you different, unique. I feel that you can't belong to anyone, even if you wanted. I know that I belong to you, but you have to continue your way: And once again, if you are ever back you'll find me loving you as much as I do today. I'm yours, but I know that you can't be mine. So, go, and follow your path," she said, caressing him and gently pushing him to get up. "I'll help you to get dressed," she added.

"I don't know when, but I'll be back," Fidelio said, as he allowed her to help him to put his pants and shirt on. "I'll fix you a cup of coffee," said she, getting dressed herself. "I'll wait for you in the kitchen."

Once alone, Fidelio sat on the bed, elbows on his knees, he rubbed his forehead with his fingers. He was confused and didn't know what to do. A part of him wanted to stay close to Candelaria, but there was something that he could not understand. Why, if he loved her so much, he didn't feel that she belonged to him? Why did he also feel this desire to go away? He felt that there was something else. Although he couldn't understand it, he knew that she was right when she said that he could not belong to her or to anyone. He had a strange sensation. A need to serve others, but how? There were still many things that he needed to learn and understand, before he could settle. He stood up, finished packing his few belongings. Now, he was certain that she was correct and he had to go. He left the room and went to the kitchen to enjoy a few more moments with Candelaria.

Later, walking towards the train station to join the sanitary brigade, the freshness of the autumnal morning, the brightness of the sun, barely over the mountains, made Fidelio feel happy. He looked around and for the first time, he noticed the tall mountains around the city, bare rock, no trees. Hundreds of birds flying on their way south covered the sky. Fidelio, taking a deep breath, felt the wonder of nature and thanked God for allowing him to be part of it.

CHAPTER VI

Miles and miles of flat, plain, dry terrain, only a few small mesquite and aloe plants grew in that desert. At the distance, Fidelio saw tall mountains, all bare rock, only a few shrubs gave them an occasional touch of green. To him, used to the landscape of central Mexico, this scenery was different, strange, mysterious, magical and attractive, but also somehow harsh, cruel and menacing.

"What do you think?" Dr. Villarreal, standing at Fidelio's side, asked. "Does this desert attract or repel you? It doesn't allow anything in between. People either love it or hate it."

"I like it," Fidelio answered. "But I couldn't say that I love it because I'm seeing it for the first time. It's so different from the landscape that I have seen until now."

"That's fair," Dr. Villarreal replied. "This land is noble with those who are willing to sweat and work it hard; to them, it will provide plenty. However, it will not tolerate laziness, those will be destroyed, then swallowed by it."

"That's also different to what I have seen before."

"I was born and raised here, before going to medical school I used to venture into it. I made friends with many of the ranchers and also with the tarahumaras. They taught me a lot about the almost magical qualities of the plants from the desert."

Dr. Villarreal smiled, looked into the distance for a moment, pensive. He then turned to the wagon train they were on. "Look at this, it's beautiful, almost a mobile hospital. To me it's like a dream that has become a reality. Because of his background, there are many who think that General Villa is semi savage. But he is intelligent, noble, understands the people, and he cares about them. He understands that war is bloody, that there will be many wounded in battle. That's why he has equipped this wagon to take care of those who need it. Of all the generals and leaders in this struggle, he is the only one who has thought about that. It was expensive to buy all this equipment. He could have used the money for his own benefit, but he has chosen to put it at the service of those wounded in battle. That's why we must be worthy of the confidence he puts in us." He paused, looked at Fidelio. "Do you understand what that means, young boy?"

"I believe I do," answered Fidelio.

"Good, I've been told that you also know quite a bit about medicinal plants and how to use them," Dr. Villarreal said, as he sat down. "Also, that in spite of being just out of childhood, you already have experience in taking care of people's ailments." He stopped, looked at Fidelio, a dubious smile on his face. "How is that so? Where and how did you learn?" He pointed to Fidelio to sit at his side.

Fidelio already knew that it was strange for someone of his age, with so little schooling, to have knowledge about the healing powers of plants. So, he wasn't upset by the question, nor by the fact that Dr. Villarreal had doubts about it. "I learned by observing the birds, frogs, butterflies, and almost any animal that I had a chance to observe. They have a lot to teach. They know which plants are dangerous and which will provide nourishment. Also, every time I found a dead one, I studied their internal organs." He smiled, looking at Dr. Villarreal. He didn't want to add that there was an inner voice that still frightened him, guiding him. "But, I want to learn more, I want to learn to use all this equipment. I will listen and follow your instructions. If I am not able to shoot a rifle, I know that I can contribute to this cause."

Dr. Villarreal laughed. "That's the way to talk young boy. Yes, I'll teach you and I know that you'll learn. You already know more than many of my colleagues. Because you have learned not from books, but from the most important source of knowledge, nature. Never change my young friend, never change." He looked outside. "We are getting close to Camargo. I know that General Villa is already preparing for a big battle, we'll be ready. Once in the city, mingle with the troops, observe them, there are a lot of young boys, like you. Learn their reasons for joining this struggle. That knowledge might become helpful when some or many of them need your help." He then looked at Fidelio with a serious expression, like a bit concerned. "But never venture too far, report every day at sunset, and be ready because we might receive orders to mobilize any time. I know that we are going to be in a battle soon, very soon. You have never been in battle before, even if one is not in the line of fire, it is not easy, it takes balls, big balls." He paused, looked at Fidelio straight in the eyes, extended his arm and squeezed Fidelio's forearm. "Let me give you a word of advice. Once in battle, even if you are not at the front, you will be afraid, perhaps scared, that's a natural reaction. It happens to all, even to the most seasoned. But, if you allow the fear to control you, then you'll be lost. Use your fear as a source of strength, then you'll be able to do your part." He released Fidelio's arm and smiled. "I don't know why, but I'm certain that you'll know how to handle the fear."

Later, walking the streets, Fidelio noticed that Camargo was a small town, compared to Torreon, but he liked that it also had wide streets and they were kept clean. Used to the pulquerias in central Mexico, always full of people, the fact that all the bars in the city were closed caught his attention. "Fidelio, hey Fidelio," someone yelled. Fidelio turned and he was surprised to see Dionaciano and some of his old classmates walking towards him, all with rifles and a belt full of bullets crossing their chest.

"Dionaciano, Pantaleon, Casimiro, friends, my good friends, I'm glad to see you all," Fidelio said, happy to see his old classmates. He noticed that, although as young as himself, there was something new in them. They seemed to be as happy as he was, and they were smiling at him, but it no longer was the childish, innocent smile of the previous years. Looking at their hairy faces, their yellow teeth, the image of a coyote that had just eaten a chicken came to Fidelio. Although friendly, their smile was that of men who had already been close to death, of men who have already killed a fellow human being.

"Fidelio, what are you doing here?" Dionaciano asked as he got close and embraced him. Fidelio returned the hug and then hugged the other boys, in a friendly way, real happy to see them.

"Are you running away from the violence of the revolution?" Pantaleon asked, smiling. "If that's the case, you are in the wrong path because Chihuahua is the place where most of the action is happening."

"No, I'm not running away from anything," answered Fidelio, also smiling. "On the contrary, I have joined it." He looked at each of them, "it seems that it has been some time since you joined."

"Yes, we did it almost from the beginning," said Casimiro. "We had been working at mines that are close by, when we heard about the assassination of Madero. We were upset, but we didn't know what to do. But when Villa captured Temosachic, a town close to where we were working, we decided to join him. We have been in many good fights since that time," he added with a proud smile.

"Yes, we have been in good fights and there will be many more." Dionaciano intervened, smiling, he looked at Fidelio and then he frowned, a worrisome expression on his face. "But Fidelio, in a battle it becomes necessary to kill in order not to be killed. We all know your courage, we also know that you don't like guns, you don't even know how to use them." He took a deep breath, looked down, in deep thought, he then looked back at Fidelio. "My dear friend, what are you going to do when we engage in battle?" he finally asked.

"I'm here to help take care of the wounded; if by any reason I must take part in a battle, God will guide me," answered Fidelio.

"That's right. You can stay back and help taking care of the wounded; that, believe me, there will be many," Pantaleon said, looking to all. "We all have seen how Fidelio can heal people and I admit it makes me feel better knowing that someone like him will be there in case any one of us is wounded." He paused, took a breath and then smiled. "I heard that my General Villa has recruited doctors and I have seen the special wagon, that they say it has been well equipped," he added.

"Great, we all know what you can do for those who are sick or wounded. Although I hope I'll never need your service, I admit that I feel safer knowing that a man of God, like you, my good friend, will take care of me in case I get wounded." Dionaciano said. The other boys nodded in approval.

"Talking about men of God, I don't like how some of our fellow soldiers treat the priests and nuns," Dionaciano continued talking. "There are many who don't respect the house of God, they ride their horses inside the churches and I have seen some of them even spit or urinate in there."

"Yes, I saw something like that in Torreon," Pantaleon added, "and I didn't like it, so I shot the one who did it."

"You did well. Everyone must respect our Saint Mother, the Church," Dionaciano said. He was going to add something when someone started yelling nearby. "Don't touch me you dirty Indian!" A tall and strong, well dressed white man yelled at a couple of Raramuri that were begging in a corner. The Raramuri were a man and a woman. Their skin was light brown and their hair was so black that it looked blue when hit by the sun rays. Both of them were young. She was dressed in a long cotton dress, embroidered with red flowers. Her belly was large and rounded. Fidelio realized that she was pregnant. She looked down, sobbing quietly. The man was tall, slender, dressed in plain cotton pants and shirt, huaraches in his feet and a red cotton band circled his head, his hair was long. He stared at the white man, but his face didn't show fear, he remained quiet, expressionless. Almost statuesque.

The white man was accompanied by two other, also well-dressed, young men. "I'll teach you to show respect to your masters," the first man yelled, the other two were laughing. The first man raised his right hand to slap the Raramuri, but he couldn't do it because Fidelio held his hand firmly.

"What you are going to teach is that you respect all," Fidelio said in a firm and calm voice.

"And the three of you are going to give them everything that is in your pockets," Dionaciano added, also with a calm voice.

The three men looked at Fidelio, who was still holding firmly the hand of the first man, and then to his companions, Dionaciano, Pantaleon and Casimiro, who were already pointing their rifles at them.

"All of it?" one of the three asked, with a trembling voice.

"All of it," replied Dionaciano.

The three men emptied their pockets and gave it to the Raramuri couple. The male took it, looked at Fidelio and his friends, embraced gently the woman and both walked away, slowly, without saying a word.

"You were lucky this time," Candelario said to the three men. "If I ever catch you again mistreating an Indian, I'll kill you."

"I hope you learned your lesson," Fidelio said. "Go home in peace."

The man looked at Fidelio and his friends with rancor. "If there is a next time, it will be different. I'll be the one teaching you a lesson that you'll never forget," he said with rancor. Then turned and walked away with his friends.

"Do you know who he is?" Dionaciano asked, after the men had left.

"Of course not," Fidelio replied.

"He is the son of Luis Terrazas, the wealthiest man in Chihuahua and until now, the most powerful," Dionaciano said, smiling. "One year ago, we would be in real trouble. But now he also trembles when he hears the name of my General Villa," he added.

"We have seen many like him, because they are rich they treat everyone like trash," Pantaleon said, spitting. "Do you remember how after the explosion of the mine where many were killed, our parents were forced to go back to the mines the following day?" Angrily he spitted again and kicked the dust. "But now it's our turn, we'll make them pay," he smiled at that thought.

"I'll never forget that day," Fidelio said. "It was hard, but we must not allow ourselves to live full of rancor, we must always remember the lesson of Jesus, our master and role model. Without accepting injustice, forgive those who trespass against us."

"Maybe you can do that. But as far as I'm concerned, I'll always hate them and I'm happy when I see them lose what they have. Then, they behave like little goats, like those folks in Gomez Palacio," Pantaleon said and laughed, showing his already rotten teeth. The others also laughed.

"It's time for us to go back to our battalion. It sure has been nice to see you Fidelio. I don't know if we'll see each other again," Dionaciano said, smiling to Fidelio. "I just hope that if we meet again, it won't be because we were wounded."

"Take care Fidelio," Casimiro, who had stayed quiet until now, said. "By the way, if you are interested in hearing mass, go to the one at 6 p.m. It's officiated by the bishop of Chihuahua, he reminds me of father Segura."

They waived farewell to Fidelio and walked away.

Fidelio observed his friends walking away. Having found them brought bitter-sweet memories of his childhood in Guanajuato. But once again, what most impressed him was how much they had changed. Although as young as himself, they were already hard, experienced in life and death, grownup men. He felt a chill running down his spine. "Would I be able to stand battle?" he asked himself. He walked a few more blocks until he reached the city square, he sat on one of the benches. Looking around, he saw the Raramuri couple coming out of the general store. The man carried a bag of flour in one arm and a package in another. Both of them walked slow, straight, with dignity. Although he realized that they had come to the city to beg for food, they looked proud.

"Indeed, they are proud people," said a man sitting in the same bench.

Fidelio looked at the man. He was well dressed, tall and slender. His hair and beard were white and his face already wrinkled around the eyes. In spite of that, there was something youthful, almost childish, in him. Fidelio had a sensation that he had seen him somewhere else. "I noticed that you were impressed by that couple," said the man. Fidelio felt that somehow, he recognized that voice.

"Yes, I was, and exactly what you just said is what impressed me," said Fidelio. "Where I come from, the Indians are humble and submissive, almost afraid of the white men, but these are different. Why is that so?"

"Humble and submissive, afraid of the white men," the man echoed Fidelio's words in an ironic tone. He smiled, showing that he was missing some of his teeth. "That's exactly what they want you to believe. These, however, are, as you said, different. They don't bother to hide what they feel about us. Although we call them Tarahumaras, they call themselves Raramuri –those who run long distance. They are a proud people. Although now peaceful, they fought fiercely the first Spanish settlers." The man paused, looking at the couple that was walking away. "Although they never surrendered, they were smart enough to understand that we have better weapons, so they have chosen to accept our presence. The Jesuits have understood them better than anyone else, and although the Raramuri killed the first missionaries, they now trust them, accept their Mission and their teaching. They are hard workers, but we have squeezed them so hard and forced them to the mountain, in the Cooper Canyon, where they now live in proud poverty. Although in winter time, they are forced to come and beg for food, they always maintain that air of dignity that bothers so many of those who, because of the lighter color of their skin, feel superior," he sighed. "There is still so much to learn." He added.

"Yes, there is," Fidelio replied pensive. The chime of the church bells calling to the evening mass, sounded melancholic.

"It's 6 p.m.," said the man standing, "the bells are calling to mass, go. Soon, it will be dangerous for the people of this country to attend one." He stood facing Fidelio for a few seconds before adding: "Remember, don't be afraid of the gift given to you, use it to benefit those in need, never try to profit from it," he smiled and walked away.

Fidelio sat on the bench for a few seconds watching the man walking away, he was impressed by the agile movements of the old man. What had he meant by his final comments? Fidelio asked himself. Although the man had left, Fidelio felt that a part of him was still at his side. As a matter of fact, he had the sensation that he always had been there. It was a strange feeling, but at the same time, that sensation gave him peace. Somehow, he now began to understand his role in the world. The sound of the bells seemed to call him, like an invitation. He stood up and walked to the church.

This church was austere, compared to those in Guanajuato and Morelia. Once inside, Fidelio noticed that there were no images or statues of saints on the walls. Only the stations of Jesus' Passion were there. He liked that. The House of God should be to worship God, he thought. He felt comfortable, it was as if he had just walked home. As Casimiro had told him, the mass was officiated by the Bishop of Chihuahua. The Bishop was a man in his mid- fifties, slender. Fidelio was impressed when he noticed that although he was wearing the usual garments for mass, these were simpler, all plain cotton. No silk or other expensive fabric. In spite of the humble garments, the Bishop irradiated a powerful inner strength.

"Brothers, the historical moment we are living is a difficult and painful one, as is any time when change is about to happen," the Bishop started his sermon. "For decades, few have accumulated power and riches, enjoying a life of comfort and opulence. Because of their wealth, they felt that they could oppress, humiliate and exploit those below them. They have used the law for their own benefit, obtaining the land that used to be communal in exchange of almost nothing. They have squeezed the small ranchers so hard that they had no choice but to sell their property for peanuts. Forcing them to become peons and, instead of paying them a fair salary, used the system of 'stores for payroll' to create a debt that forces the peons and peasants and their families to become literally property of the owner of the hacienda. But now, the silent cry of the oppressed majority has reached the ears of God and He has allowed the social tension to explode. Although President Madero was himself a member of those who had benefited most from the system, he was one of the few in his class that realized that there is a need for change and he tried to accomplish it as peacefully as possible. However, those who have benefited from the previous regime felt threatened by any change and so, they plotted against him and cowardly killed him. Some have just accepted it and submitted to the new oppressor. But, many others have rightfully revolted and we are now in the middle of the fight between these two forces.

Regardless of who wins, this struggle will cause a change. But the question is: What kind of change? Will it benefit the majority? Will there be opportunity for all to progress and move up in the social ladder? Or it will be a change that, once again, benefits a few at the expense of the majority? That is the danger of it. Things could change just to become the same as they were. Let's pray that the change will be real and for the benefit of the majority, that the upcoming change be worthy of all the pain and suffering of today."

Fidelio was deeply impressed. What he heard was so different from what he had heard before. After the mass, he went and asked to talk to the Bishop. A young priest looked at him suspiciously and asked him for the reason of his request. Fidelio explained that he had just arrived from Morelia and he had never-before heard a priest, much less a Bishop, preaching in favor of the revolution. The priest smiled sympathetically. "Follow me," he said.

Fidelio was walked through a corridor that connected the church to the Bishop house. He was again impressed by the austerity of the Bishop's quarters, simple and rustic furniture. A large, plain wood crucifix was the only decoration. "Your eminence, this young man is intrigued by your sermon of today," the priest introduced Fidelio.

The Bishop, who was talking to another priest, turned to look at Fidelio and gave a friendly smile. "How can I help you, son?" the Bishop said, pointing to a chair inviting Fidelio to sit.

"Your eminence, I heard the Bishop of Morelia denounce General Huerta as a criminal, but at the same time, he asked us to pray for peace, he did not approve of an armed rebellion. But during your sermon, you seemed to be supportive of it." Fidelio explained.

"I understand your confusion. I'm a peaceful man, however, there has been so much oppression by a minority. It's true that the idea was to make the land productive, and indeed that has happened, but this production benefits very few, the majority remains poor. The system has created a handful of families that are extremely wealthy and live in opulence, while most barely subsist and what is worst, the system created by the liberal laws, makes the social movement almost impossible. The children of the peon are condemned to be peons, they make the land productive, but they remain poor. The productivity only benefits the owner who keeps his peons ignorant, so they can remain just that, peons. That's the reason why the wealthy despise school teachers, or priests who teach people that they have rights and that by learning they could improve their situation and move up in the social ladder. However, here, in Chihuahua, the circumstances are a bit different than in most of the country. Here people had to fight against the Apache and Comanche to build their ranches, they are used to fighting and to be free, but, once again, taking advantage of the liberal laws, they were forced to sell cheap, they were robbed and forced to become peons. That's why it's here that the social tension exploded first. Madero understood that the situation was ready to explode, and it was necessary to channel all that tension. He was trying to do it through democracy, a bit naïve in my opinion, but anyhow well intended. But he was not given a chance. He was cowardly assassinated. Now there is no way to prevent violence. You ask me, how is it that I'm talking in favor of the revolution? There are occasions when violence becomes necessary and we are living in one of those. This revolution brings hope for the poor, those who were forced to remain at the bottom of society; now, hopefully, they will have a chance to improve their situation."

"But, you also said that there is a risk that things could change just to become as they were before, how is that possible?" Fidelio asked.

"That's a good question. Yes, it may seem confusing. But there are many examples in history that teach us that the change may be only in the oppressor. So, for the majority the things change only to remain the way they were; as an example of what we have just talked about. The liberals fighting against aristocracy, have just created a new one. And that is the danger that is being run here. We already have seen some of the generals taking possession of some of the most productive haciendas, only to become themselves the new boss. No change there. General Villa, although far from being a religious man, is a charismatic leader, and an honest man. He seems to care for the people and already has done some good, here, in Chihuahua. But, unfortunately, he is not the only one. There are many other leaders, many of them hate the Church. It could happen that these people take control, just to continue the oppression of the majority, for the benefit of few, new patrons. That is why we must pray for a real change."

"I believe I understand," said Fidelio, "but, changing the subject, your eminence. It caught my attention that the walls of the church are almost bare. There are no images of saints."

The Bishop smiled. "I'm glad you noticed that. The saints are people whose example we all should follow. I admire them, and as almost everyone else, I also have one or two who are my favorites, Saint Francis and San Ignacio, if you care to know. But I want people to understand that the church is a place to worship God."

"Yes, that is true," said Fidelio, nodding.

"Now, my son," said the Bishop standing up, "I hope I have cleared your doubts, if you excuse me, I have other duties to attend."

"Your eminence, allow me just one more question, please," Fidelio said.

"Of course, what is it?"

"You are the Bishop; however, this is not the cathedral, how is that?"

The Bishop smiled. "That is true. The reason I'm not in the city of Chihuahua is because it's now occupied by the Federals and, as you can assume, they don't like my position. Now, I must leave."

"Yes, of course," said Fidelio, standing up and kissing the episcopal ring.

It was night when Fidelio arrived at the train station. Dr. Villarreal was in the wagon, preparing some of the equipment.

"Good that you are here," Dr. Villarreal said when he saw him, "maybe you could help me to put everything in order. General Villa has ordered that we leave tomorrow to Chihuahua, you'll have your baptism of blood soon. Please, hand me those bandages there."

Fidelio handed the bandages and helped to prepare everything to be ready to assist those wounded in the upcoming battle. As they did, Dr. Villarreal explained to him the use of the equipment, the proper care of the wounds. "The most important thing in the care of a wound besides stopping bleeding is to prevent an infection, and to accomplish that, we must keep the wound clean," Dr. Villarreal repeated this until he was sure that he was understood. Fidelio listened but didn't want to say that he already knew that. However, he paid careful attention when Dr. Villarreal explained about the use of bee honey, cactus like aloe, and other dessert plants to accomplish the above- mentioned purpose.

"You have been a great help, thank you." Dr. Villarreal said smiling, once they were finished. "I like that you really paid attention to my explanation, now tell me: How was your day in town? Was there something that you found interesting or different from what you have seen thus far?"

"Well, yes, there were many things that happened today," Fidelio replied. "I found several of my childhood friends from Guanajuato, they have also joined the revolution." He stopped, thoughtful. "They have changed," he added after a moment.

"What do you mean?" Dr. Villarreal asked.

"I don't know, they are no longer the same children I remember."

Dr. Villarreal smiled. "Of course not, you say they have joined the revolution, probably they have been already in battle. They have learned what it is like. One has to kill in order not to be killed. Our most primitive instincts flow in battle. No one is the same after taking part in a battle. So, you can't expect them to be the same innocent children they once were."

"I understand that, but there was something else; something that you, for instance don't have. It's obvious, by what you say that you also have taken part in battle, but you don't have the same menacing look that my friends now have."

"I believe that I understand what you mean. War and killing have a different effect in each one of us. Some, like me, take it as a necessary, but hopefully temporary evil, but there are others who learn to like it and almost do it by sport. You will meet all of them. And I wonder, how will it affect you?"

Fidelio looked at him, a concerned expression in his face. "I have asked myself the same question, and the possibilities scare me."

Dr. Villarreal smiled, touched Fidelio on the shoulder. "Young man, I can tell that you are strong. There is something in you that makes you different, I can't say precisely what is it. Yes, being in or even just witnessing a battle will have an effect on you, we can be certain of that, but, somehow, I'm also certain that the effect on you will be for good." He paused for a moment, took his hand from Fidelio's shoulder. "I appreciate the confidence you have in me. Although there is a difference of age, I can tell that we are going to get along just fine. Now tell me what else did you find in this city?"

Fidelio told him about his experience with the Raramuri couple and his conversation with the Bishop.

"Yes, the Raramuri, or Tarahumara, as we call them, are an interesting and proud people. Personally, I have learned a lot from them. They have a better understanding of illness and health than we have. There are many things that we are just beginning to learn in that sense. And as for your conversation with the Bishop, I can tell you that he is a good man, I like him, but there are many here who hate him for his progressive ideas and his open support of the revolution. Maybe we'll talk a bit more about religion some other time, for the time being we need to rest. Tomorrow we are leaving to recover Chihuahua from the federals." He stood up. "Rest well my young friend," he said, before leaving.

CHAPTER VII

It was a cold late November morning when they arrived at the Consuelo Railroad Station, close to Chihuahua City. A strong wind chill blew freely in the plain terrain of the Chihuahuan desert. Fidelio, used to the year-round spring-like weather of Guanajuato and Morelia, felt the cold like needles pinching all the way to his bones when he left the wagon. He shivered, and rubbed his arms. In the blue-sky, flocks of ducks and swans, drawing several perfect "V", were flying towards the south. Looking at them and knowing that their destiny was central Mexico, Fidelio, shivering, blowing his hands and moving around, almost dancing, to warm himself, wished he could join them.

"What's wrong, Fidelio?" Dr. Villarreal, who had disembarked before, asked, laughing. "Is this cold wind bothering you? Here, have a sip of this, it will warm you up," he added, offering him a bottle filled with a clear fluid.

"What is it?" asked Fidelio, taking the bottle.

"Sotol", Dr. Villarreal replied.

"Sotol?" I never heard of it.

"It's the result of the distillation of the agave plants, common in this part of the country. It's our version of the tequila."

Fidelio sipped it, grimaced, coughed and almost jumped, after he had swallowed it. "Wow, that is harsh!" he said giving the bottle back to Dr. Villarreal.

"I know, but, did it warm you up?"

"Yes, it did and, as a matter of fact, it has fully wakened me up."

"Good, I'm aware that you are already knowledgeable about a lot of herbs, soon you'll have the chance to learn more about the wonderful effects of the dessert plants." Dr. Villarreal stopped smiling, looked at the distance. "Chihuahua is just a few miles away. From here, General Villa will lead the attack." He frowned, "It won't be easy, Chihuahua is well fortified and Orozco and his men have just reinforced them. They are brave, fearless and hate Villa and his followers," he grimaced. "The hate is reciprocal."

"Who is Orozco?" Fidelio asked.

"Pascual Orozco was one of the first to support Madero and his cause. He was pivotal in the capture of Ciudad Juarez that led to the resignation of Diaz and the triumph of the revolution. He could have been a great leader; however, he is prone to flattery and desire of wealth and power, thus he easily fell in the web of the Terrazas' group. They convinced and financed him to rebel against Madero. After the assassination of Madero, Orozco accepted the bribe offered to him by Huerta and has turned against the revolution. In spite of that, here in Chihuahua, he is still a dominant figure and there are many who believe in him. In a way, I feel sorry for him. He had the chance to occupy a prominent place in history and instead he has chosen to be remembered as a traitor to the cause for which he once fought." He spitted, pulled his pants up and looked to the train wagon conditioned as a hospital. "Fidelio, let's concentrate in the forthcoming battle. This wagon is to remain here, ready to receive the wounded. Our task is to plan a way to get them in here as soon as possible. Do you have any ideas?"

Fidelio looked to a herd of mules in the corral of the station. "If we could use those mules, and find some wagons, we could carry the wounded from the battle field to here."

"Excellent idea, I'll be sure that we get the necessary wagons." Dr. Villarreal looked to the field where some women and children were busy picking up dry wood, while others had already made fire and roasted a young goat or had a kettle with fresh coffee or maybe, beans. Others were preparing tortillas, the rhythmic clapping of their hands to flatten the dough sounded joyous. "Look at those women with their children, I doubt that there is any other place on earth where an entire family goes to war. General Villa does not really like it, but he understands that if he does not allow it, the men won't come. And remember, they are all volunteers. Anyhow, they have proven to be an asset. For instance, they prepare the meals for the troops, even Villa takes advantage of that. To prevent being poisoned, every night he eats the food prepared by one of these women," he smiled and turned to Fidelio. "Your task now is to organize these women and children to help us carry the wounded from the battlefield here."

Fidelio nodded. "Yes, I believe I can do it."

"General Villa is planning to attack in two days. I understand that it's a short time, but be sure to be ready by then. I'll go now to secure the necessary wagons."

Fidelio smiled. "We'll be ready."

He walked towards the fire places. The men were helping to roast the goats and chicken, while the women and children took care of the fire. "That coffee and those beans smell good, and that goat looks delicious," said Fidelio as he approached. "I wonder. Could you share some with me?" he asked smiling to the man and woman who were getting the food ready.

"Of course," answered the man, smiling in a friendly way and pointing to a saddle for Fidelio to seat. "Probably you don't know me, but I know you." The man continued. "You are the altar boy who helped Father Segura in Guanajuato," he laughed and looking to his wife he pointed to Fidelio. "Look Vieja, this is the boy who threw a stone at our compadre, Benito."

The woman looked to Fidelio with respect, her eyes wide open. She crossed her chest. "And he got cured from his cough and wheezing," she said, almost in a whisper.

"I know that you are a man of peace," the man said. "What made you join the bola?"

Fidelio gestured, shrugged his shoulders. "Like the rest of you, I also want justice for all," he answered.

"Yes, I understand that, but I know you don't like weapons and this is a war. How are you going to help?"

"Taking care of the wounded," he replied.

"Oh yes, yes, thanks be given to heavens!" the woman said, jubilant. She looked to her husband. "Remember, Viejo, when you told me that you were going to join 'the bola,' I told you that the children and I will follow you. Then you said: 'What will happen to you and the children if I get wounded?' I said, the Virgen of Guadalupe will take care of all of us." She smiled, nodding, a triumphant expression in her face. "Well, now you see that She has sent us this child of God," she finished pointing to Fidelio.

On hearing this, Fidelio's face flushed. He was embarrassed by what the woman had just said. For a moment he considered walking away; but immediately he reminded himself that he was there to convince them to help in the transport of the wounded.

"I just hope I could help those in need," he said. "As a matter of fact, I hope you realize that you are already doing a lot to accomplish that goal," he added addressing the woman.

"How is that?" the woman asked. "Yes, I know that there are some women and a lot of children who have joined the troops, but, for most of us, all we do is to cook for the men and wait, hoping that they would return safe. I wish we could do more."

"As I said, just by cooking and being here you are already doing a lot. But yes, there is another way you could help."

"Like what?" the man asked, interested.

"Like helping in the transport and care of the wounded," Fidelio replied.

"Yes, I like that!" the woman said, jubilant. "I'm certain that most of the women and children will also be glad to help. Just let us know what we have to do and we'll do it."

"With the help of all of you, those who are wounded in the upcoming battle will get the medical attention they'll need. Let's get all together so I can show you how to help in carrying the wounded from the battlefield to where they will be helped," said Fidelio.

"Children," said the woman, calling to her children. "Go and call all of your friends, meanwhile I'll go and get the women." She turned looking to Fidelio. "Wait here, we'll be ready in just a moment," she covered her head with her shawl and rushed to the nearby women, calling them.

Two days later, they rode the wagons, conditioned as ambulances, to where the troops had concentrated, ready to attack Chihuahua City.

"I don't know how you did it, but these women and children seem to be enthusiastic with the job of carrying the wounded back to our train," Dr. Villarreal said to Fidelio. "I knew that most of the women and children already know how to handle the mules and how to drive those wagons, but by what I see, they are also prepared to carry the wounded to those wagons."

"They might be poor peasants, but they are intelligent and creative, most of them already know how to take care of wounded people. All I did was to explain them what is needed," said Fidelio, smiling to Dr. Villarreal. He turned to look at the city. "It looks so quiet and peaceful."

"It seems that way, but they are ready and waiting for the attack," Dr. Villarreal replied. "We know that they have fortified the city and have placed their cannons in those mountains. Also, they have more men than we do. We have cut their supply of fresh water. This afternoon at 5 p.m., we'll attack from the south and the west," he looked at Fidelio. "Battles are violent, cruel, menacing, men become like wild beasts, don't let it get to your nerves, be ready to offer help to as many as we can. Do you understand, my young friend?"

"I hope so," replied Fidelio.

The attack started that afternoon, at 5 p.m. Fidelio and Dr. Villarreal, standing on top of a wagon stationed in a promontory, observed how an infantry line of four thousand men advanced like a wave. From the distance, it reminded Fidelio the marching of ants. The men were able to advance to the skirts of the bare mountains where those defending the city had posted their artillery. However, Fidelio noticed that once they arrived there, they suddenly stopped. Those that were in the frontline, seem to be trapped in an invisible (to Fidelio) web. Many of them seemed to be convulsing. "What is that holding them and why are they convulsing in such a way?" Fidelio asked himself. He also noticed at that point they had become an easy target for the enemy's artillery. He was impressed by the courage of the men that in spite of being an easy target for their cannons, they kept pushing forward. When hit by the artillery shells, bodies of men flew in pieces, and that image made Fidelio shiver, a cold sweat running through his body, he felt nauseated but he couldn't move his eyes from the battle field. He noticed that now he was sweating. The fight continued until night fall. The attack seemed to have stopped, but the artillery in both sides continued for several hours.

"I can see that you are seriously impressed by being so close to a battle. You can now imagine how much worse it is for those who are in the front. However, there is something that makes men continue fighting in spite of the immediate danger they are in," Dr. Villarreal told Fidelio. "Now, although the artilleries are still bombarding each other, we must go and pick those who are wounded," he looked at Fidelio. "However, remember that there is nothing we can do for those who are already dead. If you think that what you have just seen was terrible, prepare yourself for what you are about to witness. Among other things, don't be surprised if you see many men, women and, even children picking on the bodies of the fallen to get whatever they might have of value. Go, take the wagons and help as many as you can. If you are able to hear the explosion of the shell, that would be a good sign, it means that it didn't hit you."

Dr. Villarreal laughed at his joke and slapped Fidelio on the back. "Go now and do your job, we'll wait here. We are ready."

"What stopped many of them so suddenly? And why they seemed to be convulsing?" Fidelio asked before leaving.

"That's because they touched the electrified wire," Dr. Villarreal replied.

It was late in the night when Fidelio, accompanied by the voluntary women and children arrived with the wagons to the battle field. The full moon illuminated the scene giving it dark purple tones that, along with the yellow, red and blues of the many small fires left as a reminder of the bomb shells made Fidelio think that it was like seeing the gates of hell. Hundreds of bodies lied on the field. The monotonous laments of those wounded asking for help, water, or in pain reminded Fidelio of the monotonous rhythm of women praying the rosary. The combined smell of powder, feces, urine, sweat and rotten flesh penetrated through

Fidelio's nose, forcing him to cough, he felt nauseated and vomited. For a moment, he was overwhelmed. There were so many bodies lying on the field. Where to start? There were men with their limbs separated, bleeding profusely, others with their bowels out of the abdomen, many with their smashed brains covering their faces, there was one with an eye hanging close to his mouth. Fidelio stood there, paralyzed by the terrible scene. "Let's hurry up and start by helping those who are able to walk to the wagons," one of the women told him, slapping him in the back, she pushed him, Fidelio reacted and walked forward.

Besides them, who were there to help those in need, hundredths of vultures feasted in the bodies and also people searching the clothes of the fallen, looking for something of value, as Dr. Villarreal had warned him. "Scavengers," Fidelio thought.

They started by helping all the wounded who were able to walk to reach the ambulances. As soon as one was filled, it was taken to the prepared wagon, where several physicians were already waiting for them. Fidelio was surprised when he saw that the women were asking the boys to urinate in those who had open wounds in the extremities. "Why do you do that?" he asked one of the women.

"Dr. Villarreal has taught us that it's important to keep the wound clean. Since we don't have water here, we ask the children to urinate on them," the woman answered.

As they continued working, Fidelio felt more and more confident. He was able to align many fractured bones and to stabilize them. Also, using sticks, pieces of cloth along with small branches of the many bushes around, he created a fairly comfortable way to transport those who were unable to walk. As the hours passed, instead of feeling tired he felt energized.

"We have to stop now. A new attack will start in a few hours. You have done a great job, now go and try to get some rest," Dr. Villarreal told Fidelio after they had worked almost until sunrise.

After five days of furious attacks, the city had resisted. The loss of lives on both sides was great, but it was worse for Villa's troops. Every time they went to carry the wounded, Fidelio was afraid of finding his friends among them, it was a sweet-bitter comfort that they were not among the wounded. It had become obvious that they had been defeated. The order to withdraw was received. They did so in order.

"We have been defeated here and Torreon is already in the hands of the Federal troops." Dr. Villarreal told Fidelio as they rested in the train wagon. We are now practically surrounded. General Villa and the other leaders are now in council. It's obvious that we are in a serious situation," he sighed, "it could even be the end of the Northern Division. However, although we have been beaten this time and our situation seems to be helpless, I have confidence in General Villa. I know that he is now feeling like a fox apt to be trapped," he smiled, looking at Fidelio. "I'm confident that he'll find a bold solution to it."

CHAPTER VIII

Everyone was tense, most were scared. They were in the middle of the Chihuahuan desert, practically surrounded by enemy troops. Except for Parral, a city close to Chihuahua City, where Villa had established his headquarters before the attack to the city of Chihuahua, they had no other place to go. Fidelio and the other volunteers kept themselves busy taking care of the many wounded, but everyone knew that, unless something extraordinary happened, even Parral soon would not be safe. Fidelio sensed fear everywhere he went, as a matter of fact, he was also concerned. Was this the end of his part in the social struggle in which the whole country was involved? Even if he was to continue, it was obvious that he would need to learn to ride a horse and probably to shoot. "God has guided me and when the moment comes, He'll let me know what to do. For the time being, I'll concentrate in helping those who need my assistance," he told himself.

"Good day Fidelio," Dr. Villarreal said as he approached, smiling, almost cheerful. He slapped Fidelio's back gently, "It's always nice to see you and, let me tell you that all of the physicians are impressed by how well the people you have trained, work. Good job, my boy."

"Thank you, but I don't believe that I deserve the credit. They already knew everything that is necessary. It has been the harshness of their life that forced them to learn how to take care of themselves and those close to them. All I had to do was to allow them to put in practice what they already knew and show them how to work together, as a team," said Fidelio.

"That might be so, but I must say that it's almost amazing, that in spite of you being just out of childhood, they respect and follow your orders and that shows that you are a leader by nature," Dr. Villarreal replied, smiling. "I'm sure that someday you will become someone important, but for the time being, thanks be given to your God, you are here helping this cause and I'm glad for that." He kept smiling, Fidelio sensed that Dr. Villarreal was about to tell him something that was relevant, and he knew that it was related to what General Villa had decided to do. But considering the adverse circumstances in which they were, why was the Doctor in such a good mood?

"Well, my dear friend, I got news from headquarters," said Dr. Villarreal, still smiling. "As I told you, General Villa understands that we are almost trapped and, like a fox in imminent danger, he has come up with something no one expected, least of all, the enemy. It's a wild and dangerous move, but if successful, not only will it take us out of the immediate danger in which we are now, but it will provide us with an open door to get the necessary supplies from the United States." Dr. Villarreal laughed and slapped his thigh, he seemed to be about to dance.

Intrigued, Fidelio frowned. "What is it?" he asked.

"The Federals believe that we are almost destroyed. So, they expect us to withdraw south or to disperse in the mountains. They are coming after us. They believe we are scared, our moral down and, since we have no place to hide, we'll run towards our final defeat. The last they expect is that we become the aggressor, move north and attack. General Villa has decided that he and two thousand mounted men will move to Ciudad Juarez, at the border and capture it."

Fidelio frowned, he was perplexed. "I don't know this part of the country. How far is Ciudad Juarez, from here?" he finally asked

Dr. Villarreal shrugged his shoulders still smiling. "It's somewhere between four to five hundred kilometers."

"You mean that two thousand mounted men will have to go that distance in this desert and not be seen by the enemy? I know nothing of military strategy, but, how is that going to be accomplished?" Fidelio insisted.

"I told you Villa is like a fox, he'll find a way. He knows better than anyone else this desert and the mountains surrounding it," Dr. Villarreal replied. "As far as we are concerned, we have to prepare because we are moving with General Chao to Parral, where we'll wait for further instructions. So, we must prepare to transport all the wounded men over there. Let's not waste any time. Those who are not able to move will go in the train wagons. You and your team will take the rest in the wagons pulled by mules. General Villa and the mounted men have already left. We are leaving this afternoon."

Fidelio found Parral almost identical to Camargo. Although he didn't like drinking, he noticed that, like in Camargo, all the bars were closed, there was no selling or offering of any alcoholic drinks in town. As he walked towards the hospital, he remembered that he had noticed the same in Torreon, but because the little time he had spent in there was with Candelaria he didn't pay attention to it. "Candelaria, does she remembers me? Would I ever see her again?" he thought and sighed.

"Fidelio, hey Fidelio, stop day dreaming," Dr. Villarreal, whom Fidelio almost bumped into as he walked towards the hospital, called him. "What are you thinking, my dear friend?"

"Nothing really, I was just wondering about something that has caught my attention," replied Fidelio.

"And what is that?" Dr. Villarreal asked.

"I noticed that here, in Camargo, and in Torreon, there are no open bars. There is no selling of alcoholic drinks," Fidelio answered.

Dr. Villarreal smiled. "Yes, that's something that has caught the attention of many. General Villa doesn't like alcohol and wherever he rules, the sale of alcoholic drinks is forbidden. Of course, it still can be obtained, and most of the people around Villa drink, but he has ordered that no officer on duty can drink, and no one wearing a military uniform is allowed to drink in public. The penalty is death. In Torreon, the federal officers that volunteered to join us were accepted. In a restaurant, Villa saw two of them drinking while in uniform and he shot both of them on the spot."

"Wow, he must be a harsh man," Fidelio said.

"Indeed, he is, but, on the positive side, let's not forget that he also cares about people. We are part of the team that he has assembled to help those who are wounded in battle. I insist that he is the only general in this struggle that has done something about it. Wherever he is in control, he allows most of the business to remain open and active, but he won't tolerate any attempt to hide provisions to force the prices to go up. Something important, everywhere he has control, the education of children must go on. He makes sure that schools are open and the teachers are well paid. Above all, he has shown that he is not looking for his own benefit, like many others have already shown. On the contrary, he always thinks about how he can help others. It's difficult to describe someone like him in a few words, nobility and brutality in the same person. Probably that's the reason he is so charismatic, we all see something of ourselves in him."

"I believe that I understand what you mean," Fidelio said.

"Well, enough of that; let's talk about our own ordeal," Dr. Villarreal said. "We have many men wounded, and in pain. You and I are going to get medicine to help them. We'll go to the field to find and collect plants and herbs that will help us to alleviate pain and heal the wounds." He looked at Fidelio, smiling; "and, at the same time you are going to start learning to ride a horse, I got you one that is well tamed and obedient."

Fidelio also smiled, surprised. "I hope I do well and don't disappoint you."

"I know that you won't. As a matter of fact, I'm certain you'll do well and, I am also certain, that both of us will learn something new about the medicinal effects of herbs." They walked towards the livery stable.

To his own surprise, Fidelio had no problems mounting and riding the horse. He even enjoyed it and felt comfortable on the saddle. Being a tall man, he was also glad that the horse chosen for him was a large one. It was a bright morning and although the sun shined in the sky, the wind flowing freely in the Chihuahuan dessert was cold, chilly; feeling it in his face and body made him feel exhilarated.

Besides the horses, Dr. Villarreal had got two mules carrying baskets and two large clay jars, filled with fresh water.

"Most of those small cacti over there are aloe. We'll cut as many as we can; if it's cut the right way, when applied to the wounds, it will accelerate their healing and at the same time, it will keep them clean." Dr. Villarreal said pointing to a group of small cacti growing wild.

Fidelio nodded approvingly, looking to the field where Dr. Villarreal was pointing. "Some of those are peyote and, also, if it's cut the right way, it will help to alleviate the pain of many of our patients."

Dr. Villarreal smiled. "I knew that we were going to learn from each other." He stopped his horse and dismounted. "The Raramuri have taught me that when one is going to cut these plants, we have to walk into the field in a gentle and respectful manner," he sighed and smiled. "I don't know if that makes any difference, but at the same time, it does not cause any harm if we follow their advice."

Fidelio also dismounted and they walked into the field.

"Look over there. Those are several bee colonies. If we collect the honey, it will help to clean and heal the infected wounds," said Fidelio, pointing to the distance.

Dr. Villarreal smiled. "That's true. The Raramuri also use it for that purpose. But, how are we going to get it without upsetting the bees?"

Fidelio smiled back, "they'll let me do it." Dr. Villarreal looked at Fidelio frowning, intrigued. "It might be so, but before you try to do that, let's get as many as we can of these peyote and aloe plants," Dr. Villarreal, still smiling, looked at Fidelio. "It might sound silly to you, but remember to thank the plant for the service it's going to provide before you cut it."

Fidelio smiled back and nodded approvingly. "I understand and I'll be sure I do as you say."

"Great, let's get the baskets from the mules and fill them up," said Dr. Villarreal, as he walked towards the mules.

"Good, we have filled all of our baskets," Dr. Villarreal said, wiping the sweat from his forehead, after they had worked for several hours. "Are you sure that you want to try to collect that honey?"

"Of course, we must accept the gifts that God has given us," replied Fidelio, as he took the clay jars, drank some of the water, offered water to the horses and mules and taking both jars with him, walked toward the bee colonies.

Dr. Villarreal stopped him, a concerned look on his face. "What are you doing? You are walking to collect the bee honey and have no protection. You are going to upset those bees, the stung of so many of them might kill you."

Fidelio smiled to him. "Don't you worry, they let me do it."

Dr. Villarreal stood watching how Fidelio walked into the bee colonies. As soon as Fidelio approached, thousands of bees surrounded him. Fidelio was no longer in sight, only a gigantic ball of buzzing bees was visible. After what seemed like a very long time, Fidelio emerged from the inside of the ball, smiling, carrying the two clay jars filled with honey.

"There is something very strange about you," Dr. Villarreal said, as soon as Fidelio was close. He sighed. "I don't know what it is, but I'm glad you are on our side. Let's ride back."

"Fidelio, Fidelio, my love, it's has been a long separation. I have missed you so much. I was afraid that you would find someone else and forget about me," Candelaria said. Smiling, she took Fidelio's hands looking at him, tenderly.

"How could I forget you? There is not a single moment in which you are not in my mind," Fidelio replied, also smiling and freeing his hand to caress her face.

"Oh Fidelio, I'm so happy to be with you again. She hugged him, her head on his chest. "From now on, I'll follow you; wherever you go, I'll go," she said, closing her eyes, sighed, getting closer.

"Yes, we'll never separate again," Fidelio said taking her by the chin and gently he lifted her head and bent to kiss her.

Suddenly, he was shaking. He opened his eyes and Candelaria was not there. "Fidelio, hey Fidelio, wake up, wake up," Dr. Villarreal who was shaking him said. "What were you dreaming? You were smiling happily. I bet it was something really good," he added, pointing to the elevation in the blanket in the mid part of Fidelio's body.

"Yes, it was something nice," Fidelio said, smiling, but with a sad look in his face. He sat on the bed and with the elbows in his knees he put his hands on his head and sobbed.

Dr. Villarreal touched him gently in the shoulder. "Don't be ashamed my friend, I understand your feelings, I have also been in love. If you want to talk about it, I'll be glad to listen. What's her name? Where did you meet her? Talk, let it come out, it will be good for you."

Fidelio lifted his head, wiped his eyes and smiled to Dr. Villarreal. "Her name is Candelaria, we met in Torreon, as you know that's where I enlisted. She is the first and last love of my life. I was dreaming of her." His face saddened. "It was so real," he added.

"Well, it's obvious that you would like to see her again and if that is so I have good news for you my friend. I believe that you are closer to that than you might think," Dr. Villarreal said smiling.

"How is that so?" Fidelio said looking at him. "We are almost trapped, at this moment, my only chance would be to survive this defeat and find my way back to Torreon."

"No, my friend, we are no longer in that situation, everything has changed,"

Dr. Villarreal said, a broad smile in his face.

Surprised, Fidelio smiled. "Do you mean that General Villa has found a way out?" he asked.

"Much better than that," Dr. Villarreal replied. "He has captured Ciudad Juarez; now we have the upper hand. We can buy weapons and I'm certain that Villa must be already planning to get not only, Chihuahua but, most importantly, Torreon".

"I believe you, but I don't understand. How did that happen?"

Dr. Villarreal laughed. "I told you, he is like a fox and just like it, he has found a way out. Have you ever heard the story of the Trojan horse?"

"No, but I would like to know," said Fidelio.

"There is a story of an army trying to capture a city called Troy. In spite of all of their superior army and more elaborate battle tactics, they couldn't break its walls. Not only the walls but also the spirit of the Trojans seemed unbreakable. So, the leaders of that army pretended to withdraw and left behind a large wooden horse. The people of Troy, believing that they had defeated their enemy, took the horse into the city. But, it was a trick; hidden inside of the wooden horse were the best soldiers. During the night, they came out and captured the city."

"You mean Villa used that same trick?" Fidelio asked. "First he would have to cover the hundreds of kilometers without been detected by the enemy. Second, although I know little about war and battle strategies, what I have seen tells me that he would have to put the city under siege and that also takes time. How did he do it in such a short period of time?"

Dr. Villarreal smiled, obviously enjoying Fidelio's disbelief. "Of course, I don't believe Villa knows or even heard that story, but what Villa did has reminded me of it. He used something similar to travel hundredths of kilometers without being detected and captured the city in an almost bloodless fashion."

"To prevent being detected," Dr. Villarreal continued. "Villa had originally planned to capture the train stations between here and Ciudad Juarez. The first one they captured was the station of 'El Cobre', very close to here. There they took control of the telegraph and, when a train full of coal, going from Juarez to Chihuahua tried to pass, they forced it to stop and it was captured. It seems that someone suggested to Villa to replace the coal with men, notify by telegraph to Juarez that the rail had been removed and that it couldn't continue. They did so, the bait was taken and the train was ordered to return to Juarez. At 1 a.m. in the morning, the train arrived in Juarez. The surprise was complete, in three hours the city was captured, and most importantly, the weapons. Our artillery has now improved. Also, Villa has now an outlet to sell the cotton captured in Torreon and buy more weapons. I'm sure that the campaign to recover Chihuahua and Torreon will start soon. So, my good friend, if everything continues this way, soon, very soon, you'll be with your love. What do you think about that?"

Fidelio smiled. "That's impressive, as you said, that man is like a fox. I really don't know what to say."

"Don't say anything, get up and get ready. We are going to join Villa in Ciudad Juarez, we'll leave tomorrow," Dr. Villarreal said, slapping Fidelio's shoulder.

CHAPTER IX

Fidelio, standing at the edge of the Rio Grande River, rubbed his arms trying to warm up. The musical murmur of the flow; the changing colors of the river, the birds flying on top of it, all combined to make it attractive. However, at the same time, its width, depth and turbulence made it look menacing. He had never seen a river like this and, looking at it, feeling the cold wind in his body, made him feel strangely excited, he felt his muscles tensing; although it was cold, he also felt warm and powerful. Surprised by this sensation, he took a deep breath. The sensation was perplexing, he felt vigorous, powerful, but at the same time, he also felt like in a fog, something similar at the night when he drank several glasses of wine. The murmurs of the flow of water started to sound like voices calling him; the blow of the cold wind also seemed to talk to him; the messages, however, were contradictory. On one side, the flow of the river seemed to talk to him in a soft, attractive, seductive voice: "Fidelio, Fidelio, your ability to heal, your knowledge of the properties of the herbs, could make you very rich, use it for your own benefit; there are many who will pay well for it. Wealth, luxury, comfort, anything you wish for, all of it will be yours. Just enter this water and you'll be taken to its northern side where there are many who will pay you whatever you ask for. Wealth, luxury, comfort are waiting for you; all you have to do is come and take it." The colors of the water created attractive images of luxury mansions, well-groomed gardens, delicious dishes, seductive bodies of women offering themselves to him. "Come, come and take me, I'm yours," a soft, melodious voice, called him; the images and the tone of the voice were similar to Candelaria's. Fidelio felt tempted, as if something pulled him, he walked towards the river.

A sudden, strong current of wind forced him to a sudden stop, he had to take a step back to prevent from falling. "Fidelio! Fidelio! Fidelio! Listen, listen," the wind seemed to yell, this voice was loud and angry. "You have a gift and, like any gift, you can use it at your own will. Yes, you could use it for you own benefit; yes, it could make you wealthy, even powerful; it could provide you with a life of riches and luxury; or, maybe, you could choose to use it to benefit those in need, to alleviate the sorrows of anyone who asks for it, rich and powerful or, a simple beggar. All of them need it. If it's used for your own benefit, you'll gain wealth, property, luxury. Yes, but in exchange of that, your life will be bitter, full of sorrow, although surrounded by luxury, you'll feel empty, miserable, you will have lost the simple pleasure of breathing fresh air; you'll no longer understand the language of the birds, the frogs, even the bees, friendly to you until now; angrily, they will sting you when you cross their way again. To keep people believing, you'll have to pretend that you know and understand nature, but nature will be silent to you, you'll have lost that connection forever; surrounded by riches, you'll feel empty, your life wasted, that's the price you'll pay."

Fidelio stood there, confused, "Fidelio, Fidelio, come and take me, I'm yours." The figures in the river kept calling him in a sensual voice. "It's all up to you now. You have to choose," the wind hauled. Overwhelmed, feeling like a heavy weight on his back, Fidelio fell on his knees. "Why, why?" he asked. "I never asked for anything, all I want is to be like anyone else, live a normal life." The river kept calling him, seductive, sensual; the wind continued asking him to choose. Fidelio pressed his head, he wept.

"Fidelio, hey Fidelio, my friend, what are you doing here? Alone," a mounted man called him.

Surprised, Fidelio almost jumped and looked back. The man had dismounted and walked towards him smiling. Recognizing him, Fidelio smiled back and walked towards the man. "Enrique, what a nice surprise, I didn't expect to see you. How are you? When and how did you get here?"

"I arrived with the troops that captured the city," said Enrique. "Now it's your turn to answer. What are you doing here?"

"Just walking and looking at the river. As you know there are no rivers like this where we came from."

"Fidelio, I was passing by when I heard a loud cry: 'Why? Why?' I turned and I saw you on your knees, pressing your head. I'm your friend, tell me what's going on, why were you yelling, asking that question?"

Embarrassed, Fidelio understood Enrique's concern. "Nothing important, it's only that suddenly I became homesick. I felt so sad that I couldn't help, but to cry and ask: Why is all of this happening? I didn't think someone would hear me," he said, smiling.

Enrique extended his arm and touched Fidelio's shoulder, "I understand, witnessing the violence of war is difficult for a sensitive temper like yours, but remember, all of it is a necessary evil to accomplish the goal of justice for all."

Fidelio had recovered his calm by then, smiled, "yes, that's what it is."

"Ciudad Juarez is also a different town than those we have been to before. Have you walked through it?" asked Enrique.

"No, not yet," replied Fidelio.

"And, there is El Paso, I believe you'll find it also different. But you'll go there another time, now let's go and eat something, I'll invite you; or maybe you have something else to do?"

"No, I'm free tonight, I accept your invitation," answered Fidelio.

"Well, let me get my horse and we'll walk to the town," said Enrique, and walked to where he had left his horse. Fidelio looked at the river, only the rumor of the flow was heard, there were no figures of it; the wind, although cold, felt gentle, like a caress.

Ciudad Juarez downtown was bustling, illuminated by kerosene lamps; bars filled with loud music and gambling; yelling came from the Palenque where cock fighting was taking place at that moment. There were many drunken men walking in the streets, bottle in hand; some of them mumbled words in Spanish, and others, in a language new to Fidelio. Since their stay at Torreon, Fidelio had noticed that the Spanish spoken in the northern part of the country seemed louder, with a sharp intonation. The language that he heard for the first time sounded harsh to his ears. Used to the soft, melodious, almost musical, tone in the Spanish spoken by the people in central Mexico, both the loudness of those who spoke Spanish and the harshness of the new language made him feel a bit upset. Women with a provocative smile sat in front of many of the bars, the excessive color in their faces reminded Fidelio of the clowns that he had seen in a circus in Morelia.

"This looks like a good restaurant," said Enrique, stopping in front of a place that looked neat and clean, with tables covered by mantles that had flowers and birds embroidered on them. "I feel like eating enchiladas, what about you?"

"I think I'll have the same," replied Fidelio.

"I'm confused," said Fidelio, once they were sitting at the table. "I know that General Villa doesn't approve drinking and gambling, I noticed that both were forbidden in the previous towns we have been, I was even told that he killed two officials that drank while wearing the uniform. However, here, I see people drinking in the streets, liquor is freely sold, there is gambling everywhere. Why is it different here?"

Enrique looked at Fidelio and grinned. "I understand your confusion; I have also asked the same question. There is a practical, greedy if you like, reason for that."

"Well, what is it?" asked Fidelio, opening his arms and looking straight to Enrique. "There is a bit of shame in the answer," Enrique said. "Ciudad Juarez is the playground for the grownup people who live in the other side of the river. Gambling is illegal there and they don't get drunk over there, they come to do it here and in doing so, they spend a good amount of money. General Villa has understood that it's a relatively easy way to get money for the cause; as a matter of fact, the cock fight place is managed by his brother. The money they get is used to buy guns and ammunition."

"Indeed, there is shame in it," Fidelio said.

"It's important to make clear that most of the people on both sides are honest and hard- working," Enrique said, as he moved to allow the waitress to place the enchilada plate on the table. The girl looked at Fidelio and smiled at him. She was an attractive young blond, tall, with large, green eyes. Fidelio saw her eyes and felt the sensation already known to him, this surprised him and made him feel a bit nervous. Keeping her eyes on him, smiling in a provocative way, she placed the enchilada plate in from of him. "Enjoy it," she said with a sensual tone of voice; she turned around walking away slowly, after a few steps, she turned and smiled at him again. Fidelio felt upset with himself, strongly attracted to her, but at the same time, confused and surprised. After Candelaria, he thought that he never could be interested in another woman.

Enrique, who had noticed it all, smiled. "It looks like all the girls we meet are attracted to you, my friend. What do you do to them?" Laughing he took the knife and fork and cut a piece of his enchilada and put it in his mouth, chewing it slowly and looking at Fidelio with a grin in his face.

"What are you talking about? There is no such a thing," Fidelio replied, a sharp tone in his voice; his face flushed.

Enrique smiled again, "now you are talking like a northerner. What is it that has made you upset? There is something in you that attracts the girls, specially the pretty ones, so once again, what is it that has made you upset? As a matter of fact, it is also obvious that you are also attracted to her."

Fidelio flushed even more; embarrassed, looked down. "You are correct, but, I don't understand why I'm feeling this way."

"Fidelio, what you are feeling is just a normal reaction, it happens to all of us; although, I realize there is something that makes you different from the rest of us, in this matter, you are just like everyone else. You are attracted to a beautiful girl. It only means that you have feelings."

"But I don't want to feel it, I'm in love with Candelaria and I wish I could only think of her,"

"My friend, you are still a boy, just out of childhood, and now you are starting to feel the temptations the world has to offer. As a matter of fact, because there is something that makes you different from the rest of us, you'll have to face many more temptations. You must be aware of that and learn to handle it, because if you don't, it could lead you astray."

Fidelio frowned, about to say something, when the girl came and put two glasses in front of them. "Sotol, aged," she said. "My grandfather prepares it in oak barrels, we offer it only to special people. For you, it's on the house, enjoy it," she smiled, looking at Fidelio as she talked.

Enrique took the glass and sipped on it, he smiled, looked surprised. "It's smooth, try it," he said to Fidelio.

Fidelio also sipped the drink, smiled, also looking surprised. "Indeed, this one is smooth, different from the one I drank before."

"Do you like it?" she asked, looking and smiling to Fidelio.

"Yes, it's really good," Fidelio replied.

She was about to say something when another customer called her. "Waitress, give us the check, please," the man called.

"Yes, in a moment," she said and started walking towards the table from which she had been called. At that moment, a couple of drunk men walked in and one of them bumped into her.

"Sweetheart, you feel good, how much would it be for a night with you?" he said and started touching her butt. The other man also started touching her.

"Leave me alone!" She replied and tried to push them away.

"What? Don't play games with me, all of you are the same, if you are here it's because you are also for sale," one of the men said, holding her by the shoulders slapping her in the face, blood came out her mouth. The man held her from one arm, preventing her from falling, raised his hand to slap her again when Fidelio, as if pushed by a spring, jumped out of his chair, pushing the man down.

Once on the floor, furious, Fidelio got on top of him and punched the man in the face, so hard, that the sound of cracked bones could be heard. The other man pulled his gun, aiming at Fidelio, but before he could pull the trigger, a shot was heard and he fell, wounded in the shoulder.

"Fidelio! Stop, you are going to kill him!" Enrique, who had shot the second man, yelled as he put his gun back in the holder. Fidelio stopped punching the man, looked at the man swollen, bruised, purple face, blood pouring from his nose and mouth, unconscious. "Oh, my God," Fidelio said and stood up, feeling ashamed of himself.

"Thank you," the young woman said to Fidelio, touching him in one of his hands. She got close, on tip-toes, kissed him in the cheek. Fidelio flushed.

"What happened here?" One of the rural police men, who walked in, guns in hand, asked.

"These men tried to abuse this girl," replied Enrique.

The rural looked at the two men on the floor. One of them, unconscious, his face swollen, bleeding through his nose, the other holding his arm, bleeding. "And, who are you?" The rural police asked, placing his gun back in the holder.

"I'm Captain Enrique Lopez, in the cavalry under Maclovio Herrera. He is Fidelio Serna, with the sanitary brigade."

The rural looked at them, then he looked back at the men in the floor and smiled. "It looks like these two will need to go to the sanitary brigade," he said, with an ironic tone, looking at Fidelio. "But, you two are going to jail," he added, pointing to Enrique and Fidelio. He then looked at the two wounded men, "and these two to the hospital, but guard them, because they also will have to answer some questions."

"But, captain, these two were only trying to defend this girl from the abuse of those," said one of the customers.

"Yes, that's is true," the blond said pointing to the fallen men. "Those started it all, I didn't give them any reason to act the way they did."

The captain looked at her up and down; smiled, whistled. "Sweetheart, with that body and that face, you would tempt anyone," he said.

"It's not my fault that God made me as I am," she said, blushing. "But, these two gentlemen were only defending me."

"They are going to jail," the rural said, pointing to Enrique, "take his gun and let's go." One of the rural police took Enrique's gun, pushing him. "Move!" he said. Another rural pushed Fidelio.

"Since you are an officer, you'll share the cell with another officer," the sergeant in charge of the jail told Enrique. "And you are going to the common cell," he added, pointing to Fidelio.

"Could we be together?" Enrique asked pointing to Fidelio.

"Silence!" You might be a captain, but once in here, I'm the one who gives the orders. Do I make myself clear?" The sergeant yelled.

"Yes, sergeant, and we'll follow your orders," Fidelio said, his voice was soft but firm, he looked down fixing his eyes in the sergeant, who was much shorter than him. The sergeant rubbed his hands that suddenly had become sweaty, looked around, nervous. "Take them away, do as I say!" he yelled and kicked a chair.

The cell where Fidelio was taken was a large, dark, humid place. It wafted a strong putrid odor. Fidelio felt nauseated as he was pushed in. He had to squint to see around. Some of the prisoners were squatting in the middle of the cell, others sat, with their backs to the wall, while others, standing up, chatted together. There were several benches, one of them was empty; Fidelio sat on it, trying to make sense of what was happening. As he got used to the darkness, now he could see. In one corner there were two men, one of them was urinating towards the wall; the other, who apparently had just finished emptying his bowel, took a piece of a rag and wiped his ass with it. In another corner, darker than the rest of the cell, two shadows moved. Intrigued, Fidelio had to squint. When he finally could see, he almost jumped, surprised. Two men were kissing and masturbating each other. Like in a trance, Fidelio could not move his eyes away.

"They are having a good time," said a man who had just come and sat at Fidelio's side, placing his hand on Fidelio's thigh and gently rubbing it.

Surprised, Fidelio looked at him as he moved away. The man was slender, tall, blond; large blue eyes, with long eye lashes; his skin smooth, tanned by the sun, long hair and a well-groomed beard. Small mouth, with sensual lips, a bright smile. Fidelio sweated, felt nervous, almost scared; strongly attracted to him, as a matter of fact, he wanted to kiss and caress him; he moved further away.

The man smiled at him, his bright eyes seemed to touch Fidelio's body with fire. "Don't run from yourself," the man told Fidelio with a soft, melodious, seductive voice. Fidelio couldn't move, breathed heavy, his body melting. The man got closer, touched his thigh again, at the touch of that hand, fire went into Fidelio's whole body; he turned to hug and kiss the man, but a hand in his shoulder prevented him from doing so; that hand felt cold. At its touch, Fidelio felt suddenly calm; his mind clear, the room was suddenly illuminated, he understood the temptation into which he had been about to fall; he looked again at the man sitting at his side, noticed how attractive he was, but this time, however, he noticed that behind that beauty there was something menacing, cruel, hard; a chill ran through Fidelio's body.

"There are people here who need your help," said the man who had touched him. Fidelio turned, looked at him, a short, chubby man with dark complexion, middle aged, friendly with bright eyes and gentle smile (although he had two front teeth missing), who also looked straight into Fidelio's eyes. "You are the young man who has been helping people to heal, I recognized you since you walked in," the man added; his voice was soothing. Looking and listening to him, Fidelio felt not only calmer, but also perplexed. "Where have I met this man before?" he asked himself.

"We have two men who are badly wounded, their wounds already have a foul smell. Could you please help them?" the man asked.

"They should pay you first, very few have your ability to heal; you deserve to earn for what you know," the blond man said, touching Fidelio's hand. Fidelio felt the heat of this hand, this time, however, the sensation upset him; he pulled away and stood up. "Show me those men," he said.

"Thank you, follow me, I'll show you," said the man. Both of them walked to the farthest corner of the cell. Fidelio could now see that there were many men in there, most were young, dark complexion, almost all dressed in rags; they looked at both of them with respect and moved away to let them pass.

Two men were lying on the floor, charitable hands had improvised a bed for them using old rags and straw. Both were shaking and sweating covered by old serapes. Fidelio touched them and almost jumped. "They are on fire," he said, concerned. He moved the serapes away and saw that they were not only dirty, but had several deep and superficial wounds in several parts of their bodies, most of which were covered by a multicolored, thick, foul smelling, fluid. The worse were in their abdomen, fortunately none of them penetrated to the bowel.

"First of all, what they need is a full bath; but there is no water here," he said.

"There is plenty of water," the man who had brought him said. "Bring the carafes of water," he said to one of the men who were looking.

"You mean, the Holly Water?" The man asked.

"Yes, the water, you fool, move and get it, fast!"

"Holly Water? Who are you?" Fidelio asked.

"My name is Aurelio Gomez, I'm the sexton of the Santa Maria church," the man answered, smiling, a calm, soothing tone of voice.

"I assume that you also have soap here," Fidelio said.

"Of course, my father is the soap-maker here," the man answered smiling.

"You are full of surprises," Fidelio said also smiling. "Can you help me to wash these men?"

"Yes, just show me what to do and I'll do it."

With the help of others present, they undressed the two men. "They need a thorough bath, use a lot of water" Fidelio said, taking one of the soap bars, wetting it and starting to bathe one of the men. Aurelio, the sexton, mirrored Fidelio with the other man.

"Now, I need to open those wounds, drain the pus and remove all of the tissue that is infected," said Fidelio, once they had thoroughly washed and dried the two men. He looked around. "Let me have that bottle," he said pointing to a bottle of tequila in the belt of one of the men that observed them.

"What? My tequila, you must be crazy!" the man yelled, stepping forwards, with a menacing attitude.

Fidelio looked at him straight in the eyes. "Give me the bottle," he said gently, extending his arm.

The man took a step back, looked down, moved a little, pulled the bottle out from his belt and put it in Fidelio's hand. "It's yours," he said, nervous.

Fidelio took the bottle, uncorked it; "take a gulp," he said to the man. The man drank a good gulp out of it and gave the bottle back to Fidelio who smashed it against the wall, chose a piece and went to one of the wounded men. Fidelio put one hand in the forehead of the man. "Relax and rest, you'll feel that I touch you, don't let it bother you. Rest; just rest, rest, rest, and enjoy it. Relax peacefully, you are a child, remember your mother's caress, that's it, just relax," as he talked, Fidelio washed his hands, took water and put it on the wounds; "wherever the cold water falls, the numbness of cold takes over, you'll feel only numbness, relax and rest." Fidelio used the sharp piece of glass, opened the infected wounds one by one, let the pus drain and carefully removed all the dead tissue, washed every wound thoroughly, leaving them open. Meanwhile the man kept quiet, eyes closed, smiling. The other wounded man was already with his eyes closed, smiling, resting. Without saying anything else, Fidelio repeated the same procedure with him. All those around, impressed, just looked respectfully, not a word said; some of the men kneeled, tears in their eyes; others mumbled a prayer.

Afterwards, Fidelio talked to the sexton. "Aurelio, if you are the sexton of the church here, how is it that you are in jail?"

"The priest under whom I was working was a supporter of Porfirio Diaz, Villa knew that and expelled him out of the country, put me in jail, although I support the revolution." Aurelio said smiling and shrugging his shoulders.

"But you said that you had recognized me; and, although I don't know you, I feel that I had seen you before."

"You have earned a reputation, the men talk about you, even here. They talk about a very tall, very young, almost a child, who has the ability to heal; as a matter of fact, that's exactly how they talk about you, they know you as 'the child'." The sexton looked at Fidelio, who perceived a tender, gentle, but powerful brightness in those dark eyes. "You are a child of God." The sexton added.

Fidelio flushed. "No, I'm not!" He said is a loud tone of voice "I'm just another man full of temptations and weakness, just like anyone else."

"Yes, that's also true," the sexton said, smiling. "I noticed that just a short time ago."

Fidelio flushed again, embarrassed. "Yes, you saved me, I was about to fall."

"Everyone has temptations, most of us don't even resist them, on the contrary, the majority looks for them, that's human nature," The sexton said. "He is beautiful, isn't he?"

"Yes, he is," Fidelio replied.

"Evil is, by nature, beautiful and attractive, otherwise it would be easy to avoid it."

"Fidelio Serna!" A guard yelled. "You have visitors."

Fidelio walked to the front of the cell. The blond girl, from the restaurant, carrying a basket with food, smiled to Fidelio as he approached.

"How are you?" She asked flushing a bit. "I got you some food, I'm sorry that you have had to go through all this trouble for me." She said giving the basket to Fidelio through a space with that purpose. "Some friends of the captain and yours have asked about you. I understand that they have talked in your favor and I hope that you'll be out of here soon; meanwhile, is there something I could do for you?"

"Yes, there is something I'd like to ask you to get me," Fidelio replied.

"What is it? I'll be glad to help with anything I can to make it easier for you." She said.

"Two or three large jars of bee honey and as much as you can get of fresh aloe," Fidelio said.

"Is that all?" She said, surprised.

"Yes, please get it as soon as possible, it's important."

"I'll be back in a short while," she said starting to walk away.

"Wait, you haven't told me your name," Fidelio said, before she could leave.

"Aurora, I'll be back soon," she replied, smiled to Fidelio and walked away.

Fidelio took the basket and apportioned the food among the other prisoners.

After Aurora had brought the honey and the fresh aloe. Fidelio called Aurelio.

"I don't know how you do it, but it's a blessing that you have clean water and soap. Keeping the wounds clean is the first and most important step. But it's not enough, we must use nature to help them get rid of the infection and heal faster. It's for that reason that we need this bee honey and fresh aloe. Come, I'll show you."

They then went to the two wounded men; Fidelio talked to the men, repeating closely what he said before to help them to stay calm and relaxed during the procedure. Fidelio then proceeded to clean the wounds, poured honey bee on them and covered them with fresh slices of aloe. Towards the end of the procedure, Fidelio said to the wounded: "From now on, when Aurelio comes and he says, 'relax now,' you will get into the same state in which you are now and relax, while he works on your wounds." Fidelio then smiled to Aurelio. "Do you think you can do it?" he asked.

"Yes, I'm sure that I'll do it," Aurelio replied smiling.

Fidelio smiled back.

"Fidelio Serna, you are out of here," someone yelled.

"I was starting to understand that there was a purpose for me coming here," said Fidelio to Aurelio. He hugged him. "Thank you, I'll never forget your help and the lesson that I learned here."

"Go in peace my friend, I'll remember your instructions," said Aurelio as he slapped Fidelio's back in a friendly way.

As Fidelio walked out the blond man stood on the side of the door, smiling. He looked at Fidelio from bottom up, a spark in his green eyes, his smile showing his well aligned teeth. "So long, my dear, we'll meet again," he said. Fidelio felt a chill run down his spine.

Outside, Aurora, Enrique and Dr. Villarreal waited for him.

"The owner of the restaurant, who is the father of this girl, has known General Villa for a long time, he and General Raul Madero talked to General Villa on your behalf," Dr. Villarreal said, smiling to Fidelio. "You proved that you'll fight if you have to, but be careful with your strength, the man that you hit is in bad shape; he'll recover though."

"Thank you for what you did for me," Aurora said, she got on her tiptoes and kissed Fidelio who flushed. Dr. Villarreal and Enrique looked at each other.

"Fidelio, I know where to find you. I'm tired and have to rest, see you soon," said Enrique.

"I also have to go, report to the brigade latter," Dr. Villarreal said. He and Enrique turned and walked away.

"I'll walk you home," said Fidelio to Aurora.

"Thank you, we live in the back of the restaurant. My father is the owner and he is also thankful for what you did in my defense; sometimes is difficult to control those drunk men and lately, it has become worse," said Aurora, taking Fidelio by the arm and getting close to him.

It was a bright, cool morning, no clouds in the sky, birds were chirping. Women were outside cleaning the front of their houses. Fidelio took a deep breath, felt at peace and thankful for the blessing of nature; as they walked a grunt was heard, coming from Fidelio's belly.

"Are you hungry? I'll fix you breakfast once we get to my home," she said. "I don't understand myself," she continued; "I know that I'm pretty. Since I was fifteen, men have been trying to get close to me, from both sides of the river. They offer money, riches, even marriage, but I didn't care, the sensation of freedom makes me happy. Some have been constant and continue trying until today. I confess that I like their attention, but none of them got anything from me. That's what I don't understand, I didn't know you, never seen you before, however from the moment I saw you, even if we didn't talk, something happened inside, I don't know how it happened, but I feel that I have fallen in love with you."

Instead of feeling happy, Fidelio felt a profound sadness. Her words were like darts to his soul. Yes, he found her attractive, he also loved her, but not in the way she meant; he loved her as he loved birds, butterflies, as he loved the entire nature. He realized that she was not interested in that type of love and he was afraid that he could hurt her feelings.

"Ah, here we are. Come in, I'll prepare breakfast for you and introduce you to my father." Smiling, she looked at him. She looked radiant. "By the way," she added, "you know my name, and I know yours because I heard it last night, Fidelio. Is that really your name?"

"Yes, it is. Why do you ask?"

"I don't know if ever I heard that name before, it's a beautiful name, suits you really well. But, come in, let's have breakfast."

Fidelio didn't move. He felt a knot in his throat, it was difficult to talk. "Thank you, but I can't stay, I must go now," he finally said.

"Why? What's wrong? Did I say something that upset you?"

"On the contrary, you are wonderful. It's just that I don't want to lie to you, or give you false hope. I love you, but not in the way that you would expect. There is something much stronger, I love something that I can't understand what it is. So, I can't give you, or anyone else, what is already taken. I don't expect you to understand it because I don't understand it myself."

She looked at him tenderly, extended her arm to caress his cheek. "I understand, my love. Believe me. I understand and I still love you. I know that I'll always feel this way towards you, and I hope that someday, I don't know how, we'll be close to each other, even if I have to share you with the entire world."

Fidelio took the hand that caressed him and kissed it. "Thank you, I wish I could offer you more than friendship, but that's all I have."

"That's more than enough for now. Now, would you accept breakfast?" smiling, she asked.

Fidelio's belly grunted. "That's the answer," said he.

Both of them laughed and walked into the restaurant.

Later, Fidelio walked back to the Sanitary Brigade. Once in there, he found a bed, lied down and, exhausted, fell to sleep almost immediately.

In his dream he found himself walking in the middle of nowhere. It was dark, he barely could see, there was no pathway, a cold breeze penetrated through his skin. He felt nervous. The dark clouds in the sky, threatened a storm. He could hear voices calling, although he couldn't understand what they said, it was obvious that they were claiming for help. The images of the beautiful blond man and the sexton appeared intermittently, they seemed to fight each other. The images of Candelaria, calling him from far away, and Aurora smiling at him, also mixed in there. There were signals pointing in different directions. It was all confusion, Fidelio looked in all directions and he saw images of war, people fighting, cutting themselves into pieces. There were merry images, people drinking and singing, images of orgies, men and women caressing. Mixed in between all these images, people suffering, mourning, their skin covered with pustules. People in pain. Beggars in rags asking for food, and, wealthy people, smartly dressed, ignoring them. Suddenly, the image of a young man appeared, surrounded by fire, but the fire seemed to come out of his body, and, this fire instead of hurting those touched by it, they got relieved. They stopped what they were doing and turned to the fire-man thankful for his touch with an expression of love and inner peace. Fidelio tried to touch the man, but he was gone; overwhelmed, Fidelio fell on his knees and wept.

"Fidelio, hey Fidelio, wake up, wake up," a voice called him, forcefully rubbing him. Fidelio opened his eyes and rubbed them, he felt the tears in them and felt ashamed. "What is it?" he asked, opening his eyes. Dr. Villarreal was the one calling him.

"You were dreaming again, my friend," Dr. Villarreal said. "Looking at your face I don't know if it was a nightmare or a pleasant dream, but I know it was something important. Anyhow, I'm sorry to wake you up, but we have to move. There is another battle in our way."

"How is it?"

"An army is coming from Chihuahua. General Villa doesn't want to risk a battle so close to the border. We are moving to face them in Tierra Blanca," Dr. Villarreal replied.

CHAPTER X

A sea used to cover it all. Thousands of years ago, the sea dried up, leaving behind only sand, miles and miles of sand. White sand, as far as the eye can see. The wind lifting up the sand makes it to dance, a wavy ballet of white figures. A cold winter morning, the Sanitary Brigade arrived at Tierra Blanca (White Sand), Fidelio among them. The troops had arrived the day before. Fidelio noticed that they occupied the upper, firm part of the terrain. The federales were seen close by; they were, however, in the sand dunes where the terrain was loose; with the loose sand above their ankles it would be difficult for them to move.

Children, skinny children in rags not a thread of hair in their faces, with almost empty cartridge belts around their chests, guns in their waist belts and in their hands, ready to enter in combat. One of the youngest walked by the sanitary wagon where Fidelio sat. The boy seemed hungry. Fidelio had some refried bean tacos with him. "Are you hungry?" he said to the child. "Here, have some bean tacos," added Fidelio, extending his arm with the tacos towards the child who took them; he barely chewed before he swallowed. "Here, have some water. What is your name?" said Fidelio, offering the child a water bag.

"Jacinto Sanchez," the child replied, after he drank a sip of water and continued chewing the taco.

"Where are you from? Where are your parents?" Fidelio asked.

"I'm from Lago Guzman, my parents were killed by the federales because my father refused to join them and my mother tried to intervene," the child answered. His pale face flushed in anger; his entire body tensed, he almost choked, coughed forcing him to spit the piece of taco in his mouth.

"But you are just a child. Do you have brothers and sisters? Where are they?"

The child grinned, looked up to Fidelio. "I have two brothers and one sister. They are also here. They also want to kill as many as possible of those damned federales."

"But, how old are you? And they, how old are they?"

"I'm eleven-years-old; my sister is fourteen and my brothers twelve and thirteen," the child answered, proudly, giving back to Fidelio the water bag.

"Do you know how to shoot? Can you ride a horse? How long have you been in this?"

"Of course, we know how to shoot, our father taught us. We learned to ride a horse before we learned to walk. After our parents were killed we joined other rebels from our town, we were a small group, but now we are part of the Northern Division. I hope the battle will start soon, we'll cut them in pieces." The child said with a firm tone of voice. A distant trumpet called. "Thank you for the tacos, I must go, get my horse, and be ready."

"Take care of yourself and God bless you," Fidelio said, waving his hand.

"The Virgen of Guadalupe will protect me," the child replied, pulling an image of the Virgen from his hat and showing it to Fidelio.

"They are only children, but they are fearless soldiers; cannons, machine guns, don't scare them. They go to battle happily and come out of it like someone who went to a ball." Enrique, who had heard the conversation, said behind Fidelio.

"But they are so young," Fidelio replied, a sad tone in his voice. "I can see now how lucky I was working for your uncle, Father Segura."

"Indeed, we were lucky. The only battles we had to fight were against other children, our classmates, with whom now we are friends. Your parents had a tragic death, but even that is different to being killed for resisting to abandon their families. Violence and a hard life has taught them to be fierce very early in their lives."

"Still it's sad not to enjoy childhood," Fidelio said pensive. "Here comes Dr. Villarreal."

"Good morning my friends," Dr. Villarreal said as he approached; he looked at Enrique. "I hope that you and your men are ready to battle. General Villa is planning to attack tonight. As you probably know, we are short in ammunition; the enemy has ten cannons, we have only two; they also have more, and better, machine guns. They are mostly seasoned soldiers, many of ours are children and women. Our advantage is that we are in the solid ground and they are in the sandy part of the terrain." He frowned. "This is going to be a bloody battle; but we can't lose it."

As the day went by, there was movement of troops on both sides. A shipment with ammunition arrived. "That ammunition is a relief," Dr. Villarreal said to Fidelio. "Let's get ready; as I said, this is going to be a bloody battle. We are going to be busy."

Indeed, everyone was busy, getting ready for battle. The wind whispered to Fidelio's ears a sad tune. The sky was clear; ducks, peacocks, goose, all flew in perfect harmony; forming several "V's". Nature seemed peaceful, pleasant.

It was a dark night; clouds covered the moon. The wind was cold. No fire allowed. Fidelio, like everyone else, shaking, rubbed his body, trying to get warm. A man came providing wool sarapes to everyone. "Here, get warm and rest. Don't smoke, they are close by," said the man, as he distributed the sarapes. Looking at him, Dr. Villarreal stood up. "Sit, Doctor. There is no need to stand up. Rest; tomorrow the battle will begin," said the man, the tone of his voice sounded like an order.

"That was General Villa," said Dr. Villarreal, after the man was gone.

The battle started at 5 a.m. in the morning. The federal cavalry attacked the villista right flank. Being mostly seasoned, fearless, soldiers, the huertista attack was violent. From his position, Fidelio could observe the battle clearly. Concerned because there were many women and children among the villistas; but he was relieved when he saw that they fought well and held their position. The battle generalized. The federales now attacked the left flank and for some time it looked like that this flank was going to give ground, but through heroic fighting, they also held the attack well. The purpose of the federal Generals was clear. They tried to surround the villistas. General Villa, on his horse, moved all around, "Keep fighting, we'll defeat them," he yelled. The federales tried to move their artillery, but, they had problems; their cannons got stock in the sandy ground. After six hours, there was a brief pause. The federales concentrated their attack in the right flank, their artillery pounded that side; their infantry, covered by their machine guns, advanced. Although the villistas held their position, many fell to the machine gun bullets; Villa sent reinforcement and ordered his artillery to fire. That stopped the advance of the federal infantry. The federales, again tried to attack both flanks; in response, Villa ordered to counterattack their middle and it forced the federales to retreat and defend their center. At the end of the day, their positions were the same.

During the night; a bright night, full moon and shining stars. Fidelio and his people went to help and transport the wounded. Once again, the putrefaction smell was present. Smell of powder, feces, urine, blood, and flesh in decay, all combined. Once again, Fidelio felt nauseated, but this time he controlled it well and continued his job. There were many wounded, many bleeding. Limbs separated from their bodies. Headless bodies. Monotonous mourning murmurs, yells for help, people crying; a sad, painful, symphony. Vultures circling the field; packs of hungry dogs and rats all around. Walking with difficulty in the loose terrain, Fidelio and his team of children and women had difficulty carrying the wounded to the wagons that had to be placed in the solid ground. Searching the fallen for wounded men, suddenly Fidelio recognized one of the bodies. It was Prudencio, one of his classmates from Guanajuato. Memories flowed to Fidelio's mind; he saw Prudencio sitting in the classroom, quiet, shy, a child with a gentle smile. Now his inert body lied in there, with a bullet in his chest. Fidelio fell on his knees, chin to the chest, crying. "Why does it has to be like this?" he thought. When he lifted his head, again, he again noticed men and women, not trying to help, but searching the bodies, dead or wounded, to rip them of anything of value. Fidelio felt rage flowing though his body, filling his mind with hate and rancor.

Prudencio's rifle was on his body's side; Fidelio took it, stood up and yelled: "Scavengers! Scavengers! Damn you all, go to hell!" He shot at them; some of those who had stolen from the fallen, fell on their side.

"Fidelio! Fidelio! Child! Child! What are you doing? Stop!" One of the women in his group yelled. She ran, took the rifle away from Fidelio who stood, frozen, sweating profusely in spite of the cold wind. He saw the vultures, the dogs, the rats and those he had just shot; the rotten smell nauseated him even more. "Child, why did you do it?" the woman asked. Fidelio didn't answer, just looked at her and walked away, shoulders down, arms hanging on the side of his body, chin to his chest, crying.

Fidelio walked back to the train wagon, his mind blank; threw himself into a hammock and, almost immediately, went to sleep. In his dream, Fidelio saw himself in the middle of a sand storm, dark sand; the wind blew away everything in its path. It was night, in spite of the dark sand, a full moon seemed to illuminate everything. Horses, donkeys, pigs, cows, flying aimlessly, blown away by the strong wind. Also flying, there were people, women, men, children, with their mouths open, like yelling, with blood flowing from their eyes. There were heads, dripping blood; searching for a body. In the middle of the storm, there was a glow and in that glow, there was someone. With difficulty, fighting the wind, Fidelio got closer. Prudencio, in the middle of the glow, smiled at him. "Fidelio," said Prudencio. "My friend it's so nice to see you again. Remember school? At the beginning, when the other children attacked you, I wished I had had the courage to defend you, but instead I said and did nothing. I was glad when we all became friends; but still I felt bad at my silence. The shame of that silence is the reason I joined this fight." Fidelio looked at him, intrigued. "But I saw your dead body, how is it that you are now talking to me?" Prudencio kept smiling, a gentle look in his face. "True, my body is death, but I'm alive; and I'm here to tell you that there is a message of peace that you must transmit, through what has been given to you. You are a healer. Ahead there is more violence; this fight of brothers against brothers will continue and, as a matter of fact, it will get worse. Because of their beliefs, people will be punished, houses, churches burned, or converted into stables; priests killed, nuns raped; all of this will come to be, but you must refrain from taking part in that battle. You are a healer. Remember, remember, my dear friend. You are a healer." The sand storm stopped. There was a sudden, oppressive calm. Prudencio's image faded away. "Why me?" Fidelio sweated, opened his arms and yelled, looking up, "I just want to be like anyone else." "Remember, remember," Prudencio's voice was heard. "But I just killed people!" Fidelio yelled back, falling on his knees, crying, trembling.

"Fidelio, Fidelio, wake up, wake up," Enrique moved Fidelio forcefully. "Come on, Fidelio, wake up." Fidelio, opened his eyes, sweating profusely, still trembling. He rubbed his eyes and looked around. Enrique and Dr. Villarreal were there; a concerned look on their faces.

"Fidelio, we heard what happened tonight," Dr. Villarreal said. "I understand why you did it. Those were robbing, coward human vultures. Several times I have thought of doing what you did today. You gave them what they deserved."

"Yes, that's true. Believe me, more than once I have also desired to shoot at them," said Enrique, rubbing Fidelio's shoulder and smiling at him.

"What I did is not right," whispered Fidelio, a sad look in his face. "I became like them by doing what I did."

"You screamed and cried in your sleep," said Dr. Villarreal. "Was it because of this?"

"Yes, mostly because of that," replied Fidelio, feeling embarrassed and upset about it.

"Perhaps you need a bit of rest, maybe you should go back to Ciudad Juarez. You could help with those we are sending back there." Said Dr. Villarreal, with a serious tone of voice.

"No, thank you, I prefer to help here, it won't happen again," said Fidelio with a firm tone of voice, looking straight at Dr. Villarreal.

"Well, Fidelio, remember. This is war and in war, ugly things happen," Dr. Villarreal said.

"I'll remember," replied Fidelio.

"I hope you'll be able to rest now. Everyone must be ready early in the morning. Meanwhile, the team that you prepared has done a great job. They have helped a lot of the wounded; you should feel god about that," Dr. Villarreal said, smiling to Fidelio.

"They are wonderful people, I'm proud of them."

"Rest my friend, the battle will continue tomorrow. All of us must be ready," Enrique said.

"I'll be ready," said Fidelio, smiling to Enrique.

They waved good bye to Fidelio and left.

Fidelio went to sleep almost immediately.

Fidelio had a profound, dreamless sleep and awoke shortly before sunrise. Feeling refreshed and energized, he went out, washed his face with cold water. The morning was also cold, the sun barely showed in the horizon casting a bright yellow-orange tone; the birds chirping in the sky. For a moment, Fidelio forgot that everyone around him was getting ready for battle, the memory of Candelaria came to him and that made him feel so happy that he started singing a love song.

The battle started early, from his standpoint Fidelio observed the events as they developed. During the whole day, the federales attacked both flanks violently and, as they had done the day before, the Villistas courageously held their positions. Knowing that so many of the Villistas were children, Fidelio was deeply impressed by the ferocity of the fight. He thought about Jacinto, the child he had just met the day before. "How he, his sister and his brothers would be doing?" he asked himself. At the end of the day, there were no changes in the position of the troops.

"We are in a precarious situation," Dr. Villarreal told Fidelio that night, before Fidelio would leave to help the wounded. "Our ammunition will only last for one day more. At this moment, General Villa is planning the action for tomorrow. I'm sure he'll surprise everyone again."

"I know you said that 'he is like a fox about to be trapped', isn't it?" Fidelio replied.

Dr. Villarreal smiled. "Go now and do your job and remember, don't let your emotions lead you."

Fidelio joined his group. He was surprised that this time the pungent odor didn't upset him as much as in the previous occasions. He was happy helping as many wounded soldiers as he could. In doing so, he didn't care for which side the wounded soldier had fought. Afterwards he went and slept peacefully.

Once again, Fidelio got up early. The memory of Candelaria remained with him, he felt as if she was close by. As soon as the sun was barely seen, the federal artillery pounded the Villista line. The federal infantry attacked violently; once again, the rebels held their ground, but, this time it was hard and difficult. The battle continued through the whole morning, it seemed that the federales had the upper hand and the defense was about to give up. An order came from General Villa: "Everyone should get a horse and get ready to attack." The signal for the attack would be two cannon blasts, one after the other. Around two in the afternoon, the signal was heard and a massive cavalry charge went on. Surprised by the strength of the attack, the federales stopped, tried to defend themselves. The cavalry attack went to the enemy's center, it was a powerful attack, reinforced from both flanks with machine gun and fusil shots. The federales resisted for a short period of time, but soon they got scared and started running away in complete disorder, leaving behind weapons and equipment. It was a complete victory for the rebels. At night, everything was quiet, with the battle field full of bodies. The putrid smell stronger than ever. Vultures circling the field; packs of hungry dogs and even wild hogs came, attracted by the smell.

"This has been not only a great and important victory, with it we have captured cannons, machine guns, trains, plenty of ammunition," Enrique told Fidelio after the battle. Several shots were heard.

"What is that?" asked Fidelio.

Enrique shrugged his shoulders, "I don't know," he said.

"General Villa has ordered that the 'colorados' and the federal officials be shot,"

Dr. Villarreal said, having heard Fidelio's question as he joined them.

Hearing this, Fidelio frowned and looked down, upset. "Who are the 'colorados'?" Enrique asked.

"Those are Pascual Orozco's loyal," Dr. Villarreal answered. "Well, we finally broke through. It was a great victory. On the dark side, there are many wounded; we have hard work ahead Fidelio, better start early."

"Yes, we'll start immediately," replied Fidelio.

Fidelio went into the battle field; joined his group and started helping the wounded. Suddenly he saw Jacinto, the child was wounded, bleeding profusely from a wound in his right arm. Jacinto was unconscious. Fidelio applied pressure in the wound, tried a tourniquet in the arm, but the bleeding didn't stop; the wound was deep into the axillae, Jacinto's breath was shallow, he was pale. Suddenly, Jacinto opened his eyes; seeing Fidelio, he smiled at him, a thankful smile; with his left arm, he pulled something from his pocket and smiling at Fidelio said: "My mother gave me this, please keep it. Thank you." He closed his eyes, gasped and his breathing stopped. Fidelio looked at Jacinto's object, it was a bright American quarter. Fidelio put the coin in his pocket, hugged Jacinto's body, rocking it in a paternal way. After several minutes; carrying the body, Fidelio got up and carried it back to the camp.

When he arrived, many of the troops followed them and helped to bury Jacinto. At the place of the burial, Fidelio kneeled and prayed: "Our Father in heaven, hallowed be your name. Your kingdom come. Your will be done on earth as it is in heaven. Give us our daily bread. And forgive us, our trespasses, as we forgive those who trespass against us. Do not lead us into temptation, but deliver us from evil. Yours is the kingdom, the power and the glory. Amen." The prayer was repeated in chorus by the troop. When Fidelio got up, he was surprised when he saw General Villa standing at his side, tears in his eyes.

CHAPTER XI

"After our victory the federales have left most of the state. We now control almost all of Chihuahua. As you are aware, Villa has left for Chihuahua City to take over as Governor of the State. Here, in Juarez, we stayed behind to take care of the wounded." Dr. Villarreal said to Fidelio as they walked towards the hospital. "It's going to be relatively quiet for some time; I'd like to take the opportunity to share more time with you. You are a smart boy, wise for your age. Yes, there are many things that I would like to talk about; although, let me warn you, we might argue."

"I would like that very much," replied Fidelio, smiling. Although a bit surprised about Dr. Villarreal's warning, he already had a clear idea about what would be the topic of conversation.

"Great, but for now, let's concentrate in our job. Afterwards we'll have dinner at Aurora's restaurant. I invite." Dr. Villarreal said.

"I like the idea and, of course, I accept" said Fidelio.

"You'll assist me in today's surgeries, mostly amputations, it's a sad procedure, but necessary to save those men's lives. By the way, you are doing a great job in helping them to cope with it."

"They have a life ahead, need support to help them to cope with the loss of a limb. It's a worthy job. But the praise should be for the women and children who spend the time helping them. I only showed them how to do it." They walked into the hospital.

That night, Dr. Villarreal and Fidelio sat at Aurora's restaurant, ready to enjoy dinner. It was a quiet and cool night.

"We had a busy but, at the same time, productive day," Dr. Villarreal started the conversation. He seemed to be happy and satisfied. "Seven cases today. Thanks to the change in the technique that you have introduced, we were able to avoid amputation in three of them. I'm proud of you. Although you are young and never went to medical school, you pay attention to details, observe and ponder what you have learned. In your own way you study hard, as hard as any medical student, and in the process, we also learn from you."

"Thanks, nature has taught me most of what I know, and of course, I have learned much since I started working with you and the rest of your team," Fidelio said, hesitant to mention that, since childhood, there was something, an inner voice, guiding him.

"Well, but it is not about medicine that I want to talk to you. There are many things in my mind that I have wanted to discuss with someone. But until now, I hadn't found anyone that I thought would be worth to bring all of this up. That is, until I met and worked with you."

"What's that?" Fidelio asked, showing interest.

"Here is Aurora, let's order dinner. What do you feel like?" Dr. Villarreal said, pointing to Aurora who approached the table with a broad smile on her face.

"Hello, Aurora," said Fidelio, smiling in a friendly manner at her. "It's nice to see you again. How have you been?"

"Wonderful now, I'm glad to see that both of you are safe," Aurora answered, smiling to them. "What would you like to eat?"

"It's a cold night, I would like something hot. Do you have pozole?" Fidelio asked.

"Yes, of course, and we are proud of our pozole."

"I'll have the same," Dr. Villarreal said, returning the friendly smile to Aurora. "Also, I have heard about the sotol you have here, please bring two glasses of it."

"Sure, but the sotol will be on the house," said Aurora.

"Thank you, I appreciate that, but only for the first round, if we ask for more, as we probably will, then it will be on me," Dr. Villarreal said.

"As you wish, I'll be back with your order in a minute. Once again, I'm happy to see that both of you are back and safe," said Aurora, looking and smiling to Fidelio before walking away.

"Let's talk," Dr. Villarreal said to Fidelio after Aurora had left. He looked serious, but with a friendly, gentle smile. Fidelio remained silent and paid attention.

"There is something I rarely talk about. As a matter of fact, few people know about what I'm going to tell you," Dr. Villarreal paused, took a deep breath, he seemed to be looking for the right words.

"My parents were fervent Catholic, during childhood I never missed mass, after my first communion and used to confess every week, so I could have communion during the Sunday mass," Dr. Villarreal started, looking seriously to Fidelio, who listened attentively. Dr. Villarreal smiled, "You might be surprised to know that I wanted to become a priest and I went to the seminary."

"Yes, it's surprising. I have never seen you in church or praying," said Fidelio, being indeed surprised.

Dr. Villarreal grinned. "Good, we are starting well. Probably you are now wondering what was it that made me change"

"Yes, what was it that made you change?"

"Well, it's not easy to explain it. First let me tell you something that makes it a bit more intriguing. I still love Jesus' teachings and they guide most of my actions. That's something that will never change for me."

"But you still don't pray or go to church," said Fidelio, now more interested.

"Gentlemen, here is your hot pozole and sotol, as you ordered. Enjoy it. Would you like something else?" Aurora said as she approached, putting the bowls with pozole and the glasses with sotol on the table.

"No, thank you Aurora, kind of you to ask," Dr. Villarreal replied, smiling to Aurora.

"You seemed very involved in your conversation, so I'll leave you alone, but just signal if you need me," Aurora said before leaving.

"Let's enjoy dinner, we'll continue our conversation a bit later," said Dr. Villarreal as he rolled a tortilla and filled his spoon with the spicy soup. "Delicious, Aurora is right to feel proud of it, go ahead, try it, I know you'll like it."

Fidelio took his spoon, filled it with the pozole and took it. "Yes, it's delicious," said he, smiling. The spicy soup made Fidelio feel exhilarated; he also enjoyed the company and looked forward to the continuation of the conversation. It was important for him as well.

"Well, to your health," Dr. Villarreal said, lifting the glass with sotol after finishing the pozole.

"To your health," replied Fidelio, lifting his glass. Both of them drank.

"Good, food like this, accompanied by a good drink, makes one feel relaxed and happy to be alive," Dr. Villarreal said. He looked at Fidelio in a friendly manner. "I believe you said you have never seen me praying or going to church, even if I love Jesus' teachings."

"That's right and I wonder about that." Fidelio replied.

"It's a bit difficult for me to talk about it. I have never discussed it with anyone else. What caused me to change?" He frowned, serious. "First, it was that I found it difficult to believe some of the aspects of the bible, especially the Genesis, it is not possible for me to believe that the universe was created with the simplicity that its described in there. Then, all that of God talking only to certain chosen people. I can't believe that God talks to anyone. The idea that I would have to teach what I didn't believe was not possible. If it was to be taught as a metaphor to explain the existence of the universe, that shouldn't be any problem, but I was asked to believe it as it is written and teach it exactly in that way."

Fidelio frowned, put his elbows on the table, and supported his forehead with his hands, looking down. He felt tense and upset because he had had the same concern, had tried to put it out of his mind, but, lately, it really troubled him.

"I am aware that talking about this might be disconcerting, probably upsetting, for you. Maybe I shouldn't have even mentioned it. If you wish, we'll change the subject." Dr. Villarreal said when he noticed Fidelio's concern.

"No, no, it's also important to me. Please continue," Fidelio said, facing Dr. Villarreal, now serious and interested.

"It gets more complex," Dr. Villarreal continued. "What I just said isn't the most important; all of it is just but a simplistic way to explain the world as we see it. As I already said, I have no problem with that. There is more, I don't believe that anyone knows God's plan. No one can explain God and any attempt to do so is just a waste of time; that's the main reason I left the seminary. But let me tell the most important of all; I started our conversation telling you that I love and follow Jesus' teachings. However, I don't care if Maria, his mother, was a virgin or not, I don't care if He is the Messiah or not, I don't care if He is the Son of God, or not. I don't even accept that if He ever comes back, His return would be a triumphal one. That's something there is no way for anyone to know it, and, that's the reason I don't go to church. I would be a hypocrite if I did it. However, let me tell you that I do pray. I pray as He taught us, I just do it quietly, as He taught us we should pray. I just love Jesus for his teachings, that's all." He took a deep breath and signaled to Aurora to serve two more glasses of sotol.

Fidelio looked at him, he felt a deep, emotional pain. He felt a strong desire to cry, he was feeling sad. "Now that I have learned that there is a dark side in me, a side that I didn't know existed; what you have just said has made me conscious of my own doubts. There are many things that I don't understand. At least you know why you changed. I am all doubtful. I appreciate your confidence, but I don't know how I could help you. Since Tierra Blanca, everything has changed for me."

Aurora came, in silence she put the glasses of sotol on the table and left quietly.

Dr. Villarreal sipped the sotol, an understanding smile on his face. "Believe me, I understand the way you feel; as a matter of fact, something very similar happened to me. It is obvious that the experiences you have lived since we met have changed you." He looked at Fidelio with sympathetic eyes, he seemed to hesitate for a moment. "It was also an unpleasant surprise when I learned that there is a dark side in me. That's something we must accept and live with," he grinned. "When we met, you impressed me as someone who is different, but I didn't think we could ever have a conversation like the one we are having now. I confess to you that I thought that probably someday I would make a joke about your belief. I admit that I have become a bit cynical about it. However,

I refrained myself not only because I respect other people's beliefs, but also because you proved to be someone who deserves respect." He stopped, smiled at Fidelio. "Hey, what has happened to you shows that you are just another man; like all of us, you have a positive, bright side along with a dark, malignant, perverse side within you; it's better to know it and accept it. Knowing what you are capable of doing will help you just as it has helped me."

Fidelio looked at Dr. Villarreal and returned the friendly smile. "Thank you, believe or not, this is the second time that someone tells me that I'm just like anyone else and that's something really good to know. You are right, knowing ourselves is an important step to improve ourselves; once again, thank you."

"Thanks be given to you. It has been good for me to talk about all of this with someone who understands these concerns. To your health!" He said sipping the rest of the sotol.

"To your health," repeated Fidelio lifting his glass and drinking it all in one gulp, which forced him to shrug his shoulders. "Wow, although smooth when you zip it, it's strong and harsh when swallowed."

"Another lesson learned today. It has been a great evening, hopefully we'll have other chances to talk more about this. What do you think?" Dr. Villarreal said.

"Yes, I also hope that we'll have many more chances to talk. This has been a mind-opening conversation for me; today I understand life a bit better. As for me, I believe that, somehow, is God who put you in my way and I thank Him for that."

"There you have it, another subject for discussion," Dr. Villarreal said, laughing.

"Well, I'm glad to see that you are happy now. From the distance, I watched you talk and for a moment, I was concerned, both of you looked so serious, almost upset," Aurora said, approaching and cleaning the table. "Would you like another glass?" she added, smiling.

"No, thank you, Aurora. Tomorrow we'll have another busy day," Dr. Villarreal answered. "Here, charge it," he added giving Aurora a couple of bills.

"Thank you," Aurora said; she looked at Fidelio. "Tomorrow I'm going to El Paso, I wonder if you could come with me."

"Yes, he has a free day tomorrow," Dr. Villarreal answered for Fidelio, who looked at him a bit surprised.

"Wonderful, please come and pick me up tomorrow at 10 a.m. in the morning." She hugged Fidelio and smiled thankfully to Dr. Villarreal.

The following day, exactly at 10 a.m. in the morning, Fidelio knocked at Aurora's door.

"You are right on time, come in. I still have a couple of things to do to get ready. Please have a seat, my father will offer you a cup of fresh coffee. I will be with you soon." Aurora greeted him, pointing to a chair.

"Would you like honey and cinnamon with your coffee?" Don Prudencio, Aurora's father, asked, showing his face from another room.

"Yes, please, but I don't want to be a bother. I can just wait here," replied Fidelio, sitting.

"There is no problem, the coffee is ready, just have to add a little of cinnamon and honey," Don Prudencio said from the other room. "It's fresh," Don Prudencio said, walking in with two clay cups, handing one to Fidelio. "Be careful because it's hot."

"No, it's just right, thank you," said Fidelio, after sipping the coffee.

"First of all, I want to thank you for defending my daughter, what you did was brave and courageous." Don Prudencio said, as he sat on a chair. "Aurora is fond of you," he added. He sighed before continuing, he frowned, looked attentively to Fidelio. "As her father, I would like to know. How do you feel about her? What are your intentions?"

"I can assure you that my intentions are honest. All that I want from Aurora is friendship, I don't offer nor expect, anything else," answered Fidelio.

"By the way she talks about you and how happy she is to see you, I'm afraid that she expects or hopes far more than that," Don Prudencio said, with a sad tone of voice. "But, drink your coffee. Please, don't feel upset or nervous about my conversation. Although young, Aurora is a strong and sensible woman. Besides, I can see that you are an honest young man and I like that." He added smiling, in a friendly manner, to Fidelio. He sipped his coffee.

"Thank you. I appreciate your understanding," Fidelio said, and after sipping the coffee, he smiled. "This is excellent coffee, I never had it this good. The amount of cinnamon you added enhances its flavor. Thank you." He took a larger gulp, closed his eyes enjoying the flavor of the coffee, while Don Prudencio smiled, satisfied.

"I'm ready, I see that you have become friends," said Aurora as she entered. "I'm ready when you are," she added looking at Fidelio.

"I'm also ready," said Fidelio standing up. "Nice talking to you Don Prudencio and thanks for the excellent coffee," he added looking at Don Prudencio.

"You are welcome, hopefully we'll meet again," Don Prudencio replied. "Don't take long, I'm sure we are going to have another busy day." He added, talking to Aurora.

"I won't be late, I promise," said Aurora, as she kissed her father on the cheek. Fidelio opened the door for her and both left to El Paso.

Fidelio found El Paso City different to any town he had seen in Mexico. He found it cleaner, better planned, many more stores and many more goods offered in them. Although most of the people were friendly or simply indifferent, he didn't like that there were some, although not directly unfriendly, to whom it was obvious that they didn't like to see a brown skin man walking along a blond woman.

"Some people don't like seeing the two of us walking together," he said to Aurora.

"They are a bit more tolerant here, but just a bit up-north, there are people who wouldn't tolerate seeing a couple like us in the street. There, we could be attacked by the mob. They would kill you and rape me for it. Here, the majority don't mind us. Those who don't like it are a minority. There is a secret society called "Ku Klux Klan," they commit atrocities against black people and, although not here, also against anyone whose skin is a bit dark. What is truly upsetting is that they call themselves Christians, they pretend they are acting in his name and use a burning cross as their symbol."

"It sounds as bad or worse that the way the Raramuri and others like them are treated in Mexico," Fidelio said.

Aurora smiled. "I didn't ask you to come to talk about these things. We have enough trouble with the revolution. I need to buy dishes for the restaurant, not to talk about politics." She said holding Fidelio in the arm. "I like to be with you, the store we are looking for is close by.

There it is, come and help me to choose the china for the restaurant," she added.

"Olson, Marcus and Co, Hardware and Lumber," read the advertisement in front of the store. Aurora walked in, but when Fidelio tried to follow her he was suddenly stopped by a tall blond man. "You have to enter through that door," he said pointing to a small back door with a signal on top of it: "Colored and Mexicans," it read.

"He is coming with me," Aurora said to the man; upset, the tone of her voice was harsh. Fidelio, as tall as the blond, looked at him straight into his eyes, the blond man couldn't hold Fidelio eyes and looked another way. "He has to enter through that door," the man said in an almost apologetic tone. "He can join you once inside, but we'll keep watching both of you," he added. Fidelio started to feel angry, he desired to punch the man straight in the nose, however, he resisted the feeling. He smiled to Aurora. "I'll meet you inside," he said walking toward the door.

They had no further trouble. Aurora selected the china, paid and they left the store. Fidelio was still feeling upset. He was upset with the man and upset with himself. He realized that he was reacting emotionally, he also was aware that if he allowed himself to continue this way, eventually, his emotions will end up controlling him. He had an intense inner conflict. There was an inner voice encouraging his anger. "You should not tolerate anyone to be rude to you. You have not only physical strength, but you know that you could humiliate that man, teach him a lesson he'll never forget. As a matter of fact, you should walk back and show him who you are." At the same time, another voice said: "You are the master of your emotions, they must not control you. What has been given to you is to serve, not to cause harm." Fidelio took a deep, slow breath and it caused a refreshing, calmer, pleasant, sensation. Enjoying it, he noticed the peaceful bright blue sky; the cool morning felt like a caress to his skin. Hundreds of yellow butterflies on their way south arrived in town. Fidelio smiled, felt happy and passed his arm around Aurora's shoulders. They walked through Mesa Avenue; it was a busy morning. It seemed that everyone in town had some sort of business to take care of that morning. He felt a connection with them, somehow, they were a part of him and he was a part of them. "It seems that everyone had similar plans as us," Aurora said to Fidelio, smiling. He was now feeling completely calm and happy. Aurora got closer to him and passed an arm around Fidelio's waist. "It has been a wonderful morning," she said. "I feel sad that it's time to go back."

Fidelio looked at her. "Indeed, it has been wonderful," he said.

Enjoying each other's company, Fidelio and Aurora walked back to the restaurant where Don Prudencio greeted them.

"Did you find the china we need?" he asked Aurora.

"Yes father, I was told that it will be ready for delivery tomorrow along with the rest of the merchandise, they said that you know what it is."

Don Prudencio grinned. "Good," he said, "knowing that, will make Hipolito happy."

"Who is Hipolito?" Fidelio asked.

"Villa's younger brother," Aurora answered, she looked at her father. "Father. Are you still involved in that?"

"We can't just watch others fighting, we must do our part," Don Prudencio replied, shrugging his shoulders.

Intrigued, Fidelio listened. Don Prudencio looked at him. "Let me explain it to you, son. Judge if I'm doing right or not. Hipolito is in charge of buying guns and ammunition for the cause; however, someone must take care of crossing it through the border. So, we designed a way to accomplish it, that's all."

Fidelio nodded. "We are at war, I suppose someone must do it," Fidelio replied.

"There you have it," Don Prudencio told Aurora.

"Father as you know, there is a huge risk with doing what you do. Now the city is under the control of the Villistas; however, there is no way to know which side is going to control it next. If you get caught, we could be punished," Aurora said, concerned.

Don Prudencio smiled happily, "there is no reason for concern and much less to argue about it. The revolution will triumph, nothing is going to stop it now." He looked at Fidelio. "What about some sotol to warm up, young man?"

"Thank you, Don Prudencio, but I must report at the headquarters. Also, thank you for the wonderful cup of coffee this morning and allowing me to accompany Aurora," Fidelio replied, smiling. He turned to Aurora. "I enjoyed the morning, I hope we'll come for dinner.

Dr. Villarreal probably has news about how long we are going to stay here, I hope it will be for long."

Aurora moved close to Fidelio, squeezed gently his right arm. "Thanks for the morning, I'm looking forwards to seeing you soon," a soothing, loving, but, at the same time, sad tone in her voice.

"Thanks to you, it was a wonderful morning," Fidelio said, then turned and walked towards the hospital. When he arrived, he found Dr. Villarreal outside the hospital. He seemed upset. "Gangrene has defeated us, in spite of our efforts, we lost two men to it," he said as soon as Fidelio approached.

"Still there is so much to learn, but we must continue" Fidelio said, feeling also upset with the news.

"I believe I have other news that you probably won't like either," Dr. Villarreal said.

"What is it?" Fidelio asked.

"The troops sent to Ojinaga, the only town the federals still hold in the state, were defeated. Villa is moving there. We have been ordered to leave and get ready for the battle over there. We leave at dawn."

CHAPTER XII

Fidelio joined the group carrying the necessary material to the train wagon converted into a full ambulatory infirmary. Shortly after midnight the train moved towards Chihuahua City. Fidelio finished cleansing and organizing the wagon where the wounded were to be received and, tired, sat on one of the long and narrow tables and looked at the dessert. He felt sad. Although his love and his body belonged to Candelaria and he knew that no one could fill his soul and heart as she did, no one could ever take her place, he had also become fond of Aurora's company. He sighed as he watched the bright full moon. The moonlight and the movement of the train created shadows, strange figures that seemed to carry a sorrow message. Fighting a strong desire to cry, Fidelio wished he had had time to say farewell to Aurora and her father. Although it was a very cold night, Fidelio, covered by a sarape felt very hot, his body trembled and sweated. Finally, he gave up and wept. The rhythmic movement of the train, accompanied by the sound of the train wheels moving on the rail and the murmur of the wind produced a calming symphony that caused him to fall into deep sleep.

Candelaria, smiling, walked towards him. "Fidelio, my love, the memory of the short time we spent together fills my days and nights with brightness and freshness, wherever I look your image is there." She got closer, so close that Fidelio could feel the freshness of her breath, her lips were so close that he moved to kiss her, but she prevented it by putting her hand on his lips, then, tenderly, she put her hand on his shoulder. "Not now, my love, I want to see myself in your eyes. Let me feel the warmth of your body, let me smell you, let me touch your face." She caressed his cheeks, his lips, "your skin is so smooth. I love every inch of your body, love your smell, love your touch, I belong to you, you are the first and the last man in my life. I'll rather die than allow anyone else to touch me." Somehow, Aurora approached then, smiling to Candelaria, who hugged and kissed Aurora on the cheek; it seemed that they had known each other for a long period of time. Fidelio was surprised, he had no idea that they were friends. Happy, and hugging Candelaria, Aurora looked at him, "Fidelio, my dear friend, it's easy to understand your love for Candelaria. You must know that both of you can count on my friendship and my love. She and I have talked and agreed that whatever happens, we will always be with you, although only through our souls for the time being. We hope that the day will come when all of us will be together." Seeing both of them close and friendly, Fidelio, although surprised, felt happy. He moved forwards to get closer to them, but, smiling, they waved farewell and disappeared. The sudden stop of the train aroused Fidelio from his sleep. The dream of Candelaria and Aurora, both of them happy and friendly made him feel energized, although it was a dark night, to him, everything was now bright and shiny. The wind outside, the murmur of the train on the tracks, provided pleasant music and the shadows danced in celebration.

"Are you awake Fidelio?" Dr. Villarreal asked, walking in and sitting in front of him. "Right now, we are in Chihuahua. We have stopped to change tracks because our destiny is OJinaga; however, the track in that direction is unfinished. So, once we arrive at the station of San Sostenes, which is close by, we'll have to transfer the equipment to a mule train, and, from there, we'll continue on horse. Come, we have to prepare what we are going to need and have it ready once we arrive to San Sostenes."

"I'm fully awake and ready, let's start," Fidelio replied, jumping and walking out.

Dr. Villarreal looked at him with an expression of surprise. "Although we are in the middle of the night, you not only look rested, as a matter of fact, you also look radiant and happy. I'll bet you had a pleasant dream."

"Indeed, it was pleasant," Fidelio said, smiling. "What do we do first?"

"Let's start with the bandages and the material we'll need in the field."

When they arrived, the rest of the personal were already working, Fidelio and Dr. Villarreal joined them. The movement of the train, changing tracks, made their operation somewhat difficult; however, Dr. Villarreal had all well-trained men, so everyone knew what to do. Fidelio felt proud in being part of the team. Once the train changed tracks and on its way, the task became easier and they worked smoothly. By the time they arrived to the San Sostenes station, everything was ready.

"Hurry up boys, most of the mule wagons will be used by the troop. We'll use two of them," Dr. Villarreal said to the health team. "Fidelio, you take care of being sure that all the material is placed in the wagons."

"We have already taken down most of it. It won't take us long to finish," Fidelio said, his body energized and happy, so happy that he started singing while working; the rest looked at him surprised, but Fidelio's happiness was so contagious that they joined him. Yells of happiness were heard all over the station, they were so loud and sounded so happy that most of the troops started singing along. The entire station became a gigantic chorus that was joined by rumbling and thunderbolts from the sky.

After they had finished, Dr. Villarreal mounted in a palomino and with another horse on his side, approached. "Fidelio, I got you a good horse, it's strong and well tamed. The order is to travel fast. We must arrive to the Hacienda de San Juan before dawn, that's where all of the arriving troops are to concentrate."

"Thank you, but you didn't have to bother, I could have traveled in one of the mule wagons," Fidelio said, as he mounted the horse.

"You must learn to mount well, be careful, because we'll travel fast and the terrain is difficult. We can't afford to stop. We must be there before sunrise. Fortunately, the full moon will make our ride easier.

Dr. Villarreal said pointing to the bright circle in the sky that seemed to smile at them.

Fidelio noticed that this horse was a bit more nervous than the one he had mounted before; however, he felt so confident and energized that he controlled the horse with ease.

Looking at him, Dr. Villarreal smiled. "Soon you'll be an experienced horse rider." He then turned towards the wagon masters. "We'll go as fast as we can, but at the same time, be careful, we don't want anything lost, let's move," he told them and, slapping Fidelio's horse in the rear, signaled to move.

Feeling the slap, Fidelio's horse almost jumped, Fidelio held well and controlled the movement of the horse. Everyone cheered and clapped. "Fidelio, you have become a good horseman," one of the men in the wagons yelled.

It was a cold night, the wind chilly, and the terrain difficult, even so, Fidelio felt warm and enjoyed the travel. The horse had learned to obey him so well that even the crossing of water streams, sand or rocky terrain, all seemed easy to Fidelio. They arrived at the Hacienda de San Juan on time. Over one thousand troops were already there. The brightness of the sun rising, the clapping of the women preparing the tortillas for breakfast and the music of guitars provided a sensation of festivity.

Villa arrived later that morning. Fidelio shared the enthusiasm created by the presence of Villa. A wave of optimism spread all over the troop, Fidelio among them. Someone started singing: "Here is Francisco Villa with all the chiefs and officers, they have come to saddle the federal mules." A gigantic chorus repeated the tune. Aware of it, Villa became sure that everyone saw him, he walked among the soldiers, shared their food, talked to almost all of them. "Feel certain that the coyote won't take this chicken from us," he told them. Wild yells of enthusiasm were heard all over the camp.

The following morning, at 6 a.m., the order to march forward was received. They had to surround the town except the exit to the Rio Grande, bordering the United States. To identify those who were friends, they would go without hat, the password was "number one." That night, at 10 p.m., all positions around the town were taken. Villa talked to the troop: "Tomorrow evening, we'll attack. You'll have two hours to take Ojinaga, be brave and move forwards, no retreat. Are you happy with this command?" Enthusiastic wild yells were the answer. A cold breeze blew from the north. Fidelio on top of one the wagons listened and observed, he and his team were ready to help those in need, regardless of their affiliation.

The following day, just before sunset, at 6 p.m., the battle started. Both artilleries blasted each other. Villistas who had infiltrated among the enemy, tolled the bells in the church, at that moment several columns initiated a violent attack. The defense was weak because few federals resisted, most of them, scared, threw their weapons and ran to the river in absolute disorder. In an effort to force them to stop and fight, their officers shot many, however, seeing that it was useless, they also ran. The Villistas continued moving forward, fearless and relentless. Soon, there were so many dead men, horses, donkeys, mules in the river, that the color of the water turned an ugly purple/gray color. Around the bodies, men and horses swimming, tried to escape but with so many dead bodies floating in the river the crossing became difficult, many drowned. Watching such a sorrow spectacle, Fidelio felt a profound sadness, he prayed: "Our father who acts in heaven…" The battle lasted less than two hours.

At the end of the battle, Fidelio and his people went through the battlefield. They found few Villistas wounded, most of those who needed help were federales. Fidelio ordered to help all, regardless of their affiliation. One of the federales looked at him, tears in his eyes. "Thank you," he said trying to kiss Fidelio's hand, who didn't allow it. "You are our brother in need, hopefully someday you'll do the same for someone else," said Fidelio. Looking around he was surprised by the figure of an old blond man, an American, also helping those in need. Fidelio was intrigued. "Is he one of those Americans who are only interested in taking pictures?" he asked himself. "But, he doesn't seem interested in taking pictures, he is helping people and talking to them. Who is this man?" Fidelio thought.

Later that day, Fidelio heard that Villa had given strict orders to respect the prisoners, most of them had been forced to join the federales. Those who wished to volunteer to join the revolution would be accepted, the rest were to be set free. On hearing this, Fidelio felt proud to be part of the Northern Division and started whistling a corrido that had become popular among the troop, "la cucaracha." As he walked through the streets of Ojinaga, he saw the same old man he had seen helping those who were wounded, talking to some of the children/soldiers. The children, dressed in plain cotton shirts and pants, showed their rifles to the American who seemed to make fun of them. The man pointed to a bucket that was about fifty yards from them. One of the children took his rifle, aimed at the bucket, fired, the shot was not even close. The American laughed loudly, patted the child's back, took the rifle, cocked it, aimed, and the bucket flew before it ended dancing. Amazed, the children clapped and congratulated the old man. Fidelio, who by then, was close enough to hear the conversation. "When you aim at something, that becomes the only thing that is important to you, don't think about anything else, you and the target must become one, aim at it and gently, squeeze the trigger," the American explained to the children. When he noticed Fidelio, looked at him from the feet up, whistled and smiled. "Young man you are one of the tallest Mexicans I've ever seen and you are also strong, I'll bet you know how to fire this thing," he said, extending his arm with the rifle for Fidelio to take it. Fidelio flushed, embarrassed, the memory of himself firing a rifle and killing someone came back to him; he sweated. "I prefer not to use it," he almost whispered. The old man looked at him, frowned, kept silence for a moment, "I understand," he finally said. He gave the rifle back to one of the children, smiling, searched his pants pocket, pulled some coins and gave them to the children. "My friends, hopefully we'll have another chance to talk," he told them.

After the children left, the man turned to Fidelio. "I saw you the other night taking care of the wounded. I believe I know why you prefer not to use a rifle," he paused, took a deep breath, like thinking what to say next. "That's because you have already shot someone and you didn't like the feeling. Am I right?"

"That's right," replied Fidelio, feeling embarrassed and intrigued.

"As I said before," the man said, "I understand, it also happened to me. The cantinas here remain open. I'll invite you to a drink, let's find a place where we can sit and talk."

They walked to the city's square, where they found a cantina, entered it and sat at a table.

"What do you drink? Because I assume you drink," said the man.

"I have tried sotol," replied Fidelio.

"Sotol?" the man smiled. "That's strong, although I would prefer whiskey, let's have sotol. Hey man bring a bottle of your best sotol," he called the bartender, who brought the bottle and two glasses, left them on the table and walked away.

"First, let's introduce ourselves. I'm Ambrose Bierce," the man said, extending his right hand.

"Fidelio Serna," he said, smiling as he shook hands with the man.

"First, let me explain why I said that I understand that you prefer not to use a rifle," Bierce said as he served the sotol in the glasses, lifted his glass and swallowed the whole fluid at once, made a gesture and smiled. "This is strong stuff. Well, let me continue, I understand it because it also happened to me a long time ago, during the civil war. I hated the feeling of shooting someone I didn't know. True, the one I shot was trying to kill me, but still it was an eerie feeling. Later, either I got used to it, or just ignored it. As a matter of fact, I know I have killed more men than I can count." He frowned, put his head down, and wiped a tear from his eyes. "I don't know you, but somehow I feel that I have to tell you something I have never talked about before. I regret having killed just because, 'I obeyed orders.' Besides, let me tell you that I witnessed the Indian massacre in California and kept my mouth shut. I'm a writer, a newspaper man, and kept my mouth and pen shut." He filled his glass again and gulped it. "Well, enough of me. You are young, don't want to shoot a rifle. Why are you here in this mess?"

"Because I want justice for all," Fidelio said, "the peons work the land from sunrise to sunset, they are paid with supplies from the hacienda's store, charged for it, so they end up in a lifetime of debt that is inherited by their children. The rich become richer and the poor remain poor and exploited. That must be changed."

The blue eyes of the old man fixed on Fidelio's face seemed to laugh. Finally, the old man laughed, a sarcastic, cynical laugh. "Do you really believe that things will change?" the man asked.

"Yes, that's the reason most of us are fighting for," Fidelio replied, upset.

"I believe you. As a matter of fact, that's what most of these poor people believe. But you seem like an intelligent man, there is something in you that makes you stand up and is not that you are tall for a Mexican, no, there is something that I can't explain. That's why I wanted to talk to you." The man looked at Fidelio attentively. "As a matter of fact, yes, I'm certain that you believe what you just said," he smiled again. "Yes, you remind me of my youth. There was a time in which I also believed in mankind." Outside someone played a guitar and sang a sad love song. The man poured another glass and again gulped all, took a satisfied deep breath, smiled to Fidelio, pointed to the empty glass. "Somehow this makes life seem better than it is," he put his elbows on the table, crossed his hands and looked a Fidelio, smiling. "So, you believe that after all this killing and turmoil, a change will come. The poor peasants will no longer be exploited and they'll receive a fair treatment and paid fairly for their hard work," he rubbed his nose, still smiling. Fidelio listened attentively, he knew that the man, although cynical, was honest and had a deep inner sorrow; Fidelio sipped from his glass of sotol. "Let me tell you what is going to happen at the end of all of it." The man continued, "some of those, who until now have been poor peasants will become the new landlords, some of those who until now have been wealthy will lose everything they had. Those who work hard, will continue doing so and remain poor. The only thing that will change is that there will be new masters," he laughed. Outside someone continued playing the guitar and singing sad love songs.

"If that's what you believe then why are you here? Why are you helping the wounded?" Fidelio asked.

The man straightened his back, still smiling. "That's a fair question," he answered. "I'm here because I love action; all of this turmoil is vibrant, it reminds me that I'm still alive. Yes. I could stay home, read, write and spend the few years I have left rocking. That would be not only boring, but also an absolute waste. I know that what I have told you about what is going to happen as a consequence of all of this fighting and killing sounds cynical. But, believe me that is exactly what is going to happen. It will end up in just a struggle for power. But, having said that, this is exciting, makes my blood flow, makes me feel that I'm still alive and somehow this is history. And being part of the history, even a tiny part, is better, much better than sitting in a chair writing about something I don't even care, or just waiting for the final moment. No, I would rather die here, in the middle of this turmoil. That would be a wonderful end, yes it would be wonderful." He looked at Fidelio, a friendly shine in his eyes. "Why did I help those wounded? Because I understand what it feels to be there, wounded, in pain and no one there to help. Ignored by those who sent them to the battle. I've seen that before, been in battles, where those who were wounded were just left there to die in the sun or worse, eaten alive by rats. No, what I did is just a small way to pay for what I could have done and didn't do." On the street, someone continued singing love songs. Bierce smiled again, pulled a cigar from his jacket, bit the tip of it, spit it and putting the cigar back in his mouth, lighted it, looking straight at Fidelio eyes, expelled the smoke, frowned, looked a bit concerned. "I don't know why I'm telling all of this to you, someone who is just out of childhood; however, something in your demeanor is different. I don't know what is it but although I'm much older than you are, you make me feel as if I were the child and you the one with experience, that's weird, really weird." He kept his eyes fixed on Fidelio. "Yes, I don't know how, but I feel that someday, somehow, you'll make a difference to a lot of people. Listening to my story has already made a difference for me. It's strange, but I feel relieved of a heavy weight on my shoulders, that now I could die with my soul, if there is such a thing, in peace." He smiled again, filled again his glass, he was about to drink it when gun shots and wild yells were heard in the street, the singing stopped, the bar doors were kicked and a slender man, sun tanned, green eyes, accompanied by two women, walked in. Although good looking, the man reminded Fidelio of a wild coyote, there was something attractive and the same time something evil in the man. They walked to one of the tables, the man almost pushed the women to the chairs and he sat in another chair smirking.

"That's Rodolfo Fierro, the railroad man of Villa, one of those close to him. It is well known that he enjoys killing. He means trouble, we better leave," Bierce said to Fidelio putting money on the table. As they got up and walked towards the door, the man looked at them, he was about to say something, when Fidelio turned and looked straight in his eyes. The man closed his mouth, looked around, somehow, he seemed confused. At the door, Fidelio heard that the man slapped the table and yelled, "bartender drinks!"

"That is a dangerous and cruel man. Him, or someone like him will be the real winner of this fight," Bierce told Fidelio.

"How is that you know him?" Fidelio asked.

"I told you, I'm a reporter, I know how to get information," Bierce answered. "Well, my young friend, our paths have crossed for a very short time, for me it was worthy. Talking to you has made clear how I want the rest of my life to be. Farewell my friend, continue doing what you are doing, even if you don't know what it is yet," he smiled, slapped Fidelio on the shoulder and walked away.

Fidelio looked at him, intrigued. What did he mean? Loud laughs came from the cantina, the street now silent, in the sky vultures flew in circles, and the cold wind brought an odor of putrefaction. Fidelio felt a heavy weight on his shoulders, oppression in his chest and loneliness in his heart.

"Fidelio, I've been looking for you," Dr. Villarreal said as he approached.

Happy to see him, Fidelio turned. "Well, here I am," he said.

"We have orders to move back to Chihuahua, in there we'll get ready to move south. Villa is already planning to recover Torreon."

CHAPTER XIII

When they arrived at Chihuahua City, they found the town mourning. People aligned in the streets to say farewell to someone who apparently, in life had been important to the town, and also, to the revolution. Villa, head and shoulders down, hat in his hands, walked leading the funeral procession. Behind Villa, eight men carried a casket, a military band playing a funeral march followed, and after them, the dorados, Villa's personal guard, mounted; they also had their hats in their hands and heads down. A misty and cold day, dark clouds covered the sun, it seemed that nature also mourned, even the chirping of the birds had a sad sound.

Fidelio and Dr. Villarreal joined the crowd. Everyone kept a respectful silence, peasants holding their hats with both hands in front of their chest, people crossed their hearts as the casket passed by. Intrigued, Fidelio asked: "Who was this man? Why is the entire town mourning him? Why is Villa leading the procession?"

"Abraham Gonzalez, who like Madero, was a wealthy and educated man. Also, like Madero, he didn't like the abuse the peons suffered in the hands of the landlords. In particular, he fought against land legally stolen; one of the first to join Madero in his struggle. A friend of Villa, even when Villa was considered an outlaw. Gonzalez was the one who introduced Villa to Madero, and, Gonzalez defended and supported Villa when he was unfairly arrested. After Madero's election as President,

Gonzalez became a minister and after the assassination of Madero he came back. He didn't recognize Huerta and started organizing the resistance against the oppressor, but at that time Orozco was the strong man in Chihuahua and he had joined Huerta. By order of Huerta, with Orozco's agreement, Gonzalez was jailed and assassinated. His rests have been recently found. Villa is giving him the honor he deserves," Dr. Villarreal answered, tears in his eyes, a sad tone in his voice.

"Did you know him?"

"Yes, we grew up together, and together we learned to shot our guns, learned to ride a horse. In our youth, we teamed to serenate our girls. We separated when both of us went to an American University; he became an engineer and I became a surgeon. Before the revolution, we met on several occasions. I have wonderful memories of our time together. When he came back, he improved the situation of those who worked for him and paid fair salaries. The majority of us loved and respected him. As a governor, he had people's welfare always in mind and that made him an enemy of Terrazas, Creel, Limantour and the rest of the landlords. People like him and Madero are those who have given sense to this struggle. In their memory, we must win."

"Indeed, a man of honor," Fidelio said. "Yes, there is honor in this struggle. The old gringo is wrong, thanks to people like Gonzalez and Dr. Villarreal, a real change will be accomplished," he thought.

"I'll have to meet with General Villa later," Dr. Villarreal said to Fidelio after the funeral procession had passed by. "You have the rest of the day free, we'll meet at the railroad station tonight. The preparation to recover Torreon has already started and we'll have to work hard to get ready. Recovering Torreon won't be easy, unfortunately there will be many in need of our services." He paused, frowned, like something was puzzling him. "Before leaving Ojinaga I was told to get ready for a surprise once we are here. I wonder, what it could be?" he added.

"I hope it will be something good," Fidelio said. "I'll walk a little through the city, I've been wanting to see it since we left Torreon."

"I'm sure you'll like it," Dr. Villarreal said, before walking away.

Walking in the streets of Chihuahua, Fidelio noticed that in spite of all the recent battles and turmoil the streets were clean and the people seemed calm, but what impressed him the most were the large mansions, even more opulent that those he had seen in Morelia. Obviously, very wealthy people lived in this town. However, the contrast with the neighboring houses was not as severe as he had previously seen in Guanajuato and Morelia. He walked until he reached the central square, sat on a metallic bench and admired the buildings around it, in particular the building of the cathedral. The air clean, the clouds gone and the sky was now bright blue; birds on the trees chirped happily. Fidelio felt at peace, extended his legs, hands behind his head, he closed his eyes and rested. The image of Candelaria appeared in his mind, it seemed that he had never left her, somehow her presence and image were always present. He relaxed, took a deep breath, enjoying the freshness of the air, he allowed his body and mind to sink in the moment.

"Fidelio, hey Fidelio, wake up, wake up." Fidelio opened his eyes and saw Enrique, Pantaleon and Dionaciano. The last was the one trying to call his attention by rubbing firmly on his shoulder. The three of them smiled at him.

Fidelio looked at them, still submerged in his deep sate of relaxation and they seemed to be part of his dream. Dionaciano slapped him gently on the chin. "Are you drunk? Come on wake up. Were you smoking grass?" Fidelio opened his eyes fully, a bit upset, they were not part of his dream. "No, I am not drunk, neither I smoked anything. I only closed my eyes to enjoy the peace that is felt in here," he said rubbing his face. He looked at them and smiled. "I'm glad to see you." He then noticed then that the three of them had captain badges on their clean shirts.

"I can see that you not only survived the battles we have been through, but you have risen to become captains. Congratulations, I'm proud of you."

"Thanks. Yes, we can say that we are now seasoned soldiers, the sound of bullets help us to ignore our fears," Pantaleon said, who smiled and then paused, frowning. "However, many of our friends have fallen. We heard how you reacted when you found Prudencio's body. You have shot a rifle, killed someone, you have also become a seasoned soldier."

"No, I have not!" Fidelio said, embarrassed. "I'll never be a soldier and I hope that I never will have to shoot a gun again."

"I'm glad to hear that," Enrique said, you are much better at healing than killing, never change my friend."

"That's true, I'll never forget that man in Guanajuato, the one you hit in his chest with a stone. He claimed that thanks to that his lungs improved." Dionaciano said. "You have a God's given gift and that's the only thing that should matter to you."

On hearing this, Fidelio felt pressure on his chest. He had never asked for it. Why him? Why couldn't he be just like anyone else? He just smiled pretending to be calm. "How is that the three of you have been promoted to captain in such a short period of time?" he finally asked, changing the subject.

"We followed orders, showed no fear in battle, others followed us, that's how," Pantaleon answered. He frowned. "We believe that we are fighting a just cause. That also helps."

"But you are frowning. Something is bothering you. What is it?" Fidelio asked.

"I don't like how priests and nuns are treated by some of our troops. There are officers that not only allow it, but they encourage and participate in it. That's something I don't like. Priests, nuns, churches, deserve respect," Pantaleon answered. "I have heard that there are places where the celebration of Holly Mass has been forbidden and those who disobey are shot. We are Catholics, hopefully it won't be necessary to fight for our right to celebrate Mass."

"Somehow the struggle in which we are involved will create a change, and through it, all of our rights will be protected. In particular, I like the way General Villa favors the opening of schools. Nuns can teach and they also help taking care of those in need and the wounded. I'm sure Villa and the others eventually will recognize it," Enrique said.

"I hope you are right," Dionaciano intervened. "Fidelio, do you remember the man in Camargo? The one that was harassing the Tarahumaras."

"Yes, I remember him well. What about him?" Fidelio replied.

"I told you that he is the son of Luis Terrazas, the wealthiest man in Chihuahua and, before the revolution, the most powerful and influential man in the state." Dionaciano smiled. "Well he has been arrested. It seems that Villa was told that before leaving, his father withdrew a large amount of gold coins from the Banco Minero, and that he hid them within the bank. Villa and others believe that his son, same name as his father, knows the exact location where the money is hidden."

"That's interesting," Enrique said. "I have heard about the wealth, power and influence of the Terrazas family, it's almost unbelievable. If what you say is true and there is money hidden, it must be a large sum."

"How is it possible that someone withdraws from a bank and hides the money within the same bank?" Fidelio asked.

"That's easy if you are the owner of the bank and the building," Pantaleon answered.

"That's true. The Terrazas own most of the land, cattle and minerals in the state. What Enrique said is real. Their wealth is almost unbelievable," Dionaciano added.

"I was among the soldiers sent by general Chao to review the bank and we found its vault almost empty. The manager said that the gold coins deposited in there were removed by Don Luis, shortly before the federals left the city. However, he can't say if the money was taken out of the building because Terrazas did it at night, when the bank was closed and only allowed some of his family to be with him," Pantaleon said.

"All that is interesting," Enrique intervened, "but all of this is mere speculation until the money is found. If found, it will be good for the cause."

"That is if someone like Urbina doesn't pocket it," Dionaciano said.

"We are fighting against the abuse of the wealthy, I wouldn't expect anyone in this cause doing something like that," Enrique said.

"Let's not be too naïve," Dionaciano said, smiling.

"It's getting dark, let's find a place to eat," Pantaleon said.

"I know where we can find the best menudo in town, its close by," Dionaciano said. He looked at Fidelio and tapped him in a friendly way on the shoulder. "We invite," he added, smiling.

Suddenly, the sound of mariachi music approached the square. A mariachi followed a large group of men and women most of whom had bottles in hand. They were a noisy group, laughing, singing, howling and yelling, a wild bunch. Fidelio recognized the man leading the group. Rodolfo Fierro. Fierro turned and looked towards Fidelio's group. Fierro was a tall, slender man whose green eyes looked brighter because of his dark skin. He was smiling, showing his perfectly aligned white teeth. A bottle of tequila in one hand, two girls hugged him. Another man walked towards Fierro, a blond man and when Fidelio looked at him, he felt pressure in his belly; he felt anxious. The same man to whom he had felt attracted to, while in the Juarez jail. Suddenly he felt the attraction again, a strong impulse to join them, like something was pulling him in their direction. The bells of the church tolled; in the sky, vultures circled. The blond man looked at Fidelio, smiled at him as he tapped Fierro's shoulder.

"I know him," he said to Fierro pointing towards Fidelio. "We were in jail together in Juarez, he is the one I told you that can heal people. Let's invite him, he'll be fun."

Fierro smiled. "Hey, you!" he yelled to Fidelio. "Come and join us," looking at Fidelio's friends, Fierro opened his arms. "And bring your friends with you, there are girls and drinks enough for everybody."

"We better go," Enrique whispered to Fidelio, putting his arm on Fidelio's shoulder and giving him a gentle push.

As they joined the group, the blond man pushed two girls towards Fidelio. "Show him how beautiful life is," he told them. The girls got on each side of Fidelio, hugged him and started kissing and caressing him. Hot, wet kisses. One of them caressed him under his shirt, her hand went down and she started caressing in between his legs. Although at first Fidelio was surprised, he enjoyed the kissing and the caresses, he hugged the girls back and returned the kisses. "Kiss like this," one of the girls told him kissing him with an open mouth, opening his mouth and pushing her tongue around Fidelio's tongue. "Wow, you got a big one," the other girl said, as she continued touching Fidelio in between his legs, she kissed him in the neck. Fidelio felt his wholebody tensing; he salivated. The women tasted to strong liquor, that and their salty saliva aroused him even more. He desired to take them. One of the girls offered a bottle of tequila to him, he took a big gulp, feeling excited he yelled; a wild, prolonged yell. The others joined him. Wolves in the wild. The circle of vultures got closer. The mariachi continued playing.

Suddenly, Fierro stopped in front of a large stone building. "This is the place where we had a gold shower," he said, laughing and pulling a handful of gold coins from his pocket.

"Tell us about it," the blond man said, smirking.

"Luis Terrazas owns this bank. El Banco Minero. Before he left town, running away from us, he knew that he couldn't take all his money with him, but he wanted us to believe. So, his son, pretending to be our friend, stayed behind. When we came to the bank, we found its vault empty. No money in it. Suspecting that the money had been hidden somewhere, Villa ordered to arrest Terrazas son and ask him if he knew anything about where the money was hidden. At first, he denied any knowledge about it. "All that I have left is the reputation of wealth," he answered to our questions. But when Madinabeytia and Torrado mounted him on a mule, took him out of town, told him that he was useless to us unless he knew where the money was hidden. They pointed to a large tree. "That's the tree where we are going to hang you," they told him. Terrazas got scared. "If you puck the ceiling, you'll be showered with gold," he told them. Indeed, once we did it, golden coins showered on us. Villa has used most of it to pay for ammunition and weapons, but he allowed us to part some of it."

"How much did Villa take for himself?" one of his companions asked.

"Not even one coin," Fierro replied.

Meanwhile, the caressing between Fidelio and the girls continued. Fidelio kissing one girl and then the other, the caresses became extreme, they didn't care about the rest and not that they were in the middle of the street. Enrique got close to them, touched Fidelio in the shoulder. "Fidelio, control yourself, we are in the middle of the street," he said. Upset, Fidelio turned around. "What do you care!" he yelled. The blond man observed all of this and smiled, his blue eyes sparkled. The circle of vultures got closer. Other people walking on the street avoided the group.

The whistling of cowboys, the sound of hooves approached. A group of mounted men guiding a herd of cows to the slaughter house were passing by. As they got close, one of the cows suddenly left the herd, ran straight to Fidelio and pushed him away from the girls, throwing him to the grass, the cow then stood by his side preventing the others to approach. Gently, the cow pushed Fidelio further away, the animal looked straight at Fidelio's eyes. Looking at the animal's face, Fidelio was surprised; the look of the cow showed tenderness, almost like maternal care. He felt that there was love in that look and the way the animal had pushed him after hitting him hard of his ribs had been gentle. He felt ashamed of his conduct and having yelled at his friend. He extended his hand to caress the cow, but he couldn't do it. A shot was heard and the cow fell, mortally wounded, Fidelio heard the flap of the vultures getting closer.

"Hey, why did you shoot the cow?" one of the mounted men yelled.

"Because it attacked my friend, because I like it for barbecue later and because I want to," replied Fierro, facing the mounted man, keeping the gun in his hand.

"We have been ordered by General Aguirre to take these cows to be slaughtered and provide meat for the troops and the townspeople. We can't give you that cow, we'll take it with us."

"Are you going to allow this man to disrespect you in front of all these people," Fidelio heard the blond man whisper to Fierro's ear. Fidelio saw the circle of vultures getting closer.

"I'm General Fierro and now you have different orders. This animal stays here."

"I know who you are, but I still have to obey General Aguirre's orders," the man said dismounting and walking towards the dead animal. He couldn't continue, Fierro shot him. "I'm the one who gives orders here," he said aiming at the rest of the mounted men. The mounted men drew their guns and so did most of those in Fierro's group. For a moment, it seemed that they would start shooting at each other. "Let's get going. You win this time General, you can keep the cow," one of the mounted men said, before whistling and guiding the herd away, the others followed him.

"We better leave now," Pantaleon said to Dionaciano and Enrique. Enrique nodded, signaled to Fidelio, who stood up and walked away with them. Distracted by the cowboys, no one paid attention to them leaving, no one except the blond man, he just grinned in a cynical way and waved to Fidelio, his blue eyes sparkled. The vultures got closer. The bells of the church tolled.

"I want you to know that I'm ashamed of my conduct," Fidelio said to his friends as they walked. "In particular, I'm ashamed of yelling at you, Enrique."

"Like the rest of us, you can also fall into temptation," Dionaciano said, hugging Fidelio in a friendly way.

"You are not like the rest of us," Enrique said. "But it's true, like the rest of us you can fall into temptation. Never forget it. And don't worry about yelling at me, I understand," he added, smiling at Fidelio.

They got close to the railroad station. "This is where we split. We have to join our regiment and you have to go back to your quarters. Take care Fidelio. Hopefully, we'll meet again soon," Enrique said. Dionaciano and Pantaleon hugged Fidelio. "We'll meet again," each of them said as they walked towards their regiment along with Enrique.

Feeling, sad and pensive about the events of the day, walked in direction of the train wagons. When he looked at the wagons, he stopped, surprised. Not only one wagon was prepared to receive the wounded, but an entire train had been conditioned with this purpose.

Dr. Villarreal, who stood close to one of the wagons talking to other men noticed Fidelio's presence and smiling, obviously happy, waived at him.

"What do you think? An entire train converted into a mobile hospital. Besides, more physicians have been hired, some of them my classmates in Baltimore. This is the important part of the surprise I was told about. So, what do you think? My dear friend.

"It's beautiful," replied Fidelio. "Now we really can take care of those in need."

"And, something that is also important. General Villa has authorized us to serve not only our soldiers, but also the community while we are at peace. You'll be important in this,"

Dr. Villarreal said, smiling to Fidelio.

"I don't believe I'm ready for it," Fidelio said. "What do your colleagues think about it? Probably they won't like it."

"You were born ready. As I told you when we met, I learned from books; you learned from nature. My colleagues? I have talked to them about it, some of them don't like it, that's true; but, most are curious, they believe that it will be a good experience for all. You'll teach them as you have taught me. Thanks to you, now I understand better the use of healing herbs."

"You are the one in charge. I'll follow your orders," Fidelio said, shrugging his shoulders, but feeling a bit nervous about what Dr. Villarreal had said. "Had he really learned from nature?" he thought. Somehow, he had been guided. Someone had taught him. He noticed that Dr. Villarreal had a Coronel badge on his shirt. "You have been promoted," he added smiling and pointing to the badge on Dr. Villarreal's shirt. "Congratulations, you deserve it."

"Thank you," Dr. Villarreal said touching the badge with pride. "This is the least important part of the surprise. Now tell me about your day. How was it?"

Fidelio told him about his meeting with his childhood friends and the events with General Fierro.

"That's one of the aspects in Villa's personality that nobody understands. If he doesn't drink and does not tolerate anyone of his officers drinking while in service; and also, contrary to the belief of many, when it comes to money, he is careful not to take anything for himself, then why does he tolerate people like Urbina and Fierro? They are not only drunkards, but the first one is a notorious thief and the second an assassin who kills just for pleasure. Both of them abuse the power invested in them by Villa, but even so he tolerates them. Everyone else is severely punished if they do just half of what these two do," Dr. Villarreal said, after he had heard Fidelio's story.

"By now, I know Fierro, and, I have heard something about Urbina, but by what you are saying there is a lot more about them. Why would you say Villa not only tolerates them but also accepts and keeps them close to him?" Fidelio asked.

"Well, both are valiant, fearless in combat and they have shown that they are also good leaders, there are many who have a tendency to obey and follow people like them. Urbina let's his men ravage freely. Others, enjoy Fierro's killing instinct. Urbina has known Villa since the time that both were outlaws. Fierro knows about railroads. Both of them respect Villa and acknowledge his leadership. Urbina kills to get advantage or when he feels threatened, Fierro kills for mere pleasure. Let me tell you what happened after we captured Torreon for the first time. Hundreds of federal soldiers were captured and placed in an enclosed yard in a ranch called Aviles. Fierro showed there, ordered them to be cornered and at his signal they were to be released by tens. Fierro was armed with a gun in each hand and an assistant loading a third gun; "If you can jump the wall, you are free," he told them and started shooting. There were close to two hundred prisoners in that yard, two jumped the wall."

Fidelio looked at Dr. Villarreal feeling sad. He kept silent. "Things will change to remain the way they were," the words of the old gringo came to his mind.

Dr. Villarreal seemed to understand Fidelio's concern. "I understand all of this is difficult to accept, but let's remember that the majority of those involved in this revolution are honest, we are honest. We are fighting for a fair and just cause, thus we must do our part to accomplish the change we all dream about," Dr. Villarreal said, trying to sound optimistic.

Although feeling sad, Fidelio smiled. "Yes, that's the least we can do," he said.

"Let's rest now. Soon we'll be moving to recover Torreon, it won't be easy. We have to make all these wagons ready and there are new people in need of training," Dr. Villarreal said, touching Fidelio's shoulder in a friendly way.

"We'll be ready," Fidelio replied, gently tapping Dr. Villarreal's hand. Dr. Villarreal turned and walked away. Fidelio walked to the wagon where he used to sleep.

CHAPTER XIV

Several weeks went by peacefully, Fidelio besides doing his work assisting to have all the sanitary wagons with the necessary supplies, he kept busy taking care of the sick among the population. Every day the amount of those seeking his services increased; the word about his healing abilities had spread rapidly. One morning Fidelio awoke to the sound of a military band. He got up, looked out and saw not only a band playing "La cucaracha", but also a well uniformed mounted guard and General Villa and the governor General Chao standing in the station. They seemed to be waiting for the arrival of an upcoming train. Obviously, they were expecting someone important, "but, who is the one coming in that train?" Fidelio thought. He took a clay jar, poured water on a clay bowl, washed his face and axillae, dried with a clean rag, put a shirt on and walked to the station. It was a bright, but cold morning; Fidelio rubbed his hands to warm them up.

Once at the station, Fidelio saw Dr. Villarreal among those waiting. He was talking to a blond man, slender, about fifty-years-old. They seemed to have an animated and friendly talk.

"Fidelio, come here, allow me to introduce my dear friend and colleague Dr. Rauschbaum, Villa's personal physician. We have been talking about the curative effects of herbs. I was just telling him about you; and precisely perhaps you could help us with the difficult case we have been discussing," Dr. Villarreal said, as he greeted Fidelio.

"Doctor, it's an honor to meet you," Fidelio said, approaching them and feeling a bit embarrassed.

"Dr. Rauschbaum and I have been friends for a long time," Dr. Villarreal said.

Dr. Rauschbaum and Fidelio shook hands. By the touch of his hand, Fidelio felt softness, gentleness and firmness; looking at his blue eyes he also perceived a caring man. "How different these blue eyes are from those I have seen before," he thought.

"Dr. Villarreal has told me about your knowledge of nature's healing effects. One of my patients has an old wound. I have tried everything I know, but the wound doesn't heal. What could nature offer to help this man?" Dr. Rauschbaum asked, looking straight into Fidelio's eyes. Fidelio felt glad to notice that it was an honest question. Knowing how difficult is for most people to admit ignorance and ask for help, "this is a wise man," he thought.

"Perhaps you could use arnica flower, nopal or bee honey, or maybe a combination of these," Fidelio replied.

Dr. Rauschbaum smiled. "Thank you. I had thought about something similar, but I must confess that I wasn't sure; believe it or not you have been of great help. I'll try a combination of those." He turned to Dr. Villarreal. "My friend, it has been a pleasure talking to you again, but I have to leave you now. I must be at Villa's side when General Angeles arrives. We'll have many other opportunities to meet and talk," he turned to Fidelio. "Young man, beware, that ability of yours could be a blessing or a curse. For the time being, I'm happy that someone like you is helping our soldiers," he added and walked towards where Villa and Chao were.

"A good and honest physician. Also, very patient. Just the right temperament to tolerate Villa's frequent bursts of fury," Dr. Villarreal said, as Dr. Rauschbaum walked away.

"Indeed, also wise and humble," Fidelio said. "I'm glad that men like him are fighting on our side. So different from those we talked about yesterday."

"I understand what you say. That's another of the many facets of Villa. He attracts both, good and vile people, perhaps he knows a way to channel the energy of all of them and that benefits the cause," Dr. Villarreal said.

"Although I have seen only Villa from the distance, like the rest of the men I'm glad to fight under him, what you have said makes sense. Somehow, he channels the energy of all of us towards a common goal," said Fidelio. "But, who is General Angeles? Why are General Villa and Chao here? Why is he received with such honors?"

"General Felipe Angeles is a career soldier, an expert in artillery. Villa and all of us are happy because he is coming just at the right moment, the right man at the right time. We have captured many cannons from the enemy, bought several more and now we have an expert in the management of this weapon. He has also shown integrity, most of the career soldiers accepted Huerta, he didn't. For that reason, he was exiled to France and has returned to join this cause."

The expected train arrived. General Angeles came out of the last wagon and walked towards Villa, they embraced each other. Fidelio admired the martial attitude of the General and by the way he walked, Fidelio knew that Dr. Villarreal was correct, this was a man with integrity and honesty. That certainty helped to restore Fidelio's hope. "If at the end of this struggle, honest men like this one are in charge the change we all hope for, it will happen," he thought. Villa and Angeles exchanged friendly words and walked away. Fidelio noticed that there was a healthy connection between the two. Fidelio thought about the others around Villa, men like Fierro and Urbina. A sentence sounded loud in his mind "Things will change to remain the way they were." "It could get worse," he told himself. Suddenly, sadness overcame him. Spontaneously, he started mumbling "Our father who acts in heaven…"

"Fidelio, are you mumbling a prayer?" Dr. Villarreal asked, smiling. "And if so, why are praying?"

"I'm praying that all of this fighting, all of this killing and violence ends with a change that helps common people," Fidelio replied.

"Maybe you are right, someday we'll have a chance to continue our conversation in this matter. But today there are important details about the movement towards Torreon. We were only waiting for the arrival of

General Angeles and now that he is here, it's almost certain that we'll start moving soon, it could be even tonight or tomorrow. Our train, we'll be among the first to leave," Dr. Villarreal said.

"I'm ready," Fidelio said. "Hopefully everyone else is also ready."

"Our team is fully ready. All the equipment is in the wagons. One wagon for the filming company has been added to our train. We'll share it with the American actors, cameramen and reporters," Dr. Villarreal said, as they walked toward the train.

"Cameramen, actors, reporters? What are you talking about?" Fidelio asked, surprised and intrigued.

"Villa has signed a contract with an American filming company to film all the battles of the Northern Division. He has agreed that there will be an actor doubling him in some of the scenes. He has ordered a wagon to be prepared for them, so they will travel and carry their equipment. You and I will share it with them and also with a couple of reporters."

"Is one of the reporters an old man?" Fidelio asked, remembering his conversation with the old American reporter in Ojinaga.

"There are two young reporters. Why do you ask?"

Fidelio told him about his conversation with the old reporter.

"There have been questions about an old American writer. I didn't know anything about it. I thought it was only rumors, but now that you mention him, I realize it's true that he has been here; but no one seems to know anything else. No one seems to know what happened to him. Do you remember his name?"

"Ambrose Bierce, or something like that. He mentioned that he was a reporter," Fidelio said.

"With all this turmoil, anything could have happened. Perhaps the American with whom we'll be traveling knows something about him; we'll have plenty of time to ask them about it. Remember, be ready, we could leave any time. If we recover Torreon, the path towards central Mexico will be open."

"I'm ready. Which is the wagon where we'll be travelling along with the Americans?" Fidelio asked.

"It's the last one in the sanitary train. I must go to the headquarters to receive orders. I'll see you tomorrow, before we leave. Take care." Dr. Villarreal said, before walking away.

Fidelio walked to the last wagon of the sanitary train. Got up and once inside he found two young men, playing cards, a cigarette in their mouths. As Fidelio walked in, they looked at him, one of them took the cigarette out of his mouth. "Are you sharing the wagon with us?" he asked in Spanish.

"Yes, I am," Fidelio replied, surprised and satisfied to find out that they would be able to communicate.

"I'm John Reed, a reporter, my friend here is Raoul Walsh, an actor who will play the role of General Villa," the man said, smiling in a friendly manner, to Fidelio. "What's your name?" he asked.

"I'm Fidelio Serna, member of the sanitary division," Fidelio answered. "What do you mean by playing the role of General Villa?" he added pointing to Walsh.

Both of the men smiled. "General Villa has signed a contract with the Mutual Company to film the battles of the Northern Division and a movie about his life. I'll play his role in that movie," Walsh answered.

"I had heard something about it," Fidelio said, looking around, in one of the corners of the wagon. He saw something like a round, hollow seat with a water container on top of it, perplexed he kept looking at it.

"That is a toilette," Reed said, smiling. "If one of us wants to empty his bladder or his bowel, won't have to go outside, he can do it here and flush it,' he said walking towards the seat, pulled a chain and water flushed through the hollow seat and away from the wagon.

Fidelio who had never seen one of those, found it amusing and smiled.

"Yes, it's amusing," Reed said. "You said your name is Fidelio? Are you the healer people talk about?"

"Yes, that's my name, and yes, I provide advice and care to those who need it," Fidelio said.

"You are much younger than I expected. I have heard a lot about you, it seems that you are a popular folk's healer. They also say that for your age, you are wise. I'm glad to have you as a travel companion. I'm sure that we'll get along well," Reed said.

Walsh got up, took his jacket and walked towards the door, Reed did the same. "Well, now that we have met, we must leave; take care, we'll see each other again," Reed said, before the two of them waved to

Fidelio, left the wagon and walked towards downtown. Fidelio looked at them, left the wagon and walked toward the place he assisted the sick.

That day, knowing that the troops would be leaving, a large crowd showed up hoping to get a consult from Fidelio; thus, he consulted until very late in the night. Exhausted from the busy day, he walked back to the wagon, as he passed along the trains he noticed that there was extraordinary movement. The wagons loaded with horses and on top of the most of them, soldiers and their women prepared dinner. He saw the cannons and counted them as he walked by, there were twenty-nine of them, one in particular called his attention, a huge cannon. "How many men has that thing killed already and how many more in the future?" he thought. When he got into the wagon, he found Reed, Walsh and two other men smoking and playing cards.

"Good evening Fidelio, welcome home," Reed greeted him. "Allow me to introduce two of my colleagues. Timothy Turner and John Williams. Friends, this is Fidelio, the healer. I bet you have heard a lot about him." The two men looked at Fidelio, waived to him in a friendly manner. "Hello, Fidelio, indeed, you are a popular man," Turner said. Fidelio waived back at them, walked to the litters, threw himself into one and fell asleep almost immediately. He felt really tired.

Gray and blue mountains, no grass, no trees, just bare rocks. Dark clouds in the sky, the environment misty and cold. Purple, orange, bright yellow colors behind the mountains. A town, empty streets; scared people closing their doors and windows; soldiers kicking doors open. Yells came from one house. "Fidelio, Fidelio, where are you?" a woman called him. Male laughs, a struggle, then silence. One of the doors opened and uniformed men came out, blood on their faces, lips swollen, scratches all over, eyelids swollen and purple, like foxes after killing a hen. Fidelio sitting by himself in the train wagon, looking through the window when Candelaria in a pink dress, smiling, walked in. "Fidelio my love, I miss you so much, but now I'll be with you forever, I'll never leave you; wherever you go I'll be there, always at your side." Surprised, but happy to see her, Fidelio got up, extended his arms and walked towards her.

A sudden, violent movement threw Fidelio out the narrow litter, waking him up. The train was moving, the campaign had officially started. "What does this dream mean?" thought Fidelio, as he got up.

He looked through the window, the train was in movement, while other trains were also getting ready to depart. Perplexed, Fidelio looked at them. It was strange, the horses inside the wagons, while the soldiers were on the roof accompanied by their women who prepared breakfast for them. It smelled like coffee, beans and hot pepper.

"Women following their men wherever they go, often carrying a child on their backs. What is even more impressive is that this is an army, an army getting ready for battle. Thousands of soldiers, followed by their women and children. To the eyes of many of us, foreigners, this would look like complete disorder, but, precisely that is what makes all of this even more impressive. There is order in it. Someone who until recently was considered a common outlaw, is the one who has put order and discipline into it. Even career soldiers follow him," Reed said, standing behind Fidelio.

Fidelio, still preoccupied by the strange dream, saw Candelaria in every woman on the roof of those trains. He kept silence and continued just looking.

"Villa has cut the telegraph service up to the north and also has ordered to stop trains going or coming from Ciudad Juarez. Although everyone knows that Villa has been preparing to attack Torreon, all of us believed that Villa would wait until after the spring," Reed continued.

Fidelio listened to him like in the distance, the images of his dream kept coming. He felt happy that finally they were moving to Torreon, maybe that's what the dream was about. Seeing the women on the roof of the wagons, he decided that once in Torreon, he, like the soldiers, would take Candelaria with him. They'll never be distant from each other. Without saying a word, feeling really tired, Fidelio threw himself into the litter and almost immediately fell asleep again. The sound and movement of the train served as lullaby to him and he had a prolonged and pleasant sleep.

When he woke up, it was night. Dr. Villarreal, Reed, Walsh, Williams, Turner and another man, unknown to him, looked at him in a funny way, as if it was some kind of joke. They sat around a table, where there were cards and glasses with liquor.

"Good evening," Dr. Villarreal said, smiling but about to burst into laughter. "I hope you had a good rest," he added.

"Good evening," Fidelio replied. "Why are you laughing? How long did I sleep?"

"Almost two days," Reed said.

"You missed a wedding. Villa was the best man. Let me tell you, that man has the energy of three horses. He danced non-stop until we left this morning," Walsh intervened.

"Indeed, he is as good dancing the tango and the polkas as he is riding a horse, shooting a gun and commanding troops. Villa is full of life. No wonder you people follow him," the man said, unknown to Fidelio.

"This is Christy Cabanne, director of the movie we are filming," Walsh said, pointing to the man who had just talked.

The man nodded to Fidelio who responded the same way.

"Look at that enormous cloud. Cloud of dust," Reed said, looking through the window. Everyone looked and indeed, an enormous cloud, created by the dust of thousands of mounted men, mixed with the smoke coming from the trains was seen in both sides of the train.

"That cloud must be about five kilometers long and at least one and a half wide," Reed continued. "Thousands of men riding to the same place: Torreon. It's going to be an epic battle, and you'll be filming all of it," Reed added, looking to Cabanne and Walsh.

"Indeed, it's going to be a great movie. Villa has already agreed that the battles will be at day light," said Cabanne.

"You'll be filming history," Reed said, standing at the window and looking at the thousands of horse riders outside. He sat. "You'll put the transformation of a country in film."

"Do you really believe that this country is going to be transformed?" Walsh asked. "Let's face reality. Most of the people in this country are illiterate. Yes, in this part of the country, people are used to be independent, but in the rest of the country they are used to have a master. One way or the other, they all follow charismatic leaders. Until now Villa has proven to be the most honest among them," he looked at Fidelio and Dr. Villarreal, frowned. "But even he tolerates criminals like Fierro and thieves like Urbina in his inner circle," he finally said.

"Yes, I do believe that we are witnessing something extraordinary. The fact that thousands, all over the country, have volunteered to fight

Huerta proves that they are ready. Villa has already shown a strong interest in correcting illiteracy. Everywhere he has had the opportunity, he has opened schools and improved the teacher's salaries. We have seen it, wherever Villa goes there is hope in the eyes of the people," Reed said. "As a matter of fact, not only Mexico, but the entire world is ready for a change."

"You are an educated man, grew up here and also have lived in the United States. What do you think?" Walsh asked Dr. Villarreal.

"I agree with Reed; the change has already started. We are fighting for something more than a mere change of government. We are fighting to let those who work the land to benefit for their work, for workers to receive a fair salary, for the right of everyone to live in peace and not to be abused by those in power. To open more schools where all children could learn. Yes. All of that is worth fighting for," Dr. Villarreal replied.

"What about those who have invested to make the land productive. Those who have made the railroad system? Those who have risked their capital? Don't they also need security? Now they are losing their investment" Walsh said.

"Those invested their money because they were given the security of a profit. They knew that they were running a risk and as a matter of fact they earned a profit paying miserable salaries to their workers," Reed said. He looked to Fidelio. "What do you think Fidelio?"

Fidelio, who had been interested in the conversation from the beginning, thought for a moment, he looked to the window. "This is a just cause, I have no doubts about it," he paused for a moment. "I have not only witnessed how the miners of Guanajuato struggled to put food in the table for their families, humidity and poisoning gases made them sick, they risked their lives to get the mineral, many of them died in the process, leaving their families begging for shelter and food," he paused again, outside thousands of butterflies returned north, wishing he would be able to join them, Fidelio smiled. "The owners, those who risked their capital, fed well their families, enjoyed balls, living in comfort. Nothing wrong with that. But, all of this fighting and killing each other could have been prevented."

"How?" Walsh asked. The rest turned to look at Fidelio, interested in the answer.

"Just if they had cared in sharing the wealth, paying fair salaries," Fidelio replied.

Everyone laughed. "God bless you, hopefully you'll remain this naïve the rest of your life," Reed said, laughing. "Greed is much more powerful than anything else. Those who have capital, care only for more capital. They consider those who sweat and work just to be able to get food inferior to them. They'll never change."

"What Fidelio said is however, true. The solution is simple," intervened Dr. Villarreal, in a sad tone of voice. "Having said that, what you said," pointing to Reed, is also true. "I know well, I grew up among those who consider themselves 'superior' because of the light color of their skin, the amount of money they have, or just because they believe that they have been born 'with blue blood'."

"Jesus taught us many years ago, but we haven't heard him, yet," Fidelio said, still wishing he could join the butterflies.

Dr. Villarreal smiled. "There are many sentences in the bible that would justify violence," he said. "But I agree with you, if we applied Jesus' teachings, even the war in Europe would have been prevented. But most of us prefer just to pretend that we are Christians."

"Take from the rich to give it to the poor?" Cabanne asked.

Before anyone could answer, a man, coming from another car, walked in. "We are arriving to Bermejillo, we'll stop there," he said. "General Villa plans to establish the headquarters there. He has ordered to be ready to receive the wounded from the battles that have already been fought at Mapimi, Tlahualilo and Sacramento. Besides, Dr. Rauschbaum said that you'll need to do something to stop the epidemics of smallpox, and yellow fever."

"Well, it seems that all of us are going to be busy," Reed said, standing up. "It has been an interesting conversation," he looked to Walsh. "Yes, I like the idea of taking from the wealthy and giving it to the poor, that's much better than taking from the poor to give it to the rich," he smiled and walked out, the rest followed him, everyone had to get ready.

Dr. Villarreal and Fidelio stopped at one of the wagons, where the whole sanitary team was waiting for instructions, while Reed, Walsh and Cabanne continued to Villa's wagon.

"I know that we are short of fresh water," Dr. Villarreal told the sanitary team. "General Villa has already ordered several train wagons full of fresh water and enough food coming from Chihuahua. That shouldn't be a problem. Are we ready to receive the wounded?"

"Yes, the operating tables are clean and ready, the instruments are also clean and ready," a young American physician answered.

"Great, we also have several cases of smallpox among us. We need to prevent the disease from spreading, do you have any idea?"

"In Baltimore, one of the professors talked about a method called 'variolation', said another of the young American physicians.

"I have heard something about it," Dr. Villarreal said. "But we are about to enter battle, can we afford to expose healthy young men to the illness?"

"Yes, it will work, God will help us," Fidelio said.

All of them looked at him, some laughing. Dr. Villarreal smiled. "God's help is always welcome, and because of it, we'll go ahead and try variolation." He looked at the young American physician who had mentioned the method. "You'll be in charge of it. Let's start immediately. Choose your team, teach them and proceed with it."

The young doctor nodded, pointed to several of the men and women present and they left.

"What about yellow fever. Any idea?" Dr. Villarreal asked afterwards.

"That won't require divine help. All that we need is to provide the men with a mixture of aguardiente, eucalyptus and yerbabuena. Men should rub it on their skin, it will prevent mosquito bite," Fidelio said. "How do you know that?" one of those present asked.

"I just know," Fidelio replied.

"Batopilas and Parras are close by, we'll get plenty of aguardiente in there. We can prepare the mixture and provide the men with it. Hopefully they won't drink it instead of rubbing it," said one of the women present, laughing.

Wagons pulled by mules arrived with wounded men.

"Let's start doing our most important job. Take those men to the operating table. Fidelio, come and help me," Dr. Villarreal said, as he walked out, the rest followed him.

CHAPTER XV

"Bermejillo, Mapimi, Sacramento, all have been captured. The peripheral defenses of Torreon that Velasco had prepared have been defeated with minimal loses for us," Dr. Rauschbaum told Dr. Villarreal and Fidelio after a busy day taking care of the wounded and those affected by smallpox and yellow fever. They rested drinking freshly prepared coffee in one of the wagons of the train hospital. "That was the easy part, those, apparently weak defenses, were prepared and designed by General Velasco, a career soldier, in charge of the defense of Torreon, basically to test our strength. Now, to take Torreon we must first capture Ciudad Lerdo and then go through Gomez Palacio. Villa, like the rest of us, expects a fierce battle."

"Do you know anything about the plan of attack," Dr. Villarreal asked.

"Not much. What I know is that Villa has prepared a plan and he has shown it to Angeles. He is waiting for his opinion. They get along surprisingly well. Although Villa has not had any military education, Angeles has quickly accepted that Villa has a brilliant military mind. As a matter of fact, he doesn't hide his admiration for him. Thus, probably he'll make a few suggestions to the plan. But, what I'm sure is that the attack will start in a few days, it could even be tomorrow. So, we must be prepared. It will be a bloody battle," Dr. Rauschbaum replied. He wiped out the sweat from his forehead. "Uuuph, the spring has not even started and here it is already hot," he added.

"It's not only the heat but also the sand storms that are common here during this time of the year," Dr. Villarreal said, smiling and also wiping the sweat from his forehead. "Gomez Palacio and Torreon are surrounded by dry, rocky, mountains. I'm almost certain that General Velasco has placed artillery in them. Indeed, we must expect a bloody combat, which means that we'll be busy."

"Indeed," Dr. Rauschbaum said, looking towards Fidelio who had remained quiet during the conversation. As a matter of fact, Fidelio was not even paying any attention to what they said. He was thinking of Candelaria and how they'll be together soon. "Fidelio, you are going to play an important role in the care of the wounded during the upcoming battles. We have been thinking that we shouldn't wait until the battle is over to help those who are wounded. If we could get the wounded here as soon as possible, that will save many lives and also it will prevent infections. We need to prepare a team to be there at the moment of the combat, help those wounded almost immediately and transfer them as soon as possible, even during the battle. What do you think?"

Distracted, Fidelio didn't replay. "Fidelio, hey Fidelio, I'm talking to you,"

Dr. Rauschbaum said, waving a hand at Fidelio's face and raising his voice.

Fidelio almost jumped, embarrassed. "I'm sorry I wasn't listening. Will you please repeat what you just said?"

Dr. Rauschbaum repeated everything he had just said.

Fidelio thought for a moment. "Of course, that could be done. I can take care of getting a team. It will be formed mostly by women and children," he replied.

"Do you mean that you would want to take women and children to the middle of a bloody battle?" Dr. Villarreal asked, surprised.

"Why are you surprised? As you know children are already among the combat troops and women have been helping, I suppose, from the beginning. These women would do anything to help their men. They are fearless. I'm certain that, if asked, they'll be happy to volunteer."

"I know for a fact that you are right," Dr. Rauschbaum said. "Assemble your team and be ready. As I said before, the battle for Torreon will start in a few days, it could be even tomorrow."

"Yes, I also believe that you are right. I don't know why I was surprised since I have witnessed how women and children have taken part in this struggle from the beginning," Dr. Villarreal said.

"Good for both of you. Now that the matter is settled, let's rest because we still have a lot of work to do," Dr. Rauschbaum said and walked out. Fidelio and Dr. Villarreal also went to their wagon to rest. When they arrived, they found Reed, Walsh and the others playing cards, but they just went straight to bed and fell asleep.

The attack started on March 22, early afternoon. A five kilometers' front, Fidelio and his team among them. Fidelio had divided his team in groups. Some would be among those in the vanguard, they were to take immediate care of the wounded, cleanse the wound, take measures to stop the bleeding, apply bandages. Others were in charge of transporting the wounded to those in the rearguard, where another team, would cleanse the wounds with fresh water before pouring bee honey and cover them with clean bandages. Also, for those bleeding from their extremities, they were to release and reapply the tourniquets before sending them to the hospital along with those who needed advanced care. Fidelio lead those at the vanguard.

It was a hot and dusty day. Since they walked behind the cavalry, the dust entered their eyes, their noses, sand went to the lungs with every breath. The order was that those on horse would advance only until they were about four kilometers from the skirt of Gomez Palacio and once there they were to dismount and advance in a disperse fashion to prevent giving an easy target to the enemy's artillery. The goal was to take the mountains around the city. As they advanced and before they had dismounted, the enemy's artillery started fire. Those in the vanguard responded to the yell "There is the enemy, let's charge!" And the cavalry charged. The infantry followed them.

The machine guns of the enemy blasted them, but the charge continued. Horses and men ran in an open field, easy target for the federal's machine guns. Fidelio was forced to advance with the infantry that had charged. The sound of the bullets flying around him reminded him of a bee colony. Seeing the many fallen around him, he realized that this time the risk was not a mere sting. The cracking sound of broken bones and skulls, the blood flowing from the many wounded, legs, arms, body parts flying around, yells of pain, the sound of bombs exploding close by, throwing dust and stones all around, spreading death and pain. "This is hell," Fidelio thought. Since they were in an open field with no place where to hide or seek protection, they had no other choice but to charge. Soon, besides catching dust with every breath came the smell of sweat, blood, feces, urine, smell of putrefaction, smell of death and suffering. If they had fear, now that no longer existed. Rage became the predominant emotion. They were no longer afraid of death; they wanted to kill or be killed. Fidelio was not the exception. Looking around for a gun, he saw the children of his team, barely twelve, thirteen or fourteen-years-old. Ignoring the immediate danger, they were busy helping the wounded closer to them. Looking at them, dressed in their plain cotton pants and shirts, huaraches instead of boots and instead of cartridge belts, they carried rough ixtle bags where they had clay jars; some full of fresh water, other full of bee honey. They also carried clean rags to be used as temporary bandages. Feeling shame, Fidelio understood, his duty was not to kill, but to help those in need. He dropped the gun that he had just lifted. A man close by yelled and fell, wounded. Fidelio ran to him. Bullets flying all around, bombs exploding nearby, rage, fear, all of that didn't matter anymore. Helping the wounded became the only thing that, at the moment, mattered.

The fallen soldier was an old man who had several wounds, the worse one had opened his abdomen. He held his perforated bowel with both hands. When Fidelio arrived, the man tried to smile, showing his few, rotten teeth. "Don't bother with me," he said. "I'll die soon. Help the others, the young ones. I'm happy to die knowing that my children and my grandchildren will have a better chance than I did. This is a worthwhile cause." He looked to the sky, exhaled, died with his eyes fixed in the sky. Fidelio looked up. Hundreds of ducks, flying north passed by, forming several perfect "V's".

"Fidelio, we no longer have water," one of the children told him.

"Urinate on the wound, rinse it well, dry it, apply the bee honey and wrap it before sending them to the rearguard. I'll ask those transporting the wounded to bring more water, meanwhile do as I said." Fidelio replied.

Shortly after sunset, the battle stopped. Although they had made it to the skirt of Gomez Palacio, no real gain was obtained; the enemy still held the mountains surrounding the city. Fidelio and his team worked until late in the night helping as many as possible. Finally, around midnight, they had transported all those who needed it to the prepared wagons and most of the death bodies back to their regiments. During the night, Fidelio noticed that besides rats, vultures, there were others taking anything of value from those fallen, this time he didn't bother with them. "They, like the vultures, have to live," he thought.

"The defenses are as strong as we expected, it won't be easy, but we'll get it,"

Dr. Villarreal told Fidelio once back at the wagon. "The good news is that Maclovio Herrera has captured Ciudad Lerdo. That one was also a fierce battle, they had many men wounded, many fallen." He frowned. "Let's rest, tomorrow we'll be busy again." Reed was busy writing his impressions of the battle using the typewriter. The rhythmic sound soothed Fidelio and allowed him to fall asleep.

For the next four days, Fidelio and his team joined the troops in multiple attempts to break the defenses. On occasions they were partially successful, but a federal counterattack recovered what they had lost. Fidelio got used to the sound of bullets flying by, bombs exploding nearby, but, he couldn't get used to the dismembered bodies, to the smell of death around him. He admired the gallant valor of the combatants and even respected the valor shown by the enemy. "Do they believe their cause is right?" Fidelio asked himself. "They are fighting to preserve the right to exploit people. That's not a right and just cause; that's why they'll be defeated." He answered his own question.

"It has been a brutal combat, many losses on both sides, but General Villa is certain that now we have the upper hand and the defenses of Gomez Palacio will fall soon. This evening we'll attack again," Dr. Rauschbaum told Fidelio, Dr. Villarreal and the rest of the group as he joined them at the wagon they occupied.

That evening, Fidelio and his team joined the infantry in the vanguard. Carefully, slowly, they advanced. Fidelio was concerned because they had to cross the same uncovered field where the enemy's artillery and machine gun had caused most of the losses. This time they were cautious and the advance was slow. Silence, almost absolute silence. No bombs exploding around them, no bullets flying around. The infantry entered the city. They found hundredths of dead bodies, soldiers, horses, mules. Street dogs and cats around them, rats and roaches all over, vultures having a feast. The wind wafted putrefaction. The federals had abandoned the city. They didn't bother to collect their death. They had concentrated all their defenses in Torreon, where they now waited for them.

"Villa has given strict orders to prevent rapine and abuse over the population," Reed commented the following morning.

"Not only that, he has ordered to distribute food, clothes to the poor. No one who asks for food will be denied," Dr. Villarreal said.

"He is a good man. It's difficult to find a leader who cares about the civilian population as much as he does. This has been a wonderful experience. I'll never forget it" Reed said.

"It has been? Why do you say that?" Walsh asked.

"Because I've seen enough. I'm going back to El Paso today," Reed replied.

"The truly important battle is about to start. Torreon is still in the hands of the federals," said Turner. Williams nodded in agreement. Both looked at Reed.

"That's true, but as I said, I've seen enough. Besides, as you well know, everything we write has to be approved by Villa's censorship," Reed replied. "I want to be free to write what I witness."

"Do as you please my friend. It has been nice working with you," Williams said and this time it was Turner who nodded in agreement.

Reed looked around. "Farewell my friends. It has been wonderful meeting and working with all of you," he said to Fidelio and Dr. Villarreal. "Keep an eye on this man, someday we'll be writing about him," he added pointing to Fidelio and looking to his peers.

Williams and Turner smiled. "Yes, probably you are right. Mexico is always full of surprises," said Turner.

"Velasco has rejected the offer to surrender Torreon peacefully," Dr. Rauschbaum said, as he walked in. "Good evening to everyone," he added waving to all of those present. "Villa is, for the time being occupied in feeding the poor in Gomez Palacio. He is also allowing the troops to rest a bit, but, the plan to attack Torreon is ready. They still have powerful artillery in the mountains, in particular in three places: The hills of Calabazas, la polvoreda and el huarache. Once we capture and silence those cannons, the garrison will be ours."

"Meanwhile, there are many wounded who need our care. We better get busy because there will be many more."

"Yes, many more. The federals will fight hard. They know, as well as we do, the strategic importance of Torreon," Dr. Rauschbaum said. He looked to Fidelio, smiled extending his arm and touching Fidelio on the shoulder. "My son, you did a marvelous job. Thanks to you many lives have been saved."

Fidelio smiled back. "Thanks to the children and women who volunteered to help."

"Yes, of course. But, you, my friend, taught them well. That's amazing. You did it in such short period of time," Dr. Rauschbaum said. "Even General Villa has noticed the difference, he asked to congratulate all the sanitary team," he added. All those present clapped. Fidelio blushed.

A man walked in and gave a written note to Dr. Villarreal. "We need to rest. The attack will start tomorrow night," he informed them, after reading the note.

The following night, three groups were assigned to capture the three main federal defenses in the highlands. Fidelio and his team joined the group ready to attack the calabazas highland, all rocks, just a few bushes grew on it. Since early evening there had been and exchange of artillery. This time, thanks to General Angeles ability, the rebels had the upper hand. To identify themselves, everyone had their arms bare; besides that, many of them had an image of the Virgin of Guadalupe on their hats. "She'll shield us," they said. The night was hot and humid, thousands of mosquitos buzzed around. "Spread around, start climbing and move forward," was the order to start the attack. After a few steps, the federals flew rockets to illuminate the field, their machine guns vomited fire. Bodies flying, bodies falling. In the vanguard, Fidelio suddenly felt a sudden gush of warm fluid on his cheek; surprised, he wiped it and saw bright red fluid, but it was not his blood; a bullet had hit a close by man in the neck and red fluid was bursting out of his neck. Attempting to stop the bleeding Fidelio applied pressure on the man's neck, looking at Fidelio the man opened his mouth, no sound came out. The man fell, dead. Fidelio looked around, a man who had been hit in the face, the bullet had blinded him, but even so he tried to move forwards when he was hit again, this time in the chest, like a round cylinder he rolled down the hill taking with him several other men trying to advance. Rage, once again, started to build in Fidelio. A rocket, once again, illuminated the field and once again, Fidelio saw the children of the team, in their plain cotton shirts and pants rushing, trying to help as many wounded as possible, the bullets flew around them, but somehow none of them was injured. Are they angels? Fidelio asked himself. Another group of young men, also, like those in his team, almost children, but already seasoned soldiers, lighted dynamite sticks and using slings threw them towards where one of the machine guns was, although they hit the target one of them received a bullet in one arm and started bleeding. No longer feeling rage, Fidelio ran to assist him, he was able to stop the bleeding and sent him to the rearguard for further assistance. From there on, it was a continuous work for Fidelio and his team. They seemed to dance at the rhythm of the machine guns and the explosion of the dynamite sticks.

Both sides fought hard, both sides showed no mercy, both sides fearless. Overwhelmed by the bravery of the attack, the federals withdrew. At sunset, the hill had been captured. Feeling victorious, the leader of the company without caring to plan a defense for the position, ordered his soldiers to rest. Meanwhile, Fidelio and his team continued helping and transporting the wounded. Suddenly, there was a counterattack. Taken by surprise, the rebels ran abandoning the just captured hill. Fortunately, for Fidelio and his team they had already transported the wounded to the rearguard. Like the rest, they also retreated.

Mounting a black horse, sweating, his face covered with white dust, Villa arrived. "Why did you retreat? Who is your commander?" furious, he yelled.

"I am," a man with the badge of major in his shoulder answered.

"Didn't you receive the order to hold the position obtained? You didn't even try. You just ran like rabbits. I could arrest you and get you through a martial court, but I'll give you another chance." He then looked at the rest of the men. "As for you, I'll give the choice. Either you'll be shot or go back and recover that hill. Well, little boys, what do answer!"

"We'll take it back! Viva Villa!" was the almost unanimous reply.

Villa looked at the Major. "Well, you heard them. Go and recover that mountain." Villa turned and looked at Fidelio and his team, he smiled at them. "Good job, little boys, continue taking care of the wound. I wish there were more like you," he said before applying the spurs to his horse to ride to another position.

The battle continued for the next five days. The number of the dead and wounded piled up. The sanitary team worked day and night. Dr. Villarreal arranged a train to transport those in need of hospital care to Parral.

"Almost one third of our men are dead or wounded," Dr. Rauschbaum told Fidelio and Dr. Villarreal during an occasional rest. "Villa is concerned about it. He is even considering stopping the attack. Angeles' opinion is that the federal are in a worse situation than we are. Velasco has proposed a truce to pick the wounded and death bodies. We have refused it because, planning ahead, we have taken care of our wounded and buried our dead. Angeles opinion is that the federals are at the point of breaking."

Two nights later. "You did a god job stopping the bleeding in Colonel Robles leg. He is already back in the fight. He, like many others is a valiant man," Dr. Villarreal told Fidelio as they rested, drinking a cup of fresh coffee. Suddenly, the night brightened, an enormous fire illuminated Torreon. "Look Fidelio, there is a big fire in Torreon," Dr. Villarreal pointed to the sieged city. Suddenly, the fire brightened in sequence accompanied by several terrible rumbles. "It seems that they are intentionally burning the ammunition. Are they abandoning the city?"

"Yes, they are," Dr. Rauschbaum said. "Villa has ordered not to attack and he has even provided them with an exit. Angeles agrees with it. They don't want any more unnecessary loss of lives on our side. Tomorrow, we'll occupy the city." Dr. Villarreal smiled and lifted his cup of coffee.

Fidelio's heart jumped in his chest. "Candelaria, my love, soon, very soon, we'll be together, and this time it will be forever," he thought.

CHAPTER XVI

Although everyone expected to find Torreon showing the consequences of the terrible battle. They were not prepared for what they found. When they entered the city, Fidelio, like most of them, felt surprised. The spectacle that the city offered was depressive; a lot worse than what they had found in Gomez Palacio. They found the streets devastated, dirty and pestilent. There were death bodies, men, women, even children, along with horses and mules everywhere, many already in frank decomposition, flies, rats and roaches all over. Hundreds of vultures, dogs, even pigs, fought the rats and each other, for the putrid flesh. In a large house, across the street from the alameda, they found four hundred severely wounded men. They were so dirty that many of them had worms in their wounds. The floors stained by urine and feces everywhere. None of them had been taken care of. A note nailed to one of the walls, asked Villa to take care of their wounded. When informed, Villa ordered the sanitary brigade to take immediate care of them. Although Fidelio desired to go looking for Candelaria, he understood that his duty was with those in need of care. He organized his team to start cleansing the wounds, bathing the men and washing the floors.

"Villa has given orders to clean the streets, bury the death and, besides that, he has placed two edicts," Dr. Villarreal told Fidelio several days later. They rested in the terrace of the large house where they took care of the wounded. "In one of them, he orders the town's people to clean the part of the street in front of their houses. If the front of a house is found dirty, they will pay a fine of one hundred pesos. In the second one, the sale of alcoholic drinks is forbidden. If someone is found drinking, the penalty is death. Besides that, looting is not allowed, those found doing so, will be shot on the spot."

"Do these apply to people like Urbina and Fierro?" Fidelio asked.

Dr. Villarreal just grinned. "I wish it would, but, unfortunately, I doubt it," he replied.

"Dr. Villarreal, I would like to ask for a permission," said Fidelio, after a moment of hesitation.

"Permission? Yes, of course, now we have everything under control. I think we'll manage," Dr. Villarreal said. "Anything in particular?"

"Yes, I would like to go looking for my girl."

"I understand. Of course, the permission is granted," Dr. Villarreal said, he looked at Fidelio and smiled. "I'll advice you to take a bath first."

Since it was early, Fidelio first walked to the market close to the railroad station only to find it closed. No food stands, no fruit and vegetables stands, no grocery stands, no one in there. Fidelio looked at the railroad station. Then he remembered "General Diaz number twenty-three, that's the guest house where we spent our days together," he thought. Walking in that direction, the image of Candelaria became so real that Fidelio felt he could touch her. He felt happy, so happy and cheerful that he danced as he walked.

"General Diaz number twenty-three, this is the place," he stopped, and happy, he took a deep breath. He noticed then that the street was clean and neat. He smiled, "Villa's edict has been successful." Although the walls of the house had been recently washed, Fidelio could see red-purple stains on it and holes, multiple holes on it. "It was a rough battle," he thought as he knocked at the door. Inside a dog barked, but no other sound. Fidelio knocked harder.

"Who is it?" a woman asked from inside.

"It's me, Fidelio, I'm looking for Candelaria," Fidelio answered. The person inside made an unintelligible sound, almost like a grunting.

"Wait, I'll open for you," the same voice said, after a moment of hesitation. The door finally opened and the face of the same woman who had greeted him the first time he had been there, showed. Fidelio noticed that she was pale, with a concerned and fearful look on her face. "Candelaria is not here," she said almost in a whisper, like she had to make an effort to talk, like she was afraid of something.

"But, do you know where I could find her?" Fidelio asked. His hands sweated.

Holding the door, the woman stared at Fidelio, tears started to flow from her eyes. Fidelio became concerned.

"Is she sick? Has she been wounded? Where is she?" he almost yelled, anxious.

"No, she is not sick, she has not been wounded," the woman replied. "She was killed, assassinated!" she almost yelled, allowing the tears to flow.

Fidelio felt a painful knot in his belly, his legs trembled. He had to make an effort not to fall. Suddenly, the day was no longer bright, it became dark for him. "No, that's not true. You are lying! Tell me that you are lying! Where is she!" he yelled, pushing the door wide open, lifted his hand threatening to slap the woman.

"It's true, I'm telling you the truth!" scared, the woman mumbled, putting her arms in front of her. "The soldiers did it!" tears now flowing freely. "We could do nothing to protect her, nothing." She dropped her chin to the chest, her hands covered her face, sobbing loudly.

Fidelio fell on his knees, shoulders down, facing the floor, also weeping loudly. "Candelaria, Candelaria, my love, where are you?" he yelled, raising his arms to the sky.

Although the sun was bright. For him everything was dark. His sobbing and yells became so loud that people started to come out. Seeing his pain, his sorrow, and knowing the reason, some of them also wept.

Gently, the woman put her hand on his shoulder. "She was courageous, she fought, she even injured some of the soldiers and she preferred death to dishonor." She said in a soothing tone of voice.

Feeling a bit calmer, Fidelio looked at her. "What do you mean? How did it happen?" he asked.

"After you left, she stayed here, in the same room that both of you occupied," the woman said, smiling to Fidelio. "She never stopped talking about you. She was so happy remembering you that she sang your name and danced every time she talked about you." She paused for a moment, the smile went away. She seemed concerned, she hesitated to continue.

"Please, continue, tell me what happened, even if it's painful. I need to know," Fidelio said.

"She helped the revolution. At the pozole stand, she would listen to the military and observed the movements of the soldiers, then she informed Villa's spies," a man said, noticing that the woman hesitated to talk.

"Someone informed the federals. We suspect that the informer was Dora Iduarte. She used to work with Candelaria at the same pozole stand and she was the lover of a federal colonel, one of the colorados. No one has seen her again," the woman continued. "One night the federals showed, looking for her. The colonel Perez Silguero, Dora's lover, was their commander."

"I know him, he is a coward. Got promotions through lies. Always runs to hide in the rearguard as soon as he even hears of Villa's soldiers," someone in the crowd intervened.

"Trying to protect herself, Candelaria locked the door, but they kicked it open." The woman continued after the interruption. "She is yours, do whatever you like with her,' their colonel ordered. Candelaria fought hard, and before they could force themselves into her, she took one of their knives and stabbed herself to death. Merciless, they pulled her body out. 'This is what happens to those who spy and plot against us,' they yelled to us and left. Once we became sure that they had gone, we cleansed the body, took it to the Guadalupe church, although with some hesitation, Father Segura, the priest, agreed for a mass once we explained how it had happened. She is buried at the municipal cemetery."

Fidelio listened in silence. Still on his knees. Slowly, he stood up, his hands clinched in a fist, jaws tight. His eyes dry, no tears on them. His face, however, revealed the pain he suffered. He looked around to all the people present. "Thank you," he finally mumbled before walking out, shoulders down, dragging his feet, looking sad, very sad. He didn't want to know the exact place of her burial, for him Candelaria was alive, she would live forever in him.

The name of Father Segura, came to his mind. "Is he the same one? The same Father Segura from Guanajuato? "Now, it would be so nice to talk to him. I need someone to whom I can talk. Someone in whom I can trust," Fidelio thought. He could see the towers of the church from where he stood. It was close by, only a few blocks away. He walked in that direction. He ignored the people on the street, but he looked so painfully sad, that most moved aside allowing him to walk by, it seemed that they also felt his sorrow.

Once he entered the church, walked all the way to the front, where the image of the Virgen of Guadalupe stood, he fell on his knees, bent his body to put face and hands to the floor. Weeping, he allowed his pain to get out. "Dear Mother, why did you let it happen? Why?" he yelled. Women praying the rosary turned and looked at him, concerned. He didn't care about them.

The yelling attracted the attention of a priest who was at the sacristy, he ran to Fidelio. "Son, my son, what is it?" he asked, as soon as he approached, kneeling at Fidelio's side.

Fidelio lifted his face and when he saw the man in front of him, he couldn't believe it. His old friend and mentor was there in flesh. "Father, oh Father Segura!" He almost jumped and embraced the priest. "Is it you, is it really you? Am I dreaming?" he said, crying louder.

The priest also acted surprised for a moment. "Fidelio, is it you? This is a surprise also for me. Yes, it's me. Father Segura, your old friend," the Father said, returning Fidelio's embrace. "Now please tell me what is hurting so much that you are yelling and crying?"

"Oh Father, it's so painful. It hurts so much," Fidelio said, still sobbing.

Father Segura keeping his arm around Fidelio's shoulder helped him to get up and gently guided him to one of the church's seats. "I'm listening, my son," he said after both of them were seated.

Fidelio told him the whole story about him and Candelaria, starting from the time he and Enrique arrived in Torreon. Father Segura allowed him to talk until he noticed he had finished.

"I understand the reason for your pain. It's a loss, a serious and important loss," said Father Segura, after listening to Fidelio. I can sense rage and rancor in you. What are you planning to do?"

"I want revenge," Fidelio replied in a hard tone. "This pain won't stop until I have revenged her death. I'll find that Colonel and make him suffer, I'll make him pay for it."

Father Segura kept quiet for a moment. "There is someone I'd like you to meet," he said getting up. "He lives close by. Let's go and see him."

The street was quiet. Although some wounded soldiers passed by, Fidelio didn't seem to notice them. After they had walked in silence for about half a block, Father Segura stopped and knocked on a door. A Chinese child opened the door and having seen who had knocked, smiled and embraced Father Segura's knees. "Father Segura, it is Father Segura!" he yelled. Other children came also running as soon as their heard the name of whom had knocked. All of them surrounded father Segura, cheering him extending their arms, trying to hug him.

"How are you my dear children," Father Segura told them, smiling happily, and also extending his arms trying to caress most of them. "Is your father around?" he asked the child who had opened the door, as soon as the children finally ended greeting him. "Yes, he is, let me call him," said the child. "Please come in and take a seat." He went to another room as soon as Father Segura and Fidelio had walked in and taken a seat.

A middle aged, slender, Chinese man came in shortly afterwards. "Father Segura, I'm glad to see you. It's has been a while since the last time you came to this, your humble home," said the man, embracing Father Segura. Fidelio impressed by the smoothness of the Chinese movements, immediately felt that he was an honest man who also had a powerful inner strength.

"Why Father Segura wants me to meet him?" Fidelio asked himself.

"With all this turmoil around us, we have been busy," Father Segura said to the man.

"Allow me to introduce a dear friend. I have known him since he was a little child, he is now a grownup man, fighting for the revolution," he added pointing to Fidelio. The Chinese put his hands together in front of this chest and bent a little, always looking straight into Fidelio's eyes. "Fidelio, this is Woo Lam Po, a dear friend. We have been friends since my arrival to Torreon," he smiled. "He is a man with great spiritual strength. It will be good for you to talk to him," Father Segura added. Fidelio instead of extending his hand for a handshake, repeated the movement the Chinese had done. Outside the children played and laughed.

"Please take a seat, my humble home is yours," Woo Lam Po said, sitting himself. "May I offer you a cup of tea?"

"Yes, it will be nice, thank you," Father Segura said and Fidelio nodded.

Woo Lam Po stood up, went to another room and said something in a language foreign to Fidelio.

Almost immediately a Chinese woman entered carrying a tea pot and cups. She served the tea in the cups, serving Father Segura and Fidelio first.

"This is my wife," Woo Lam Po said to Fidelio who stood up and repeated the movement he had just learned from Mr. Woo. The woman responded smiling and bending a little before leaving quietly.

Somehow Fidelio felt comfortable. The house was full of calm and tranquility. Like an island of peace in a sea of violence.

Woo Lam Po, looked at Fidelio in a friendly manner, waiting for him to start talking.

"Fidelio, tell Mr. Woo what you have just told me," said Father Segura.

Without hesitation, certain that he was among friends, Fidelio started telling Mr. Woo the whole story between him and Candelaria. Tears flowed freely as he talked. Remembering Candelaria and how the plans he had made for a future with her had been broken, Fidelio felt miserable. Nothing made sense for him anymore. He wanted an explanation, a justification for all the suffering. Above all, he wanted revenge. Mr. Woo allowed Fidelio to talk freely. Finally, Fidelio bent and put his head between his knees. "Why, why, why all this has happened? Why God has allowed it to happen?" he yelled, sobbing loudly.

Woo Lam and Father Segura said nothing. Woo Lam waited until Fidelio had recovered himself. "I understand your pain, you have lost something of great value. Your plans for the future are broken and you would like not only an explanation but also you want revenge. You believe that punishing those who have caused your pain and suffering will make you feel better, or at least you will make them feel the same way you are feeling now. Yes, revenge is always tempting." He paused. Like in a deep thought.

Fidelio felt intrigued; looked at Mr. Woo waiting for him to continue.

"We came from China, crossed the sea. Running away from hunger, war, famine. We came looking for peace, looking for a place where we could work and prosper. For a place where we could raise our children without the fear of them being killed or taken away from us," Woo Lam continued looking at the distance, listening to the laughs of the children playing outside. He paused again.

Although Woo Lam didn't show emotion, Fidelio sensed that the memory was painful; thus, he kept silent.

"We thought that we had found that place here. Thus, a large number of us chose this town to settle. In the beginning, we had no problems. We worked hard, supported each other, and thanks to it, many of us became prosperous. As a community, we saved, and soon we had enough to open our own bank. But our success created resentment among those who had come before us. We are different, have different customs, even if we speak the language, we do so with a different accent. Soon, we became the target of many who blamed us for the poverty of others. Some started to hate us and in the Independence Day our farms, our stores, along with those of the Spanish immigrants, became the target of looting and hatred."

The memory of how in Guanajuato and Morelia, the mob used to loot the commercial properties of Spaniards during the month of September, came to Fidelio's mind. That memory caused embarrassment and shame, but he kept silent and continued listening.

"The revolution came," Woo Lam continued. "In May 5, 1911, there were speeches blaming us for the poverty of many. "It would best to get rid of all of them," one of the speakers said. That month, in May

11, the maderistas attacked and in May 13 the federals abandoned the city. As soon as the federals left, a mob started looting all the commerce, in particular that of the Chinese," Woo Lam paused, he now looked sad, his eyes to the floor; he crossed his hands in front of his chest, took a deep breath.

"The violent looting lasted two days," he continued. "Their target were foreign properties, but there was special hatred against Chinese. It was not only the Chinese commercial properties that were attacked, but also their homes. Chinese people were dragged out of their homes. Men, women, children, young and old. All were attacked, kicked, women raped, their age didn't matter to the mob." Woo closed his eyes, rubbed his hands, making an effort not to show how painful it was for him to remember. "The mob showed no mercy, many were decapitated, many were stabbed. Others burned alive. Some were tied to horses that pulled in different directions so their bodies were thorn into pieces. Heads were used as playing balls. Someone took a three-years-old child from the legs and smashed his head against the wall."

Fidelio could see the scene clearly, his hands sweated. He sobbed, the image was too clear, too painful. Somehow, he was there, he felt like he was part of the multi-head, unintelligent monster, he could see himself being one of those that showed no mercy, the cruelty of the mob was his own. He now desired Woo Lam to stop, but he couldn't say a word.

"Finally, Emilio Madero's troops entered the city, he ordered his soldiers to shoot anyone who attacked a foreigner. In particular, he ordered to protect the Chinese people. That put an end to the looting." Woo Lam ended. His face didn't show resignation, it showed calm, deep, inner peace.

Fidelio felt intrigued by Woo Lam's calmness. "What did you do afterwards? Did you ask for punishment of those who provoked or participated in the riot?" he asked.

"Madero ordered an investigation, some were punished. The Chinese government also intervened. An apology was given. One of the main instigators was killed during the riot by the same mob he had incited to violence. Now, we just want to live in peace," Woo Lam answered.

"But, is that enough? Are you satisfied? What about the person who killed the three-years-old child?" Fidelio asked.

"That person will have to live with his conscience," Woo Lam replied. "Seeking revenge only feeds itself. Responding unjustified violence with more violence, generates even more violence. A mob in a riot is a non-thinking monster, once it stops those who participated in it eventually will receive the consequences of their action, they'll punish themselves."

"How can you remain calm with something like that?"

"A mob is the one that caused it. As I already said a mob is a stupid monster, it doesn't think, it just reacts. In a mob, no one in particular is guilty, all of those taking part of it are, however, guilty. It's afterwards, when everyone becomes themselves again that they see what had happened, they see their own crime. They now have to live with their conscience. Getting angry does not change the fact that it happened, getting angry does not alleviate the pain, only worsens it."

"But we are in a revolution precisely to prevent and revenge abuse."

"Indeed, you are. Sometimes there is a change just to go back to the way it was. We saw that happening many times in China."

Confused, Fidelio stopped arguing. He had heard the same sentence so often, by so many different people. He just looked at Woo Lam, perplexed.

Woo Lam smiled to him in a friendly way. "What I have just said does not mean to ignore what has happened, but to learn from it. Also, it does not mean indifference. We have responded by opening our homes to those in need, we keep our commerce open, we don't hide provisions to raise the price. That is also a way of fighting and, I would argue, a more efficient way. And, yes, I admit that there are occasions in which the use of violence becomes necessary, but even then, one needs to know when it's enough. Your leader, General Villa seems to understand it, but there are many others whose only wish is to take the place of those they are fighting against."

Still perplexed, Fidelio, however, couldn't argue anymore. He sensed that there was something powerful in Woo Lam words, something he still couldn't grasp. At the same time, the rage and desire for revenge he had felt was almost gone. He now knew that there is another way to respond to violence. A different, probably more powerful way. He smiled to Father Segura and Woo Lam. "Thank you," he said to both of them. He got up. "I must leave now," he added, looking at both of them. "Father, thank you, once again you have been a lightning rod to me. And to you, Mr. Po, you have taught me a lesson that I'll never forget and for that, there is no way I could thank you enough." Woo Lam looked at Fidelio, put his hands in front of his chest and bent his head a little, smiling in a friendly way. Fidelio responded in the same manner and walked away. Outside the children continued playing and laughing. Fidelio noticed now that some of the children were blond, some black, others Chinese and Mexican, all having a good, happy time.

Walking back towards the house in the alameda, Fidelio noticed men who had lost some part of their body. Some had lost one arm, others one or even two legs, many had lost their eyes. Although he had been taking care of the wounded, it seemed to him that he had seen them for the first time. He thought about all that he had seen dying. "Is all of this loss worth it?" he asked himself. Once at the house, without saying anything, he walked straight to where his few belongings were, took a bag and packed them.

"What are you doing?" Dr. Villarreal asked, noticing Fidelio's action.

"I'm leaving," Fidelio replied, in a calm tone of voice.

"Are you going to become a deserter? Why?"

Fidelio looked at him, thought for a moment. "If it becomes to that, yes, I will be a deserter," he finally answered.

Dr. Villarreal looked at him, frowned. "You are a good man. You must have a darn good reason for what you are about to do. I won't ask about it, but you will not become a deserter, I'll not allow it."

Defiant, Fidelio looked at him. "Are you going to stop me? Are you going to arrest me? That won't do it. I won't take part in this killing anymore."

"No, my friend, you won't be arrested and no one is going to stop you. What I'm going to do is to give you a letter saying that you have served and you leave with honor," Dr. Villarreal replied. "Now, tell me where are you going?"

"I'll go to Loma Sola. My sister Antonia lives there."

"In the middle of the desert. There are many minerals in there. Good luck, my friend. Maybe, someday, will meet again," Dr. Villarreal took a piece a paper, wrote on it, put a seal and handed it to Fidelio.

Fidelio took the note, put it in the bag and embraced Dr. Villarreal, "thank you for everything," he said and left. Dr. Villarreal just looked at him.

CHAPTER XVII

A hot sunny day in the middle of the desert. Few mesquite and huisache bushes, with no place to hide from the burning sun rays. Goats eating placidly gobernadora and huisache leaves and some tunas, the thorny fruits of cactus. Fidelio, under an improvised roof made using mesquite and huisache sticks kept together by threads of ixtle, sat over a rough ixtle carpet, he played the flute while a dog slept at his side. The heat didn't bother him, he enjoyed the peace and solitude of the place. Suddenly, a rattling noise called his attention and he jumped, looking to where the noise had originated. Scared, the goats ran –some of them jumped, away from where the noise had come; but one of them wasn't fast enough. With a lighting speed a rattlesnake had bitten her in her rear thigh. The goat baled, scared and in pain. The snake lifted its head getting ready to bite again but before it could do it, Fidelio grasped the serpent's head from behind. Feeling the strong grip, the trapped snake moved trying to free itself, its tail rattling, the dog barking at it. Holding the grip Fidelio turned the serpent's head toward him. He looked at the snake straight into its eyes. "Not my goats, I'm their shepherd," and then he released the grip and let the serpent go. The snake just slid away.

Fidelio turned his attention to the injured goat. "Relax my dear friend, I know you are in pain, but first let me see. Where is that bite? Ah, it's here, in your rear thigh." Fidelio, caressing the goat, kept talking to it with a soothing tone. The goat just lied down, silent and calm, like sleeping. Fidelio, kneeled at the goat's side, did a slight cut where the serpent had bitten, squeezed the wound allowing it to bleed almost freely. He looked into his ixtle bag, pulled a clay jar filled with a gray/green colored ointment. Fidelio took some of the ointment and rubbed it over the goat's wound. "There you are, my friend, the snake's poison won't harm you now." He said standing up, smiling. He looked toward the position of the sun. "It's getting late. We must be at the ranch before sunset. Go, get the goats and let's start walking home," he said, talking to the dog that immediately ran barking to the goats and moving them to a pack. The injured goat as soon as she heard the barking dog, got up and joined the rest of the herd.

As he guided the herd back to the ranch, Fidelio kept whistling. He felt happy and enjoyed the peaceful life of a shepherd. Some horsemen galloped close by. Seeing them, Fidelio thought about the time when he had been with the sanitary brigade of the Northern Division. He didn't miss it, he preferred the company of the goats, the wild animals of the desert and his dog, but the memory of his friends came back. Dr. Villarreal, Enrique, his classmates from Guanajuato, came to his mind. Three years had gone by since he had arrived at Loma Sola and he hoped that his friends had survived the battles they probably had fought. As he walked, a huisache larger than the others, got his attention, it was a late bloomer. Fidelio walked to it, made a cut in the trunk and using a clay jar collected the oozing gum; he also picked as many flowers as he could; he was planning to use both to prepare ointments that he knew will help healing the wounds of the animals under his care. "Thank you," he said caressing the trunk of the shrub, after he had collected enough material.

As he continued walking, he began thinking how, few months after he had left, the battles in Paredon and Saltillo, had happened near Loma Sola and how tempted he had been to rejoin Villa's Northern Division. But the memory of Candelaria had prevented him from doing so. He had learned about the capture of Zacatecas and how the usurper, Victoriano Huerta, had left the country, but how afterwards the revolution had become a battle between the different factions of the movement. He knew that Villa had been defeated by Obregon and how that defeat had made the once powerful General of the Northern Division, officially an outlaw, once again. Thinking about all of this, Fidelio became concerned about the person he respected the most, Father Segura. Although in Loma Sola there was peace, he had also heard about how churches were converted into barracks for the soldiers and some, into stables. Monasteries had been forcefully opened and the nuns forced out, many of them after being raped. Some priests had been killed, many expelled out of the country. "Is Father Segura safe?" he asked himself.

Once in the ranch, Fidelio, helped by his dog, guided the goats into the corral and once in there he proceeded to milk some of them. Doing so, he felt again cheerful, the unpleasant memories faded away. "Ah look at it! How beautiful is the milk you are giving us!" he said to one of the goats, as he squeezed her milk into the bucket. "Would you agree, Gus?" he asked the dog, that replied by barking and wiggling its tail. Fidelio started whistling, the dog seemed to follow the rhythm by wiggling its tail.

"Fidelio, you look happy, as a matter of fact, you are always happy, no matter what. I envy you for that," Antonia, Fidelio's elder sister, who by now was a childless widow, said as she walked into the corral.

"Good evening, Antonia," said Fidelio, getting up and greeting her. "Look how beautiful and healthy this milk is. With it you'll make delicious cheese," he added showing her the two buckets full of the white liquid.

"Yes, it is beautiful, we'll get wonderful cheese out of it and some of it will sweeten the coffee I have prepared for you," she said, smiling to him and taking the buckets from him. "Don Seve is coming to talk to you, it seems that at the San Rafael mine a rich deposit has been found; and it seems that they are going to need more miners to exploit it. His compadre, Don Antonio, the owner of the mine, came to talk to him and he asked for his help to get miners. Don Seve knows that we are from Guanajuato and that our father was a miner; so, he thinks you might be interested in the job. They pay well. Although, I know that Don Seve would miss you. I have heard him bragging to his friends about how well the goats respond to you and the way you keep them healthy and productive."

"Fidelio, I'd like to have a few words with you," Severiano Garza said, the owner of the ranch, as he approached them. A tall, slender man, about sixty-years-old, white hair and a large white moustache.

"Don Seve, glad to see you. I'm at your service," Fidelio said.

Severiano, "Don Seve" as he was called by all of those working for him, hesitated a moment, looking at Fidelio in a friendly way. "Fidelio, my son," he finally started. "My compadre, Don Antonio, whom you know well, has asked me to help him to find people willing to work at his mine. He pays well, as a matter of fact, much better than I'm paying you. Your sister has told me that both of you are from Guanajuato and your father was himself a miner. I thought that, perhaps, you would be interested in the job. Although, as you probably know, it's a dangerous job. I'll hate seeing you leave because I know I'll never find another shepherd like you, but it's up to you. Think about it and let me know."

"Thank you for thinking about me, Don Seve. You get me by surprise. Actually, I have never been a miner. But, precisely because our father died in a mine accident, I admit that I would be interested in becoming one. And, for that reason, I believe that I have a clear idea how dangerous mining is. On the other hand, I love my job, always surrounded by friends. Yes, I'll think about it and, of course, I'll let you know before anyone else."

"Today is Wednesday. Think about it until the weekend and let me know your decision," said Severiano. He looked at the goats and smiled. "Since you became their shepherd, we have not lost a single goat; as a matter of fact, the herd has increased as never before. Yes, I'll hate seeing you leave, but I promised my compadre that if anyone of my worker's choses to become a miner I'll respect it and you won't be the exception. Remember, however, that you must let me know no later than Sunday." He looked at the distance and frowned. "A dust storm is approaching, secure the goats and close your doors and windows as tight as you can," he smirked. "Even if we do that, as we all well know, the dust will find a way inside," he said, waived at them and walked to his own adobe house.

Fidelio and Antonia looked at the dark clouds approaching, secured the gate of the corral and ran into their shack, closing the doors and windows. The wind whistled and, as Severiano had said, the dust penetrated the shack under the door and through the narrow space between the windows. "This is the difference from Guanajuato; in here, when we see dark clouds we get sand instead of water," said Antonia, smiling to Fidelio who smiled back at her and sat on a bejuco chair.

The following Sunday, all the ranch employees joined together to pray the Rosary and share the Sunday meal, a custom that had been started by Fidelio since his arrival and later shared and encouraged by Don Severiano, who was a childless widower and enjoyed the company of those working for him.

"Don Seve, I have reached a decision," Fidelio told Severiano after the Rosary. Both of them enjoying a glass of lemonade enriched with chia seeds.

Severiano drank a little of his lemonade, looked at Fidelio, a bit concerned. "Well, what is it?"

"I'll go and work at the mine," said Fidelio, looking serious.

Severiano looked down for a second, he then turned his head and looked at Fidelio, straight into his eyes. He was almost as tall as Fidelio. "I respect your decision, although I must tell you that I don't approve it; not only because we'll miss you, not only me, but I believe, that you will also be missed by the herd and the animals in this desert." He paused for a moment keeping his brown eyes straight into Fidelio's eyes, he looked concerned.

"Although the conditions in a mine have improved, and I know that my compadre Antonio has invested in making it a bit safer, it's still a very dangerous job. There are many risks, collapse of the mine, fire, the heat, suffocation and even drowning in the water that leaks into many of the tunnels. Not only that, there is also the risk of illness. Miners live a short, often, a sad, almost breathless, life. Also, I must tell you that my compadre had just sold half of the interest in the mine to the English. I don't know if they'll have the same concern for the miners as my compadre does. Is there anything that would make you change your mind? Have you thought about all of this?"

Fidelio smiled to him, he could see that Severiano was seriously concerned and that his concern was not because he was leaving, he felt that it was almost the concern of a father for the safety and well-being of a son. "Don Seve, thank you for your concern. Yes, I have thought about all the risks that you just mentioned and it's precisely for that reason that I believe that I must go. It has not been an easy decision because I love being a shepherd and I love the open air. In here I have found the peace that I needed, but now it's time to change and face life. Thank you for your concern. It's been a gift from God finding a patron like you."

"God bless you my son," said Severiano, as he hugged Fidelio who hugged him back. "Be careful in that hole and don't take unnecessary risks," he added holding Fidelio by the shoulder.

It didn't take long for Fidelio to realize that mining was not only a harsh job, but even more risky and dangerous than he had expected. At his arrival, he was assigned to be an assistant to those in charge of blasting the rock with dynamite sticks. His job was to break the rock by drilling it, this allowed a dynamite stick to be inserted in order to blast the rock and obtain material and, at the same time, advance in the perforation of the tunnel.

"Fidelio, it seems that you hardly sleep. When you come out of the mine, you are always the last to leave, it seems that you want to be sure that everyone has come out safe; and in the morning, you are the first one to arrive," said She Ling Wong, a Chinese miner, in a broken Spanish, rubbing his hands to warm them up. Although it was summer time, the desert before sunrise is cold. At the distance the orange colors behind the mountains announced the proximity of the sunrise.

"I'm just learning this job; thus, I need to observe what you and the rest do," Fidelio said, smiling to She Ling. "I'll help you to prepare enough candles and slime, so by the time the rest arrive, they'll be ready."

As the miners arrived, they used the slime to hold the candles on their hats. When lighted, the candle provided a bit of illumination, enough to free their hands and allow them to perform their job.

"Who got these candles and slime ready!" Geronimo Saavedra, yelled kicking the candles and throwing some of the slime away.

Saavedra, a lean short man in his mid-thirties had been working at the mine for several years and had gained influence over other miners. As a matter of fact, before Fidelio's arrival, Saavedra had been elected the leader of the recently formed union. He looked around until he saw She Ling and Fidelio. "What? Do you think that by doing this you'll impress the English people? Let me tell you. They don't care about us, they don't even like Chinese or Mexicans. All that they care about is how to exploit us. They pretend to pay us well; in return we, like them, will pretend to work," Saavedra said, in a burlesque tone.

"That's the wrong attitude," Fidelio replied. "We must prove to them that we are as capable as anyone else to do the job; that we can do it even better than them. That's the way we can get them to listen to us and improve the conditions of the mine and by doing that, it will make everybody's life safer, and, at the same time, it will be easier for us to negotiate better salaries. Doing as you said, will only reinforce their idea that we are lazy and dumb."

By that time the rest of the miners had already arrived. Listening to their argument most of them approved what Fidelio had just said; but some looked at Fidelio with rancor and supported Saavedra.

"Too much talk!" yelled Robert Eager, an American engineer, who was the assistant to the English manager, and also in charge in processing the material once out of the mine. "It's getting late and many of you have not applied the slime and candles on your hats, do it quickly and get into the mine. Thank She Ling and Fidelio for having it ready for you."

Saavedra kept looking at Fidelio with rancor and spitted to the floor as he walked into the mine. "You'll feel sorry," Fidelio understood Saavedra's mumbling.

"Probably this is how Jonah felt when he entered the giant fish's mouth," thought Fidelio, as he entered the mine tunnel. The tunnel was dark, and the candle barely illuminated enough to allow them to see what was immediately ahead; the torches hanging on the side of the mine walls, didn't help much. The mine was hot and humid, and an acidic, stingy waft welcomed Fidelio and the miners. The rails in the floor helped them to guide themselves. Fidelio, like the rest of the miners, wore only a plain cotton shirt and pants; huaraches with no socks. He also carried his ixtle bag with clay jars filled with the ointments he had prepared to heal wounds, if he ever needed; he also had clean rags. Inside the mine, besides the heat and humidity, the floor was muddy. Fidelio got along well with those in his team; as a matter of fact, he was pleased to know that they were a real team, looking after each other. As they walked into the mine, they could hear horses whining.

"Rogaciano and the horses are waiting for us," said Fulgencio, Fidelio's team leader. "Fidelio, help him with the horses and get the train ready. Afterwards follow us. We'll go ahead and start the drilling and blasting. That way we will get enough material ready to fill the cars. Today, you'll help Rogaciano with the horses."

In the penumbra, Fidelio, mainly guided by the horses whining, the clear in their eyes and Rogaciano's candlelight walked toward them. "Rogaciano, how are you and our friends today?" Fidelio said as he got close enough.

"They had started to get nervous, waiting for their morning apples that you have got them used to," Rogaciano replied smiling to him.

"Here you are, my friends," Fidelio said to the horses as he pulled two apples from his ixtle bag and gave one to each of them. He whispered in their ears as he put the apple in their mouths.

"I have tamed horses my whole life. When I first attempted to get these two into the mine they resisted and were almost violent. But since you came and whispered in their ears, they even seem to be happy walking into this darkness that used to scare them so much. I don't know how do you do it, but I'm certainly glad that you are here; and as you can see, they are much happier," said Rogaciano, in a happy mood. A blast was heard, although a bit stronger than usual, used to it, they didn't pay attention and kept getting the horses and the train ready. However, this time the blast was followed by a noisy rumble and yells. Fidelio sensed that something had gone wrong. "Follow me," he said and walked as fast as he could into the tunnel where the sound had originated.

When Fidelio got to the end of the tunnel, he found several of his team mates sitting, others lying in the floor, injured. He took a quick look at them and was happy to see that their wounds were superficial, none of them had a serious injury. He was about to ask what had happened when he saw Fulgencio lying on the floor with a deep wound in his head, immobile. Fidelio almost jumped to his side, Fulgencio's eyes were wide open, his face almost entirely covered with blood and mud. "Fulgencio! Fulgencio!" yelled Fidelio. He didn't get an answer. Fidelio put his hand on his neck, feeling for pulsations, there was none. Crying in silence, Fidelio closed Fulgencio's eyes. Pulled a rag from his ixtle bag and gently, cleansed Fulgencio's face.

"After we had drilled, Fulgencio had some difficulty putting the dynamite stick and the line was also shorter. I tried to warn him, but he ignored me," said Jonas, a black miner. "That happens when one is a black man, nobody listens," he added.

"God has protected you Fidelio. If Fulgencio hasn't asked you to help Rogaciano with the horses, you would have been the one drilling and placing that stick," said Marcial, another of the miners in the team.

Other miners approached, Saavedra among them. When Saavedra saw Fidelio, made a gesture of disgust and spitted. "This is your fault!" he yelled. Fidelio just looked at him and decided to ignore him. He got up, lifted Fulgencio's head and shoulders, "Help me with his legs," he asked Jonas and between the two of them placed Fulgencio's body on one of the cars of the wagon that Rogaciano had brought. Fidelio got in front and guided the horses out of the mine, the rest followed him. "Our father who acts in heaven..." Fidelio started praying, the rest of the miners joined him, but not all of them. Saavedra and his followers remained silent.

Six months later. Fidelio, now a lean and muscular man thanks to the heavy work performed at the mine, walked into the mine's office. He had been called by Charles Peabody, Chief engineer and manager of the mine. A tall, slender, blond, blue eyed with thick glasses, English man.

"Fidelio, when you had just joined, because you had no experience in mining I was concerned about your own safety and also the safety of those working along with you," said Peabody, in Spanish, with a heavy

English accent, he smiled at Fidelio and nodded. "And yes, I was also concerned about productivity. But you surprised all of us and learned quickly, in particular, you have become an expert in both the use of explosives for the extraction of the material and its transport through the rails. Eager has told me how remarkable is the way that the horses and mules respond to your command and to our surprise, productivity has increased," his face now became serious, watching Fidelio's reaction to what he had just said.

Fidelio looked back at Peabody, through the thick glasses his blue eyes looked much larger. During the last six months, he had learned more about the dangers of the mine and had lead the miners in asking for safety measures, thus, although he sensed that Peabody was honest in what he had just said; and had a clear idea about the purpose of the meeting, he remained silent and waited for Peabody to continue.

"I'm also pleased that after that accident in which we lost Fulgencio, we haven't had any other accident," Peabody continued, now smiling in a friendly way to Fidelio. "Most of the other miners agree with your concerns for safety and, as you well know, most of your demands have been approved; including the payment to Fulgencio's wife and assisting her with their children; and yes, I'll agree that what you have asked for has helped to increase safety and we are glad for that. But, I must tell you that I have also received complaints about you. Some of your co-workers don't seem to like you and what you have done. In particular, those who have been with us longer than you. Probably by now you know who they are."

Fidelio frowned. Shortly after his arrival, he had noticed that some of the miners resented his interest in the job and his effort to improve it, and that their resentment had increased when most of the other miners became friends with him and supported his ideas. Although Fidelio preferred to ignore those who criticized him and just do his job, he felt a bit concerned. By the way Saavedra and some of his followers behaved, he sensed that the blast in which Fulgencio had lost his life had not been an accident. Someone had changed the dynamite sticks. He also sensed that they were already plotting something worse.

"Well, to make it short, I called to let you know that we are pleased with your job and your progress and we have decided to promote you to team's captain," Peabody continued. Although Fidelio had already thought about the probability of been offered the promotion, he still felt a bit surprised and frowned.

"Of course, your salary will also increase," Peabody quickly added noticing Fidelio's reaction.

"It's not the money," said Fidelio. "It's just that I'm a bit surprised. I know that there are others interested in the position. Some of them have been working in here longer than me."

"We are aware of that. Robert is who proposed you for the job, Don Antonio is pleased with it and I also agree. We hope that you'll accept it."

Fidelio knew the responsibility of the job, he didn't shy from it. As a matter of fact, he already had some ideas about how to improve it. He thought for a moment. "Yes, I accept," he said.

"Wonderful, Don Antonio will be pleased when I inform him about your decision," Peabody said, extending his hand. Fidelio took it and they shook hands to close the deal, no papers signed and Fidelio didn't ask for it, he knew that Peabody was a man of honor.

Fidelio started to walk out. "Fidelio, I almost forgot. There is something else I'd like to talk with you," Peabody said, before Fidelio reached the door. Fidelio stopped and turned around concerned.

"Yes, what is it?" he asked softly. Peabody coughed a little, hesitant. "This is something personal," he said. "I've been observing you and I noticed that although there is no priest or pastor around, you have started some sort of religious service on Sunday and most of the miners assist to it. Well I want to tell you that's what has given me the idea that perhaps you could help me."

"Yes, I'll be glad if I can help you in any way," Fidelio replied. He could sense that it was important to Peabody, something concerning someone close to him.

"My wife, who is in England taking care of our children - two boys and one girl," Peabody said. He hesitated again, a bit nervous, took the bottle of whiskey he had on his desk, poured himself a little in a glass and drank from it. "I'm sorry, would you like something?" he asked pointing to the bottle. Fidelio moved his head and hands in a negative way. "Well, my wife has become sick and needs rest. She is moving with her mother, but they won't be able to take care of the children. Two of them, one of the boys and the girl, will be coming here for a couple of months and I want to ask if in your free time, you could show them around here."

"Yes, of course," Fidelio said. "I like children."

"Good, in a couple of weeks they should be arriving in Monterrey. You'll pick them at the train station there. I'll arrange with Thomas, the chauffeur, to drive you there, that way you'll meet them and start getting along. Thank you for your help."

CHAPTER XVIII

A few weeks later, at sunrise, Thomas, the black driver, drove the car to pick Fidelio in front of the shack he occupied.

Although he had seen the automobile of the company, a large black Packard, Fidelio was hesitant to board it. The rumbling of the powerful twelve cylinders' motor made him nervous. He was afraid that it could explode any moment. After a moment of doubt, he finally boarded.

"Have you ever been in an automobile before, Fidelio?" asked Thomas in a broken Spanish with a heavy English accent. "I noticed that you seemed afraid to board it," he added with a broad smile, his white teeth shining. "There is nothing to be afraid in it. On the contrary, a machine like this will transform the world."

"No, this is the first time I'm in one of these. I have seen you driving around. To me this machine seems like something magical," Fidelio replied. "Where did you learn to drive it?" Although the lack of road, the loose sand and the many rocks around made the travel bumpy, Fidelio felt that it was smooth, with a lot more comfort and speed than traveling on a horse or a mule wagon as he had done before. He liked it even better than traveling by train. The leather seats impressed him, softer, much softer than being seated in a wagon. "This is like flying," he thought.

"I learned to drive in England," Thomas answered to his question. "But over there it was a Rolls-Royce. That's a real automobile," he added showing his smile. Fidelio found Thomas pleasant. Although they had never talked before, he felt like he was talking to an old friend.

"You speak exactly like Mr. Peabody. Are you also English?" Fidelio asked. He was curious, Peabody was blond and Thomas was really dark, he had never seen someone as dark as Thomas, even Jonas' skin color was lighter.

"I assume that I'm English, although I was born in Nigeria, which is in Africa. But since my father was taken to work in England by his master, I grew up in England and learned mechanics. For that reason, during the war I had the opportunity to drive one of the first tanks, an armored war-automobile. After the war, I was hired to work in a coal mine in Wales, there is where I met Mr. Peabody. He is a good man and boss. When he told me that he was coming here and offered me to come along, I almost jumped to accept. Mexico over there sounds like a mysterious and magical place, although dangerous. Let me tell you that I like it here, people treat me well, even with respect, and I even like the nickname almost everyone calls me, 'el negro Tomas,' I know it's friendly, not offensive here, and besides, that's the color of my skin," Thomas smiled, shrugging his shoulders; he seemed to be really happy. Fidelio admired the way Thomas drove, avoiding holes, thorns, rocks and animals. At the distance, several deer looked at them. However, this was the first time he had heard about a war somewhere else. Different to the one in which he had recently been involved. "Is the whole world in turmoil? Are dictators somewhere else?" he thought. "Tell me more about the war you were in. Why did you have to fight?"

"The war? I don't even know why or what was it that we were fighting for. It was a terrible and dirty war. At least I got to drive a tank, but the majority of the soldiers spent most of it in filthy holes. Epidemics were rampant. I believe that as many men died because of illness as they died because of bullets. What made it worse was that nobody seemed to know the reason or the purpose of all that killing, other than 'we are fighting for our country'," Thomas replied. He frowned for a moment and then smiled. "It's fun to drive in this terrain, reminds me when I was driving in Belgium during the war, but over there I drove a tank with no tires. Here, I have had several blown tires already," Thomas said maneuvering to avoid a coyote eating a rabbit. Almost immediately there was an explosion and Thomas had a hard time preventing the automobile to roll over; he laughed. "There you have it. It seems that I called for a blown tire. You'll need to help me to change it."

One of the front tires had been punctured by a sharp piece of an animal carcass. "Darn, it's going to be difficult to change it. The terrain is too sandy and loose," said Thomas, after he had looked at the flat tire sunk in loose sand. Upset he kicked the sand. As he did, he uncovered a small snake. Scared, Thomas jumped.

"That's a harmless snake," Fidelio said, laughing. "What is wrong with the tire?"

"I need to change it, but to be able to do it, the car needs to be lifted. The terrain is so loose that it doesn't allow the jack to hold firm and lift the car," Thomas explained kicking once again the sand. At the distance, a squirrel seemed to enjoy the scene.

"I believe that I can help you with that," Fidelio said. He looked around and collected a bunch of huisache sticks, cut several branches of a small cactus, using his knife, he stripped one of the cactus branch into cords that he then used to tie the huisache sticks and the cactus branches together, creating a firm carpet. "Where is that you'll need to place the jack?" he asked Thomas.

"Right in here," said Thomas pointing to a place near the middle of the automobile. Fidelio wiped away some of the sand and placed the carpet under the car. "Let's see if this is firm enough for the jack," he said to Thomas who put the jack over the carpet. It held firm enough to lift the car; thus, Thomas could unscrew the tire just to find out that he didn't have enough space to remove it.

"Wait a little," Fidelio said, when he realized what the problem was. He went to the front of the car and lifted it one extra inch. "Is that enough?"

"Yes, it is," said Thomas, who quickly removed the flat tire and replaced it with a new one. "You can let it go now," he said, as he placed the screws.

"Man, you are not only resourceful, but you are also strong," Thomas said, once they were back on their way to Monterrey. Fidelio didn't reply, he just admired how skillfully Thomas handled the car.

"Your question about the war has kept me thinking about it," Thomas said, after they had drove in silence for a while. "It was a bloody war. Thousands of men died and I assume that many lost everything they had. We were told that we were fighting for our country, for our pride. But, in the end, all the countries that took part in it were devastated; kingdoms and empires were blown away. Well, maybe, it's a god thing that England, my country, is now the richest and most powerful country in the world. I assume that's good. But, was it worth the thousands of young men who died and the many more who ended up disabled? I don't know and maybe I shouldn't care." He shrugged his shoulders again.

Fidelio looked at him. "Thousands have died and many more have become disabled," he thought. Those words brought to his memory the battles in which he had participated not long ago. "Was it worth it?" he asked himself in silence. "I hope so," he answered himself.

"If you don't have any more questions, let's talk about something more pleasant," Thomas said, cheerfully, after a moment of silence. "When you get to meet Mr. Peabody's children, you'll like them. But let me warn you, they are energetic and don't shy away from trouble."

"That's fine with me. I like children. I'll love to play with them," Fidelio replied.

"Chances are they'll play you," Thomas said, laughing. "There is the Saltillo-Monterrey trail. At least it resembles something like a road, we'll go a bit faster once we reach it. A lot of curves, but if we don't get another flat tire, we'll make it on time to wait for the children at the train station."

They were getting close to the mountains, the landscape had already changed, Fidelio noticed that the type of cactus in here were larger and with a different shape; the large number and shape of these cactus seemed to him like an entire army extending their arms to the sky, praising God.

Once they reached Monterrey, Fidelio noticed that although it had some similarities to Torreon and Chihuahua, the streets here were narrower and covered with cobblestone. There were some other differences, the streets were clean and since the revolution had almost spared it, all the buildings were intact. Like in Chihuahua and Morelia, the government buildings were impressive and so was the Cathedral. Fidelio also noticed a large number of chimneys on top of the buildings were much larger than he had seen before; he could feel the energy of the town. Although at the time Monterrey was still a small city, Fidelio had the impression that soon it would become one of the most important towns in the country. They traveled along the Santa Catarina River that, since they were in the dry season, was merely a stream of water. Looking up, Fidelio admired the saddle mountain, the city's symbol. "It's majestic," he thought. They finally reached the train station and parked in front of it.

Fidelio and Thomas joined the people already waiting for the arrival of the train. "I hope it's on time," someone close to them said. "That doesn't happen often," another person replied in a sarcastic tone. "Well, believe it or not, here it is, just on time," another one said, laughing.

Rumbling, blowing dark smoke, whistling, almost like bragging, the train arrived at the terminal. "It rains and it's foggy in London at this time of the year, but here it is hot and humid. I wonder how the children would like it here with this type of weather," Thomas said, as he wiped the sweat from his forehead. "There they are!" he added, waiving his hand.

Fidelio who was also feeling uncomfortable with the heat and had his white cotton shirt dampened by profuse sweating almost jumped, surprised when he realized that Peabody's children were no children but those who left the Pullman car and were now almost running toward them, smiling to Thomas. They were two young people, about his own age. A young boy and a still girlish young woman, both red haired, both handsome; their clothes also a bit dampened by sweat.

"Thomas, how nice to see you. You look well, it seems that Mexico is agreeable with you. How is father?" said the young man, smiling to Thomas and extending his hand to him.

"Yes, indeed, you look well Thomas," said the girl also smiling to Thomas and looking to Fidelio, who perceived a special shine in her bright blue eyes that sent a current though his spine. He liked her red hair arranged in a ponytail.

"It's nice to see that you both are finally here. Your father is well and anxiously waiting for you. This is my friend Fidelio, your father asked him to help us to look after both of you, while you are here," Thomas said, shaking hands with the young man and pointing to Fidelio.

"Please to meet you Fidelio, I'm Preston," said the boy, in a broken Spanish extending his hand to Fidelio who reciprocated. As they shook hands, Fidelio felt that Preston was not only athletic and energetic, a bit rebellious but also, like his father, honest and trustworthy. "This is my sister, Victoria," Preston added.

"Hola Fidelio, call me Vicky," she said speaking also in Spanish. Her full face brightened with her otherwise mischievous smile. Looking at her, Fidelio, once again, felt a spark running down his spine that caused goosebumps on his skin. He felt embarrassed and hoped that no one would notice.

"You got plenty of luggage, fortunately the Packard has a large trunk, I believe it will accommodate all of it," Thomas said, looking at the luggage carried by a porter. "The car is this way," he added walking towards where they had parked the automobile.

Once they were on their way back, Preston and Vicky looked at the landscape. "It all looks strange and mysterious, so different from England and Wales," said Preston. "I had never seen these type of plants, mountains all rock, no trees on them; this is going to be interesting."

"But it's so hot," said Vicky, wiping her forehead with a silk handkerchief. "Are there horses? I would love to explore this land, but I would need someone to guide me."

"Fidelio knows this territory well, he could guide you," said Thomas.

"Well, I'm looking forward," she said, looking at Fidelio.

The car bumped and Thomas had to maneuver to keep control and avoid hitting a couple of wild horses that jumped in front of the car and ran away. Preston smiled admiring Thomas' ability while Vicky cheered and turned to look at the horses. "Wild horses! I love it. Fidelio, you'll have to take me where there are herds of them," she said jumping on the seat, happy. Fidelio hearing her, smiled. She was so different to Candelaria and Aurora, but precisely that difference made her attractive. That made him a little nervous. "Yes, we have plenty of wild horses around us," he said to her.

"We are almost there," said Thomas, smiling. "I'm glad that you have enjoyed the ride. I'm sure your father will be happy to see both of you."

"And we'll be happy to see him," Vicky said, cheerful. Her red hair sparkled when hit by the sun. Fidelio looked at her. "It seems that angels are also involved in fire," he thought.

The night was falling when Thomas parked in front of Peabody's home. It was a large adobe building surrounded by palm and huisache trees. The house was fresh thanks to the large windows, the north/south orientation of the building to avoid the sun from hitting directly, and the shadows provided by the trees surrounding it. Peabody, who apparently had heard the motor of the car approaching waited for them in front of the house.

As soon as Thomas parked the car, Vicky jumped out and ran to hug her father. Preston followed and also hugged him.

"Did you have any problem?" Peabody asked Thomas in English.

"None," Thomas replied.

"Good," he embraced both of his children, "I'm glad you are here. You'll find this place different to all you have known until now, but, I know you'll come to like it and enjoy it, as I have. Thomas will drive you wherever you want to go," he added before turning to look at Fidelio. "Fidelio, it seems that some members of the union are trying to cause trouble. They have complained about you getting the position of the team's captain, bypassing some who started here before you did. We know we have made the right choice, but it will be a good idea for you to concentrate on the job at the mines." Peabody said to Fidelio, speaking in Spanish.

"But father," said Vicky. "He promised me to show me where the wild horses are."

"Well, maybe he could do it in a weekend," Peabody replied. "What would you say, Fidelio?"

"Yes, I'll be happy to guide her; as for what it concerns to the job at the mine, I'll just concentrate on it. I don't want to be the reason for trouble. If there is someone else who wants the job, he may have it and I'll obey him," Fidelio replied. "Is there anything else I can help you with, now?"

"No, thank you. As I said the job is yours, we know you are the right one. Go home and rest," Peabody answered.

"We'll be seeing you Fidelio, have a good night," Preston said, waving at him.

"Remember you'll have to take me to see the herd of wild horses," Vicky said, also waving at Fidelio.

Thomas smiled, "remember that you have a friend to help whenever you need me, just call and I'll be there."

"Thank you, I'll remember it," Fidelio replied.

Fidelio left and walked toward the adobe shacks the company provided for the miners. Jonas, Rogaciano, Marcial and others had an animated conversation in front of the shack occupied by Fidelio.

"Fidelio, we need to talk," Rogaciano told Fidelio, as soon as he arrived. "Saavedra has been trying to make you responsible for the accident that killed Fulgencio. He has been talking in getting the union to oppose your promotion to the team's captain. Everyone knows that what he says about the accident is not true, but he hates you," his voice firm, energetic. "We have come not only to warn you, but to let you know that we support you. Everyone knows that since your arrival safety has improved, production has increased and thanks to that our salaries raised; besides, you have made us proud of our work. That's why he and his followers hate you so much. Before your arrival, they had control over us, they knew how to scare us. But since your arrival we have learned that we can fight back. The blast that killed Fulgencio was an attempt to kill you and to spread fear among us. We know that."

"I left the place where I was born because I didn't like how I and my people were treated; as if we are trash. I did several jobs before coming to the mine." Jonas intervened. "Don Antonio, who is a nice man, offered me this job. He has treated us well, but from the beginning, I didn't like the way Saavedra and his friends took advantage of his noble character. When the English took over, they imposed discipline. Saavedra and the others have continued acting the same way and that has caused problems with the administration. Then you arrived and started talking about pride in the job and, we also noticed how you got the company to improve safety. We have become conscious about our right; Saavedra and his friends have lost power. We no longer listen to their frequent complaints about the company and their motto: "If they pretend to pay us, we'll pretend to work." But he is still the leader of the local branch of the union. You must be careful, they might try something against you; we'll cover your back from now on." He tightened his fist to put emphasis on his words.

"They are spreading rumors about your friendly relationship with Eager and Peabody; that you have accepted bribes, and, that you are their puppet, that's why you have been promoted to the team's captain. We don't believe them. We are now aware that they have pocketed the union's money; we realize now that when they threatened strike they forced the administration to bribe them. They are corrupt and expect us to be submissive. Well, that's no more." Intervened Marcial, also with a firm tone of voice.

Fidelio listened to them. "The legality of unions is one of the reasons we fought the revolution," he said. "As long as the unions are used to benefit and improve the quality of life of the workers, to be part of the union is good. We must not fight the union. We must work to keep it within its purpose. The union must benefit all, not only those who get to the top of it."

Jonas looked at him, his black eyes showed how intense were his feelings. "Yes, you are right, this is about us, all of us. I can see how if we maintain a common purpose, all of us, we'll benefit. But Saavedra and his friends are only looking how to use us for their benefit. I ran away from masters who abused me, but now, here, those who are supposed to be on our side have become the new masters. We have allowed it until now, we'll not allow it any longer. Being a union's member is a good thing, as long as we work as such, otherwise, we've just got different masters."

Fidelio looked at him and looking at his eyes he knew that Jonas was a natural leader, a leader for just causes. He was glad that all of them were on the same side.

"Thank you, friends. For the time being we must continue working the same, doing our best. The company is not our enemy; if they benefit, we'll also benefit. Yes, we must fight for what is fair. As for Saavedra and his friends, I'll wait for them to bring the charges against me at the next union meeting. Now, we all need to rest. Thank you for your friendship. I'll meet you tomorrow at the mine. For now, let's pray for guidance," he said holding hands with them.

The following morning before dawn Fidelio, as it had become routine, helped She Ling to get the slime and candles ready. As they approached, the miners applied the slime and candles to their hats, happy to find it ready for them. When Saavedra arrived, and looked to the slime and candles ready, frowned, spitted in disgust but still, like the rest, applied the slime and held the candle in his hat. He turned and looked at Fidelio and She Ling. "You two are traitors to the union. You and those who are like you are enemies of the union and all, will pay for it," he yelled, pointing to Fidelio and She Ling who just looked at him, but didn't reply. Fidelio walked into the mine along with the members of his team. The day went without trouble, they were able to blast enough to widen the tunnel following the main vein and in the process, they found a new, apparently richer, vein. In the evening, as they walked out of the mine, Fidelio noticed Robert Eager standing up, just out of the mouth of the tunnel. He seemed concerned. Looking at him, Fidelio sensed that he had bad news.

"There was an accident," said Eager. "The load of one of the upcoming cars somehow fell on She Ling," nervous, he moved around, rubbed his hands, looking down. "He is now at the infirmary. We are seriously worried, both of She Ling's legs have open fractures." Saavedra and some of his friends grimaced and looked at each other. Fidelio recognized a newcomer, standing at Saavedra's side. But, for the time being, his main concern was She Ling's health.

"Get clean, boiled water, huisache sticks, branches of cactus and threads of ixtle," he said to those close to him. "Come and help me," he said to Jonas as he walked toward the infirmary followed by Jonas and most of the miners. Once in the infirmary, they found She Ling lying on a bed all bruised with bone protruding in the middle of both legs, obviously in pain, jaws tight, making an effort not to move. Petra, his Mexican wife, seated at his side, holding his hand mumbled a prayer, tears in her eyes.

"Petra, please go and get the clean boiled water that I already asked for, get as much as you can. Also, you know where I keep the bee honey and tree oil, please get it for me.

Meanwhile, Jonas will help me. With God's help, we'll find a way to assist She Ling," Fidelio said to her, as soon as he walked in; he then turned to all the miners who were trying to see what was happening, "please, wait outside," he told them. After the room was clear, Fidelio turned his attention to She Ling. "Hello, my good friend. Jonas, you and I are a team now. Is that agreeable with you?" Fidelio said, in a soothing voice. She Ling nodded, trying to smile.

"Good, it has been a hot day, isn't it? I bet you still feel the heat. Remember? In days like these we used to go to the waterfall in Santiago. How much we enjoyed the cold water, so refreshing. Now, just close your eyes and imagine a nice cold bath at the waterfall in Santiago. You have been there many times, imagine it, how nice, and how cold the water is. Cold water, cold water numbing your whole body." As Fidelio continued talking in a soothing, rhythmic tone, She Ling closed his eyes and showed a pleasant, relaxed smile.

As Fidelio continued talking, he signaled Jonas to help him to uncover She Ling's legs. By that time, Petra had already delivered what Fidelio had asked for, and had left to wait outside. Fidelio, helped by Jonas, used the water to wash thoroughly the open wounds in the legs. His voice was so soothing that even Jonas eyes started to close, Fidelio slapped him gently on the face and signaled him to stay alert. After the wounds were clean, Fidelio poured honey bee that he had previously mixed with other healing herbs. After that, he signaled Jonas to hold She Ling by the hip and, always talking in a soothing, melodious tone, he pulled the legs from the feet until the fractures were aligned. She Ling barely frowned at the pull. Fidelio then wrapped the wounds and using the huisache sticks, the agave branches, all threaded with the ixtle cords, he created a combination of cast and lever that not only immobilized She Ling's legs but, at the same time, maintained the fractured bones aligned. "Now rest, sleep peacefully, from now on every time I sang the word 'bu-tter-fly', you'll go to sleep and relax as you are now. Rest, rest, rest." "Bu-tter-fly," Fidelio sang again, "you'll respond only to my voice, no one else, only to my voice."

Jonas, who had assisted Fidelio, looked at him with an expression of astonishment and disbelief. "I've seen the work of other healers, but none like you. God must be with you," he said.

It was late in the night when Fidelio and Jonas walked out of the infirmary. There was a full moon and a pleasant breeze freshened the night. Petra waited for them. "How is he?" she asked.

"He'll do well," Fidelio replied, extending his arm and touching her shoulder gently. Most of the miners had also waited and looked to Fidelio in a friendly manner, but he sensed a negative vibration; looking around he saw how Saavedra and his followers looked at him with rancor. Someone, whispered something to Saavedra who then whispered something to one of his friends. Fidelio now recognized the man who whispered to Saavedra, it was the same one who had tempted him in the Juarez jail, the same one that had accompanied Fierro in Chihuahua, although Fidelio still found him attractive by now he identified the presence of his real enemy.

At the distance a mountain wolf howled.

Peabody, accompanied by his son and Eager walked in. "Bobby has told me about the accident. We had almost one full year without accidents. In this particular case, it seems that there was a human error involved. We'll look at it and, if necessary, we'll do whatever is needed to prevent something like this from ever happening again. If there is responsibility, we'll also look at it," Peabody said in a loud voice, talking to all; he then turned to Fidelio and smiled at him. "We have got a Doctor from Monterrey to come and examine She Ling. Good job, Fidelio," he added.

The brilliant full moon that had illuminated the night until then was covered by clouds, darkness ensued. "Fidelio is a traitor, an enemy of the union, out with him!" one of Saavedra's companions yelled. At the distance, a mountain wolf howled.

CHAPTER XIX

For the next couple of weeks, they had a difficult time at the mine. The pumping system failed and as a result, the water level raised making it not only difficult but more dangerous than usual for the miners. The level of water raised to above their knees and the miners, besides being forced to work on a muddy and slippery ground, they had also to be concerned with the leeches and rats; and on top of that, the excess humidity made it difficult for them to keep the candles in their hats lighted. It was hot inside of the mine and because of the excess of flowing water, it was difficult to deliver fresh water to the miners. In spite of all the difficulties, Fidelio and his team successfully perforated the rock and safely placed the dynamite sticks, blasted, and sent out several loaded cars of the mineral. Every evening, after the ten hours' shift, once they got out of the mine tunnel, they had to wash their legs with fresh water. Many of them had a hard time removing the leeches.

Rogaciano approached Fidelio while they walked out of the mine after a heavy day of work. "Fidelio, do you have a moment? We need to talk," he said.

Fidelio stopped. "Yes, of course. What is it?" he replied.

"Saavedra and his new counselor have been spreading lies about you. They blame you for Fulgencio's accident and also accuse you of helping the administration by increasing productivity. They have done nothing about the failure of the water pumps. Most of us know that he and his followers care only about filling their pockets. We are also aware that it has been you, Jonas and She Ling who have spoken and cared about our safety. We are also aware that thanks to the increased productivity, our salaries have been raised. But, that new Saavedra's counselor, with his sweet talk has created doubts among some of the miners. The majority of us, however, remain on your side. But, you must be prepared," said Rogaciano.

"I'm not too preoccupied about how they are going to attack me. At the moment, I'm more concerned about the malfunction of the water pumps. That is right now the main problem, too many are falling sick because of it, and it needs to be fixed as soon as possible. I know Jonas has already talked with the administration about it; we need to show support for him. As far as that new Saavedra's counselor, I know he is the real enemy. Somehow when the time comes, I'll be ready for him." Fidelio replied.

"The blast that killed Fulgencio was not an accident, neither was what happened to She Ling. Knowing that you were in charge of drilling and placing the dynamite stick, the sticks were replaced to cause a more powerful blast. It was meant to kill you. What happened to She Ling also was not an accident. That blond man tried to bribe She Ling by offering him the position of treasurer in the union, however when it became clear that She Ling is not corrupt, as they are, they decided to eliminate him. Simulating accidents, it's one of the many ways they have used to keep control of the union."

"Yes, you are right on that. I'm also aware of their methods. You are also right when you say that a new leader is necessary. He should be someone who cares about all. What do you and the rest think about Jonas?"

"He is a good man. But, we were thinking of you."

"Thank you, but I know I'm not the right one for that position. Jonas is capable and strong. He is honest and cares for all and yes, you are right, even when he doesn't have to get involved, he does when he believes that it's a just cause. I have no doubt that he is the best man for the job."

"I believe you are right. I'll talk to the rest. Yes, Jonas has been here for more than two years and during all this time he has proven to be not only friendly, but has shown that he cares about all that happens in here. He is always ready to help and offers his assistance. Also, he knows well the mining job and has proven to be an honest man. In the beginning, there were a few that had concern about him because his skin is darker and he came from up-north, but we all come from so many different places and most of us here also have dark skin. No, that won't be a problem. We know him well. Yes, I agree with you, he'll be a good candidate," Rogaciano stopped, frowned, looking in front of him. "There comes Peabody and Eager. The doctor who came from Monterrey is with them," he added, pointing to the three approaching men.

"Fidelio, we are looking for you," said Peabody, in his broken Spanish. "This is Dr. Gonzalez, from Monterrey," he smiled looking proudly to Fidelio. "As soon as he examined She Ling, he seemed surprised and wanted to know who had aligned the fractures and applied that cast. When we told him that you are the one who fixed She Ling's fractures, he immediately asked to meet with you and talk about the care given to She Ling."

Fidelio nodded respectfully to Dr. Gonzalez. "I'm at your service," he said.

Dr. Gonzalez, a middle aged, slender and short, almost bold man with friendly brown eyes, his white linen suit stained with sweat, smiled to Fidelio. "So, you are the one who applied that cast. It's a clever idea. Where did you learn to do it? I had never seen anything like that. It's obvious that it's improvised and that you used what nature provides. That's something all of us should learn to do. Could you teach me?" he said, as he wiped the sweat from his forehead and face.

As usual when someone praised him, Fidelio felt a bit confused and embarrassed. "I learned by observing nature and yes, I believe I could show you how to do it." Once again, he preferred not to mention that an inner voice guided him in everything related to healing. Although this time he knew that the man in front of him would be open to it.

"When I was notified about the accident and asked to come, I came expecting to find a man with multiple exposed fractures; and I was almost certain that, by the time I arrived, the wounds would be seriously infected; and we would have to transport the poor man to Monterrey and forced to amputate his limbs in order to save his life," Dr. Gonzalez said, looking at Fidelio with admiration. "But, to my pleasant surprise, the fractures are no longer exposed, the wounds are clean and healing well. It seems that he'll recover and walk again. There is no need to transport him anywhere. You did an admirable job and he should just continue with the care you are giving him." He paused and turned to Peabody. "You are lucky to have this young man with you. You know, at his age I was studying about fractures at medical school and even today I don't know of anyone who could have done as good a job as this young man has done without any formal training."

"Yes, we are well aware of Fidelio's value," Peabody replied.

"Well, instead of talking about our patient, we should go and look at him," Dr. Gonzalez said to Fidelio.

"Yes, of course. Just give me a minute to talk to my friend, Rogaciano. He is also She Ling's friend and like everyone else here, he is also interested in the outcome of all of this," said Fidelio touching Rogaciano's shoulder. "We'll continue our conversation later." He said to Rogaciano, who nodded showing respect for those present and walked toward his shack, while Fidelio and Dr. Gonzalez walked to the infirmary; Peabody and Eager walked toward the failing pumps.

"Fidelio, let's talk a bit," Dr. Gonzalez told Fidelio after they had examined She Ling and were out of the infirmary. "What I told you before is true, that's how I honestly feel. However, I also feel compelled to warn you. That strange and admirable natural ability that you have," he frowned and paused for a moment, jaws tight. "For many of my colleagues, would be a matter of concern and for most of them, it will cause jealousy and envy. Once it's known that you have this ability, instead of learning from you, they'll attack you. Having said that, I encourage you to continue doing what you are doing. As it is right now, you have much more to offer to those who are ill than we, supposedly learned men, can. I'm aware that for us there is still a lot more to learn, in particular to learn from nature. There is so much that we don't know. But it's hard for most of us to accept that. What has impressed me the most is that you don't brag about it, you just use it.

You even seem to be humbled by it. That's the sign of an honest man." He smiled and looked at Fidelio directly in the eyes.

Fidelio knew that he was sincere, so he just smiled back at him, grateful for his comment.

"Well, I'm leaving now. I can see that there is no need for me to come back. Just keep doing what you have been doing until now. You have kept those wounds clean and that's part of the key to your success. I have the feeling that I'll hear a lot more about you. Good bye and take care not only of those in need but, yourself also," Dr. Gonzalez said, extending his hand.

"Thank you," Fidelio said, as he took Dr. Gonzalez's hand.

A car's horn was heard and the company's Packard, driven by Thomas, approached.

Dr. Gonzalez boarded in the back seat, waved to Fidelio and tapped on Thomas' shoulder, who smiled and waved to Fidelio before driving away.

Fidelio stood there, looking down, pensive. Concerned about what Dr. Gonzalez had just told him. For some time, he had also wandered about this ability given to him. "What was the purpose of it? Why was it given to him?" Although he felt proud of it, somehow, he was also afraid of it. He remembered the river in Juarez, he remembered what had been offered to him and the idea of a life of wealth, luxury and carnal pleasure still tempted him.

"Fidelio, hey Fidelio, you are just the one I'm looking for," a melodious feminine voice with an English accent took him away from his thoughts.

Fidelio turned and saw Vicky approaching. Looking at her white face surrounded by her bright red hair, her smile showing her pearly teeth, Fidelio found her attractive, very attractive, so attractive that he felt pressure raising in his underwear; he felt a little embarrassed. He hoped that she wouldn't notice the bulk in between his legs.

"You promised to take me where the wild horses are," she said still smiling at him. Her wet, heart shaped lips, seemed like a fountain of fresh, delicious water. Fidelio had to make an effort to prevent himself from taking her in his arms and satiate his thirst.

"Yes, I haven't forgotten. I'll take you this Sunday," he said, still feeling nervous.

"Good, it's a beautiful evening, let's walk along," she said placing herself on his side and taking his arm.

"Fidelio! Fidelio! Come quickly! It's Jonas. He has been stabbed!" yelled Rogaciano, as he approached running.

"Oh, my God!" Vicky yelled in English, taking away her arm from Fidelio. "Go Fidelio, you are needed in there," she added, in Spanish, this time.

Fidelio followed Rogaciano to the group of shacks that housed the miners and their families. The night was clear, there was a full, bright moon in the sky. They found Jonas lying in front of his shack, his head resting on the lap of his Mexican wife, who caressed him tenderly, sobbing quietly. Jonas had his eyes closed, the dress of his wife soaked in blood.

"Jonas, what happened?" asked Fidelio, as he kneeled in front of Jonas.

Jonas opened his eyes and smiled to Fidelio. "I'm done, my friend," he said. "I ran away from where I was born trying to find peace. Once I got here I found a wonderful woman; thanks to her I have found peace for my soul. However, I have also found that hatred and exploitation of men by men happens everywhere; and what is worse, exploitation by someone who claims to represent us, but in reality, he's only looking after himself. Take care my friend, there are some who hate you, those men really despise you and they'll do anything to harm you and those who support your ideas and goals."

"Do you know who did this?" Fidelio asked.

"This evening, Saavedra's men came and asked to talk with me. They seemed to be friendly, and so I agreed. They tried to convince me to join them. They offered money and a position in the union. I refused their offer and while I was explaining my reasons, one of them caught me by surprise and stabbed me in the back. But the real enemy is Saavedra's new counselor, Saravia is his name. He is the one who has been promoting hate since his arrival. Some time ago, he tried to convince me to join them. When I made my position clear, he smiled, with that cruel and cynical smile of him. "You'll be sorry," he said. Well, he got that wrong, I'm not sorry. Jonas laughed quietly.

Fidelio felt hate, hate not only against Saavedra who was only an instrument. His hate was against the evil one, who somehow appeared to be following him. He was the real enemy. He looked at Jonas and was impressed by how calm he was. "Let me look at your wounds," said Fidelio to Jonas who smiled at him. "Not even you could do something about this," said Jonas, as he turned to show his back to Fidelio.

Jonas had been stabbed several times in his back. All deep, he was bleeding profusely. Fidelio realized that indeed, there was nothing he could do to prevent the end that would occur soon. He looked up. Vultures were already circling. A deep sensation of impotence, rage, profound rage invaded him. He just tightened his jaws and looked up.

"Fidelio, the Lord is fair and just. Don't blame him. I know I'm dying, but there is a purpose for my death. Use it, use it my friend," Jonas, who had turned and was again resting on his wife's lap, said. Then he looked up. "Look at those beautiful birds, they'll guide my soul to Him, my Lord and my Master," he added and closed his eyes, smiling. Seeing that his wife bent over him and kissed him, sobbing quietly. Fidelio remained kneeling, also sobbing quietly; he felt a profound sadness. What was the purpose of his ability to heal? If he couldn't use it to benefit good men like Jonas? "Hail Mary, full of grace, the Lord is with thee…" Maria Consuelo, Jonas' wife, started praying as she got up, extended her hand and touched Fidelio's shoulder. The rest of the women followed Maria Consuelo's lead and kept praying. In silence some men approached, lifted Jonas body and took him inside his shack, someone had already cleansed the table where the men put the body; Maria Consuelo, as she kept praying the rosary, pulled Jonas best clothes from a drawer and, helped by other women, changed his clothes and combed him. Other women prepared coffee. "That's what happens to those traitors to the union," someone yelled at the distance. Some of the miners turned, upset, Rogaciano signaled them to remain calm.

The women inside the shack kept on praying the Rosary while the men gathered outside, Fidelio joined them. Although the majority of the miners were there, it was obvious that there were some who either approved what had happened or were too scared to join them. "Those who are not here are a bunch of cowards," said one of the men, angrily, he sipped from his cup of coffee. "We must crush them, destroy them," he added.

"My death has a purpose, use it, use it my friend. Those were Jonas last words," Fidelio said to them. "Hate towards our enemies won't help. We must understand Jonas' advice and use this tragedy to honor him. Yes, we must defeat our enemy. And our enemy is the evil one. He is our real enemy." At the distance an owl screeched, Fidelio smiled after hearing that sound. "God will guide us when the moment comes," he added.

"Since your arrival, you have guided us mainly by example. You don't talk too much, but have shown the way. I really don't understand what you mean by what you just said, but I trust you and follow you," said Rogaciano. A murmur of approval was heard; the owl screeched again. The full moon shined on them; they looked at each other surprised, suddenly, they all felt at peace, calm, resolute.

"The union meeting is in two days, we must prepare for it," said one of the miners.

"Yes, we will," Fidelio said. "But for the moment, let's concentrate in honoring Jonas and pray for the peace of his soul. Real men pray the Rosary, let us pray," he added holding the hands of those close to him, they all did the same. A human chain was formed. "Our father who acts in heaven..." Fidelio started praying, the rest of the men joined him. The owl called again, this time it was a smooth, gentle call.

They prayed the whole night, everyone stayed. Jonas was buried the following day with the presence of Peabody, accompanied by Preston and Vicky, Eager was also present. Saavedra, Saravia and their friends didn't join the procession, but looked from the distance. Clouds covered the sky protecting them from the sun. After Jonas had been buried, Peabody addressed those present.

"Jonas was a good and honest man; an excellent miner and we also, want to honor his memory. First, let me tell you that we understand your concerns regarding the safety of the mine and how the failure of the pumping system makes it a lot more dangerous for all of you. Almost immediately that the problem started, Jonas came to talk to

Robert and myself and he kept insisting on it, almost every day. We know that he had no official position to talk in your name, but he cared, so he did talk for all of you. It's for that reason that the mine will stay closed until the problem is fixed. Your salaries will continue to be paid as usual." A murmur of approval was heard, the miners looked at each other, happy with the news. "Also, I know that you are concerned about Jonas' wife and children," Peabody continued. "I have talked to Don Antonio and the other owners of the company. They have agreed to provide Maria del Consuelo, enough so she can support their children and as long as they obtain good grades, a scholarship for their education has also been approved," the miners applauded approvingly. "We want to show that we appreciate what you do and I hope our relationship will continue as it is until now," Peabody ended.

"Even after death, Jonas continues taking care of us," said Rogaciano.

"We also must honor him," replied Marcial.

"Yes, he has shown us the path, we'll honor his memory at the meeting," said Rogaciano.

CHAPTER XX

A hot and dry morning, no clouds in the sky, the sun showed all its splendor and power. Slowly, the miners gathered in the place that had been improvised for the union meetings. A simple roof made using palm leaves had been placed to protect them from the fiery sun rays, the shadow provided and a gentle breeze, made the heat tolerable. Rough wood benches had been placed for the miners to sit and in front, a table with few chairs for the leaders of the reunion; on top and a little behind the table, facing the benches, hanged a message that read: "The triumph of the Revolution has granted us with the right to union to fight and prevent the abuse of workers by the capitalists" had been written on a large piece of cloth. Rogaciano, Marcial and others smiled leeringly as they walked in and read the written sentence. "Today, an additional sentence will be written on it: 'And the right to fight against abusive leaders'," said Rogaciano to Marcial. Fidelio also walked in and sat at the front, smiled and shook hands with those close to him. Saavedra accompanied by the rest of the Executive Committee walked in and sat at the front. Saravia came after them accompanied by several men who walked and spread around, surrounding the sitting miners. Saravia sat at the front table.

"The meeting is open," Martin Rodriguez, the union's secretary, read. "The only item for discussion is the expulsion of Fidelio Serna for treason to the union. Everyone here has witnessed how he has been working with the administration to boycott the benefits obtained by our leaders with so much difficulty." The majority of those present responded to this with a murmur of disapproval, some of them booed. Most of the miners looked at each other, upset about what had been said.

"How can you prove what you just said? Since his arrival, Fidelio has worked shoulder to shoulder with us. Contrary to you, that have done nothing but to benefit yourselves, Fidelio has obtained real benefits for all of us," said Filomeno, one of the older miners, standing up and pointing toward those sitting at the table. As soon as he finished talking, two of the men who had come with Saravia, moved towards the bench where he sat; almost immediately, three of the miners stood and placed themselves within them and Filomeno.

"We won't let you scare us this time!" yelled Panfilo, a young miner who had worked with Fidelio at the ranch. A murmur of approval was heard.

"Those who are against the decisions made by the leaders of the union will be punished by removing them from the protection and safeguard that the union provides," said Martin Rodriguez, in a loud, menacing tone of voice.

"Who is the coward that stabbed Jonas!" asked Rogaciano, standing up.

"Which one of you ordered it?" Panfilo also asked.

"Jonas was one of those who, together with Fidelio and others, have been working along with the administration and by doing that, they have helped to boycott the efforts of our leaders. Although he was a traitor to the principles of the union, we are sorry for what happened to him. That incident will be investigated later and those responsible will be punished accordingly. For the time being, we must not get distracted from the main reason for this meeting; we'll concentrate this reunion on reviewing the charges against Fidelio Serna, who has shown to be the worst of all. As a matter of fact, he is the cause of all the recent problems we face." Rodriguez replied. Saravia looked at him, smiled and nodded approvingly.

Juan Mendez, a well-known follower of Saavedra and a member of the executive committee stood up. "We all have seen how well Fidelio

Serna has mingled with those in the administration. He jumps at their minimal request. Since his arrival, he has been against the policies of the union, everyone here have witnessed how he has argued with our leader and has promoted hard work, which is contrary to the strategy we had been following before Fidelio's arrival." Again, with a cynical smile, Saravia looked at Mendez and, once again, nodded approving what Mendez had just said.

"Before Fidelio's arrival, you told us that 'we had to pretend to work' and that way you'll put pressure on the administration to obtain benefits. If any benefits have been obtained thus far with that policy it has ended up in your pockets, while we received nothing. Fidelio has shown that by doing our best, we not only increase productivity, but also, it has given us pride in what we do. Pride in a job well done; and yes, by working hard and with pride we have seen real benefits for all of us. In the last weeks, the pumps failed and what did you do? You did nothing. It was Jonas and Fidelio who talked for all of us to get it fixed. It has been thanks to those like Jonas, She Ling and Fidelio, who truly have represented us, that we have seen real improvement in the safety and working conditions. You have done nothing but filled your pockets!" said Marcial, standing up and pointing to those in the front desk. Almost everyone clapped enthusiastically.

Two of Saravia's men who had been standing in the sidelines, moved toward the place where Marcial and Rogaciano sat, but once again, they were prevented to get close by several of the miners who stood in front of them. Disconcerted, Saavedra looked to Saravia who signaled to him to say nothing. Suddenly, the sound of a rattlesnake was heard, the serpent slid quickly toward where Marcial sat. Scared, those in its path moved away, but before the snake could get close to Marcial, also suddenly, coming from no- where, an eagle flew in and took the serpent away. Holding the snake within its claws, the eagle went and stood in a pole close to where Fidelio sat and, although the snake tried to fight back, with a quick stroke of its beak, the eagle captured the snake behind its head, killing it. Seeing that, Saravia blushed, disgusted made a fist and hitting with violence the table, stood up and walked away.

"Where are you going?" Saavedra asked him with a trembling voice.

Saravia stopped, turned, looked at Saavedra. "You are now on your own," he replied and, before leaving, he signaled to the men who had walked in with him; they followed him.

"Out, out with all of you!" yelled Rogaciano, standing and pointing to all of those sitting at the executive committee table.

"Yes, out with all of you, traitors to the real cause. You have done nothing but benefit yourselves, we don't want you anymore! Get out!" someone in the back also yelled.

"Comrades, comrades, stay calm. I hear and understand your discomfort; but we must stay together, that's the only way to accomplish the purpose of the union. Everything will be done as you wish from now on," said Saavedra, in a conciliatory tone of voice.

"You are right in what you are saying, we are strong together. You have just witnessed our power and now, we'll to start by barring all of you from the union," said Marcial, pointing to those at the table.

"Yes, out with all of you," many voices yelled.

Saavedra, disconcerted, looked at those sitting with him at the front table, expecting and hoping that someone would say something. "Out! Out! Out!" the miners kept yelling. Some of them started throwing stones at them. Scared, Saavedra and all of those at the table, got up and ran away.

Noticing that Saavedra and all his followers had left, the miners clapped excitedly and hugged each other with enthusiasm. Getting rid of them had been much easier than they had expected.

"Wow, everything was so well orchestrated. Who planned it? Where and when did you guys do it?" someone asked.

Rogaciano and Marcial looked at each other. "Did you plan it?" they asked each other.

"No, I didn't," both of them answered almost in unison.

"Then who did it? Was it you, Fidelio? When did you do it?"

Fidelio stood up, smiled at them, "No, I didn't plan anything," he replied.

Rogaciano looked at those who had stood up and placed themselves in between Saavedra's hit men and those in danger. "Who told you to do it?" he asked them. They just shrugged shoulders. "It just felt that it was the right thing to do, so we did it," one of them replied.

Marcial turned to Panfilo, "you said 'we are now prepared'. Why did you say that?"

Panfilo looked at him smiling, he pointed to the men who had stood protecting those in danger. "It just seemed like the right thing to say," he replied.

"You were right when you said, 'God will guide us when the moment comes'. Indeed, God has not only guided us, but I believe that the snake and the eagle are messages from Him. You are a man of God," Rogaciano said to Fidelio. A murmur of approval was heard, all of them looked at Fidelio with respect who had also been wondering: "How did it all happen?"

Hearing and seen that reaction, Fidelio blushed. "No, no, I'm just like all of you, just another man, I seek justice and try to do well, that's all," he said.

Marcial seemed to notice Fidelio's embarrassment. "Now we should concentrate on deciding who is going to be our next leader?" he said in a loud voice and raising his arms to call everyone's attention. Everyone sat again. "I'm happy to propose someone who has stood for us many times, we all know him well, I'm talking about Rogaciano," Marcial continued after all had sat, pointing to his friend. "Yes, he is the right one," someone in the back yelled. Most of them clapped approvingly.

Rogaciano looked at Marcial and smiled at him. He stood up. "Thank you. I appreciate your confidence in me; but I must tell you that I honestly believe that our dear friend, Marcial is the right one to be our leader. He has always shown courage and disinterest, he has always put the majority's welfare before his own. He is the one we need at this moment."

"Both of them are excellent candidates," said Filomeno, standing up. "Both of them have shown, as Rogaciano said, courage and disinterest. Both of them have shown that they will consider the benefit of the majority before their own. Today, they have also shown that they can work together, as a team. Therefore, I propose that both of them be elected as our co-leaders."

Everyone clapped and yells of "hurrah, hurrah, hurrah! Yes, that is the best we can do. Rogaciano and Marcial our new leaders," was the answer to the proposal.

Smiling Marcial and Rogaciano, looked at each other, shook hands and then embraced. Facing their peers, they raised each other's arm. All cheered and clapped, standing up, Fidelio joined them.

"It seems that it's unanimous," said Filomeno, laughing. The eagle, standing on the pole, opened its wings and flew away.

Walking out, Fidelio saw Preston and Vicky waiting outside. Noticing the enthusiasm of the miners as they walked out, both of them smiled. "It seems that everything went well," Preston said as Fidelio, accompanied by Rogaciano and Marcial, approached. "We saw Saravia leaving with several men, they seemed upset; then Saavedra and others came out running, they seemed to be scared. They all left in a couple of trucks they had brought yesterday evening. They drove towards Monterrey," Preston added.

"I hope you were able to free yourselves of those ugly people. And if so, who is your new leader?" Vicky asked, smiling and almost jumping cheerfully, sharing the enthusiasm of the miners.

"Yes, we have freed ourselves of that band of thieves, all of them have run away, hopefully to never return," Rogaciano replied, smiling to them.

"Rogaciano and myself will share the honor of leading the union," said Marcial, passing an arm around Rogaciano's shoulder.

"That's wonderful, I have known both of you for a short period of time and what I have seen, from both of you, is enthusiasm and desire to serve. I believe everyone will benefit from it," Preston said. "By the way, I have been working with Robert Eager in fixing the pumping system. I believe that we have found the problem, it will be fully fixed in a couple of days. Would you like to come and see it?" he added.

Rogaciano and Marcial looked at each other. "Yes, of course, that's good news. Let's go and see it," said Marcial, and Rogaciano nodded approvingly.

"We'll talk later," Rogaciano said to Fidelio.

"Yes, we need to talk, we would like you to be a member of the executive committee," said Marcial, also talking to Fidelio. The three of them walked toward the pump, leaving Fidelio to accompany Vicky.

"Fidelio, when are you going to take me to see the wild horses? Remember, you promised," Vicky asked as soon as they were alone.

"Yes, I remember, tomorrow is Sunday and there is no work in the mine. If you agree we'll leave early tomorrow morning," Fidelio replied.

During his life as a shepherd, Fidelio had had many opportunities to observe the herds of wild horses roaming in that desert. He had observed their habits, understood their language and had learned how to befriend them. He found that when treated with honesty, respect and an open mind, the horse is a trustworthy animal; by understanding them he had even learned how to tame them and, although most of the times he preferred walking, he had become an excellent horse-rider.

The following day, before sunrise, Fidelio mounted in a bay stallion, guiding a saddled pinto mare, rode to Peabody's house where he and Vicky waited for him. Preston was also present. There was a gentle, fresh breeze, the air was clean. Fidelio enjoyed the freshness of the dew at that hour and the smell of what for many, was a desert. Fidelio knew otherwise, the place was full of plant and animal life. The mountains, although apparently bare rocks provided ground that allowed the growth of life. Fidelio knew all of it well. That morning, Fidelio felt a bit nervous, he felt strongly attracted by Vicky and knew that the attraction was mutual. Seeing her father and brother with her and greeting him, gave him hope that he and Vicky wouldn't be left alone, he hoped they would accompany them. That calmed him.

"Hello, my friend," Peabody greeted Fidelio, as he approached. "Would you like a cup of coffee, before leaving?"

"Yes, thank you," Fidelio replied, as he dismounted. "I'm glad that you and Preston are coming with us." He noticed, however, that there were no other horses ready and his anxiety returned.

"I'm afraid that we'll disappoint you," said Peabody. "But we have noticed that the pumping system needs more work than we had expected. The needed parts just arrived. Preston, Eager and myself will be working on it today. Vicky has been planning on this trip almost since her arrival and, although we tried to convince her to postpone it, she is like her mother, a stubborn girl and always gets her way," Peabody smiled and hugged his daughter in a fatherly manner. "What about that cup of coffee?" he added.

"Yes, of course, I'll be glad. If you prefer I could get a couple of miners, who also know the place well, to go with us," said Fidelio.

"That won't be necessary," said Vicky, taking Fidelio by the arm and guided him into the house. The aroma of fresh coffee, combined with Vicky's perfume, excited Fidelio; he hoped no one would have noticed; Vicky, however, noticed it and smiled.

After drinking the coffee, Vicky took a small basket filled with muffins just baked, dried meat, fresh fruit, a bottle of water and another bottle of wine. "We won't be hungry," she said to Fidelio laughing. She hugged her father and brother, hanged the basket on the saddle and mounted the pinto mare. "Let's go Fidelio," she said.

"Be careful, you know that wild animals also follow the herds, wolves and puma in particular, but even coyotes," said Peabody.

"Yes, we'll be careful. We'll be back before dawn," Fidelio replied, as he mounted.

"Let's see if you can overtake me!" said Vicky, putting the mare to full gallop. Fidelio followed her. Preston and his father looked at them and smiling they walked into the house.

Although Fidelio had become a good rider, he had difficulty keeping up with Vicky who was an expert and had full control of the young mare. She laughed and enjoyed watching Fidelio trying to follow her. After a while, she slowed her horse to a trot allowing Fidelio to catch with her. They trotted in silence for a few minutes.

"You know. I've riding a horse since I was a child," said Vicky. "But I know little about wild horses. The horses I've known have been always in a stable, they were born there and are easily tamed. Tell me more about how is that there are wild horses in here. I know that there were no horses in this continent, they were brought by the Spanish conquerors, but that's as far as my knowledge about it goes."

"I didn't know that," Fidelio replied. "I can tell you that the horse is a noble animal. They tend to group in small bands, even when you see large herds, in reality they are always in small bands; several mares and one stallion per band."

"Mmmph, male dominance. I don't believe I like that," said Vicky.

"Well, it's true that the stallion gets mating privileges, but his role in reality is to protect the herd and be sure that everyone stays together. The real leader of the band is a mare, a dominant mare. She is the one that choses the direction to go, and the safety of grazing places and watering holes. She always drinks first and then allows the rest to drink."

"Now, that's really smart; that's the way it should always be," said Vicky, laughing, radiant, making the mare she mounted on to dance. Fidelio admired her ability in controlling the horse. "How is that the stallion gets mating privileges?" she asked.

"By showing strength," Fidelio replied. They were getting to an elevated place from where Fidelio knew they could see most of the plain. "There they are," he said as soon as they reached the top pointing to a small lagoon where a large herd of horses rested and drank water. Several stallions at the periphery watched to provide the alert for possible pray animals.

"How do people call these beautiful horses?" Vicky asked, admiring them.

"Mustengos," Fidelio replied.

"'Mustengos?' Why are they called that way? What does it mean?"

"It's an old Spanish word. It means horses without owner."

One of the horses in the periphery, leading a group of stallions, a brown with patches of black, approached a band of mares drinking at the edge of the lagoon. Movement that the dominant stallion of that band, a palomino, noticed and immediately galloped to position him between the approaching male and the mares. "Look Fidelio, it seems that they are going to fight for the girls. This is exciting," Vicky said, the mare she mounted, danced, apparently sharing her enthusiasm. Fidelio smiled and looked attentively, he knew that most often the movement of the dominant stallion would be enough to deter the invader. This time, however, the young stallion seemed decided to challenge the old one. Previously, Fidelio had observed that usually it was a group of young stallions that challenged the dominant one. This time it was one against one; he had never witnessed one single stallion challenging another one. The lead mare turned around and looked at the two stallions facing each other, kicking the dust. This also called Fidelio's attention.

The stallions, their necks straightened, their ears pointing forward, galloped to each other, clashed, biting each other furiously. They were about the same size and weight, an even fight. The older stallion, however, seemed to be a more experienced fighter; suddenly moved to the side and kicked the young one right on the belly, the strength of the kick pushed the brown stallion down, leaving him at the mercy of the old one. The palomino looked at him and turned, allowing the young one to stand and leave, defeated.

"That was a good fight, that horse is noble. He refused to finish the defeated horse. I have not seen that happening among humans," Vicky said, her face flushed and sweat covered her upper lip.

"The young one will try again, that's their nature. Contrary to humans they are not fighting to get power, they only want to have their own band. Remember in the herd the one that has real power is the leading mare. In this particular case, it seems that, somehow, she encouraged the young stallion to try," Fidelio replied.

"She is a smart girl. Let's rest here," Vicky said, smiling cheerfully, as she looked at him and dismounted and sat. Fidelio followed her.

They sat watching the horses, the morning was fresh; although the sun was already up, the clouds in the sky provided a protective shadow for them. The breeze played with Vicky's red hair that sparkled thanks to the brightness of the morning, her head seemed to be surrounded by fire. Looking at her, Fidelio found her more attractive than ever; watching her, he didn't care anymore about the horses, his eyes were fixed on her hair flowing freely, her face also shined, even the freckles in her face seemed to shine, her full lips curved in a heart shape form, her long neck, the wavy form of her breasts under her shirt moving up and down with every breath, the narrow waist and the rounded lines of the rest of her body. Everything about her seemed to Fidelio like something magical, he had a hard time believing she was real, he thought that an angel was sitting there with him. She turned and smiled to him; to Fidelio her lips looked like a juicy red strawberry asked to be bitten. He could no longer resist the temptation, without even thinking his arm moved, hugged her and took the fruit offered to him. Like she was waiting for it, she responded with intensity, with passion, a long-wet kiss. She pushed her tongue forwards, licking Fidelio's tongue, he responded with the same; to him this was the most delicious fruit he had ever eaten. Her hands moved under his shirt caressing his chest, she moved down and went under his pant and caressed him. "Allow me to enjoy you," she whispered. She started kissing his neck, pulled his shirt and licked his chest, licked the sweat from it, while her hand kept on caressing his hard, firm organ. Fidelio put his hand under her neck and gently he pushed her down, placing her back on the grass, pulled her blouse up, caressed her firm breast, and he started kissing and licking them, to finally suck her nipple; she pushed his and hers pants down. Fidelio got on top of her and penetrated her, she yelled softly, "ah, yes, yes that's it, my love, my sweet Mexican love," she whispered in his ear, Fidelio pushed harder, making her to scream with pleasure, both of them sweated, the hard, firm part of him into her soft and pliable part, both became one, both moved rhythmically, a wild, frenzy dance; Fidelio felt that all of his energy flowed down into her. Afterwards, as he got dressed, he looked up and noticed that a mountain lioness was standing, close by, observing them. The puma kept observing Fidelio, she seemed to be calm, but there was something like a reproach in its eyes; it seemed to say "Fidelio what have you done? So soon have you forgotten me?" Embarrassed, Fidelio couldn't sustain the lioness look and looked in another direction; he knew, however, that the puma would remain calm.

"Let's seat and enjoy our lunch," Vicky said after dressing herself. "Oh, my God!" she yelled jumping scared, when she noticed the lioness now looking at her. "Look Fidelio, a mountain lion. What are we going to do?"

"Nothing, don't be scared, she won't hurt us," Fidelio reassured her.

"What do you mean by 'nothing'. How do you know that it's a 'she'? And if that's so, why is she just there, looking at us?"

"She'll stay there, she won't hurt us as long as we don't threaten her. I've been long enough in this desert to distinguish male from female and, she is looking at us because, believe or not, she is jealous of you and upset with me. I happen to agree with her, what just happened, shouldn't have happened. It's my fault."

Vicky looked at him, upset, tears started to fall from her beautiful, large, green/blue eyes. "What do you mean, 'it shouldn't have happened?' To me it was wonderful, something of which I had dreamed. Yes, I dreamed of it almost since I met you and the desire increased the better

I got to know you. I, not only admire you, but I love you. Do you hear me!? I love you!"

Fidelio looked at her, a serious, sad, expression on his face. "That's exactly the reason I said it shouldn't have happened. I can't love you. You, or anyone else. At least not in the way you would expect, and deserve, to be loved. There is something else, I don't know exactly what, but I can't love anyone in particular. Yes, I in a certain way I love you. I find you beautiful. As a matter of fact, I believe that you are an angel sent by God." Now upset, he looked up, raised his fist. "Why, why are you doing this to me, to us!" He yelled to the clouds.

"What? Do you believe that God has something to do with this and that is God who somehow wants to keep you? Are you crazy?"

"There have been other occasions in my life that I have believed that I must be crazy. But now I know that I'm not. There is something else, I fell in love before, she is dead and I had the purpose to remain loyal to her memory. I know the lioness is here to remind me of my purpose and precisely that's the reason she is not a physical menace for us."

Vicky looked at him, upset. She threw away the basket with the food. "So, what just happened between us, means nothing to you? To me it meant a lot. I'm now ready to stay here, in what is to me a foreign and mysterious country. I'm now ready to follow you wherever you go, no matter the circumstances; that's the way I love you. Whether you or I, like it or not, now I belong to you."

Fidelio looked at her, tears flowing down, he fell on his knees and opened his arms in despair. "I'm sorry, there is nothing I can offer you; not even myself. I'm serious when I say that I don't know what to do and what should I do. I can't belong to you, even if I want it, I can't." He dropped his head into his chest sobbing."

The lioness walked toward Vicky, who just looked at her and didn't move. Once close enough the lioness just rubbed her body gently in Vicky's legs and then, tenderly, licked her hands. Vicky walked toward Fidelio, bent on her knees and embraced him, kissing him tenderly and licking his tears. "Fidelio, somehow, I understand. I'll love you even if you can't love me. Somehow, I now understand that you belong to all, but no one in particular. I have seen what you can do and somehow, I understand that even that does not belong to you," she said. The lioness moved close to them and sat in front of them, her attitude seemed gentle, tender, protective, like a mother.

Vicky got up. "Come Fidelio, let's go back. I'll always treasure in my heart this day; from now on, every time I see a horse, I'll think about you," she smiled looking at the mountain lion. "And every time I see a cat, I'll think about you," she added caressing the lioness. A gentle breeze blew her hair freely, the sun rays shone on her. Fidelio looked at her and was surprised how she now reminded him about Candelaria, he loved her and because of it a profound sadness invaded him. Why couldn't he belong to anyone?

They mounted and letting the horses trot at their own leisure they went back. Pairing her horse with Fidelio's, she took his hand and smiled at him, tenderly; he answered by caressing her hand. By the time they reached the camp the sunset rays provided a magical lighting to it, with the orange, purple sun rays the rocks in the mountains seemed like jewels, the shacks and adobe houses shone, even the few bushes were bright, the whole camp seemed to be floating in the light, a pleasant and peaceful image; but when they arrived the magic disappeared. There were soldiers in the camp.

CHAPTER XXI

Most of the soldiers surrounded the building of the administration and the houses of Eager and Peabody. The miners and their families had been taken out of their shacks and all were crowded outside of the administration. Although the children played, most of the men and women were fearful and nervous by the presence of the soldiers. A full moon shone in the sky. Looking at the dark brown faces of most of the soldiers, Fidelio thought about the federales and the 'colorados' who had fought at the side of Orozco, all of those against whom he had fought during the time he had spent with Villa. "Who won the revolution?" he asked himself. The soldiers looking at them waited until they had come close to Peabody's house and once they had approached, one of them stood in front with an extended arm ordering them to stop. "Who are you? What is your business in here?" asked the soldier.

"My name is Fidelio Serna," replied Fidelio. "I'm a miner here and she is the daughter of Mr. Peabody, the manager of the mine."

The soldier looked at them, he kept looking at Vicky who frowned, upset by the lascivious way the soldier looked at her, not trying to disguise how he felt. Like a coyote in front of a fat chicken. Finally, the soldier smiled showing the few, remaining rotten front teeth, yellow-brown in color. "Go ahead, they are waiting for you," he finally said.

Having heard about their arrival, Peabody and Preston waited for them out of the house; two officers stood by their side. "Vicky, Fidelio I'm glad to see that you are coming back safely," said Peabody, after Fidelio and Vicky had dismounted. Vicky seemed concerned, as a matter of fact, she looked scared.

"What happened? Why are the soldiers here?" she asked, running and embracing her father who returned the hug and kept his arm around her, a protective gesture.

"Nothing for which we have to be afraid," Preston said, caressing her hair tenderly.

"What is it then?" Vicky asked. Peabody and Preston looked at Fidelio.

"Are you Fidelio Serna?" one of the officers with the ensign of a captain in his shirt, asked.

"Yes, I am," Fidelio answered.

"There is a report that you promote and induce praying the rosary in public. Is that true?"

"Yes, it is true,"

"Are you aware that religious manifestations in public have been prohibited and that it could be punished even by death?"

"No, this is the first time I hear about it. Why is that so? What is the danger of it?"

The captain looked at him, the expression of his face was friendly, even sympathetic to Fidelio. He shrugged his shoulders, "I'm a soldier. I don't ask questions, only obey orders." He kept looking at Fidelio. "During the revolution, I got wounded and although I fought in the federal side, you transported me out of the field and had my wound taken care of," he grimaced, something close to a smile. "I won't forget that. For the time being, I'll leave it only as a warning. But you must stop praying and encouraging others to pray in public. Remember all public religious manifestations are forbidden by law. We have strict orders to capture and punish those who disobey the law."

Fidelio looked at him. "Is it possible to prevent the nightingale from chirping? Can you stop the rooster from announcing the sunrise?" he asked, smiling at the captain.

The captain spitted nervous. "You have been warned. Had it been anyone else I wouldn't have hesitated to take that person to jail, I could even order to shoot him; I won't do anything like it this time, but don't force us to come back. Next time, it might be that someone else is in charge, someone who owes nothing to you. Remember that well, I know that even among Villa's soldiers there were many who didn't like you." He looked to Peabody, "you are also warned. No religious manifestations are allowed, if that happens you might have to get a new crew. Or the mine might be closed." He looked at the lieutenant at his side. "We are done here. Get everyone in formation." The lieutenant looked at the captain, he seemed about to say something, but just saluted. "Sergeant, get the troop ready!" he yelled walking away.

"Fidelio, there is someone else here waiting for you," Peabody said, after the soldiers had left.

"Who is it?" Fidelio asked, intrigued.

"I believe, she is your sister," replied Peabody, smiling and pointing to Antonia who walked out of the house, tears in her eyes; she hugged and kissed him on the cheek.

"Fidelio, I was scared when I saw the soldiers and learned that they were looking for you and the charge against you. At the ranch, everyone is upset for the prohibition to pray and assist to mass; however, somehow God seems to take care of you and He sent that captain who knows you and at least for now he has left you in peace," said Antonia, embracing him.

"Remember, 'Thy will be done.' We just have to accept His will," Fidelio replied, as he returned her embrace.

"The reason I came looking for you is this letter, received at the ranch. It's from Enrique," she said giving him the letter. Fidelio took it and read it.

"Enrique is now the foreman in a ranch, close by, in Espinazo. He has married and they just had a child, a baby boy. Enrique is asking me to go and help them to take care of the child." Fidelio said, after reading the letter. He turned and looked at Peabody. "This man has been more than a friend for me; to me he has been almost like a father. If he needs me, I feel that I must go."

"We'll miss you," said Peabody. "But, probably, under the present circumstances it's for the best," hearing this, Vicky cried and ran into the house.

Peabody and Preston looked at her, concerned. "She has got fond of you, now she is upset, but somehow, she'll get over it; it will pass. We'll have to go back to England soon," Preston said to Fidelio. "Take good care of yourself. It has been an amazing experience meeting you and watching what you can do. Even in England, physicians don't accomplish as much as you do. Considering that you use only what nature provides."

Upset and nervous as usually happened when someone mentioned what he knew was a gift, Fidelio just shrugged his shoulders. "I only do what I can, please say farewell to Vicky from me," he said to Preston, then he turned and faced Peabody and Eager. "I learned a lot working in the mine. I don't believe that there are many who care about their miners the way you have done while I've been here, please continue treating them as you have done until now, as what they are: People, good people," he told them.

"Your attitude has shown all of us that it's possible to find common ground. A ground from which all of us can profit and share the benefit. I know that the miners and we, at management, are thankful to you," Eager said, extending his right arm and pressing Fidelio's shoulder in a friendly way.

Fidelio and Antonia walked away, as they left, the miners surrounded them, cheerful to see that Fidelio had been let free. Happy to be surrounded by friends, Fidelio felt thorn, for one side he knew that he could be of help to improve the safety and the health of the miners; on the other side his friend, who he knew also cared about him, called for his help. Somehow, he also knew that the time to leave had come.

"Fidelio, we became preoccupied when we learned that Saravia and Saavedra had reported you to the authorities in Monterrey. We thought the soldiers had come to take you with them," Rogaciano told him.

"Many of us wanted to fight and defend our right to worship God as we see fit and prevent them from taking you with them. However, the presence of our families tied our hands. It was a difficult situation for all of us," Marcial added.

Listening to them, Fidelio realized that it would be safer for them if he left. "Thank you for your concern my friends," he said. "But, I must tell you that I have decided to leave. It will be much safer for you if I'm not around anymore. I'm almost sure that they will leave all of you in peace, if they know I'm no longer here. But beware, Saavedra, or someone like him, will try to take over the union once again; don't let it happen." All of those who heard him stood still, disconcerted, they looked at each other, surprised by what Fidelio had just said.

"What do you mean? Are you leaving us? Now that we have got rid of those who ripped us pretending to work for us. We need you now more than ever, you have showed us that there is a way to keep the union honest and fulfilling its purpose," Filomeno said.

"You said it right," Fidelio replied. "You have learned that the union is good for all if it is kept within its purpose, now you can do it." Fidelio grimaced shrugging his shoulders. "As a matter of fact, you know a lot more about unions than I do; let me tell you that I knew close to nothing about it when I came here. Besides, by what has happened today, you have learned that it would be dangerous for all of you if I remain here."

"Where will you go?" asked Marcial.

"Not far, to Espinazo, where I'll help a good friend of mine and where I'll continue to work as what I'm, a shepherd."

Arid, almost completely dry landscape, the blazing, fiery sun rays instead of a clear and bright environment made everything seemed hazy, phantasmagoric, like covered by a light veil. At a certain distance, it created the impression that the cactus and mesquite bushes floated, everything seemed so bright that created the impression that a mixture of orange, yellow, purple flames covered the entire landscape, an explosion of hazy colors. It felt hot, so hot that even the lizards chose to remain underground. Few mesquite and gobernadora bushes, small cactus plants, the terrain was mostly sand, firm in some places, loose in another, dry sand, like powder, surrounded the few miserable shacks, some of which had adobe walls, most, however, had walls and roofs built with carrizo sticks covered with mud that had quickly dried under the blazing sun rays. Although by then Fidelio had gotten used to living in the northern Mexico desert, he had never been in a place where everything seemed so dry. When he arrived at Espinazo, a tiny town in the middle of the desert, a place where the railroad train stopped to replenish water, he noticed that besides few bushes the town had only one moderately large tree, a mesquite tree, known in the region as "pirul". Around the only water well there was a small mud pool. The only building that seemed to have some solidity, was the house of the owner of the hacienda for whom Enrique had become the foreman.

In spite of the apparent hostility of the environment, although all seemed sully, Fidelio felt that somehow, the place welcomed him; by now an expert in the medicinal benefits that nature has to offer, he could see that he could make use of the apparent scarcity of plants in the area, most of them with medicinal properties. He felt that he would be able to get the most out of the place. As a matter of fact, he immediately felt comfortable, he had arrived home. Although he had never been in a place like this, he belonged here. Somehow the place seemed familiar to him, he felt that the sun rays caressed his skin, tenderly like saying, "welcome home, you are finally here, we've been waiting for you."

"Fidelio, my dear friend, I'm so happy you chose to come," Enrique welcomed Fidelio, embracing him. "Above all, I'm happy to see that you are well and healthy. It has been several years since the last time we saw each other. Let me tell you that, in Torreon, I looked for you and to my surprise someone told me that you had left. Later, I found Dr. Villarreal and he explained how it was that you departed. Afterwards, in the middle of many battles, I often wondered about you, concerned how you had managed. Fortunately for me, once we established ourselves in here, I remembered that you told Dr. Villarreal that you were going with Antonia, that's why I addressed the letter to her and now you are here," he smiled again, holding Fidelio by the shoulders. "Look at you. You are now a grownup man, you look healthy and strong, it seems that life has been good for you." Fidelio listened to him, also happy to once again, join his childhood friend.

Keeping his arm around Fidelio's shoulder, Enrique pointed to a young, attractive woman. She smiled to Fidelio, while rocking a crying baby in her arms. "First let me introduce you to my wife, Petra and our son," Enrique said, she nodded in a friendly way, smiling to him. She caressed the baby trying to calm him, but the baby just kept crying.

Fidelio, smiling back to her, extended his arm and caressed the baby. The child, responded to Fidelio's caress getting quiet, moved his arm to touch Fidelio's hand and smiled. Noticing the baby's reaction to Fidelio's touch, Petra looked at him, thankful.

"Later I'll introduce you to Don Teodoro, the owner of the hacienda. I'm sure that both of you will get along." Enrique said, taking one step forward, also happy with his child's reaction to Fidelio's touch. "Since we met, you have shown to be different, and what makes you special is that it seems that something supernatural accompanies you. Don Teodoro strongly believes in the existence and influence of spirits and when I talked to him about you, he asked a lot of questions and when I told him about your gift for healing and that I expected you to come, he became interested, I would say almost excited, about meeting you."

Fidelio frowned, a bit surprised and concerned. Although by his own experience he was aware of the existence of something powerful guiding him, something that until now, he didn't understand. Had "spirits" helped and guided him? He didn't believe that could be the answer to his own doubts.

"Don Teodoro has agreed that you'll help Petra taking care of Ulises, that's the name of our son, and also, you'll work with the other shepherds. For the time being let me show you around." Enrique added.

Fidelio found Marcelino, Prudencio and Jacinto, the three shepherds already working in there, in a friendly manner; he also found it interesting when they mentioned that besides taking care of the goats they supplemented their income by collecting candelilla and ixtle. He asked them a lot of questions about those, wishing to learn as much as possible about how they obtained and processed them, he would use that knowledge for healing purposes. Afterwards, Enrique took him to the large adobe and brick house occupied by the owner of the hacienda.

They found Theodore Von Wernich, a German immigrant, a blond, chubby man with friendly blue eyes, already at the door waiting for them. As soon as they approached, he walked forward extending his hand to Fidelio.

"Welcome," he said taking Fidelio's hand with both hands. "I'm glad you have come. You may believe it or not but I had expected your arrival for some time, the spirits announced that someone with healing abilities would come." He smiled noticing the expression of surprise in Enrique's face. Fidelio just smiled, he already felt that he belonged there, somehow, he felt that he had been searching for it, and now the whole place made him feel welcome, although he still couldn't understand the reason for it. "Spirits guided me to this place," Von Wernich continued, "long before Enrique's arrival, spirits announced that a military man would come and he would bring someone who would convert this arid, apparently unfriendly desert, into a place of hope and healing. So, when Enrique told me about your healing ability, that provided credibility to what the spirits had announced."

Hearing Von Wernich, Fidelio felt embarrassed, by what he was hearing. He felt that something extraordinary was expected from him. "Thank you," he finally said. "But I'm just another shepherd. Besides that, I'll help Petra and Enrique to raise their child. Hopefully he'll follow on the footsteps of his father and become an honest man."

Von Wernich looked at Enrique and laughed, happy, he patted Fidelio on the shoulder. "Just as you said Enrique, he is a humble man." He turned and looked at Fidelio smiling in a friendly way. "Yes, you'll work as a shepherd for as long as you want, but somehow I feel that it won't be long before your services as a healer will be called for. You have a destiny, we all have one and yours is truly important. But now come inside and have a cup of coffee."

Von Wernich's adobe house was spacious, with large rooms, the roof was high with large doors and windows to allow free flow of the wind, that made the house feel fresh in the summer, while by closing the doors and windows in the winter the house would be warmer. They sat in comfortable and fresh chairs made with a combination of bejuco and ixtle fibers. "These chairs are designed and hand made by the local peasants," said Von Wernich, while a man and a woman, served coffee and sotol for everyone. "Enjoy, this sotol, also a local product and it's excellent. A toast to this great and wonderful country, that soon peace and prosperity come to it," he added lifting his cup. "To your health," Enrique and Fidelio said lifting their glasses.

"Don Teo (such was the tender and respectful name used by Von Wernich's employees and friends when they addressed him) I am curious. How is it that you believe in spirits?" Enrique asked.

Von Wernich looked at him, his blue eyes sparkled. "I'm glad you asked me that," he said. "Most of the people would believe that it's something foolish and indeed I'll admit that there are many who have taken advantage of people credibility to exploit them, but believe me it's real. There are spirits and we can learn a lot through them. In Europe, the most educated people believe in them." He paused for a moment, frowning. "But, it must be taken with respect, otherwise it might become against the one who is abusing it." Fidelio listened to him, although he didn't believe that "spirits" could be called at will, he agreed with the idea that when something is not fully understood, it should be taken with respect. He chose to remain quiet and listen.

"Perhaps you take me for a fool," Von Wernich continued, "now you see me in here, this land for me is a foreign and mysterious land, different, very different from Germany, the place where I was born and grew up. I loved that country, admired and loved the Kaiser. I believed in him and I believed in what we were taught. The Kaiser and the nobility in Germany and Europe was so because of the divine design." He grimaced. "The suffix 'Von' before my name, Wernich, means that I'm supposed to be part of the nobility, thanks to it and by hard work I raised within the Imperial bureaucracy. Because of my position, I had to travel, mainly to France and it's there where I learned for the first time about the spirits. At the beginning, I was skeptical about it. But, believe me, this is something serious. It was in one of those sessions that I learned that all men are created equal, there is no such a thing as 'hereditary nobility.' Also, I learned about the upcoming of the big war and the end of the Kaiser, the Czar and the Austro-Hungarian Empire as a result of it. It was fortunate for me that I left before all of that happened," once again, he grimaced. "I didn't escape violence. I came to Mexico in the middle of the revolution. But at least here, I hope that the change will be to benefit the common people."

"That's why many of us joined the rebellion, however, now I'm not so sure. I know that the religious manifestations are forbidden. Forbidding people to worship God as they have been taught; how could that benefit the common people?" Fidelio said.

"It would be safer for all if we don't talk about it, Fidelio," Enrique intervened. "Don Teo, is it true that Madero started the revolution because spirits told him that he was called to bring democracy to Mexico?"

The question caused Von Wernich to grimace again. "Yes, I believe so. As a matter of fact, I met Madero in Paris, at one of the spiritual meetings. I believe it's now safe to tell you that he is the reason I came to Mexico. The Kaiser had interest in the Mexican revolution and my job was to cause enough problem for your neighbor in the north, so it would be prevented from entering the European war. Well, that plan didn't work well, for the Kaiser, at least." He laughed, then looked at Fidelio. "Enrique is right, it will be best for all of us, if, for the time being, we stay out of the religious conflict."

Fidelio thought for a moment, then turned and looked at Enrique and Von Wernich. "Nothing will prevent me from praying and thanking God every day," he said, in a defiant tone.

Von Wernich laughed loudly, slapped on his thigh, "that's the right attitude! You are a man of conviction, I like that and I'll support you," he said. If we say that we shouldn't talk about it, it is because it's safer. As you know walls can hear."

"Yes, I agree, let me tell you that I haven't changed my conviction. Petra and I pray every day, but we do it quietly. However, I thank you for reminding us that we must defend our right to worship as we have done until now. But, for the time being, all of us will just do the job for which we have been hired," said Enrique.

"Probably so," Fidelio said. "For now, I would like to remain what I'm, a shepherd."

"I believe that somehow, this desert will show you the path to follow, it's not only the goats that need a shepherd," said Don Teo, laughing.

CHAPTER XXII

Several weeks later, Fidelio looked at the goats and smiled. Under his care they had gained weight, reproduced, the herd had increased and the milk production was abundant. Although he knew that goats easily adapt and learn to eat almost whatever nature has to offer, he also had learned how to find places where his goats would get the most nutritious and healthy food. He loved them and enjoyed the simple life of a shepherd. He sat and relaxed, everything seemed to be peaceful. He even considered taking a nap, when Gus, his dog, barked calling his attention to one of the goats, Fidelio looked at the goats and frowned. One of his goats seemed sick, lying down. Fidelio got up and examined her. Although the sun was blazing, at the touch the goat felt cold, very cold and dry. She grinded her teeth. Fidelio knew that she was pregnant and he noticed that she was bleeding, he understood that the pregnancy was lost. Although Fidelio's proximity calmed her, he realized that she had acquired a serious infection, which was not only the cause of her illness and loss of her pregnancy, but he also became conscious that the infection could spread to the herd. He had to prevent the spreading of the disease. First, he had to keep her apart from the rest. He could not prevent her from expelling the lost pregnancy. He knew that the placenta and the fetus would be highly contagious. If any of the animals, including his dog or scavengers were allowed to eat or even lick the expelled conception they would get the infection and spread the disease. He knew that it would be necessary to slaughter the diseased goat, and also, burn her body, preferably before she aborted. All these ideas flashed through Fidelio's mind. Shaking and in tears he looked up, opened his arms, praying for help. He had been given the gift of healing, but this time there was nothing he could do to save the goat and her pregnancy. Even worse if he didn't act, the infection could spread not only to the rest of his herd, but to the rest of the animals, even to the other shepherds and their family. But he loved the goats under his care. Just thinking about what was necessary to do made him feel nauseated and he vomited. He had now a responsibility for the rest of the herd, it was his duty to prevent the spread of the illness, but he felt that he couldn't do it. Feeling a heavy weight on his shoulders, he fell on his knees, with arms open to the sky and yelled, a wild yell, he sobbed bitterly.

"Why are you crying and yelling, young man?" A dark skinned old man asked. He was dressed in humble, raggedy, plain cotton shirt and pants, and had a worn-out palm sombrero on his head and a rough, also worn out, leather huaraches covered his feet.

"Who are you? Where do you come from?" Fidelio asked, surprised, looking at the old man.

The old man smiled, as he took of his hat to remove the ixtle bag around his chest. "I collect candelilla and from the distance I saw your herd, so I decided to walk this way hoping to share lunch and converse with someone. As I approached, I heard you crying. Are you crying because of what has happened to this goat?" he asked pointing to the diseased animal.

Fidelio nodded, still sobbing.

"She is sick, very sick, she has lost her pregnancy and she is about to die. I guess you already realize that," the old man said, putting his hand on Fidelio's shoulder. "You also know what must be done, but you hesitate to do it. You realize that she has a contagious disease and that in order to prevent it from spreading to the rest, you'll have to slaughter her and incinerate her body. Of course, you also have to bury the ashes," the old man said, a serious look in his face. "I know. It's difficult. I've been a shepherd and yes, I know, one falls in love with the herd. One takes care of them, feeds them, sometimes one has to assist them to deliver and when possible one also heals them. But then, occasions like this come, and one does not want to do what must be done. Yes, I know about all of that." The old man added in a calm, soothing voice, gently massaging Fidelio's back and neck as he spoke.

Fidelio turned to look at the man, intrigued by what he had said. It seemed that the man had read his mind. The gentle massage made him feel calm and relaxed. Looking at the man he had the strange feeling that he had seen him before, as a matter of fact he felt that he loved him; something like a child loves a loving father.

Fidelio sat. The gentle soothing brown eyes of the old man gazed at him. "Yes, you know that this goat must be sacrificed. Believe me, she already knows that this is the end for her. Besides, she is also suffering and you must put an end to her suffering." The goat grinded her teeth, she was shivering. "Let's move her away from the rest of the herd," the old man said. Somehow, like she understood, the goat got up and moved several yards away, to a hole that somehow was fully covered by a bed of fresh lechuguilla leaves, all of them blossomed with beautiful small white flowers. The goat walked into it and laid down on them. Fidelio, who had followed her was surprised and looked at the old man, who just smiled at him, a calm, gentle smile. "Use your knife and put an end to her suffering," said the old man.

Tearful, Fidelio nodded, kneeled at the goat side and with a quick movement, he cut the goat's throat. The goat didn't complain, she just put her head on the leaves. Fidelio felt surprised when he noticed that as she bled, the white flowers slowly absorbed the blood and became pink. He could not stop sobbing. The old man stood by his side. "We are not done yet," he said. "We must now collect dry lechuguilla leaves and mesquite sticks, burn her remains and afterwards cover the hole, we must not leave any temptation for the scavengers."

"I have noticed how hard all of this has been for you. It's a lesson for you and you must get used to it. Soon there will be many more occasions in which you'll face difficult situations like this one. Illnesses that you won't be able to heal, situations in which you'll know that the end for that life has come. But even in those circumstances, your duty will be to bring acceptance and hope, ease the transition. Learn from all those occasions, and also from those in which you'll succeed in returning health and prolonging someone's life. A lot will be asked from you and that won't be easy. Your time is approaching and you are now ready for it," said the old man to Fidelio once they had covered the hole with the goat's ashes. Fidelio looked at him, perplexed.

"What do you mean?" Fidelio asked.

"You'll find out soon. It won't be easy. You'll be loved and praised by many; but, also, you'll be attacked, insulted and you'll be the subject of many lies and slander. Don't let anything like that take you away from your duty. You'll be a beacon of hope for many. And also don't let the praises get over your head, learn from your apparent failures and do as much good as you can," the old man answered. "Now, I'm an old man and I'm tired. Do you have fresh water and something to eat?" he added smiling.

"Yes, I do, I have dry meat, goat cheese, hot pepper and tortillas, besides a jar filled with fresh water and I'll be glad to share it with you. But I still have questions about what you said. Why me? I'm happy with being only a shepherd. Is there a way to keep me what I am, what I want to be?" Fidelio said, concerned, distressed.

The old man shrugged his shoulders, smiling to Fidelio. "You'll continue being a shepherd, only that now it won't be goats that you'll have to take care of. But, you'll always have the choice. You have been given a gift, the gift of healing. By now you know that it has limits. The way you use it is up to you. It could make you wealthy, very wealthy and powerful, or you could use it to benefit as many as you can. One way or the other it will be hard work, many sleepless nights; it's up to you. You could even try to walk away, but you already own the gift, it will always be with you. It's best to accept what you have been called for, although there will be times in which you'll feel it is a burden, I believe that you'll know what to do when the time comes. Now, what about dinner?"

"I'll prepare it," Fidelio said, getting up and walking to get dry sticks to make fire to prepare the meal. He understood that there was no reason in arguing. Although he was now concerned. How was he going to be a beacon of hope in the middle of the desert? In this place where there was so much poverty? He chose not to ask anymore and prepared the meal.

"I'm tired, wake me up when it's ready," the old man said, putting his ixtle bag as a pillow, lying down and falling asleep almost immediately. Fidelio took a sarape and covered him.

Once the meal was ready, Fidelio awoke the old man. They ate in silence. The old man chewed slowly, he seemed to enjoy the taste of the food, even to Fidelio this simple meal tasted different, he also enjoyed it and in spite of the apparent silence, Fidelio felt communion with the humble old man. He felt that something more than his body had been nourished.

"Thank you, it has been a delicious meal. Now, it's time for me to leave. Good bye, my dear friend, you are now ready. Be strong," the old man said, walking towards a couple of donkeys carrying baskets full with fresh candelilla leaves. Fidelio was again surprised that he hadn't noticed the donkeys before. The old man waved good bye, took the donkeys and walked away mumbling a song. Smiling, Fidelio waved back and then turned to collect the herd and walk back to the ranch. At the distance the bare mountains seemed to shine under the sunset rays.

When he arrived to the humble village, he noticed that several hand propelled carriages had been stationed in the railroad tracks. Several men seemed distressed, they talked to Enrique and Von Wernich, one of the men seemed as if he was about to cry, upset and nervous. From the distance, although he couldn't hear them, he sensed that they were talking about him. Someone in their family needed assistance; when they noticed his presence, Enrique pointed to him; one of the men, tears in his eyes, ran to him. "You need to help us!" the man almost yelled. Fidelio stopped, signaled the goats to the corral, they obeyed.

"What is it? How can I help you?" he asked the man.

"We need you to come with us. Come, hurry, there is no time to waste!" said the man in a loud voice, taking Fidelio by the hand and pulling him towards the carriages in the railroad track.

"Wait. You still haven't told me. How can I help you?" Fidelio said, freeing his hand.

"My wife, my wife needs help. That's why we came looking for you. Please, hurry up," the man insisted, taking Fidelio by the arm and pointed to the carriages, sobbing.

Fidelio frowned. "She is with child, in labor," he said.

The man looked at him. "Yes, but I didn't say that. How do you know?"

"It doesn't matter," Fidelio replied, smiling gently to the man. "How long has she been in labor?"

"Three days. She says that she no longer feels the baby moving. Dark and thick green fluid is coming out of her. The women who have been trying to help her, say that she might die. The shepherds told us about you, that's why we come looking for you. Please hurry up," the man said, pointing once again, to the wagons on the railroad track.

Fidelio felt the man's anguish, "let's go," he said walking with him towards the wagons.

It took them thirty minutes to get to the small ranch. As they arrived, Fidelio noticed that the house was a large adobe house with high ceiling and large doors that also served as windows. The house had several rooms in it. It was clean, the earth floor of the house firm and neatly swept. A tall and robust woman, brown hair, fair skin, lied on a bed. Her face and entire body covered with sweat. Although it was obvious that she was struggling, she looked calm.

As soon as Fidelio walked in, she smiled to him. "So, you are the boy, whom the shepherds talk about. I hope that indeed you can help. I've been trying to push out this baby since yesterday, it does not come out. I never had any difficulty delivering my other children; but his time I know something is wrong and won't come out no matter how hard I push. I need help."

Fidelio, looking into her eyes, walked toward her and took her hand.

"What's your name?" he asked.

"Maria Zapata de Rios, to serve God and you," she answered.

"Maria, you are strong, I can see that. I can help you. God will guide me. I know that you also feel His presence. He is here with us. Let your body rest, rest, rest. You have worked hard, you need to rest, let your body rest, allow your eyes, your body, your mind, to rest, rest and relax." She closed her eyes, extended her legs and fell into a deep sleep.

Gently, Fidelio palpated her abdomen, he frowned. He then uncovered her legs and palpated in between her legs, the frown in his forehead got deeper, what he felt confirmed his abdominal exam. The baby was not only very large, but also was positioned transversally. He had to choose. He could open her belly, he could try to get the baby's feet and hope he could pull the baby out, or he would need to cut the baby and deliver him piece by piece. He decided to open her belly.

He looked at her husband, who had remained at his side. "The baby is sideways and large, very large, that's the reason she didn't deliver. I'll have to deliver the baby through her belly. I'll need clean water, soap, a glass bottle, needles and fine silk thread. Can you get all of this?"

The man looked at him surprised, doubtful. "Yes, we have all of that, I'll get them for you," he said, after a moment of hesitation.

Once he had obtained all of what he had asked for, Fidelio uncovered her belly, washed it, washed his hands, broke the bottle glass, chose the sharpest piece, and he used it to cut through her belly and delivered a baby boy, dark purple in color, no movement. Using the silk thread, he closed her abdomen. During the entire procedure, she maintained an expression of peace, not a sound, or complain.

"Go to sleep now," Fidelio told her after he had finished. "Sleep, rest and relax. You are tired. You need the rest. Tomorrow, when you wake up, you'll be rested and calm. Of course, you'll mourn the loss of your child, that's natural, you are a mother. But now, just sleep, rest and relax."

"She'll recover. For now, she just needs to rest. She may move and walk around, just don't allow her to do any heavy work. I'll be back in ten days to remove the stitches in her belly. I'm sorry there was nothing I could do for your child. There is now an angel in heaven looking for you," Fidelio told the man who looked at him with tears in his eyes.

"Thank you, thank you. How can I pay you?" he said, took Fidelio's hand and tried to kiss it.

Fidelio moved his hand to prevent the man from kissing it. "You must thank God. This is His work. For me, just order them to drive me back, that's enough pay."

"My name is Manuel Rios. Although it might not show, I'm a wealthy man. I could give you several horses, or, if you prefer, I could pay you with money," said the man, pointing to the nearby corral, full of already tamed mustangs.

Fidelio looked at the horses, then turned and looked friendly to Manuel. "Those are beautiful horses, but I really don't have any use for them; also, I don't need any money. As I said, all that I ask you is to order your men to take me back," he smiled at him. "But, there is always a way to help. Share your God's given wealth with the poor."

CHAPTER XXIII

"Since Fidelio helped Maria Rios with her difficult delivery, and the fact that she survived the surgery, the word has spread and now the women of the region are coming asking for his assistance. Fidelio has become very busy. It's amazing how these people who don't allow any man to even look at their women, now they bring them here and ask Fidelio to help them during the delivery of their children. Both, husband and wife feel safer with him," said Teodoro Von Wernich to Enrique as they sipped coffee in the terrace of the main house. A pleasant late summer evening, a gentle fresh breeze announced the proximity of rain and the fall.

"Yes, that's one of the many surprising aspects of Fidelio, he inspires trust and confidence. For that reason, he has become busy assisting the local women to deliver. But, as you are well aware, almost since his arrival, he has taken care of some of the shepherds, the candelilla and ixtle pickers; and now all of them come looking for him to take care of their illnesses. That's the reason we see a lot more activity in town. My friend has become popular," Enrique said, smiling as he lifted his cup and sipped his coffee.

"As I have told both of you, the spirits had predicted this. But, I must admit that I'm surprised. This seems to be bigger than I thought," said Von Wernich. He grimaced, ironically. "But, what the townspeople are saying has also surprised me. Have you heard what they say?"

Enrique grimaced back. "I don't know about spirits. I have known Fidelio since both of us were children. He always has had that ability; he has gotten the gift of healing. Yes, I have heard what people say. They are talking about some kind of hermit who, a long time ago, chose this desert to worship the lord and, apparently, he was also a folk healer. "Tata Santito," that's how they call him. The legend, orally passed from one generation to the next, says that this man predicted, two hundred years ago, the appearance of a miraculous healer in the middle of this, almost desolate desert."

"That's what the folk people say and probably they are right," said Von Wernich. "Nevertheless, I have decided to allow Fidelio to serve the people. The least I can do is to let him take care of the shepherds, peasants, cowboys of this hacienda and also of those who work in the neighboring haciendas."

"They are not the only ones who come. There are folks coming by train, every day people from other towns arrive. All come looking for Fidelio," Enrique said. "It's going to be necessary to provide these folks with supplies and probably, shelter."

"Yes, and if this trend continues, it opens an opportunity for an honest business," Von Wernich said. "All of this is good and I'm happy to have had the opportunity to live through it. But, there is something else I want to talk to you about, something that is important for me." His face turned serious.

"Yes, what is it? Don Teo," Enrique asked, moving forward to pay attention.

"I know I said that we shouldn't talk about how the government has forbidden all public religious manifestations. But, I have become aware that churches are being converted into stables or military barracks. That convents and seminars are being forcefully closed. That there is persecution of priests and nuns, in particular those who are foreigners. It's well known that many of them have been shot, hanged; nuns have been raped. Although, I'm not a religious person, I can't pretend that this is not happening and look the other way. I already did that once in my life and I won't do it again. I want to help those who are been persecuted. The fact that more people are coming here creates an opportunity for them to travel here. We are close to the border. We can help them to escape."

"I'm glad that you think that way. Yes, although it's true that the Catholic hierarchy supported Huerta's government, the majority of us, Catholics, fought on the side of the revolution. The new government blames the Catholic Church for all the country's problems. Although here we are in relative peace, I know that there is tension and violence in many parts of the country. Not only priests and nuns, but also common people are being shot just because they assist to mass. The situation might end in another civil war," Enrique replied.

"Do you believe that we should tell Fidelio about our intentions?" Von Wernich asked.

"I know Fidelio, he is always ready to help those in need, even if that endangers him. But in this particular case I believe it's best to keep it just between us," Enrique replied.

"Good. Get men to build small cottages. We'll lease them to whoever needs a place to stay; and, of course, we might also use them as temporary shelter for those who are running away from persecution," Von Wernich said, as he lifted the coffee jar. "More coffee?" he asked.

"Yes, please," Enrique said, extending his clay cup. "Here is Fidelio," he added pointing to the entrance.

"Don Teo, Enrique, I would like a word with you," Fidelio said, walking in. He was dressed with simple, humble, white cotton pants and shirt, rough leather huaraches.

"Of course, Fidelio. What is it?" Von Wernich said, looking in a friendly manner at Fidelio.

"I'm afraid that I no longer can continue taking care of the goats. Every day more people come, asking for help. I believe that it's my duty to help them," said Fidelio, with a humble tone of voice.

Von Wernich looked at him, keeping his sympathetic smile. "Of course, Fidelio, precisely, we have been talking about it. From now on you'll be in charge of taking care of the sick. No other duty for you. As a matter of fact, if you need someone to help you collecting, preparing, or whatever you think is necessary, Enrique will take care of providing the men that you might need. Besides that, the warehouse we have been using to store candelilla, may be cleansed and prepared for the pregnant woman to stay."

"Thank you, that will help, there is something else I would like to ask for," Fidelio said.

"Yes, what is it?"

"I'll need the space under the Pirul. In there, I'll receive the people. Also, I would like to ask that the pool must be reserved to bath those who might be helped that way."

Von Wernich nodded approvingly, "that won't be a problem, that space and whatever you need to help are yours. As a matter of fact, we have also talked about building some cottages where those who come from far can stay."

Fidelio smiled, hesitated for a moment, "once again, thank you. That's great help, but still there is one more thing," Fidelio said, hesitant.

"Something else?" Von Wernich frowned, intrigued. Enrique looked at Fidelio, also intrigued.

"Yes, some of the people that have come looking for help, own a circus. God granted them to improve. They are thankful and have asked if there is something they own that could help to assist in the healing of others; and indeed, they have what I need; a mountain lion. It's not truly dangerous, they have removed its claws and fangs. But I already know how I could use it," said Fidelio, smiling.

Enrique and Von Wernich almost jumped from their seats. "A mountain lion? Are you sure, Fidelio?" Enrique asked.

Fidelio smiled at them. "Yes, I'm sure."

"Well, although I don't see how a mountain lion could help to return health, if you say that you already have an idea how you are going to use it, I'll allow it. But keep it in a cage," Von Wernich said, lifting a finger to put emphasis in his words.

"Yes, I will, and once again, thank you," Fidelio said, smiling and slightly bending in a humble way.

"No, thanks to be given to you," Von Wernich said, standing up. "You are a humble person and it shows. However, you are the one for whom people come looking for help. That would have happened wherever you are, because it's you who have that gift and you don't even try to take advantage of it." He walked and hugged Fidelio, Enrique also stood up. "Yes, Fidelio, thank you. We'll do whatever is necessary to help you," he said, touching Fidelio's shoulder.

"Fidelio, there are many waiting for you," one of the peons of the hacienda walked in.

"Do you want us to tell them that you are resting and you'll see them later?"

"No, I'll be with them right now. They have come from far," Fidelio replied.

He walked towards the pirul tree, where around one hundred people waited for him. When they saw him, respectfully they separated opening a path for him to walk through. Seeing their faces, he saw many disfigured by leprosy, tuberculosis, malnutrition and mental diseases. Many of their bodies deformed by chronic illness. Looking at them, Fidelio noticed that many of them were in the terminal stage of their illness. "To them, at least you can offer hope and comfort," he remembered he had been told. Although he felt sad about it, he also knew that he would have to learn to accept it. However, he also noticed that there were many to whom he could offer a real difference, to whom he could help to restore their health, to whom he could offer more, much more than only hope and comfort. "As long as there is one for whom I can make a difference, all the effort will be worthwhile," he thought. As he passed through, many of the ill people extended their hands trying to touch him. Fidelio allowed them.

Fidelio saw their pale faces, sunken eyes, swollen extremities, skin covered with sores, other full of warts. "So much suffering, there is much to do. God will guide me," he thought. A chair had been placed under the pirul; Fidelio sat on it and signaled to a man to approach. The man had his legs wrapped in bandages trying to cover the sores of his skin. Fidelio removed the bandages, took a branch of aloe, cut it, gave it to the man and asked him to bath in the pool using the open aloe instead of soap. The next man had painful warts in his feet, Fidelio covered them with banana peels and put bandage to hold the peels in place. "Leave them over night, change them tomorrow, soon you'll be better," he said to him.

Then came a woman, about thirty-years-old, pale, very pale, and eyes sunken. Fidelio looked at her. "Dear sister, you are bleeding too much," he said. She fell on her knees. "Thanks heaven, you know," she said. "I have consulted many doctors, they say there is nothing that can be done, you are my last hope, please help me," she added.

"You'll improve, the bleeding will stop," said Fidelio, taking a bottle with a tincture and giving it to her. "Five drops of this in a half glass of water every night, before you go to sleep, will cure you.

"Thank you, my child, God has sent you. God bless you and God bless the mother who carried you to life," she said sobbing, still on her knees, she kissed Fidelio's hand.

"Woman, you must thank God, not me. He loves you and He'll be the one healing you. God bless you," said Fidelio, as he helped her to get up.

Fidelio continued working non-stop. The night came, someone lighted torches, no one left, all waited patiently until their turn came. Most of them were poor peasants, shepherds, cowboys, many of them just accompanied their sick relatives, all hoping for help. Many came from the nearby villages or haciendas and had just walked or mounted a horse to Espinazo. Many others arrived by train, among them there were some who were better dressed, obviously economically fluent. Fidelio treated all the same, paid the same attention to all. There were some who offered to pay for the service received. "Give to the poor, never ignore those who extend their hands to you," Fidelio replied, in those instances.

Although the night was dark, Fidelio didn't stop. He continued under the light of the few torches. People patiently waited for their turn and, when the orange colors of the sunrise appeared in the horizon, Fidelio still continued under the pirul, listening, giving advice about the use of the healing herbs. Many received ointments, or beverages previously prepared by him. Most of them, after talking to Fidelio left smiling, happy and comforted. Some left comforted, but sad. Fidelio never gave false hope, but he always provided understanding and comfort. Even so, few left disappointed.

"In order to recover your health, you must stop smoking. Eat more fruits, onions and peppers, work hard and above all, stop cheating others. Think about the common benefit, instead of putting your interest first," Fidelio told a man who had come because of a chronic cough.

The man looked at him upset. "I traveled here from Zacatecas, waited in line since yesterday, just for you to tell me that!" he yelled.

"The cure is within your reach. I can only give you advice. You are the only one who can really help yourself. It's your choice," Fidelio replied with a soft, but firm voice. The man looked at him and walked away, upset.

Fidelio observed him walking away. "In reality, the most important person to help all of you are yourselves," Fidelio addressed those who waited. "If you are not willing to help yourselves, there is little I can do for you," Fidelio added.

"Fidelio the train has arrived with more people looking for you," Prudencio, one of the shepherds, told him.

"Be sure that there is food and water for them and also try to help those who have chosen to stay," Fidelio replied. "Everyone will receive attention," he added.

"Aren't you hungry, child?" Prudencio asked.

"Just get me water and a large slice of cantaloupe, please," Fidelio replied.

"You have been working since yesterday, you must rest," Prudencio said, concerned.

"How can I rest when there are so many in need? It's my duty to continue," Fidelio said, as he signaled for the next patient to approach.

"I'll bring you what you asked for," Prudencio said and walked towards the main house.

"Besides water and cantaloupe, I got you coffee and bread, just out of the oven. I'll leave it here," Prudencio said, when he came back. Fidelio smiled thankfully. Later, he gave the bread and coffee to an old man who had been waiting for long. Fidelio drank the water and ate the cantaloupe at intervals, as he listened to the people's complaints.

Fidelio remained under the pirul consulting those who patiently waited to be seen. It was mid-afternoon when he left to prepare the ointments and herbal products he knew would help in improving the health of those in need. He got absorbed in his job and did not notice the arrival of Von Wernich, who approached limping and grimacing in pain as he walked.

"Fidelio, are you busy?" he asked.

Fidelio turned and as soon as he saw Von Wernich, he knew that he had come in need of help. "No, Don Teo, never busy for you. How can I help you?"

"I didn't want to bother you with my problems. I've had a wart in my foot for a while. I confess to you that I have consulted several physicians in Saltillo and Monterrey. If anything, they only got it worse and, now the pain makes walking almost impossible. Could you help me?"

"Let me see," Fidelio said. Von Wernich sat, removed his boots and showed his feet to Fidelio who examined him in silence. In the plant of the left foot, Von Wernich had chronic warts that had become infected and an abscess had formed.

"Yes, I can help you," Fidelio said. "Close your eyes and imagine yourself as a child, imagine that childhood place where you felt happy, secure and protected. You are that child again, imagine that place of peace and enter it. Relax and enjoy it. It's a chilly day, but you feel comfortable, allow the cool breeze to caress you. There is a fountain, you have bathed in there many times and you know that the water is cold. Put your feet in the water. It feels nice and comfortable to feel the cold water in your feet." As he talked, Fidelio took a sharp piece of glass and opened the abscess in the foot, letting the pus drain. Afterwards, he applied an ointment he had already prepared mixing honey bee and aloe extract. On top of it, he placed a banana peel with the white towards the wound and finally applied bandage around the foot. "You'll need help to go back home, tomorrow I'll change the bandage," he said after he had finished.

"Von Wernich opened his eyes and looked at his foot. "Wow, I felt nothing and there is no more pain."

"I'll call Juancho and Prudencio to help you to go home. I'll treat your foot again tomorrow."

For the next seven days, besides taking care of those who arrived by train, mule or horse, Fidelio also took care of Von Wernich.

"Fidelio, you truly have a gift, now I can walk without pain, my feet have healed, the infection and the wart is gone. This is something that the entire world must be aware of. To be sure about that, I've written to the most important newspapers in Mexico. Soon the entire country, the world will know the wonder that is here in the middle of this desert. You are an angel of mercy," Von Wernich said, enthusiastically.

Fidelio frowned. "Don Teo," he said. "I'm happy to see how well you have responded to the treatment. But it's not me who should be praised, but the Lord who is the one that has given me this gift. I'm happy to help as many as I can, but I would prefer that all of this had stayed within us, there is no need for the newspapers."

"Non-sense," Von Wernich replied. "Besides I already passed the information to them and I have paid a full page to let everyone know what you have done, not only for me, but for all of those who keep coming, looking for help and getting it."

Once again, Fidelio frowned, serious. "Not all of them, many come here just to die," he said.

CHAPTER XXIV

"Every day two to three hundred people arrive by train and that's not counting those who come by other means of transport. People are coming from every corner of the country. Besides, there are many who come from the border states, mainly Texas and New Mexico. I know there are some who have come from Cuba," Enrique said to Von Wernich in a chilly November morning as they stood looking at the people leaving the train that had just arrived from Saltillo. The cold wind forced those who left the train to rub their arms.

"Well, I must admit that this is much better than what I had hoped for," Von Wernich said. "Besides thanking Fidelio for what he did for me, the main purpose of publicizing his ability to heal was indeed to attract people to travel here. As we have talked before, that makes it less risky for those running away from persecution to come. Once here, they can join those going to the north side of the border. My contacts in San Luis Potosi and Zacatecas have informed me that we should expect a group of nuns and priests arriving soon. It shouldn't be difficult to recognize them, they are foreigners. They'll be here soon, maybe in this train."

"The cottages that we built to lease for people who had to stay got occupied almost immediately after they were built. Now, most of those who for one reason or another, choose to stay are forced to improvise their shelter. They have built bush shacks and cover the holes with rags, or even with their own clothes. Although, I'm not an expert, I believe it's a matter of concern because many of them have contagious diseases. I know that the authorities in Monterrey and Saltillo are already paying attention to it," Enrique said, preoccupied.

"Yes, that's a matter of concern. However, I'm impressed by how well Fidelio has organized the way he provides his service. He has separated those with leprosy and other contagious diseases. He performs his surgical procedures in a room that he has managed to keep amazingly clean, and besides that, the area where women labor and deliver is also a clean place where he only allows the immediate family in. He insists in keeping everything clean and he himself washes his hands often and encourages all of those who assist him to do the same. Besides the gift of healing, Fidelio has shown to be an excellent organizer."

"When we served in the Northern Division, Fidelio organized and trained the team in charge of helping and transporting those wounded during battle," Enrique said. "He is a natural leader."

"Townsfolk say that Fidelio has the soul of a child and has never been with a woman. Do you know anything about that?" Von Wernich asked.

"Well, I can tell you that in different circumstances, Fidelio would be happily married by now. But, don't tell that to anyone, let them believe what they believe," Enrique replied. Something among those leaving the train called his attention. Von Wernich noticed it and looked in the same direction.

A young couple, both of them blond, left the first-class car guiding a blind child, about eight-years-old. They seemed disconcerted looking at the poverty and desolation of the small village. Looking around, the young man noticed Enrique and Von Wernich and signaled his wife to follow him.

"Excuse me, sir," the man addressed Von Wernich, with a heavy accent that denounced him to be a recent immigrant from Spain. "We are coming from Veracruz looking for the man whom the people call 'the Child.' Is this the place?"

"Indeed, this is it," Von Wernich replied. "Is he the reason you come here?" he asked pointing to the blind boy.

"Yes, it's because of him. We have consulted several physicians in Veracruz and Mexico City, all of them agree in that they don't know what is wrong with him and that there is nothing they can do to help him."

"What happened? How is it that he got this way? Was he born blind?" asked Enrique.

"No, his sight was perfectly normal until last year. When we arrived at Veracruz, he made a lot of friends in the neighborhood. Last year, during the celebration of Mexico's independence, he and his friends played with fire crackers. One of them exploded before he could release it. Since then he has been blind. We read in the newspapers from Mexico City about the amazing cures of this Child and decided to come. We hope he'll be able to help us. Almost all of those who arrived with us have come for similar reasons. There are so many people." The man answered, preoccupied; his wife upset, concerned. She caressed the boy who in spite of his problem remained calm; he even seemed to be hopeful listening to the many people around them.

"As you can see, thousands are already here, waiting for Fidelio. All are like you, expecting something short of a miracle from him. Until now, he has managed to see almost everyone that have come. But, it's impossible to say when you'll get your chance," said Enrique.

"It doesn't matter how long it takes, as I said, he is our hope. We'll wait. Is there a place where we can stay?" asked the young man, looking around.

"Unfortunately, no," Enrique said. "People who has stayed, have built their own shelter. I'm afraid you'll have to do the same."

The couple looked at the humble shacks recently built, "we'll do that. Thank for your help." They walked away.

"People come here because they have faith, faith in Fidelio. It's not only that they have read or heard others about Fidelio's gift. It's impressive that the common denominator for all of those who come, it's the faith they all show. That's powerful," Enrique said, looking at the couple who walked among the recently built huts, trying to choose a place where they would build their own shack.

"Indeed, it is. It seems that some of the people that we have been waiting for have arrived," Von Wernich said, making a gesture in direction of the train, where three women and two middle-aged men, disembarked from the second-class wagon. They seemed to argue among themselves, one of them pointed in the direction of the main house. "Let's find out," Von Wernich added, starting to walk toward them. Enrique followed him.

"Friends, you seem to be lost. Probably, we can help you. What are you looking for?" Von Wernich told the group as he and Enrique approached them.

"By your accent, I gather you are the man we are looking for," said the elder of the women, in Spanish, with a heavy German accent.

"Yes, you are probably right," Von Wernich said, smiling. "How could I help you?"

The woman pulled a rosary from her neck and showed it to Von Wernich and Enrique.

Von Wernich extended his arm signaling her to cover the rosary. "We have been waiting for you. Would you like to have breakfast with us? My house is the one you just pointed to," he said extending his arm, showing the way.

"Yes, it's been a while since we had a real meal," one of the men said, a grunt sound came from his belly. The five of them followed Enrique and Von Wernich to the main house where they were served breakfast.

"Thank you, those scrambled eggs with hot sauce were excellent. Since we left San Luis, we haven't had a good hot meal," said the woman with the German accent, the two other women nodded agreeably. The two men smiled.

"Well, reverend mother, I'll say that the gorditas we have been eating along the way were also good. For me they were the equivalent of the manna God sent to the Jewish people. He always takes care of his people," one of the men said.

"I'm happy to see that now you feel secure and talk lightly. But, in reality, how did you manage to escape? What is truly happening?" Enrique asked, as he served more coffee in the clay cups.

The faces of the five, showed grief. Tears rolled down for one of the women. "We had a convent and a school in Patzcuaro. One day the soldiers came in and closed our school and the convent. They forced everyone out. Some attempted to rape the nuns. Fortunately, their Captain was an honest man and didn't allow it, but I'm aware of others who weren't as lucky as we have been," said the elder nun.

"Mexico is a Catholic country, how is that things have come to be this way? Why this persecution?" Von Wernich asked.

"It's a long story, Mexico has not progressed to its potential. Peons, farmers, workers are abused by those who are wealthy and have some power. The church failed to denounce it and, after Madero's assassination, the hierarchy, in a pharisaic way, decided to support what they thought would maintain the status quo of the Church with the government. Although one could understand their reasons, we must by now realize that it was a mistake, a serious mistake. They knew the way Huerta seized power. It was not only a serious mistake, but a stupid one. I'm sorry to say that, but we are all paying the consequences. It fed those who were already blaming the church for the country's situation," said the elder of the two men. The elder nun frowned, the other two nuns opened their mouths, surprised on hearing such criticism of the Catholic hierarchy.

"I'm surprised to hear a priest criticizing in such a way those who are your leaders. 'Obedience,' isn't that one of the vows you must make when you become a priest?" Von Wernich asked.

"Obey? Yes, we didn't like it, but we obeyed. However, that doesn't prevent us to see what has happened. We come from Sonora and as far as we are concerned, all the work done with the Yaqui in Sonora and the Raramuri in Chihuahua is now nullified, and all of this is happening when there is so much to do, to help them to get out of their poverty. At the same time, we must recognize that the actual government is not truly honest when they say they want to help the poor. All of this has become a way to tighten the grip and maintain power," said the priest, upset.

"During the years of war, we started to see how some of the troops under Obregon and Elias Called ravaged some churches. During those years, in Sonora, at least, there were moderate men like Maytorena and Adolfo de la Huerta, who controlled them. Unfortunately, the group commanded by Obregon and Elias Calles is the group that finally has seized the power in Mexico. Zapata was assassinated by Carranza's orders. Carranza was then assassinated under Obregon's orders. Villa, De la Huerta, and Buelna, all of those who could be an opposition force have also been assassinated or forced to emigrate. The rest of those with some influence, have just been bought. Even under Obregon there was hope for a truce, but after his assassination, the radical Elias Calles has been unleashed. Temples have been ravaged, some have been converted into schools or public libraries. Unfortunately, those are the least, most are used for barracks or stables. Many priests when captured have been shot on the spot. On our way here, we saw hundreds of hanged men along the railway," said the younger priest, in a sad tone of voice. "The hate is worse against those priests and nuns who are foreigners; that's why we have to leave the country. Hopefully it won't be long before we can return. I love this country," he added.

"It seems that we got rid of a despotic dictator just to get a worse one," Enrique said, also in a sad tone of voice. "So many men died fighting for justice. I wonder what my old classmates are doing. Knowing them, I'm certain they have joined the rebellion."

"Although there are no battles here and the persecution is less severe, we are a part of the movement of resistance and we'll help you to get out of the country safely. Although, as you will find out, Fidelio starts his healing sessions praying. That puts all of us in danger, but he won't stop," Von Wernich said.

"The fame of this Child is already known. I know that there is concern in the Church's hierarchy. For the time being, because of the struggle with the government, they have chosen to keep silent about this. But, as I already said, there is concern," said the young priest.

"In that aspect, I would fancy that's something in which both, government and church agree, neither are happy with what is happening here," Enrique said. "We received a notice that a commission is coming to investigate the sanitary condition here."

"Now that you mention that," said the young priest. "What is really happening here? You are surrounded by a large shantytown. Although I'm not a physician, I noticed that many of those who travel along with us have little hope, they seem to be in terminal stages of their illness. Also, there are many with contagious diseases. So many of them in the same place, with so little water and such a miserable condition. It doesn't require much knowledge to realize that there is a real danger for the beginning of an epidemic situation."

"God protects this place, as He has protected us. I can see now the reason why he brought us here," said the elder nun.

"What do you mean?" Von Wernich asked.

"This Child, as the people call him, is obviously a child of God and God is the one who has guided us here in order to help with the Child's mission. We are going to stay here," she replied with a firm tone of voice, the two young women looked at her, surprised.

"But are you aware of the risk that you and your sisters are running if you stay here? You, in particular, are a foreigner, and there is no way you can disguise that," Von Wernich said.

"There is nothing to disguise if your child accepts we'll stay, that's God's design and we must obey," the nun replied. This time the younger nuns smiled approvingly.

"We applaud your decision," the elder of the priests said. "Personally, I wish I could also stay, but in our case we would only endanger the extraordinary accomplishment of this man, who I understand is humble and remains so."

"That's true," Enrique said. I have known him since childhood. He is humble, and as a matter of fact, he has not lost it."

"But Mother, what could you do? How could you help Fidelio?" Von Wernich asked.

"We have been taught about nursing. In the convent, we must take care of ourselves; I'm sure the Child will find us helpful. I know that we have been brought here for a reason and that reason is not to escape the persecution, but to help in God's work."

"As you already have noticed there is no suitable place to accommodate you, if you chose to stay. You'll be on your own in that matter," Von Wernich said.

"As a matter of fact, there are already some volunteers working with Fidelio, I'm sure he'll receive you with gratitude and that you'll find that there is plenty to do," Enrique said. "I'll take you to him."

"I'm sure that the sisters, as myself, are eager to start serving. Let's go and meet him now," the elder nun said, standing up. The two younger nuns also stood up as the priests did.

"I'd like to meet him too. We'll go with you," one the priests said.

"Good, let's go and find him. At this hour, he must be under the pirul," Enrique said, taking a last sip of his coffee and standing up.

The pirul was just a few steps away from the main building. They found Fidelio surrounded by hundreds of hopeful people. Fidelio lead a prayer of the rosary. The nuns and the priests, smiling and nodding approvingly, looked at each other and joined in the prayer.

"Child, you know that the public religious ceremonies are forbidden. We have talked about it before, for sure the authorities are going to be informed," Von Wernich said to Fidelio as they approached.

"It's only through prayer and faith that those who can be healed will be healed. There is no way to silence the voice of the Lord," Fidelio replied.

"Yes, Child, you must continue with your mission, don't allow anyone to stop you. God is with you," the elder nun said. The other two nodded agreeably.

Fidelio looked at the three women and smiled in a friendly manner to them. "We have been waiting for you. Yes, your help is much needed and it will be appreciated. You'll be in charge of the women in labor and also, you'll help in assisting in some of the surgeries. But, today just follow me and pay attention." Von Wernich, Enrique, the priests and nuns, all looked at him surprised.

"How did you know that they are here to volunteer their services?" one of the priests asked.

Fidelio just shrugged his shoulders and smiled, "the Lord works in many ways."

CHAPTER XXV

One year later, in a chilly winter morning, two men disembarked from the train. To fight the bitter cold wind, they jumped while they rubbed their arms and face in an attempt to warm up a little.

"This must be the place, it's more desolated, miserable and dry than I had thought," said one of them, looking around. Hundreds of miserable shacks everywhere they looked, many sick people just sat, trying to get some of the sun rays to warm up.

"Yes, we are in the right place. We'll find the man they call 'the Child' here. I wonder if, once they find out the reason we are here, we'll be welcomed," said the other one. "I would say that's our man," he added pointing to a pirul tree where Fidelio, dressed in a long white robe, a red heart pierced by an arrow embroidered in the chest part of the robe, was sitting. Around his waist, a rough ixtle cord; barefoot, he called someone to get close to him.

"Yes, that's exactly how I had imagined this 'child'," said the first man, smirking. "What is he doing?"

Fidelio had started rocking a man in a swing, but intentionally, Fidelio bumped and pinched the man as he came down. Obviously, that had upset the man, who turned and looked at Fidelio in a menacing way.

"Why that man doesn't say anything?" asked one of the two men.

The other shrugged his shoulders. "I don't know."

"Child, that hurts. Stop doing that!" yelled the man in the swing, who apparently had had enough bumping by Fidelio. Everyone in the crowd clapped. "Alleluia, alleluia, praised be the Lord," started singing some of those present.

"What happened? Why is everyone praising the Lord?" one of the two newly arrived men asked a woman also dressed in a long white robe.

"That man came here because he was mute," she replied, smiling, obviously happy, but not surprised.

"What? Do you mean that man was mute and now he can speak? the man asked, disconcerted. "I don't believe it. It must be a trick."

The woman turned, looked at him, still smiling. "He's not the first one, many others have come in a worse condition than him and most like him, have recovered their voice. You just saw it. It doesn't matter if you believe it or not."

"Yes, you are right, even having seen it, still it is difficult to believe. Do you know the child?" the man asked.

"Yes, I'm one of the many who have volunteered to help him."

"My name is Jacobo Dalevuelta, I'm a reporter and he is Agustin Casasola, a photographer. We are here sent from the newspaper 'El Universal' in Mexico City. Could you introduce us to him?"

The woman, who was one of the nuns, looked at them. "Yes, as a matter of fact, he has been talking about your arrival, come with me, he is expecting you."

"What do you mean when you say that he is expecting us?" Casasola asked. "How did he know?"

As she walked toward the pirul, the nun turned and smiled at him. "I just know that he has talked about the arrival of two men who come to witness what is being done here. You are not the first one to show surprise by his abilities. There are others who have come here with the intention of 'unmasking the tricks performed,' but it's always him who surprises everyone. After witnessing what he can do, some have chosen to stay and help. Here we are," she said, as they approached.

Fidelio, at the time pointed to a paralyzed woman. He took an orange from a bag full of fruits and threw the orange to her, she caught it, peeled it and ate it. Fidelio smiled at her.

"You'll have to move for the next one," Fidelio told her. The nun touched Fidelio's shoulder who turned and looked at her. "What is it, Sister?" he asked her.

"Child, these two men are from a newspaper in Mexico City."

Fidelio looked at the two men. "You are welcome. Open your eyes. Go whereever you like and tell people what you have seen, be sure to tell the truth," he said to Dalevuelta. Fidelio then looked at Casasola's camera. "Take as many pictures of whatever you like, but be sure to give me copies, because if you don't, none of them will come out."

"Thank you, child. We'll report only the truth," Dalevuelta said. Casasola started taking pictures of Fidelio and the shanty town. "But, also we would like to have a conversation with you. We hope you could explain to us in detail, exactly what it is that you are doing here," added Dalevuelta.

"We'll have time for that," Fidelio replied, as he turned noticing the blind child and his parents. He walked in their direction.

Noticing that Fidelio walked towards them, the mother of the child came forward. "Child, God bless you. We heard about you and have traveled here from Veracruz, our son needs your help, he…" Fidelio signaled her to stop talking. "There is no need for you to tell me what is wrong with him. I already know and I can tell you that he'll recover his sight," Fidelio told her. Then he proceeded to gently massage the boy's eyes as he looked to the sky in deep concentration moving his lips, like praying, but no sound was heard. After a few minutes, Fidelio addressed the young boy: "You are healed, hand me a handkerchief to cover his eyes." After applying the handkerchief, he turned to the boy's parents. "Remove the handkerchief at sunrise tomorrow," he told them. Then he turned to see the paralytic woman. He went to the bag with fruits, chose an apple and threw it to her a little farther than the previous one. She had to move to catch this one, Fidelio smiled. "You are already improving," he told her. Casasola took pictures and Dalevuelta wrote in his notebook.

"Move, everyone move out! The Child will receive me, even if he doesn't want. I'll break anyone who tries to stop me!" yelled a strong, young man. Pushing those in front of him and forcing his way through. An elder couple behind him, trying, unsuccessfully, to control him.

Fidelio signaled to let him approach. "What's wrong, son?" he asked the man. "Why are you pushing people?"

"Child, this is my youngest son. During his childhood, he was gentle and well-mannered with everyone. He did well in school. However, as he has grown up, he has become violent and troublesome. He is always picking fights, even with us, his parents who love him. It seems that the devil has entered him," said the woman who had followed the young man, as she tried to hold her son's hand, who moved his hand away in a rude manner.

"Nothing wrong with me, mama," said the man, in a harsh tone of voice. "My strength has proven to everyone that they have to obey me, even you and my father. No one will prevent me from taking advantage of it."

"You'll learn to use your God's given strength to serve Him," Fidelio said to the man with a firm tone of voice.

The man laughed. "My strength is to serve me only and only me!" he yelled at Fidelio, showing his large fist to him.

Fidelio smiled gently at him. "There is no need to be afraid."

"Afraid? Me afraid? I'm afraid of nothing, you and everyone else should be afraid of me!" said the man, upset.

"Afraid of nothing? Let us test how valiant you are. Do you agree?"

"What do you mean?" the man asked, now hesitant, frowning.

"It's simple, you just follow me," Fidelio said, with a soothing tone of voice.

The man smirked. "I'm stronger and more courageous than you are, I'll follow you to hell, if that's what you want."

"Wonderful, let's go," said Fidelio, walking into the cage where the mountain lion was. The man followed him and as soon as he walked in, the mountain lion roared and jumped to the man's chest putting him down and getting on top of him.

"Aaaayyy, Take it away from me! Get me out of here!" yelled the man, scared and crying. He tried to move, the lion kept on top of him. Kneeling, Fidelio caressed the lion that moved away from the man and caressed Fidelio's cheek with its head. Surprised, the man got up.

"Are you afraid of a little cat?" Fidelio asked.

The man bent his head, embarrassed. "You have shown me that I, like everyone else, fear something stronger than me. I have learned the lesson. You are right, from now on, I'll use my God's given strength to serve the Lord and protect others. Thank you, Child, you are truly a man of God," he said, walking out of the cage. When Fidelio walked with him out of the cage, the young man's parents took Fidelio's hands, trying to kiss them, Fidelio stopped them.

"You must thank God, everything I do is because of Him," he told them, making the signal of the cross to them. Casasola took pictures; Dalevuelta wrote notes.

Two young women dressed in long white robes embroidered with the pierced heart in the front part of it, helped two men who carried a middle- aged man, in an improvised stretcher. The man looked at Fidelio with sadness. "Child, I'm beyond help. God has taken away my limbs, His will must be obeyed. This is how I must pay for all my sins."

Fidelio, without saying a word, uncovered his legs and taking oil, he started massaging the man's legs; as he did, he mumbled a religious song. Those who heard him, started singing along with him. "Ay, virgin of hope come! Help me to save my soul, because I suffer in pain, Ay little virgin pray Jesus for him and me, I want to be His love and be the eternal captive of His love."

"God has seen that you repent, He has forgiven you. Now you must forgive yourself and your sins will be forgiven," Fidelio told the man after a few more minutes. He then turned to the women in the long dress, "he'll need to be treated again tomorrow. Be sure he is carried back."

More pictures were taken by Casasola and more notes were written by Dalevuelta.

Fidelio moved forward to assist another person. Dalevuelta signaled to Casasola to stay and interview the paralytic man.

"You look like an educated man. Where are you from?" Dalevuelta asked the man who, surprised, looked in another direction, sobbing silently. Tears in his eyes.

"Leave him alone, please," said one of the two men who helped the man in the stretcher. "He has suffered enough, please don't ask him anymore questions. That only will increase his sorrow."

"It's fine, I'll answer your questions," said the man to Dalevuelta. "Talking about it, probably will help me," he said to the man who had talked. "You can say that I'm an educated man, and indeed, I'm a physician, practicing in Torreon," he answered Dalevuelta's question.

"How is it that you lost the use of your legs?" asked Dalevuelta. "I noticed that your legs are strong."

The man smiled sarcastically. "At the school, I used to play soccer."

"How is it that you became unable to walk?"

The man shriveled, tears flowed down his cheeks. He opened his mouth in an attempt to answer, but no sound came out of it. One of the men who carried him rubbed his shoulder.

"Calm, Pancho, there is no need to go through this," the man said.

"Yes, I must," replied the man called Pancho. "One day, I was on call at Torreon's Civil Hospital. The day had been calm so I decided to accept an invitation to a party. Once in there I had a good time and drank more than I should. Close to midnight I was called to the hospital, in one of the nearby haciendas there had been a machete and gun fight. There were several men badly wounded. I meant to go, but I drank too much; my friend, who gave the party, helped me to shower and gave me strong coffee. But by the time I arrived at the hospital, it was too late. Three men had bled to death. I was able to stop the bleeding in one of the men, but he developed a serious infection, his legs became gangrenous and I had to amputate his legs in a futile attempt to save his life. It's all my fault and I deserve to suffer for it."

"Did the Child know anything about this? Have you talked to him before today?" Dalevuelta asked.

"No, today is the first time I talked about it. I had never seen the Child before."

"How is that you decided to come?"

"A colleague from Monterey told me about what Fidelio had done to save the leg of a miner in a mine close by."

"How do you feel now?"

"After the massage, I now feel my legs. I already feel better."

Intrigued, Dalevuelta frowned. "The Child has no medical education.

What do you think about what he is doing here?"

The man looked around, to those suffering, many of them in terminal stage. "At least he offers them hope, for most of these people that's more than we, who went to medical school, can offer them," the man replied.

"Thank you for answering my questions," Dalevuelta told the man. "We must catch up with the Child," he told Casasola.

The night came and Fidelio, under the dim light of torches, continued helping as many as he could. He didn't stop to eat or rest, even so, he seemed to be full of energy. A woman tended to her husband who lied on the floor, only by the light in his eyes those around him could tell he was still alive. Fidelio kneeled on his side, without a word he uncovered the man's belly, pulled a bottle from the ixtle bag that he hanged around his shoulders, poured some fluid into his hands and massaged the man's belly; several scars from previous surgeries became visible. Fidelio smiled to the man as he massaged him. "Now rest for a while. When you are ready, eat a banana," he told the man when he finished, leaving some bananas at the man's side.

"But, Child, for days, he has not tolerated any food," the woman said, before Fidelio left.

Fidelio turned, "he will now."

A group of men pushed those around Fidelio in order to facilitate that a man in uniform could get to Fidelio. "I'm General Peraldi-Carranza," said the man in uniform. "I have heard about you and against the advice of my Doctor and my family I have decided to come to ask for your help," he stood firm in front of Fidelio. "I've been here for almost a week and I don't appreciate to be forced to wait," he added.

Fidelio looked at him, a sad expression in his face. "You are welcome to stay, if you wish, but it would be better for you to get in peace with your creator. God have mercy on your soul, there is nothing I can offer you," he told the man as he made the signal of the cross to him and started walking away. He stopped yielding to a procession of mourners praying the rosary. They carried four rough wood caskets to the newly created cemetery. Casasola took pictures and Dalevuelta wrote notes.

Fidelio then climbed to the roof of one of the adobe houses and from there he threw oranges, apples, bananas and other fruits to the multitude that followed him. Those who were hit by one of the fruits jumped expressing their gratitude to the Child. There were some, who, when hit by the fruit yelled: "Thank you Child, my pain and sorrows are gone, thank you." The multitude started singing the same song, they had previously sung.

The orange-yellow rays of the sunrise found Fidelio assisting those in need. Casasola and Dalevuelta looked exhausted. Fidelio, who had been working non-stop, seemed fresh and full of energy, like he had slept for several hours and eaten a hearty meal.

"Child, when do you rest? When do you eat? You have been working non-stop since we arrived yesterday morning. Aren't you tired?" Dalevuelta asked.

"They come from far away looking for help, there is no time to rest," Fidelio answered.

"That might be so for you," Dalevuelta said. "But, my friend and I are just common people. We arrived just yesterday after several days of travel to get here, we need to rest and eat. Is there a place where we could just do that?"

"Enrique, the foreman of this hacienda will find you a place," Fidelio said signaling to one of the peons of the hacienda. "Prudencio, take these men to Enrique, they need hostage and food." Fidelio told the man and he was about to continue his work when at the distance a child's voice was heard. "I see! I can see now!" cried the child. "Alleluia! Blessed be the Lord!" Many voices were heard. Intrigued, Dalevuelta and Casasola looked at each other.

The parents of the blind boy and the boy himself approached Fidelio. The woman threw herself at Fidelio's feet taking his hand and kissing them. "Thank you, Child, thank you," she said, crying.

"How could we pay what you have done for us?" asked the father of the boy.

"Praise and thank the Lord. He is the one who has allowed your son to be healed. Give to the poor as often as you can," Fidelio replied and turned to continue his work.

Dalevuelta and Casasola followed Prudencio to the main house; they had to stop to allow another funeral procession to pass by. Casasola called Dalevuelta's attention to the man whose belly Fidelio had massaged standing up and eating a banana.

CHAPTER XXVI

It was almost noon when Enrique met the reporters in front of the house he now occupied alongside the main building. Although in the early morning hours the day had been very cold, the absence of clouds allowed the blazing sun rays to warm the desert. Casasola and Dalevuelta had to remove their jackets, the day had become hot. Children chased thousands of butterflies passing by on their way south and that made the town look almost cheerful.

"Don Teo, the owner of the hacienda and myself have been already informed about your arrival. I assume that by now, you have realized that the Child does not hide anything. He'll allow you to witness what he is doing here. If he welcomes you, of course we also welcome you. Is there anything I can do to make your stay pleasant?" Enrique told the reporters.

"Yes, of course, we would like to find a place where we can stay. We have traveled for several days, and since our arrival, yesterday, we accompanied the Child witnessing his activities. We would like to refresh ourselves and rest," Dalevuelta told Enrique.

"I believe Don Teo won't oppose if you stay at his house, there are several bedrooms in there and he lives alone," Enrique told the reporters. "I assume that you must be hungry. Petronila, Don Teo's cook, will prepare you something to eat, whenever both of you are ready." "Whose tent is that?" asked Casasola, pointing to a large military tent erected in one side of the main house.

"That's the tent prepared for General Peraldi," Enrique replied.

"I remember that the Child looked at him yesterday. 'It would be better to make peace with your Creator,' he told him," Casasola said.

"Among the many abilities that the Child has, is that he recognizes when the end is close by. He does not offer false hope. It's sad for me to inform you that the General died last night. A few hours after the Child saw him. I had an opportunity to meet him when Villa and Carranza were in friendly terms and, of course, we talked during his stay here. He was an honest man and a real patriot," Enrique said, in a sad tone of voice.

"Indeed, I interviewed him while he was in Mexico City," Dalevuelta said.

"Will he be buried here?" Casasola asked.

"No, his body has already been taken to Cuatrocienegas, his birth place," Enrique replied.

"We came here convinced that this Child would be just another quack; thus far he has surprised us in a favorable way," Dalevuelta said. "He was already working when we arrived yesterday morning and he has continued non-stop through the night and was still taking care of people when we left. Does he work this way all the time?"

"Yes, sometimes he works several days and nights non-stop. 'People travels here from far, they come here looking for help. It's my duty to serve them,' he says" Enrique replied. "But, you must be tired, it would be best for you to rest. I'll show you your room."

Later that evening, Dalevuelta and Casasola, fully rested after several hours of sleep, joined Enrique, Von Wernich and two other men for dinner. Enrique introduced the reporters to Von Wernich and pointed to the two men. "Friends of Don Teo," he introduced them. They all shook hands and sat at the table, where coffee had already been served.

"Is the Child still working?" Casasola asked.

"Yes, he's still working, he is too conscious of his duty and tries to help as many as possible; if he could help it, no one should have to wait for his assistance," Von Wernich answered.

"But he has to sleep, eat, urinate and empty his bowel, like everyone else," Casasola said.

Von Wernich smirked, the two men also looked interested in the answer. "He eats from the bag of fruits he carries with him, or whatever people offer him, lies down to sleep whenever he feels exhausted and of course, urinates and defecates like everyone else. He has to be careful though, when he urinates people try to catch his urine and drink it."

"Ouch, that's dirty," one of the men said.

Dalevuelta looked at the two men, moved his hand to his chin, frowning like in deep thought. He then looked at Von Wernich and Enrique, hesitant to say what he was thinking. "At the risk of being an unpleasant guest, but as a reporter, I have found that it is best for me to be open and honest to those around me. I noticed that both of you traveled in the same train by which we arrived yesterday. You don't seem to be sick and you don't look Mexicans. What has brought you here?"

"You should try these scrambled eggs with chorizo," intervened Enrique, pointing to the plate that Petronila carried and had started serving. "The chorizo is prepared here by one of our peons, it's excellent," Enrique added, nervous.

Dalevuelta noticed Enrique's nervousness. "There is no need to be nervous. You are priests, aren't you?" he asked the two men, who were now confused and only looked at him while nervously trying to find an answer.

Dalevuelta raised his right hand in a calming gesture. "There is no need to be afraid. Although I'm not a religious person and agree with the government in many of the reasons to be against the Church, I disagree with the persecution and the violence employed against you people. My friend here and I have discussed about it often and both of us agree that people should be free to practice the religion they chose to believe. As a matter of fact, we have noticed that this is a place where God is continually praised," Dalevuelta smiled in a friendly way to the two men, then he turned to look at Von Wernich and Enrique. "I can guess what you are doing," he added. "You are taking advantage that so many people are travelling here; so, the religious people who are persecuted can come safely and from here, you'll help them to cross the border. Not only that we won't denounce you, but we'll help as much as we can. Am I correct? My friend," he asked Casasola.

"Yes, you are," Casasola replied. He took a sip of his coffee and smiled to all. "Now, let's try those scrambled eggs with chorizo. Let's see if your chorizo is as good as the one from Toluca."

Von Wernich, Enrique and the two men laughed, relieved. Petronila, who had followed the conversation, also happy, served them more coffee.

After dinner, they enjoyed a glass of sotol. "Is this tequila or maybe mescal?" Dalevuelta asked.

"No, this is sotol. It's also from agave, as tequila and mescal are, but this is the agave from this region and the method of distillation is also a bit different," Von Wernich answered, proudly.

"You sound proud," one of the priests said.

"Yes, I'm proud of this my new fatherland and proud of what we are doing here," Von Wernich replied.

Dalevuelta looked at the two priests, with a friendly expression. "If you want to share with us your experiences, we'll appreciate. I promise nothing of whatever you say will be sent to the newspapers. However, later, when all this turmoil has passed, it will become an important historical information. Even then, if I would choose to publish it, your name will never appear and how it was that we met. The secret of Espinazo will never be revealed."

The elder of the two priests, sighed. "To officiate mass is the best part of being a priest. He took bread and gave to His disciples. 'This my body,' the priest paused. Then He took the wine and served it to them. 'This is my blood. Do this in my memory.' He added. Not to be able to follow His order, it's the hardest part for me." He crossed his hands in front of his chest, a sad look on his face.

The younger priest also had a sad expression on his face. "I agree with that. But I believe that something good will come of all of this. We must admit that the Church often has forgotten that Jesus showed a strong preference for the poor. That He preferred to serve them and choose not to get involved in the political situation of His time." His face was now blushed. "He warned us. He was clear when He said: 'Because of me, you'll be persecuted'," he said. He looked at the shantytown around them. To all the people suffering. "What is happening here is extraordinary. It seems that He wants to show us that He remains around us. 'What you do for those who have nothing you also do it for me.' He said. I wish I could stay here," he added and sighed.

"But many have died defending the right to practice the religion they love and chose to follow. How many did we see hanging from the telegraph posts on our way here? Hundreds, maybe thousands. Not only men, but also women and children were hanged. Nuns have been raped," the elder priest said, raising his voice, upset.

"You must admit that there have been many priests who have abused. There are many stories of women and children abused by priests. It's not only the political aspect of all of this," intervened Casasola, with a serious expression on his face.

"Enough of all of that," Dalevuelta said. "This discussion is leading us nowhere. Both sides have reasons for it. We'll concentrate only in the work of the Child and that's all we are going to report about. It's getting dark already and it seems that the Child is still working."

It was almost dawn of the following day when Fidelio started to feel exhausted, he hadn't slept or eaten for more than three days. Everywhere he looked around, he saw ill people who were waiting for an opportunity to receive his treatment, or at least his advice. A lot of them invalid, blind, deaf, mute, disfigured, many of them at terminal stage, many of those waiting had no chance to recover and Fidelio knew it. "I must continue, there is so much to do, so many people come here hoping for a cure, or at least, hope to find some comfort in their suffering, although their suffering makes them closer to God," he thought. "My tiredness and hunger means nothing. I must continue." He bent his head and rubbed his forehead fighting his exhaustion.

"You look exhausted Child, and certainly you are tired. Come and rest here," one of the bystanders told him with a gentle, loving, tone of voice.

"Yes, Child, it's time to rest. Eat a bit of this soup that I just prepared for my family, it will be good for you. This man is right, you need to rest," said a woman, offering him a bowl full of a healthy looking, vegetable soup. Fidelio took it, sat, ate the soup, laid down and almost immediately closed his eyes and fell into deep sleep.

Fidelio found himself standing in a boulevard. It had wide streets adorned with beautiful and colorful flowery plants in the middle and trees with luxuriant foliage on the side. Modern automobiles passed by and the attractive women in them smiled in a coquettish manner to him. A bit embarrassed Fidelio paid attention to his clothes. He was surprised to find that he was dressed in an elegant cashmere suit, he smiled when he looked at his shiny black shoes and the silk tie around his neck. The entire neighborhood was elegant. The large houses were surrounded by well- groomed gardens. Fidelio realized that somehow, he now belonged to the high society and he was respected, even admired. He felt important and being taller than the majority of those around him, he straightened his back and walked around, grinning proudly.

An elegant automobile stopped and a man dressed in a white linen suit accompanied by a beautiful blond woman came out smiling in a friendly way to Fidelio. "Fidelio, my friend, it's nice to see you. You look well and I can see that you are doing better than well. That healing ability of yours really produces eh? Everywhere we go people talk wonders about you," the man laughed, a vulgar and noisy laugh. "And they pay well, don't they?" he added in an ironic tone of voice and slapped Fidelio on the shoulder.

Fidelio, his smile gone, didn't answer. He couldn't remember where he had met this man, but he was certain that they had met several times and the way he acted meant that they knew each other and, by his attitude, they were in friendly terms. Indeed, since he had decided to leave Espinazo and had established his practice in Mexico City. He had become wealthy, very wealthy, people respected him, even physicians were happy to refer patients to him – for a small fee, of course.

The man grinned, he was attractive, very attractive, Fidelio started to enjoy his presence. "Let me introduce you to Leticia, she is beautiful, isn't she? You'll find her even better than any other I have brought to you."

Fidelio almost jumped, surprised. "Other women, what other women?" he asked himself.

The man noticed Fidelio's surprise. "Come on my friend, there is no need to act between us," he said as he got closer to whisper in Fidelio's ear. "As for her, you'll enjoy her. She knows about all the other women and she doesn't care and she won't talk, your image of chastity will be maintained. But as you'll understand that will cost you a bit more. She has an expensive taste. You understand that, don't you?"

Suddenly, Fidelio recognized the man, but he felt tempted; tempted by the beautiful woman, tempted by the promise of pleasure and the enjoyable presence of the man. However, at the same time, he felt nauseated and disgusted. Although it was a cool day, he felt hot, terribly hot, he sweated and, besides all that he now felt a sudden urgency to urinate. He saw a church close by and somehow, he hoped that he would find a restroom in there. So, he ran in that direction. The noisy, vulgar laugh of the man and the woman followed him. As he entered the church, the nausea and the urgency he had felt, disappeared, the sweat gone, in there he felt calm, protected. Feeling now a sensation of peace, he walked to the altar and weeping he fell on his knees. "What have I done? Why did I abandon Espinazo? Why did I fail Candelaria? How could I have forgotten her?" He asked himself. "Fidelio, Fidelio, my love, I'm with you, as long as you remember me, I always will be at your side," he heard Candelaria's sweet voice. He felt now calm, he got up and walked out of the church.

When he left the church, he was surprised to find that he was now in a little town, close to Guanajuato; it was night. A procession, mourning procession passed by. Men walked with their chin to their chests, women and children weeping, a long funeral procession, hundreds of caskets carried to the cemetery. The mourners monotonously prayed the rosary. Mounted in white horses, skeletons in dark military uniforms, flanked the procession. The sound of a solitary drum, pacing the rhythm of the procession, was heard at the distance. It was a brilliant night with a shiny, full moon in the sky. Fidelio moved aside to allow the procession to pass. Intrigued, he asked himself, "What is this funeral procession? Who are these people? Who are those dead? Why are so many mourning and so many dead?" As the funeral procession passed by, Fidelio noticed that the mourners were dressed in long black robes.

"Interesting procession, isn't it?" A man dressed in an elegant charro suit adorned with pure silver buttons asked Fidelio.

"Yes, but what is it for? Who are these people?" Fidelio replied.

The man grinned in a cynical way. "This procession is for those who have died fighting to close churches, monasteries, rape nuns, kill priests and punish those who dare to oppose the law. But, the interesting aspect of this procession is that the majority of the caskets are occupied by the latter, those who oppose the law," the man laughed, a cruel, sardonic laugh. "But there is even more," the charro continued, "there are also those who have been sick, unable to afford a doctor, many of them would have had a chance, but, let's face it, it's true that there are many among them for whom, certainly, there was no hope. Not even you or anyone else, could have done anything for those."

Fidelio looked at himself and noticed that he was now dressed in simple peasant clothes. He shivered and felt sad. Sad for all of them, he wished there was something he could do about it. In silence, he started praying. He had seen so many dying, so many suffer. "God is near those who suffer," he said.

"God? Who is He? Where has He been? If He cares about those who suffer why does He allow them to suffer and die in misery? No, it seems to me that He has abandoned them. Ha, and they still claim for Him, that's ridiculous."

"God is always present. Yes, He allows suffering but if we think about it, we'll realize that He came to live and suffer along with those like these and he told us that we should look for Him on those who suffer and are punished for no fault of their own. We have chosen to ignore Him and we have chosen not to see Him although He continually manifests Himself in the sunrise, in the sunset, in the sky and in the earth. He is always present and that's why they seek Him," Fidelio said, with a firm tone of voice. Someone in the procession started singing a song praising the Lord.

The man in the charro suit grinned sarcastically. "You speak well, that and your healing ability could make you not only wealthy, but also powerful. Are you interested? It would be easy to arrange that," he said with a seductive smile. Fidelio felt a profound attraction for him, a sensation he knew he had felt before, now more intense than ever before. Somehow, he saw himself famous, wealthy, everything that money could buy at his reach; pleasure, all kind of pleasure at his disposal. "Yes, it's there at your disposal, just reach for it and you'll get it," the man told him, embracing Fidelio tenderly.

Although the contact of the man attracted Fidelio and he was tempted by riches, the melody sang by the mournful and the procession made Fidelio disgusted with the idea of obtaining riches because people suffer, he wished to help them regardless if he was paid or not; he realized that wealth was unimportant for him. He moved away from the man. "Thank you, riches are nothing when the soul is lost," he said.

The man kept his smile. "People could even believe that you are the second coming of Christ," he added. Suddenly a powerful chorus singing alleluia was heard. Fidelio felt important, straightened his back, took a deep breath, the idea tempted him, really tempted him; that was even more attractive to him than all the wealth in the world. The idea that he could be like the Christ, seemed true to him; after all, wasn't He who had taught him and guided him towards healing since his childhood? Yes, that was the reason, now all of it seemed to make sense. Fidelio smiled happy when suddenly a mare left the procession and ran towards Fidelio pushing him down; with Fidelio down, the mare put herself in two legs ready to crush him. Fidelio got scared, really scared, it seemed that the mare wanted to kill him. A woman walked out of the procession and positioned herself between Fidelio and the mare, seeing her, the mare calmed down and followed the woman; as the woman walked away with the mare she turned so Fidelio could see her face, her disfigured face by leper; she smiled and as she did Fidelio saw the image of a man, a young, bearded man, his face clean, no sign of leper. Fidelio felt humbled, really humbled, he got up, looked at the man in the elegant charro dress. "Jesus has never left. He is present in all of those who suffer, I'm nothing more than one of His followers," said Fidelio.

Furious, the man spitted and walked away.

Fidelio felt someone rocking him; he turned trying to ignore whoever was rocking him.

"Child, Child, wake up, wake up there are many still waiting to see you."

Fidelio awoke, looked at all of those waiting for him, the purpose for his life now clear to him. "Let's pray and thank the Lord," he said.

CHAPTER XXVII

In Monterrey a large group of local physicians, along with others, who had traveled from Saltillo and Torreon, met to discuss what was happening in Espinazo. The meeting had been called by the Health Council of the State of Nuevo Leon under Dr. Francisco Vela. Among those present were Fidelio's old friend and boss, Dr. Villarreal, and, also present was Dr. Gonzalez, who had met Fidelio while he worked at the mines.

"What has been happening for the last few years and continues happening until now, close by, just a few kilometers from Monterrey and Saltillo, is a disgrace for the practice of medicine and a threat for the health of the entire population in both states, Coahuila and Nuevo Leon. I would dare to say that the threat is not only for these two states, but for the entire northern Mexico, and it's also embarrassing for all of us. The purpose of this meeting is to hear your opinion and try to establish a common plan of action. In the name of the Health Council and mine as head of the Council, I'd like to thank all of you for leaving your busy practice and showing up. If any of you has had any experience with the matter of discussion, or if you have an opinion, please state it now, the floor is open to all of you," Dr. Vela, standing up in front of those present, said as an introduction for the meeting, he then sat behind a table positioned in front of all those present.

"What you have just said is the sad and upsetting truth. We all should be embarrassed for what is happening in that place. Hundreds of sick people, with all sort of contagious diseases. Tuberculosis, leper, syphilis, typhoid fever, I could go through the entire book, are now there in that filthy, unhealthy place, where water is scanty and in reality there is no medicine for them, only filthy, untested herbs. That man and that place are a disgrace for the practice of medicine, an embarrassment for us as physicians and a menace for the entire population," said one of those present, almost yelling, standing up and forcibly pointing his finger to where he imagined Espinazo would be.

"What my distinguished colleague, Dr. Aguayo, and you, Dr. Vela, have said are indeed a sad reality. But, let's face it, what is it that we could do about it? People believe in him, they will travel there even if we oppose it," said another of those present without standing up, morbidly obese and because of it, his breathing was shallow. "The best we can do is to ignore it. He'll fade away, like many other folk healers. If the ignorant people want to believe in him and in his fake healing, let them believe it. They are just that, ignorant people, and we all know that's how the populace is," he added, with a despiteful tone of voice.

"That's what we have done with the hundreds of fake, itinerant folk healers. Everyone knows that they are just a fake. Even those who consult them know that. Indeed, it's true, eventually they fade away and are forgotten," said Dr. Aguayo, a bold and skinny man, around forty-years-old. "But, what is happening now in that filthy place is different. We can't allow this turmoil to continue, we have the responsibility of stopping this fake healer. He is not only killing those who go there seeking for his help, he is also killing our practices. Thanks to him our offices are almost empty, while he gets thousands of patients and he can't see them all. This has to stop!" he added, foamy saliva running out, like a rabid dog. Some of the audience clapped in approval, those in front of him, used their handkerchiefs to wipe the saliva Aguayo had spitted into their heads as he talked.

Dr. Villarreal stood up, his hair had now a touch of gray and had few wrinkles on his face. He looked serious and stood erect. His whole demeanor inspired respect. Since he was well known and respected among the medical community, everyone stood silent, waiting for him to speak. "I hear and understand what has been said by those who spoke before me. It's true, there have been and still are, many who abuse the credibility and faith of the people; even people who are supposed to help the sick, the weak, the poor, deceive and abuse them. But let's analyze the matter of discussion; in reality, what is it that we are witnessing? Why is all of this happening? And, in reality, what is the cause of all this? His voice, although clear and calm, put emphasis in the questions he had asked, he paused for a moment looking around to all of those present.

"We know for a fact that not only our country has suffered from the plague of itinerary false healers, they are everywhere. I saw some of them during my stay in Baltimore as a medical student. It's true, they pretend to have the answer and the magical solution to all mankind's problems; those of you who studied in Mexico City, know the story of the infamous Dr. Merolique. It's also true that these men, and some women included, abuse the trust and faith not only of the common people, but as we all well know, even some of those who claim to be well educated follow and support them, many of the last, who are wealthy enough, even invest in them; they happen to be a good business. We also know that many of those who claim to have found the magical potion, hold a legitimate title, and I'm sure that all of us here know someone, perhaps some of you even had dinner with one of them yesterday evening. Now, let's face our reality. What do we really offer? I know a good number of so called physicians who still deny the cell theory, who doubt that bacteria are the cause of most contagious diseases. Yes, our profession has made a tremendous progress, in particular during the second half of the last century and it continues during the present, but we are only starting to learn and understand disease. Even Joseph Skoda, the master clinician, not long ago, after giving a brilliant talk about tuberculosis answered 'it doesn't matter', when asked about treatment," his face flushed, his back straightened and his voice became louder and powerful as he spoke. "And, today, the answer to that question remains the same; other than sending people to the mountains, we still don't have a cure. The same happens with many other illnesses, we don't even know what cancer is, we don't have a cure for leper; there are many among us who still believe in leeches, and even worse, there are many who still use them. Fidelio, somehow, has learned about the healing properties of herbs. Herbs! We don't even want to look at them, much less to study their pharmaceutical potential. We must realize that there is much we don't know, that we must look openly at every possible alternative to help us to fulfill our duty. What do we offer to those with cancer, tuberculosis, leper, syphilis, and many other illnesses? Fidelio is not an itinerant healer, he is not seeking for patients, but they are the ones who seek for him. He does not pretend to have a title, but I have worked with him and I know for a fact, that that he knows the human anatomy much better than many of us. He does not pretend to have found the magical elixir that will cure all illnesses, but he has learned about the healing potential of the herbs in the desert and also, he offers them hope, he offers them consolation in their suffering. In reality, what we should be discussing here is how can we improve? Fidelio is not the enemy, his presence and his popularity only show us that we still have a lot to learn."

"Which side are you!" yelled one of those present.

"You are a traitor to our profession. How do you dare to compare that false healer to some of us? We have earned our title, we spent years in medical school!" yelled someone, sitting in the back. Dr. Villarreal stood silent.

"Colleagues, let's not start a fight. Everyone has a right to express his opinion," said Dr. Vela, as he banged the table with his fist and standing up.

"But it's important that man is stopped and sent to jail for fraud!" yelled Dr. Aguayo.

"Yes, Fidelio is pretending to be a doctor, when he barely knows how to read and write," another one added.

Dr. Villarreal once again, stood up. "Yes, it is true that Fidelio never went to medical school. But that doesn't mean that he has not studied. I know for a fact, that he has spent years studying the effects of herbs and plants. I know for a fact that he has studied and thought deeply about all that nature has to offer. How many of us can claim the same? How many of us continue studying and learning every day? Many of you, years after graduation, continue practicing 'as the professors taught us.' It happens that many of the so-called professors also practice as their professor taught them. I have worked with Fidelio and I know that he thinks about the rationale of what he is doing and changes when he observes that something doesn't work. I wish we would do the same."

"In Mexico City, Dr. Neumayer, who is a Professor at the National Medical School, has given a public demonstration of how easy it is to create the illusion of healing in those who are naïve, and that's what is happening at Espinazo," a third one intervened.

Dr. Gonzalez raised his hand and stood up. "Would you like to say something, Dr. Gonzalez?" Dr. Vela asked him with respect.

"Yes, I would like to express my personal opinion," Dr. Gonzalez replied. "I happen to know Fidelio and I have observed his methods. I know that he does not claim to be a physician, but, as Dr. Villarreal said, he knows the healing potential of herbs. I have witnessed some of his treatments and believe me, many of us would wish to have his ability," he stopped, smiled and looked in the direction of the one who had talked before him. "As for the also infamous Dr. Neumayer, everyone knows that he is one of those Dr. Villarreal just mentioned, a fake healer with a medical title." He paused for a moment, took a deep breathing before continuing. "Also in Mexico City, the French physician, Charles Marceau, regarding Fidelio's abilities has stated and I quote, 'it would be medical folly to negate in the name of science (as we know it today) the cures of the spiritual forces of the world' and he added, 'because all of life is based upon illusion or suggestion, we doctors have not tried to understand the nature of our successes (and our failures), there are many things that happen in medicine (and in the world) that are today completely unexplainable. If the truth be known, many have died because of our blindness and inability to treat many illnesses.' I happen to agree with him!" Dr. Gonzalez finished, looked defiantly around him before he sat. Many of the present looked at each other with disgust.

"I didn't expect that from you, Dr. Gonzalez," Dr. Vela said.

"Often the truth is unpleasant," Dr. Gonzalez replied. "But what must be said, has to be said. Having said that, there is something else I'd like to add," he stood up and looked around. "How many of us would go to the country, to those small, filthy and poor places, like

Espinazo? We prefer to stay in the comfort of a city. Which one of us would go and practice there?" he added and sat down. Everyone stood silent.

"Dr. Vela, The President Elias Calles is in an actual tour around the country. There is a rumor that he is planning to stop in Espinoza and consult with the Child. What can you tell us about that?" asked one of the present, standing up.

"Unfortunately, that's true," Dr. Vela replied.

"Has anyone tried to stop him? That would encourage more people to travel to that place," said the same one, concerned.

"Yes, of course we have tried to stop him from going there. We have explained to him the risk of contagious diseases, hopefully he'll listen to us," Dr. Vela replied. He looked around waiting for someone else to speak. "Well, it seems that the matter has been discussed enough, for the time being," he said after no one said anything. "The newspapers in Mexico City, which are cynically commendatory of his work as those in our cities which report only the negative aspects, do nothing but to give him free publicity and accomplish nothing else but to encourage people to go there and that's also a problem," he paused for a moment, sighed before continuing. "And, as you probably know, we have tried to bring Fidelio to trial, but since he doesn't claim to be a physician and he does not prescribe medication and uses only herbs, the judge decided that there is no legal case against him. So, we must seek another course of action," he paused again, sighed again and continued. "Since it's also obvious that today we won't be able to reach an agreement regarding a common plan of action, I plan to visit the place, incognito. I'll inform you of my findings after I return from the place. For the time being, I'd like to thank you all for your presence," he added, standing up, he banged the table with a gavel and walked out of the room.

Meanwhile in Espinazo, Fidelio, standing up on the roof of the house that Von Wernich (with contribution from the wealthy people whom Fidelio had helped) recently had built for him, looked to the thousands of recently arrived people. He knew that many of them had terminal illnesses, whose condition was so serious that doctors had already given up. Their illness in a terminal stage and doctors claimed that nothing else could be done. Of course, Fidelio was also aware of the many who had chosen to stay and receive their daily dose of herbal remedies and besides them, there were the pregnant women who had come to deliver in Espinazo. Most of those women had hope that Fidelio would be the one assisting at their delivery. Thinking about that, Fidelio sighed, it was a relief for him to know that at least one of the many volunteers, most of them nuns running from persecution, who had also chosen to stay and help Fidelio, would assist the women at the time of their delivery. Thankfully, the great majority would have a joyous, happy result. But Fidelio already had learned how easy it was for them to get serious complications. Even among that group, there were a few who had died as a consequence of bleeding, convulsions or fever; there was nothing he, or anyone else, could have done to prevent it.

Looking at the crowd, Fidelio felt overwhelmed. "So much to do, there are so many in need of help, and so little I can really do for them." He looked around and saw the hundreds of crosses in the two newly created cemeteries, looking at the recently built monuments in there, the freshly excavated tombs, Fidelio felt pressure in his chest and almost fainted and fell from the roof, however he controlled the sensation in time.

The crowd that adoringly looked at him, hoping that at least he would throw fruits to them – there were many who had cured, or at least improved, when hit by one of them, gasped, "Child, is there something wrong with you?" someone among the crowd yelled, honestly concerned.

Fidelio turned his attention to them, opened his arms as a gesture of embracement and smiled at them reassuringly; he made the sign of the cross blessing them. Happy and reassured, the people started singing an anthem praising him. Listening to it, Fidelio felt overwhelmed, embarrassed, looked again at the cemeteries and the chest pain returned. "Have I failed those?" he asked himself.

He looked farther away to the desert and remembered his days as a goat shepherd. The memory of the anguish, impotence and despair he had felt when some of those seeking his help, passed away, especially those who had died while he held them in his arms, he remembered how at that moment, they looked at him and even then, they smiled at him, thankfully.

"Why Lord?" he asked in silence, tears in his eyes. "Why didn't you allow me to continue being just that, a goat shepherd? Now there is so much to do, so many in need of help. So many come here with hope, but so many come just to die, there is so little I can offer them. Why? Why? Why?" In anguish, he looked to the sky, it was a clear morning with few clouds lazily floating in the bright blue. Somehow, in the white, like floating cotton, clouds, Fidelio saw clearly the image of Candelaria, lovingly smiling at him. Fidelio felt that the image tenderly caressed him, reassured him. Fidelio closed his eyes and smiled, filled with a sensation of peace, of love, love for Candelaria, love for those who had come, even love for those whom he knew despised what he was doing. Love, love for all, above all love for God, an immense love and inner peace. Acceptance. "If this is what you want, thy will be done," he thought. "It's not for me to ask your reasons, only to obey."

He then looked at the town and smiled again. Although most of the people had to live in improvised shacks, built with the few available resources of the region, there was order. The streets were wide enough to allow the pass of wagons and people to walk, each street with a name, the people took care of the cleaning of the front of their shacks and also, there was order and above all, peace. People respected and helped each other, every one shared what they had with the rest. "There is no doubt," Fidelio thought, "although there is suffering, God has looked at them and offered them hope, hope that's something I cannot and will not, deny them, yes there is much to do; let's do it." Smiling and feeling energized, he turned and walked down the stairs.

An upcoming train whistled, announcing its arrival. People started disembarking. As he walked toward the pirul, looking at those who disembarked, he recognized some of his friends from Guanajuato. Father Segura and two of his old childhood classmates, Pantaleon and Dionaciano, had left the train looking around, nervous, like scared street dogs, fear on their faces. Fidelio and Enrique, who happened to be at the station, and had also recognized them, happy, ran to greet them. Fidelio noticed that Father Segura had lost weight, he looked almost starved; Pantaleon and Dionaciano looked much older; Pantaleon had a scar in his face, they also seemed to have starved. The three of them looked everywhere, nervous, afraid, they seemed to expect that suddenly someone would jump at them, or someone would shoot at them. Fidelio and Enrique greeted them.

"Father Segura, Pantaleon, Dioanaciano, I'm so happy to see all of you again," said Fidelio as soon as he approached, opening his arms like trying to embrace the three of them. Enrique embraced Father Segura. "Yes, I'm also happy to see you, and above all, happy to know that you are safe. In here you'll be safe, there is nothing to worry about. We'll take care of the three of you, as we have done with many others, who arrived before you and will continue coming," he said. The five of them embraced each other, Pantaleon and Dionaciano wept loudly and blew their nose.

"You need to rest and I'm sure that you are hungry," Enrique said, concerned about the appearance of his friends. "Let's go home, since we are always expecting guests at home, my wife has prepared dinner. She'll be happy to meet you all. We'll talk after you have eaten and rested. Fidelio, are you coming with us?"

"I'll meet you all later, there are many waiting," Once again, he embraced his friends. "Enrique will help you, we have a lot to talk about, hopefully, we'll do it tonight," he added before leaving. Enrique, Father Segura, Dionaciano and Pantaleon walked towards Enrique's house.

"We are exhausted, I don't know about the two of you, but I'd like to lie down, I mean if that's possible," Father Segura said when they arrived.

"I also need to rest and I hope I'll be able to sleep," Pantaleon said.

"I'm exhausted, need to rest or I'll fall down," Dionaciano said, almost falling asleep in there.

"You need to eat something first, afterwards I'll take you to where you can rest. There are beds with clean sheets in the recently built house for Fidelio, which he almost never uses. Follow me," Enrique said, as he walked towards Fidelio's house. They followed him.

That evening, feeling refreshed and rested, Father Segura, Dionaciano and Pantaleon, joined Enrique and Von Wernich for dinner. "Is Fidelio coming?" Father Segura asked.

"I wouldn't be sure," replied Von Wernich. "Once he starts, he works non-stop. Sometimes for several days in a row. He doesn't stop to eat and sleeps whenever he almost falls, exhausted. I wonder how is that he gets the necessary energy to maintain that rhythm of work. He seems obsessed, he wants to help all, but at the same time, he knows that's not possible. Fortunately, lately, many who came looking for help or accompanying someone else, have volunteered to stay and help," he paused for a moment, reflecting. "But even with that help, Fidelio is the one who people come looking for, he is the one who has the gift to heal, and believe me, there are many who heal, just by his presence."

"He is good, always has been," Father Segura said. "God supports him."

"Yes, we have known that since we were children," Pantaleon said. Dionaciano nodded agreeably.

"I'm sure, however, that Fidelio will find time to join us. He would like to find out about you and what you have been doing since the last time he saw any of you," Enrique said. He then looked to Father Segura. "I'm sure it has been hard for you in particular, Father."

Father Segura frowned, a sad and painful expression on his face. "Yes, indeed, it has been hard. Twice I've been taken to face the firing squad. Twice, at the last moment, God has sent what I would call a guardian Angel to stop it and save me. Although I'm now well aware that it has become dangerous, I've promised that I'll continue doing what Jesus asked us to do in his memory, even if that means that it will be the last thing I do," although pale, his cheeks became red and brilliant, he smiled.

"Even those who participate in mass are apprehended and many of them hang in the telegraph posts. But we'll continue the fight to protect our right to worship God," Pantaleon said emphatically blasting the table as he spoke, his cheeks blushed. Dionaciano nodded approvingly, also blushed, jaws tight.

"You are among friends now, but I must admit that there is danger even here. There are priests and nuns who have chosen to stay and help

Fidelio's work. For that reason, we have not one, but several masses every day. Until now, nothing has happened, but we must be alert," Von Wernich said.

"We joined the revolution for justice and fairness, we didn't join it to be denied our right to worship God," Dionaciano said.

"One way or the other, here you are safe. We have made arrangements through which, those who wish to escape persecution can cross the border and be safe. Many nuns, Mexicans and foreigners, have chosen to stay, once they saw what is being done here," Enrique said.

Father Segura looked at him. "There is something that worries me. During the travel, listening to the people I noticed that many of them consider Fidelio much more than a simple healer. That's worrisome." He frowned rubbing his forehead, concerned.

"Now that you mention it, he indeed is more than simply another folk healer. He has proven to be much more than that. People believe that he is something like a saint, even there are some who consider him a new Messiah, and that's good because, although Fidelio refuses to accept any form of payment, most of them are willing to pay. Nothing wrong with accepting that," Von Wernich said, smiling.

"It's hard for me to believe that Fidelio would like to take advantage of the gift God has given to him," Dionaciano said.

"And he doesn't," Enrique said. "But, at the same time, people are willing to pay and that has helped, not only to build Fidelio a house (which he almost never visits), but also it has allowed us to help those who are running away from persecution. Many priests and nuns have been saved thanks to Fidelio. Also, we have built the ward where the pregnant women who come here deliver and stay. There is also a school. So, you can see that the money has been used for a good reason. Fidelio, of course is aware of it, although I believe he has mixed feelings about it."

"Fidelio has accepted his mission. Precisely for that reason he has gained enemies. We know for a fact that there are many physicians who hate him and they have tried to stop his work. Several times they have tried to take him away for a trial, but those attempts have failed because they have been unable to show that Fidelio lies to people. He insists in that he is only offering hope, and he more than fulfills his word," Von Wernich said.

"The mere fact that he has continued for this long and, as we can see, people keep coming, speaks for itself. Also, and most importantly, the fact that in the middle of the religious persecution he has been allowed to worship in public, means that God is with him," said Father Segura, crossing his chest.

"Good evening to everyone," said Fidelio, smiling, as he entered the room accompanied by a man. "I'm sorry if I left you for a while, but, we have been busy," said Fidelio, pointing to the man with him. "This is Dr. Vela, he just arrived from Monterrey. He'll stay with us for some time. Please let him move freely; show him everything and let him go wherever he chooses," said Fidelio to Enrique and Von Wernich, who nodded agreeably. Enrique grinned when he noticed the gun in Dr. Vela's belt.

"Please have a chair, Doctor," Von Wernich said, pointing to a chair.

"You won't need that in here," Enrique said to Dr. Vela, pointing to the gun.

"I hope not," Dr. Vela said, sitting down.

"Would you join us Child?" Von Wernich asked Fidelio.

"Maybe later," Fidelio said, walking towards the door. "Someone who considers himself important is coming. We must prepare for him," he said before leaving.

Dr. Vela almost jumped in his chair, surprised. "How does he know that the President is coming?"

CHAPTER XXVIII

That winter had been particularly cold and that February morning was not the exception. Although the sun shone in the sky, the cold howling wind, blowing from the north penetrated to the bones. The humble shacks with walls of sticks and palm leaves barely protected their inhabitants. Fidelio visiting those receiving treatment, found sad news. In spite of the warm herbal remedies, provided daily, several elders had died from respiratory illness; some of them had come accompanying a sick relative and because of the weather and poor housing they had become ill. From experience, Fidelio had learned that in the winter the elder were particularly vulnerable to the cold weather, and during those months he spent as much time as possible providing warm herbal beverages to all, but in particular to those coughing and sneezing. Also, he made sure that during the cold months of the year, the children and elder people received grapefruit and other citric fruits.

"I'm sorry to say that we have lost some," Sister Theresa, one of the nuns who had volunteered to stay, informed Fidelio. "But thanks to your remedies, many have been cured and many others have at least improved; and, even more importantly, we have prevented many from getting sick. Don't get discouraged Child, there is no way we could have prevented those, it's just nature. This is the way it has happened for years; the winter months are bad for children and old people. But, once again, thanks to you, many have been cured, and, you have prevented many from getting sick."

"I'm not discouraged sister. I understand that it's only through His will that we can succeed. He'll show us the way to improve what we have done until now," Fidelio replied, looking to the railroad track.

"Are you expecting someone, or something?" Sister Theresa asked, also looking in the direction of the rail tracks.

"Yes, someone is coming. He'll arrive today."

"How do you know it?"

Fidelio shrugged his shoulders. "I just know."

"Do you know who is coming?"

"Yes, the one who ordered yours and other monasteries closed, who has ordered persecution of priests and nuns, who has forbidden mass and all public religious manifestations. He is the one arriving."

"But, we celebrate mass here and people are always singing religious hymns; although many of the latter are dedicated to you. Many pray the rosary every night, and you know that we encourage it," Sister Theresa said. "Aren't you afraid, Child? After the convent was closed, I was scared, that's the reason I came here. Running away from persecution. But, after seeing what God has done here, through you, I'm no longer afraid. I hope, however, that he comes in peace."

"He needs help. Just like everyone else, and we'll give it to him," Fidelio said, smiling.

At 3 p.m. in the afternoon, the presidential train, nicknamed "Olivo", arrived to Espinazo. Several soldiers came down, pushed the curious people away and then aligned. After them, the Nuevo Leon state governor, Aaron Saenz; the minister of war, General Juan Andrew Almazan, in military uniform full of medals, descended from the train and respectfully waited. After a few minutes, Mexico's President, General Plutarco Elias Calles, dressed in civil clothes, came down. An improvised musical band played the 'Zacatecas march'. Fidelio standing, smiled to the President, while the people, curios, observed. Many were nervous.

"Welcome, Mr. President and all of you," Fidelio greeted them, opening his arms, welcoming the President and his companions. "God will grant the healing you need, if you are willing to receive it."

The president looked at him, intrigued. "Do you know why I came here?"

Fidelio, looked into the president's eyes and smiled friendly. "Once again, God will grant you to be healed if you are willing to receive His gift. Open you heart and come with me," he said as he guided them to a close by shack.

Frowning, jaws tight, the president followed him and so did Andrew Almazan and Saenz.

"Now, Mr. President, please take your clothes of and enter the bath," Fidelio told Elias Calles once they were inside the shack, signaling the bath tub already prepared with warm water and herbs on it.

"That's not the way to talk to your President!" yelled Andrew Almazan.

"This time I believe that's in my best interest to do as he says. Please wait outside General. And you too," said the President to Andrew Almazan and Saenz, a tranquil tone of voice. They looked at him, disconcerted, but left after a short moment of indecision. "I'll call you if I need anything," the President added.

The President took of his clothes and entered the bath. Fidelio noticed the nodular lesions and ulcers in the President's skin. "This water is hot," said the President as he entered the bathtub.

"Yes, indeed. That's the way you need it. Just wait, after a few minutes, you'll get used to it and you'll find it comfortable," Fidelio said, as he prepared a mixture of herbs with bee honey and, once ready, he dropped the mixture into the bathtub.

"Aaaaah," somehow I now feel relaxed," said the President, closing his eyes, letting his whole body sink into the water.

"This mixture and the infusion I'm going to prepare for you will help with your ailment. You are already beginning to notice its benefit. You already feel that you are healing. To help your soul to heal along with your body, perhaps, you'll agree to answer the question. Why are you persecuting us?"

The President opened his eyes and smiled. "You mean why am I persecuting those who have abused the trust of our ignorant people?"

"I'll agree there have been abuse by some members of the church and that those deserve to be punished. But you can't deny that also a lot of good has been done. In Guanajuato and Morelia, for example, I noticed that the education was mainly imparted by religious people."

The president smirked. "Did you have access to it?"

Fidelio smiled back to the President. "I did, but that is not important. Besides, by now you have realized that trying to prevent people to worship God as they see fit, does not help in any way. How many have died in this unnecessary struggle?"

"Many, that's true. Most in the rebel side and many more will die. The fight will continue until all the churches and monasteries are closed and the public religious manifestations stops. Religious frenzy along with it. And, most importantly, before they are allowed to resume services, the church will have to be subordinate to the State." Fidelio poured a bit more of the herbal and honey bee preparation into the bathtub. Outside, the people started singing a religious anthem. The president frowned.

"Do you mean something like that?" Fidelio asked, smiling in a friendly manner to the President, as he continue pouring the herbal preparation.

The President ignored Fidelio's question, closed his eyes, smiling, relaxed. "Somehow this feels good. I never felt any improvement with all the blood-letting and the medication that has been prescribed for me."

"As I said at your arrival. Your body and soul will heal, but in order to accomplish it, you must forgive yourself," Fidelio said, as he took a sponge and started rubbing the president's back. Outside, the singing of the religious anthem became louder.

"You know that I could order this place to be evacuated and all of your activities closed."

"Yes, we all know that. It really doesn't matter. Everything is God's will. You may pretend that it's yours. I already know that regardless of where I'm if God wishes to use me, the mission will continue. You are already feeling His power. You already feel better. Stop the persecution of those who choose to worship God. Forgive those who affected you in your childhood, and above all, forgive yourself."

Dr. Vela walked into the room. "Mr. President, in the name of the medical community I want to apologize for this mess. We can offer you better services in a scientific way," he said, breathing heavily.

The President looked at him and laughed. "In a scientific way? What does that mean? Your colleagues have already tried and prescribed many different potions, creams, and pills, blood-letting. Some even dared to suggest the removal of all my teeth and several organs. Of course, I didn't agree to the latter. But, I allowed them to do everything else. What have they accomplished? Nothing!" He pushed himself almost out of the tub and looked at his skin. The nodules had significantly improved, the ulcers almost gone. He smiled. "Do you see this? A simple bath and a conversation has done the ..." he stopped, nervous.

"The miracle? Isn't that what you expected coming here?" Fidelio asked.

The president turned to Fidelio, his eyes sparkled, menacing. "A miracle? I don't believe in miracles!" he almost yelled.

"There must be some trick, Mr. President," said Dr. Vela, a grin on his face.

The president now turned to him. "A trick? Do you call this a trick?" he said, showing the improved ulcers on his skin. "No, there is no trick to this. But, also there is no miracle!" He yelled again, now turning to see Fidelio. "How did you accomplish this? It's only a warm herbal bath and a little of conversation and this has happened," he looked at his healed body. "How did you do it? You must be expecting to obtain something for you in exchange of this. What is it?"

"Yes, in this case I would like to ask something from you, Mr. President," Fidelio replied.

Elias Calles laughed, a sarcastic, cynical laugh. "Well, that's expected, nobody does something for nothing. Why should you be different? What is it? Money? Power? Just name it. If its money, I can make you wealthy, very wealthy, one of the richest men of the country. Is it power? Yes, I also can provide that. Just ask and I'll be sure you get whatever you ask for." He sat back in the bathtub.

Fidelio smiled. "There is only one thing I would like to ask from you," he said in a calm tone of voice.

"Well, what is it!" Elias Calles almost yelled.

"Save your soul," Fidelio replied, in a firm, but calm tone of voice, looking straight into the president's eyes.

Perplexed, both, the president and Dr. Vela looked at Fidelio. "What are you talking about?" asked the president.

"Stop this nonsense religious war. Stop killing people just because they choose to worship God. You can't rule over their souls," Fidelio replied, keeping his eyes in the president's.

The president stood up, upset, his jaws tight, his face blushed. He took one step out of the large bucket where he was taking the bath, looked into his clothes where he had a revolver; stopped, took a deep breath and moved towards the bucket, sat in the water, now trembling, the ulcers in his skin had reappeared. "I didn't start this war," he said. "It was them who disobeyed, they started it. It was them who keep trying to influence the decisions of the government. They can worship, as long as they follow the rules. If they had obeyed, nothing would have happened."

"Priests have been killed just because they performed mass. Many innocent people, including women and children have been killed just because they assisted at mass. How can that be justified?" Fidelio said, now in a firm tone of voice.

The president lifted himself, almost stood up. Jaws tight again, salivating, his eyes reddened. "You know that I could put you facing a firing squad, for talking to me like that. I'm the president!" His muscles tense. Suddenly he started trembling, looked at his body, the rash and ulcers in his skin increased in size, new ampules appeared. The expression of his face changed.

"Mr. President, this man is nothing but a quack. Stop this and leave now. As you can see you won't improve with this fake treatment," Dr. Vela intervened, a shadow of a grin in his face.

Elias Calles looked at him, tears in his eyes, he then looked at his skin.

"What you see in your skin is only the manifestation of what is going on within your soul," Fidelio said. "Your illness lies in your soul. You can heal yourself, just forgive yourself, and stop hating yourself. Heal your soul and your physical illness will also improve. You can do it, Mr. President," he added, with a calm, secure, soothing tone of voice.

The president, now sobbing, let his body immerse in the bathtub, the tension in his muscles gone. Suddenly, he yelled, a painful, sorrowful cry. Tears now flowed freely.

"That's it. Relax and allow your negative emotions to flow out of your body," Fidelio said, maintaining a soothing tone of voice. He approached the president and started applying an herbal ointment to the president's skin as he murmured a melodious tune. The president closed his eyes, a calm expression on his face. He smiled.

At that moment, General Andrew-Almazan entered, a gun in his hand. "I heard the president's yell," he said, pointing the gun to Fidelio.

"Relax, General, everything is well in here," the president said, in a calm tone of voice, smiling to the general. "I thank you for your concern and the speed of your response to my cry. You may leave now, as you can see, I'm well taken care of," he added.

Dr. Vela, not knowing what to do, just stood in the corner. Andrew-Almazan put the gun back in the holster and started walking out.

"General, wait a minute," said Elias Calles, in a firm tone of voice. "There is something else I want you to take care, as soon as possible."

Andrew-Almazan stopped and turned facing the president. "Yes, sir. What is it?"

"Find a way to end this stupid war. No more people hanged. Stop the persecution of priests."

Dr. Vela and the general looked at him, surprised.

"But, Mr. President, you must know that that there are priests and nuns in this place. As a matter of fact, I have witnessed several public religious ceremonies during my stay in here,"

Dr. Vela said, upset.

"That's true. Since we arrived here, I have noticed several who I'm certain are foreigner priests. It seems that this is their route of escape," said Andrew-Almazan.

"Yes, I also heard the religious anthem. But, I forbid any reprisal against these people. As I said, general, this war is over!" said Elias Calles, a firm tone of voice.

Obviously hesitant, Andrew-Almazan looked at the president. "Forgive me for asking, Mr. President. But, are you certain?"

"Yes, general, I'm certain!"

Andrew-Almazan clicked his heels. "It will be done as you order, sir. Permission to leave, sir."

"There is one more thing, and this must be clear," said the president, looking at general Andrew-Almazan and to Dr. Vela. "This conversation never happened. Understood!"

"Yes, sir," Andrew-Almazan said clicking his heels again.

"Good," said Elias Calles. He turned to look at Dr. Vela and smiled to him. "I could silence you, but I know that you'll also keep silent about this."

Scared, trembling, Vela just nodded his head.

"Both of you may now leave. I want to continue with my bath," he turned to Fidelio.

"You too, my friend, just stay outside, I'll call if I need you. I want to rest."

As soon as they all had left, the president sank in the bathtub keeping only his head out, closed his eyes, smiling. He started humming "la Adelita," a popular song among the troops.

CHAPTER XXIX

"All of us wonder. What happened between you and the president? He not only looked happy when he left, but to our amazement, he ignored the singing of religious anthems and all the religious manifestations happening here during his stay," Enrique said to Fidelio, shortly after the president had boarded the Olivo train and left. Enrique, Von Wernich, Pantaleon, Dionaciano and Father Segura had joined Fidelio during one of his short periods of rest, at Von Wernich's house. They all sat and enjoyed a cup of fresh coffee.

"His health improved, that's all," Fidelio replied, shrugging his shoulders and calmly smiling at Enrique.

"But, you look so calm, you act like nothing has happened here," Father Segura said, looking at Fidelio as he put his cup on the table. "Everyone is aware that something extraordinary has happened here. Something that no one would have expected. The president stopped in the middle of what is probably Mexico's driest place. A town that before your arrival, few knew it exists. Like most of us, you are the reason he came; and, apparently, he found what he had hoped for. I repeat Enrique's question, what happened? General Andrew-Almazan noticed the nuns and priests here. People just ignored the presence of the man who ordered the religious persecution and, loudly, prayed the

Rosary and sang religious anthems. Andrew-Almazan and his men did nothing about it. They just ignored it. Why?"

"Yes, the president found what he came looking for. He found that his ailment comes from within, he found that the real illness is in his soul. He accepted the Holy Spirit invitation to redeem himself," Fidelio said, in a soft tone of voice. Smiling, he looked to father Segura, Pantaleon and Dionaciano, "and, regarding the religious persecution. It's over. We are free to worship God as we always have done," he added.

"Alleluia! Indeed, something extraordinary has happened here," Father Segura said, standing up. "Praised be the Lord," he added raising his arms and looking up. The rest, surprised, looked at Fidelio with respect and admiration.

"I know that you are not kidding, what you said explains why they ignored the religious manifestations here," Von Wernich said. "Your enemies consider you just another folk healer, but you are much more than that. God is within you and people have already noticed it. Many of them are already worshipping your image," he added pointing to the shanty town.

Fidelio frowned, for a moment tightened his jaws, concerned. Serious, he looked at Von Wernich. "They shouldn't do that," he said, he then looked around, "and everyone must do his best not to encourage it. Yes, finally, I have understood that I have received a gift. But now it's also clear to me that I don't own it, my duty is to take care of what I don't own. It's a gift given with the purpose to provide comfort and hope to those who suffer. I'm only His instrument, that's all," he said, moving his hands to add emphasis to what he said, a sad tone of voice. He paused for a moment. "Only God should be worshipped. No one else!" he added, this time with a firm tone of voice.

"Since the day Enrique proposed you to be an altar boy, I noticed something special in you. I must admit that this is much more than I could ever have imagined. You are right, God has chosen you to be His instrument on earth. I'm glad that you are humble enough to recognize it, and I agree with you that only God is to be worshipped," Father Segura said. He stood up, walked toward Fidelio and touched Fidelio's forehead. "God bless you my son," he added.

"Thank you, Father," Fidelio said, taking Father Segura's hand and kissing it, "you have been a good teacher to me."

"I have learned much more from you," Father Segura said, bending and kissing Fidelio's forehead. He returned to his chair and sat.

"They are already singing anthems that anonymous authors have dedicated to you, and you know that people believe that just by touching you they'll heal. You also know that there are many who try to catch your urine and drink it; people already worship you, there is no way we could stop it and that's why they are giving," Enrique said.

Overwhelmed, Fidelio bent his head, he felt sadness, profound sadness. He bent covering his face with his hands, in deep thought. "I must confess that it's all my own fault," he said, wiping his tears as he raised his head. "I noticed how people reacted, and it made me feel good, important. It fed my ego. The evil one tempted me and I took the bait, now I see it and what is supposed to be a blessing has become a curse, for me, at least." He stood up, straightening his shoulders, he raised his head. "Worshipping my image is like worshipping false idols, it must end," he added. A whistle announced that a train had arrived at the station. Dark clouds covered the sun.

"What do you mean by saying that it must end?" Pantaleon asked, concerned.

Fidelio shrugged his shoulders, "I really don't know how it will end. What I do know is that I'm not distinct from anyone else, nor am I special. Yes, the gift of healing has been given to me, but, I'm not the only one, others have received a different gift, no one of us is special, we are all but one. God is in all of us, we need each other, that's what I now know and understand. I also know that as God has guided me until now, He'll continue showing me the way. Now, I must go and take care of those waiting," he said and walked outside, toward the pirul. Noticing him, the multitude started singing a praising anthem. Fidelio smiled to them. Hundreds of butterflies flew around the town.

As Fidelio walked, something at the train station caught his attention, he recognized some of those arriving, Dr. Villarreal, his friend and mentor, accompanied by Antonia and a woman, dressed as a nun, had just disembarked and asked someone for directions. Happy, Fidelio walked towards them.

As Fidelio walked towards the station, Dr. Villarreal noticed him. "Fidelio," he yelled, waving his hand. Antonia and the nun also waved, smiling, also happy to see him.

"Aurora!" Fidelio couldn't prevent himself from happily yelling as he recognized the woman dressed as a nun. Happy, he almost ran, Antonia and Aurora, ran toward him.

"Fidelio, it's wonderful to see you again, "Aurora said, hugging him, her face shinning with happiness. Fidelio reciprocated and then he also hugged Antonia and Dr. Villarreal.

Although Antonia smiled and seemed happy, Fidelio hinted sadness in her. At the distance an owl shrieked, hearing it Fidelio looked up, vultures flew in circles and thousands of butterflies flew on their way north.

"You are a nun," said Fidelio, pointing to Aurora's outfit.

Aurora smiled, radiant. "Yes, and I thank you. Meeting you helped me to listen and answer to God's call."

"But, wearing that outfit in public could endanger you," said Fidelio.

"Yes, I'm aware of that, but I don't care, I love God and I love being a nun, that's why I'm here, to serve those in need. I'm a nun, also trained as a nurse, that's why I asked to be sent here," Aurora said, a radiant smile on her face.

"She told us that, and I still don't understand it," Dr. Villarreal said. "How is it that your superior agreed to your petition to come here? I'm also concerned about you wearing that outfit in public. When I mentioned it to you, you told me that you became a nun in El Paso, that's the other side of the border, nuns are safe there. But, I'm sure your superior knows that Mexico has become a dangerous place for nuns and priests."

Aurora smiled. "Yes, it wasn't easy, but they agreed when I told them that God is the one guiding me."

Those around them started calling to Fidelio for help, some touched him. Fidelio turned and noticed a woman carrying a sick child in her arms, the child cried bitterly. Fidelio extending his arms, took the child, humming a song, he caressed the child. The child smiled, closed his eyes and went to sleep. "He'll get better now," said Fidelio to the woman giving the sleeping child back to her. Fidelio turned to his friends.

"Yes, there is so much to do and so little time to do it. Go to the house, Enrique and Don Teo will help you. There is much to talk. I'll meet you tonight" said Fidelio to them, pointing to the main house.

"You are amazing," Dr. Villarreal said, admiring what Fidelio had done with the baby. "I'm here also to help and to tell you that knowing you and being aware of what you are doing, has also helped me to understand that it's me who must improve. Thus, I have returned to the Church. Now I go to mass and I also try to help as much as I can. I agree with you that this gift, this ability to heal, it's a God's given gift. It's true we obtained it through different paths, but I'm now certain it's a God's given gift."

"I've come to help as much as I can. I'm looking forward to start," Aurora said, tenderly rubbing Fidelio's shoulder before leaving.

"Yes, there is a lot to talk about, I hope soon we'll have a chance," Antonia said, a sad expression on her face. "Also, Don Antonio gave this letter addressed to you, it's posted in Wales," she added giving Fidelio an envelope who, a bit surprised, took it.

After they had left, Fidelio, desirous to read the letter, walked to the house that Enrique and Von Wernich had built for him. At the moment, he desired solitude. Once in the house, he walked to an empty room, sat in a bejuco chair and opened the envelope. In it, besides a hand-written letter, he found three drawings. One of a horse, another of a mountain lion and the third one of himself. Smiling, he admired the drawings for a while, still smiling he opened the letter and read it.

"Dear Fidelio,

I hope that somehow, you'll receive this letter. It's the first and last that I'll ever write to you. I want you to know that you are, now and forever, in my mind. I'll always treasure your memory and I know that I'll love you until the end of my days. No, don't be concerned about this, the memory is a happy one and I'll keep it that way. I'm also aware that for me, you are a dream, a wonderful dream and I know it will remain just that. I have accepted the proposal of a good man and tomorrow I'll be married. I'm certain that my marriage will be a happy one, because I'll always be loyal to you and him. If I happen to have a son, I'll call him Joseph, somehow that name reminds me of you.

Farewell my sweet dream.
Yours forever.
Vicky."

Fidelio closed his eyes and thought about the three women who had left their mark in him. Three wonderful women. A bit sad, the image of them came to his mind. He smiled, thankful for their love, thankful for having had the opportunity to meet them, thankful for their sweet memory. Their memory was, however, bitter-sweet, by then he already knew and understood that mankind was his family, he belonged to all.

As he thought about them, the image of another woman came to his mind. The image of Antonia, his sister. She looked sad, concerned and it was not because of the letter. Fidelio felt that she had sad news from the mine.

Although concerned, Fidelio went into the maternity ward and assisted in two healthy deliveries, then he went to the surgical area, where Sister Teresa had already prepared two people who needed removal of large benign tumors. After performing the surgical procedures, Fidelio walked to visit those with leprosy and other contagious diseases. He became certain that they had received their daily herbal remedies; wherever he walked in he was received with reverence and gratitude. Some sang anthems praising him. "They should praise God," Fidelio thought.

After sunset, Fidelio walked into Von Wernich house to meet with his friends. He wondered about the news from the mine.

"Fidelio, we are glad that you have found the time to meet with us," Dr. Villarreal greeted Fidelio as he walked in. "Antonia just finished telling us what happened at the mine where you used to work. What happened there reflects what is happening in the rest of the country. It seems that in many aspects we are back to where we were before the revolution."

Enrique, Von Wernich, Pantaleon, Dionaciano, Father Segura and Aurora, were also present, they all sat around a table, sweet bread and a jar of fresh coffee on it. All those present seemed upset.

"What is it, Antonia?" Fidelio asked, taking a seat in front of his sister.

Antonia wiped away a tear. "Shortly after you left, Don Antonio and the English sold the mine. The new owners didn't approve the benefits given to the miners. After they took over, almost immediately, Mr. Peabody and Mr. Eager were fired." She stopped, obviously upset, making an effort not to start crying. "They cancelled all the benefits previously given to the miners. Of course, Marcial and Dionaciano protested and threatened with strike.

The new owners hired a man, Saravia is his name, an attractive, soft spoken, but evil man. Shortly after the arrival of this man, Marcial was found dead. The explanation given was that he had choked, but most believe he was poisoned. Dionaciano and the miners proceeded with the strike, there was violence. The army came, under the command of a Colonel recently arrived from Torreon, a man known in there because of his cruelty. Almost as soon as they arrived, the soldiers surrounded Dionaciano's house and shot him to death along with his wife and children. They pretexted that Dionaciano had fired at them. Everybody knows that Dionaciano didn't like guns, he never owned one. Scared, the miners have been forced to return to work and Saavedra and his group are back as leaders of the union. They are ruthless and I heard that they have sworn revenge against you. I'm scared, worried about your safety."

Overwhelmed, sad, Fidelio looked down, rubbed his forehead. "Things will change to become the way they were," he mumbled. "Don't worry, God is my shield," he said, in a loud voice, lifting his head, almost defiant.

Dionaciano hammered the table with his fist, "it seems that we fought for nothing. Things are the same as they were. Different masters that's all."

"Sadly, in many aspects, that's true," intervened Dr. Villarreal. "Like before the revolution, the President has absolute power, he is the one who decides who'll be governors, representatives, judges, and of course he only appoints those who'll obey him. Besides that, the main reason for the civil war we have just lived, happened because he tried to put the Church under the control of the state. Somehow, he has realized that he won't accomplish that. That's why he has agreed to the treaty with the Church."

Fidelio listened with his eyes closed, chin to the chest and his right hand on his forehead, a profound sadness had overcome him. Outside people sang anthems dedicated to him. Fidelio, surrounded by people who loved him, people who praised him, felt lonely.

"Madero, Carranza, Zapata, Villa and many other leaders of the revolution, all of those who could oppose the new government, have been assassinated, or bought. We must accept that the result of the revolution is that we just changed dictator. As long as they bribe those in charge, companies can get away with anything, something like what we just heard. We know, for instance, that the oil companies are allowed to have their own army," added Dr. Villarreal.

"However, I must add that in spite of that, there are some positive signs. People have shown that there is a limit in what they'll tolerate and that gives me hope that, somehow, Madero's dream of democracy, someday it will become a reality in Mexico. There are more schools, art has been made available to all."

"Amen to that," Father Segura said.

"But, changing the subject, regarding your job here, Dr. Vela, in Monterrey has talked to the press about your activities," Dr. Villarreal continued, talking directly to Fidelio. "Unable to prove anything bad about what you are doing here, he pretends to show you are just as a well- intentioned, naïve person, playing to be a physician," he smiled as he said this, then he became serious. "What has happened here has made many of us aware of the real need for medical assistance for the majority. Gomez Morin, a good friend of mine and a true revolutionary has become interested and has proposed the creation of a National Health System, somehow the president is also interested. Gomez Morin has already asked if I would be willing to help. Of course, I will and I'm not the only one. What has happened here has helped to increase awareness for the need of it."

"That's good news. I'll pray for it to become a reality," Father Segura said. "For some, like Dr. Vela, what is happening here, is difficult to understand. As a matter of fact, it's difficult to understand for the majority of us, it beats reason," he continued. "Just look outside, almost thirty thousand people are here. In a place that less than fifteen years ago, few knew it exists. All because the son of a miner, a goat shepherd who has received the gift of healing, is here."

Outside, the people continued singing religious anthems, most of them praising Fidelio.

"Many come here just to die," said Fidelio, standing up, he looked to Antonia.

"Dionaciano and Marcial were good friends, honest people, I'm sure they are with God now. It's not up to us to question God's reason for what has happened. I assume that's why He has given us freedom," he then looked around. "As for me I must continue taking care of the gift I don't really own," he looked outside. "That's the reason they are here. Now I must go and serve them," he added, before walking out.

"Fidelio, wait," Aurora said, running to his side. "I'd like to go with you. As I said, I'd like to help as much as I can."

Fidelio turned, smiled at her. "Sure, come along."

CHAPTER XXX

Fidelio and Aurora worked side by side until dawn. "Aurora, thank you. Having you at my side has been a great help. I'm glad you have chosen to come and help. It's obvious that you not only care, but you have been well trained as a nurse and also, I can see that indeed, this is the right path for you. Wherever you go, you'll be loved and useful. This is the last surgery for tonight. Go and rest now, I'll continue by myself, besides, Sister Teresa and the other volunteers are already here," Fidelio said, as he applied the final stitch in a wound made to remove a mass in the back of a woman.

"I'll rest when you rest," Aurora replied.

Fidelio turned and smiled at her. "I'm used to this, but you are not, it doesn't make any sense for you to overdo it. Just go and rest. We'll meet later."

"But, what about you? We have been working the whole night. You also need to rest, you can't just keep going. Sure, all of these people need you, but they need you healthy, rested and strong," Aurora said. Anxious, almost upset, she turned to Sister Teresa. "Please help me to make him understand that he also needs to rest."

Sister Teresa smiled, "believe me, we have tried," she replied in a soft and tender tone of voice.

"Go and rest Aurora, you'll be much more helpful once you have rested. Later, you and Sister Teresa could continue helping Dr. Villarreal in this ward," Fidelio said, having finished stitching the wound and started washing his hands.

When they left the ward, a woman carrying a bowl of soup approached Fidelio. "Child, you must be tired and hungry. I noticed how you have worked the whole night. Please accept this soup. I just prepared it and all in my family would like to share it with you," she said, in a humble, loving, tender, caring, tone of voice.

"Thank you, it's kind of you, I'll enjoy it," Fidelio said, as he took the bowl, sat and drank the soup. He chewed the vegetables.

"Indeed, he is just a child. This is the way it is almost every day. He eats whatever the people offer him and rests whenever the exhaustion overwhelms him. Don Teo and Enrique built a house for him, but he almost never uses it," Sister Teresa said to Aurora. "You must be tired, go and rest, there are plenty of volunteers, besides there is so much to do. You'll need to be rested to really help. None of us can keep up with his pace," she added, gently touching Aurora's shoulder with one hand and pointing to Fidelio with the other.

"She is right Aurora, go and rest," Fidelio said getting up, he burped, smiled, "that was a delicious and nutritious soup," he added, touching his belly. Aurora and Sister Teresa smiled back at him.

"You are right, I need to rest," said Aurora. "I'll be back as soon as possible. I want to serve."

"I'll go with you," Sister Teresa said.

Fidelio turned and started to walk toward the pirul when a well-dressed couple approached him. "We noticed how you enjoyed that soup," said the man. "We just arrived yesterday, but, it has been a while since we have been observing what is happening in this town. All over the country, and even beyond its border, people are already talking about your sainthood. There are many who believe that Jesus is in you, that you are the second coming of the Lord. Many already praise and worship your image. We are among them. We have come here because we believe that everyone should know who you are. Thanks to you a new church is about to start, with you at its center. It's just amazing. A new covenant. We are wealthy. We offer not only our wealth, but the wealth of many others like us. To show that we mean well, we can assure that all these people and those who are about to come will be fed. Everyone who comes looking for your help will be fed healthy and nutritious food. What do you think?" said the man, showing his bright, well aligned front teeth.

Fidelio looked at them. The couple was attractive. Blond, bright blue eyes, their dress elegant and amazingly clean. He felt strongly attracted to them, in particular to the beautiful woman. She reminded him of Vicky, but, with a stronger sensuality in this one. The already known body feeling came to him, their proximity made him feel exhilarated, energetic. He thought about what the man had said. To be the creator of a new religion, a new and different church. The idea that Christ had resurrected in him, made him to feel important, superior. That would explain why he had been given the gift of healing. Jesus healed to show that The Father was with Him. Fidelio looked at the cassock he wore, looked at the shanty town. Like Jesus, he had chosen to spend his life at the service of the poor, like Jesus he didn't ask for retribution for healing people. Yes, maybe, indeed, Jesus was within him. Fidelio straightened his shoulders, stood tall. Yes, everything seemed to be clear now.

"Thank you for coming. Everyone will appreciate if you provide food for them," Fidelio replied.

Still smiling, the man extended his hand and touched Fidelio's shoulder, the hand felt warm, almost hot. As soon as he felt the touch, Fidelio felt the heat running through his entire body, he felt strong and powerful. He looked around, saw the people in the shanty town, he had power over all of them, he had the power to heal them. The woman also got close and putting her arm around Fidelio's shoulder, pushed her body onto him. Her body was hot. Fidelio felt desire for her body, to become one with her. "I'm yours, my love," she whispered at Fidelio's ear. "Since I learned about you, I have loved and wanted you. You are so powerful, so wonderful, you can have whatever you want, including me. You can take me whenever you wish." She caressed him. Feeling her contact, Fidelio ignored everything else. He wanted her, he wanted to feel the heat of her body. He felt dizzy, drunk with passion and desire. Vultures circled on top of them. Suddenly, a heard of goats approached bailing noisily, a large buck ran apart from the herd and ran straight to Fidelio, at full speed hit him in the butt, pushing him down, got on top of him, bailed facing Fidelio. Its breath was cool, fresh, mint like. Surprised, Fidelio looked at the buck and his surprised increased when he noticed that the buck's eyes looked like Candelaria's eyes. The goat looked straight at him and then turned its face looking towards the couple. Fidelio followed its gaze and looked at the couple. This time he saw their real image. They looked old, decrepit, long nails, and their wrinkled skin looked like melting wax. Fidelio felt ashamed of himself. Once again, he had fallen into temptation. At the same it became clear to him who he really was: A common man with a gift, a gift not different from the gift given to Father Segura and many others, a gift to serve those in need. A gift which he should take care of, but he didn't own it. Thankful Fidelio caressed the buck that, bailing turned around and went back to the herd. Still ashamed, Fidelio got up and doing so, he looked again at the couple, who once again, seemed to be a pleasant attractive couple, but no longer attractive to him. He knew who they were and what they wanted. Without a word, he just walked away. They didn't try to stop him, they just grinned, a sarcastic grin. Dark clouds covered the sky, lightening illuminated the vultures flying around the couple. Butterflies surrounded Fidelio.

While Fidelio walked, he noticed that people threw flowers at his path, while others fell on their knees putting their face to the earth as he passed by. Although he tried to stop it, they continued doing it, everywhere Fidelio felt the presence and influence of the couple. "This is not what God wants from me," he thought.

Ahead he saw Dr. Villarreal, Father Segura and Sister Teresa. They looked at a pamphlet with an image on it. They seemed upset. "This is your image Fidelio," Father Segura told Fidelio as he approached, showing him the image in the pamphlet in his hand. "Yesterday morning, a couple arrived. They seem to be wealthy, very wealthy. They have been feeding people, giving pamphlets with your image and saying that they should worship your image and pray to you for a miracle," Father Segura added.

"Besides that, they have others selling your image along with candles, encouraging them to worship it. It's selling well, hundreds already bought them," intervened Dr. Villarreal. "I'm sorry to say it, but it seems that someone has found the opportunity for business, a profitable business."

"No one should worship false idols and that's what this image is!" yelled Fidelio, taking the picture from Father Segura and tearing it into pieces. "Only God is to be praised!" he added.

"Amen," the three replied in chorus.

"But, this has already started. What could we do about it?" Sister Teresa said.

"I must make everyone understand that like any other person I have weakness, temptations. That I'm just another common man," Fidelio said.

"But, the reality that everyone knows is precisely that you are not just another common man. You have the gift of healing, and by now we all know it," said Dr. Villarreal. Father Segura and Sister Teresa nodded agreeably.

"Even so," said Fidelio, "I'm just one of many of God's instruments. God, not the instrument, should be worshipped. I'm nothing else than a little ripple in the ocean of God's love. Worshipping someone like me is like confusing a little sunbeam with the majesty of the sun, and compared to God even the sun is nothing."

"That's right," Father Segura said, extending his arm and touching Fidelio's shoulder. "However, we must face the reality, people believe what they believe and the evil one knows how to manipulate it. That's what we are facing now."

"Whatever it is. I won't take part in it," said Fidelio. "All of you could help, you from the pulpit," he added touching Father Segura's hand. "You as a medical doctor and you as a nurse and a nun," he added looking at Dr. Villarreal and Sister Teresa. "Faith it's what has made people improve. Faith in God, not in the instrument. Yes, I have learned about the medicinal effects of nature, but that has always been there. Others have used it before me. People must realize that." He looked around to the shanty town. The three, newly built, cemeteries. He sighed. "Thousands have come here, just to die. There was nothing I could have offered them, except a little comfort for some. There are so many in need, so many. It's just overwhelming. Now this has become something larger than me." He thought for a moment, and smiled. "All of this is just a dream, a dream from which we'll awake soon. Somehow this has to end."

"What are you talking about?" said Aurora, who had just arrived and had listened to what Fidelio had said. "You won't do anything to harm yourself. Will you?"

Fidelio grinned. "No, of course not," he said. "Someone else will take care of it," he thought. Dark clouds covered the sky, a misty rain started, vultures circled, a butterfly rested on Fidelio's shoulder.

"Fidelio! Fidelio! Great news!" Enrique yelled at Fidelio as he and Von Wernich approached. A broad smile on their faces. Cheerful, they almost danced as they walked toward where Fidelio and his friends stood.

Looking at them Fidelio had a momentary flush on his face. He felt sad. On their faces, he could read the reason why they were so cheerful.

"Probably all of you already know about that wonderful couple that arrived in yesterday's train," said Enrique as he and Von Wernich got close. "They are not only beautiful, but they are also generous. This afternoon they approached us and mentioned how impressed they are with what you have accomplished here. They are particularly impressed how people are already worshipping your image, they call you a saint, a reformer. They are certain that here a new church has started and they are enthusiastic about it, so enthusiastic that they offered a donation for the new church, and we couldn't believe the amount of money they donated. One hundred thousand pesos! Can you believe it?"

"Just image all that we could do with that money," intervened Von Wernich. "Besides that, a lot more will come. It's just great!"

Fidelio tried to smile at them. "Until now we have been able to manage well. I agree that there is a need, but thanks to the volunteer work and yes, those who have given a voluntary contribution have also helped. I acknowledge that I received a gift, a gift that truly doesn't belong to me, but to the one who gave it. To God and only to Him. Of course, in return, I have encouraged everyone to praise the Lord. The Lord, not me, much less my image. Until now what has been voluntarily given has been well used to provide the service. But we have not sold anything or encouraged anything else other than praising the Lord. No profit has been obtained. Now you come excited because you see the probability of profit. No, no money will be accepted for that purpose. You'll have to give it back"

Enrique and Von Wernich face's flushed, upset. "But, just imagine what could be accomplished with all of that money and the wealth that could be obtained. People already believe. That's what is truly important," Von Wernich said.

"Think about what we already have received, and there is more, much more coming. We have been assured of that. Besides, I must tell you that since their arrival, suddenly, there have been some who claim that your soul has entered them, they claim to share the gift and already there are many who believe and follow them," Enrique said.

Sad, Fidelio looked at them. "You have fallen into temptation. God bless and forgive you," he thought. "That's not God's work," said he with emphasis. He paused for a moment. "Until now, what has been accepted has been only for the purpose to serve those in need. We won't accept anything destined to a different purpose, much less for a profit," he added.

"What do you mean?" Enrique asked.

"No money for a new church, or worshipping other than God, will be accepted," said Fidelio, in a firm tone of voice.

"What about the one hundred thousand pesos that we already got?" Von Wernich asked.

"You'll have to give it back," replied Fidelio.

Upset, Enrique and Von Wernich looked at each other. "You are wrong Fidelio. I hope you won't regret it later," Enrique said.

"Yes, this is money that is going to help many. We won't give it back," said Von Wernich. He and Enrique walked toward the main house where the blond couple in shiny white clothes waited for them.

Feeling a profound sadness, Fidelio just looked at them. "Thank you for all the good you have done. I forgive you for what you are about to do," he thought.

Aurora watched them walk away. She turned to Fidelio. "Fidelio, you deserve all the respect and love in the world. You have accomplished wonderful things in this place, in the middle of nowhere, but you are just a man. You know that I love you, and it's for that reason I must insist in saying that you are just a man; a man to whom God has given the gift of healing, but that's all."

"Aurora is right," Father Segura said. "Don't fall into the temptation they are offering you," he added.

Dr. Villarreal nodded in agreement to what Aurora and Father Segura had said.

"By now I'm well aware of the privilege God has given to me, but I have also become aware in that I'm not the only one. Every-one of us has received something from God. I, like anyone else, need the help of others. None of us is an isolated entity. I would be a fool if I take undue advantage of what has been given to me. If anything, I'm just another of God's instruments," said Fidelio.

"But, you must be careful now. Because you don't agree with their plans, you have become a nuisance for them," Father Segura said.

"I'm well aware of that, but I'm also aware that this process has already started. This wonderful dream must end before it becomes a nightmare," said Fidelio smiling to his friends. He then looked to Dr. Villarreal. "There are many who would benefit from your surgical expertise, Sister Teresa and Aurora will help you. There are many waiting for assistance, let me take care of them and help as many as possible," he added and started walking toward the pirul.

Just before approaching the pirul, Fidelio noticed Enrique and Von Wernich in a heated conversation with the blond couple, as they talked Enrique pointed toward the shanty town, the man smiled and nodded agreeably to what Enrique said. Seeing them, Fidelio smiled, he knew they were talking about him, he knew that they no longer had use for him. Now they had those who claimed Fidelio's soul had entered them, that's all they needed. For them Fidelio had become a nuisance. How to get rid of him was the point of their conversation.

Fidelio worked non-stop two days and nights. The third day he felt tired and hungry, a child, one whom Fidelio had never seen before, approached him. "Child," said the boy, "my mother has noticed how you have been working hard, she believes you must be tired and hungry. She has prepared this soup for you." Fidelio looked at the child, noticed his rosy cheeks, sparkling green-blue eyes, clean, amazingly clean, shiny white clothes. The soup seemed to be nutritious, fragrant. Fidelio noticed that Enrique and Von Wernich accompanied by the blond couple observed from the main house.

"Thank you," said Fidelio, "and also, thank you mom, please."

The child grinned. "You are welcome, my mom will be happy to know you have accepted what she prepared so carefully, for you," he said and ran in the direction of the main house.

Fidelio felt exhausted, the aroma of the soup guaranteed a good taste, somehow the plate felt warm, his belly grunted, his mouth salivated. He sat and prepared to eat the delicious soup.

"Fidelio! Stop! Don't take that soup." Antonia yelled as she, Aurora and Sister Teresa rushed toward him.

"That soup has been prepared by that woman," said Aurora, moving her head in direction to where the blond couple stood. "I don't trust them. They seem pleasant, have smooth manners. They are good looking, really good looking. But, they use it all to encourage people to praise you, not God and I don't like that."

Fidelio smiled to them, "I'm aware of that and, like you, I don't like what they are doing either. But, at the same time, I realize that it's an irreversible process. It already has started and it's clear that as long as I'm here it will become stronger and stronger. My mission has come to an end. I know that."

"But, if you take that soup you would have given them what they want. They'll defeat you, the whole purpose of what you have done here will be lost," said Sister Teresa.

"No, on the contrary. What has happened here has opened the people's eyes. Some, like the one Dr. Villarreal mentioned, have become aware of the need of medical and social assistance for those less privileged. Something is already being done. But, does it matter if they defeat me? They can't defeat God. What they are doing and encouraging is to worship images, not God and I won't be part of that."

"You are right, but still I won't allow you to eat that!" said Antonia, smashing the soup plate with a stick.

Fidelio smiled tenderly at her. "Thank you for your concern. You have been a wonderful sister. I love you. But, what is going to happen is going to happen. It's something that is already written. Anyhow, it doesn't matter." He pulled a coin from his purse, an American quarter and gave it to Aurora. "Take care of that, please. Keeping it has reminded me that everything is temporal. Life is just a dream."

Aurora took the coin and put it in her pocket. "Thank you, I'll keep it close to me," she said.

"Now, if you excuse me. I'm tired," said Fidelio, closing his eyes and lying down. He fell asleep almost immediately.

"He needs rest," said Sister Teresa. "Let's let him rest and we need to do the same." She signaled to a person close by for a sarape, covered Fidelio with it and they walked away.

Green grass, bushes with multicolor flowers, fruits hanging from the branches of leafy trees. Lazy clouds floating in the deep blue sky. Fidelio rested on the grass. Candelaria sitting at his side, caressed his hair. "Fidelio, I'm so happy. We are together again," said Candelaria as she took his hand, lifted it to her lips and kissed it.

Happy, smiling, Fidelio turned to look at her, "yes, I've missed you so much. It's lonely when you are not around, your love has been the most wonderful part of the dream that my life has been. This time we'll stay together forever, nothing could separate us now."

Candelaria bent down, their lips touched, a soft, tender kiss. Fidelio put his head on her lap and closed his eyes. A profound, restful, dreamless, sleep.

When Fidelio woke up, he found that Enrique sat at his side. "Back at the dream," thought Fidelio as he got up and looked at the shanty town and noticed several crowds surrounding men who dressed cassocks, similar to the one he wore. The building of something like a mausoleum had started, Fidelio then turned to Enrique. "You seem concerned, Enrique. What is bothering you?" Lightning cracked at the distance, dark clouds covered the sky, a storm approached.

"I'm ashamed of myself," said Enrique, avoiding Fidelio's eyes.

"What do you mean?" asked Fidelio in a friendly tone of voice, sitting and looking straight at him.

"I saw when that woman prepared the soup for you. I knew her intention and did nothing to stop her. I want you to know that and ask for your forgiveness," said Enrique, facing down.

"I knew it already," said Fidelio. "There is no need to ask for my forgiveness, I have already done so, you must forgive yourself." Lighting increased. A hot, humid wind blew in.

"During all of these years, since we met, I have learned to love and respect you. When we met, I was the one who lead, but now, the table has turned. You are the one who has grown and matured to become the leader. I not only respect you, but I also love you. Now, my only desire is that you get the recognition you deserve. You are a natural leader. The new church will put you in the right place," said Enrique.

"The feeling of love and respect is mutual you know that. And you also know that the church in which we both grew up and served is the one that follows Jesus' teaching. There is no need for a new one."

"But think all the good we could do, all the money that could be obtained, think what we could accomplish with it. I'm now convinced that's the reason you received the gift of healing. Already there are many who believe that Jesus is in you. Also, already there are several men and women who claim to share your spirit. People believe in them and are throwing lots of money at them. Oh, Fidelio, there is so much we could do with that."

Fidelio grinned sadly to Enrique. "Jesus has never left us, He is everywhere. As a matter of fact, He is in each one of us. His message is clear where we should look for Him. He said, 'every time you feed the hungry, when you provide drink for the thirsty, you are doing it to me.' He is in all of them," said Fidelio pointing to the shanty town.

Enrique frowned. "You are right," said he, still avoiding Fidelio's eyes. "I almost forgot, I had the women to prepare soup for you. I watched them preparing it, I can assure you that nobody added anything strange to it. Here it is. It's for you, enjoy it."

Fidelio smiled, "thank you," he said, taking the bowl of soup and took a bit. "Indeed, it's good. Once again, thank you, I really was hungry," he added and took more from the bowl. Fidelio sat. "I'm tired. I'll finish the soup and rest a bit more." Rain started to fall, the lighting increased.

"That's good. Rest, I'll watch while you rest," said Enrique smiling.

Fidelio finished the soup, put the plate beside him, lied down and closed his eyes. Enrique covered him with a sarape and walked away, sobbing. The lighting increased, heavy rain satiated earth's thirst.

Lazy clouds floated in the bright, clear, blue sky. At a short distance, Fidelio saw a beautiful forest, happy, he walked in that direction. Radiant, Candelaria ran toward him. "Fidelio, my love, my eternal love. We are together now," said she, embracing him and guiding him into the flowery garden.

"Indeed, now we'll be together for eternity," said Fidelio, passing his arm around her shoulder and letting her guide him.

www.ingramcontent.com/pod-product-compliance
Lightning Source LLC
LaVergne TN
LVHW041750060526
838201LV00046B/960